W9-ARC-835

FLASH FIRE

ALSO BY TJ KLUNE

The House in the Cerulean Sea
The Extraordinaries

FLASH FIRE

TJ KLUNE

TOR TEEN

A TOM DOHERTY ASSOCIATES BOOK
NEW YORK

FLASH FIRE

Copyright © 2021 by Travis Klune

A Tor Teen Book
Published by Tom Doherty Associates
120 Broadway
New York, NY 10271

www.tor-forge.com

Tor® is a registered trademark of Macmillan Publishing Group, LLC.

The Library of Congress Cataloging-in-Publication Data
is available upon request.

ISBN 978-1-250-20368-7 (hardcover)
ISBN 978-1-250-20370-0 (ebook)

Our books may be purchased in bulk for promotional, educational, or
business use. Please contact your local bookseller or the Macmillan Corporate
and Premium Sales Department at 1-800-221-7945, extension 5442,
or by email at MacmillanSpecialMarkets@macmillan.com.

First Edition: July 2021

Printed in the United States of America

0 9 8 7 6 5 4 3 2 1

This story is for those who never considered themselves extraordinary.

Trust me, you are.

FLASH FIRE

A swift, severe fire caused by a mixture of air and a flammable substance.

FLASH FIRE

FLASH FIRE

Fic: A Pleasure to Burn
Author: PyroStormIsBae
Chapter 36 of ?
137,467 words
Pairing: Pyro Storm/Original Male Character
Rated: R (Rating is finally going up!)
Tags: True Love, Pining, Gentle Pyro Storm, Happy Ending, First Kiss, More Than First Kiss, Fluffy Like a Cloud, So Much Violence, Evil Shadow Star, Bakery AU, Private Investigator, Anti-Rebecca Firestone, Hands Going Under Clothes, !!!, Naked Party and You're All Invited

....

Chapter 36: Burn Me Up

Author Note: Yes, finally an update! Sorry it's taken so long. I got busy with the holidays and my amazing boyfriend, who is pretty much the best person in the entire world. And then school started up again. But I promise this won't be abandoned. Thank you for all the comments on the last chapter! I read all of them. (Even the bad ones. Question: Why do you do that? What's the point of leaving mean comments? Let me live, damn.) Things are heating up for our heroes—in more ways than one!—and I'm finally giving you a point of view from Pyro Storm like a bunch of you asked for! Thank you to my BF, who beta read this for me (even if he told me it wasn't physically possible for Pyro Storm to have an eight-pack). Thanks!!!

Pyro Storm sat perched on the edge of the building, surveying the city stretched out before him. He knew its diseased heart, the curdled blood that ran through its dark veins. He loved this city, his mistress. He would do anything for it.

Almost anything.

He didn't look back when the door to the roof opened behind him. He knew who it was.

"Pyro Storm," a deep, sexy voice said. "There you are. I was looking for you."

"Nash," Pyro Storm growled seductively. When he'd stumbled into Nash Bellin's bakery-slash-private-investigator agency months before, injured and dazed, he'd only been looking for help to stop a group of master thieves threatening their fair city. He hadn't known then that Nash would be the biggest thief of all.

Because he'd stolen Pyro Storm's heart.

"What are you doing up here?" Nash asked.

"Watching," Pyro Storm said. "Waiting." The lights from the city below him stretched out as far as he could see.

"For what?"

Pyro Storm shook his head. "You wouldn't understand."

"Because I'm not an Extraordinary," Nash said bitterly.

Pyro Storm whirled around, hands curling into fists as he jumped off the ledge onto the roof. "No," he snarled. "It has nothing to do with that. You don't need to be an Extraordinary. You're already a world-famous baker-slash-private investigator. You do enough, Nash."

Nash looked away, throat working. "Then why won't you talk to me? I tell you how I feel about you, that I lo—"

"Don't," Pyro Storm whispered hoarsely. He didn't deserve to hear such sweet words. Ever since he was a child, born in fire, he'd been a loner. To form relationships meant to make targets of those he cared about. It had happened before. Once, he'd let someone in to see the person behind the mask. It had ended in tragedy. The first man he'd ever loved, Jacoby Middleton, had been taken too soon by the machinations of evil.

As always, Nash knew what he was thinking. "This is about Jacoby, isn't it?"

Pyro Storm turned back toward the edge of the roof. He stared stoically into nothing. *Don't let him see you hurting,* he thought. *Don't let him see how much you care.*

"I'm not him," Nash said. He sounded as if he'd moved closer. "I'm sorry you lost him when he turned out to be the villain called Smasher Man, who smashed everything in sight, including orphans on field trips. You had no way of knowing."

"I was blinded by my feelings," Pyro Storm said roughly. "I can't let it happen again." He shuddered when Nash's hand fell on his costumed shoulder.

"I'm not evil," Nash whispered, and Pyro Storm had to force himself not to ravage him right then and there. "I won't turn out to be a super villain. All I want to do is bake scones, solve crimes, and—and love you."

There it was, out in the open, with no way to take it back.

Pyro Storm was strong and brave and kind and very attractive. But even he couldn't stand against true love. It was too big a foe. He'd already lost.

He turned and stared into Nash's bright, beautiful eyes.

"Nash," he said, pulling him close. "This is dangerous."

"Danger is my middle name," Nash said, because it was true. Nash Danger Bellin. It was a family name. "I can handle you." His hands went to Pyro Storm's strongly muscled chest, sliding down slowly to his almost-eight-pack. *"All of you."* His hands went lower. And lower. And . . .

Pyro Storm kissed him—he had no other choice. Nash grunted as Pyro Storm licked into his mouth. They were finally about to become one. Pyro Storm felt Nash's many muscles in his arms and chest and marveled at how strong he was. Nash worked out a lot, and it showed.

"I want you to give it to me," Nash panted. "Right here on the roof. You aren't my first, but I want you to be my last. Show me how an Extraordinary does the *do.*"

Pyro Storm felt like he was burning up from the inside out. He stepped back from Nash. He began to strip slowly, unfastening his cape and letting it fall to the roof. He then bent over, sliding off his boots. The rest of the costume followed. He was about to take off his mask when Nash breathed, "Leave it on. I *like* it."

And then he had an arm full of Nash Danger Bellin, and they rubbed their groins together hotly.

To be continued . . .

....

Comments:

ImSoExtra(ordinaries) 13:45: IHKJREITHJ!!!! THIS IS FIRE. OMF GOD. THEY ARE GOING TO HAVE SEX ON A ROOF IN THE DARK. YES. YES. YES. PLEASE UPDATE NOW!!!!!!!

LetPyroStormSmash 14:04: I made an account just to tell you I love this story so much and to make a request! Can Pyro Storm dump Nash and get back with Smasher Man? Even though he's mentioned in this chapter for the first time, Smasher Man is already more interesting than Nash. Love the rest! (Except for Nash.)

WTF6969 14:12: Why haven't you mentioned the police in almost ten chapters, especially since Nash was working with them at the beginning? Please don't tell me you're turning into one of those social justice warriors.

TacosAreFun 14:37: Ignore WTF6969. They're commenting on every Extraordinary fic like this.

ExtraExtra 15:17 In Chapter 17, you said Nash's middle name was Rebel. Now it's Danger? Also, why have you never revealed who Pyro Storm's identity is in this fic? He's always wearing a mask, no matter what. And now they're going to have sex while he's wearing a mask? That's creepy. Unless it's a BDSM thing? If it is, you need to update your tags so people aren't caught off guard.

FireStoned 16:12 ANTI-REBECCA FIRESTONE IS THE MOST OFFENSIVE TAG ON THIS STUPID SITE. I AM REPORTING THIS FIC. YOU HAVE TRIGGERED ME BECAUSE I LOVE HER AND SHE IS THE BEST PERSON. HOW DARE YOU TRY AND MINIMIZE HER CONTRIBUTIONS. SHE SAVED THE CITY

ALONG WITH PYRO STORM. REBECCA FIRESTONE FOR PRESIDENT. NOT EVERYTHING IS GAY!!!!!!

SoundOfJazz 16:26 Hi! I found your story! Gibby says hello and that your story is filled with lies. Please don't write about having sex because it'll make us very uncomfortable. I love you!

ReturnOfTheGray 17:15: PyroStormIsBae, no.

1

Nicky, *yes*," Seth Gray groaned, and Nick had never been prouder
of himself in his entire life. Granted, he'd also never been more
turned-on, and he couldn't quite focus because all the blood had
left his brain and traveled south, but *still*. Hearing his name come
from Seth's mouth in that way was apparently enough to fry all
the remaining circuits in Nicholas Bell's brain.

Sweat dripped down the back of his neck as he shifted above
Seth, who was lying on Nick's bed. Seth's glasses were crooked, his
bow tie partially undone, his dark hair a mess of curls. His sweater
was rucked-up, revealing a sliver of pale skin. Seth's cheeks were
flushed, his lips swollen since Nick had been attacking them for the
last twenty minutes. Nick thought they'd gotten this making-out
thing down pat.

However, a conundrum now presented itself: stop while they still
could, or keep on going into the strange, unknown land of Putting
Hands Under Clothes for a Nice Time. They had the house to themselves; it was Saturday and Dad was out to lunch with the Chief of
Police Rodney Caplan and Officer Rookie to talk shop. Nick wasn't
necessarily supposed to know what *shop* meant, but he wasn't stupid, no matter the overwhelming evidence to the contrary, given
certain . . . actions he might've taken last year (or, to be honest, all
the other years of his life). He'd seen the posts on social media calling for reform and defunding, people marching in the streets demanding change, and though he'd always been proud of his father,
valid concerns were being raised, and rightly so. Dad didn't talk
much about it—at least, with Nick—and neither did Cap or the
Rook, no matter how he asked. This frustrated Nick to no end.

Especially since he'd spent the morning with Dad, driving around in the new, unmarked SUV he had been given as part of his job as the lead in the newly formed Extraordinaries Division, listening to music on Nick's phone he'd connected via Bluetooth when they ran errands. Talk about overkill. Nick treasured the time he had with his dad, but he was certainly capable of side-eyeing the fact that the seats were leather and heated, and for what? To keep Dad's ass warm while he worked? Seemed like there were more important things to worry about.

Speaking of Dad.

He probably wouldn't be back for hours, especially if they got a couple of beers into them. Seth had come over to help Nick with his homework (trigonometry *again*), and they'd promised to stay downstairs, Nick smiling innocently at his father, who had eyed them both up and down with a stern expression. Seth squeaked, as he was wont to do, his abilities to create fire out of nothing be damned.

And they had *meant* to only do homework. Honest. Nick wasn't failing or anything, but he had a test coming up that he wasn't quite ready for, and he wanted to get as much done as he could, seeing as how it was Valentine's Day and homework was in no way romantic in the slightest. They had plans later with their friends—a double date of sorts—and he'd decided to be responsible. Mature, even.

The *problem* with that was, of course, Seth. Seth, whose brow had been furrowed as he'd looked down at the textbooks and papers spread out on the table. Seth, who'd been munching on pretzels while saying something about the sides and angles of tri-angles. Seth, who was quite possibly the hottest dude in existence, so much so that if Nick didn't put his face on Seth's face again in the next five minutes, he'd probably die.

"Hey," he'd said, interrupting what he was sure was the most boring explanation of mathematics in the history of the world. "Can I show you something in my room?"

Seth had wiped the salt from his lips with the back of his hand. "What?"

Nick had leaned forward, chin in his hands. "It's a surprise."

"Surprise," Seth had repeated. He'd sounded dubious, which, okay, yeah, sometimes Nick's surprises, while well-intentioned, ended up exploding. Literally. But this was going to be a good surprise. With potentially *good* explosions.

(And since he was always and forever a prude, he'd flushed at his own audacity.)

But he wasn't to be deterred. He'd stood from the table. "Come on. It won't take long." This wasn't a lie. If it progressed further than it had before, it'd probably be over very quickly.

"Your dad said we couldn't go upstairs while he wasn't here," Seth had reminded him, as he'd stood too.

This was true, yes. But when Nick had reminded Dad that a bedroom wasn't necessary when it came to getting down to bidness (Nick's words, which he'd immediately regretted), Dad said he was going to get plastic tarps to cover all the furniture so they didn't leave boy stains. Nick, of course, had been sufficiently outraged.

Dad had made things worse by taking out an empty spritz bottle from underneath the sink, filling it with water, and saying if it worked on dogs in heat, it'd work on boys as well. And then he'd sprayed Nick in the face.

Nick loved his father more than anything, but he was convinced his sole reason for existing was to ensure Nick would remain a virgin for the rest of his life.

Which was fine with Nick, at least for now. Yes, he had a hot boyfriend who had superpowers and went by the name Pyro Storm, and *yes*, his body looked amazing when he was in chinos *or* his Extraordinary costume, *and yes*, Nick loved making out with said hot superhero boyfriend, but he wasn't quite sure if he was ready to take it to the next level.

It hadn't helped that he'd done what he always did when he didn't know something: he researched it exhaustively. And boy oh boy, was that a mistake. It was confusing being turned-on and also slightly horrified at the same time, especially when he'd come across an article titled "How to Be a Good Bottom" that involved detailed instructions and illustrations about things like the proper way to perform enemas to avoid any side effects, and wearing gloves for prepping so one's fingernails didn't cause damage to the interior of the anus.

And that didn't even begin to cover the wide and terrifying world of being a modern queer man in the twenty-first century and all that came with it. Was he a twink? A twunk? A power top? A power *bottom*? A bear? An otter? (He didn't have enough body hair for those last two, but he wasn't ready to rule anything out yet.) Did the heter-oh-noes have to deal with this? If not, then it was homophobic in ways Nick couldn't even begin to articulate. How *dare* straight people avoid these little boxes.

He kept on clicking, and it was about the time he was mired deep in an unintentional exploration of furry culture (people dressed up like wolves and goats and chickens and how *awesome was that*) that he realized he was probably in over his head.

He was sixteen years old, dammit. He didn't need to be a power goat twunk. He had ADHD and a healthy libido, which didn't really leave room for anything else.

Which was why the surprise Nick had for Seth was simply tackling him onto the bed and sticking his tongue down his throat. Seth, for his part, squawked, protested once through a mouthful of Nick, then gave up entirely when Nick bit down on the skin under his ear, which immediately turned him into putty.

Nick was by no means an expert, especially since his first experience had been with a villain who'd ended up trying to kill him, but Seth's appreciative noises and the grinding of his hips meant he wasn't *too* bad, right? And Seth tasted like pretzels, which should not have been as hot as it was. Oh god. What if he had a food fetish? What were they called? Foodies? Shit. What if he was a foodie?

Nick remembered what he'd learned on Reddit about safety and consent. "We don't have to do anything you don't want to. You have a right to say no, and I will respect that decision."

Seth laughed quietly. "Really. How generous of you."

"I know," Nick said, distracted by the way Seth's sweater was pulling up even higher. Another inch or two, and his belly button would be exposed. Was that hot? Nick thought it might be, but he couldn't be sure. Did he have a kink for belly buttons? What a terrible realization to have at this exact moment. He was having a hard enough time knowing he was a foodie.

"Nick," Seth said.

"I'm not thinking anything weird!" Nick blurted as he looked up from Seth's stomach. "I don't want to cover you in chunky peanut butter and eat it off you!"

"What?"

"Nothing," Nick said hastily. "Forget I even said that. Let's talk about something else. How are you? I'm fine, thank you for asking. Would you like to take off your pants and stay awhile?" But then the idea of having to take off his *own* pants entered his head, and he couldn't quite catch his breath. This was both exactly what he wanted and still moving way too fast, all at the same time. He didn't know how to reconcile the two, and the indecision made his brain hurt.

"Hey, hey," Seth said, reaching up and grabbing his forearms. "Nicky, look at me."

Nick did, trying to calm down before he spun out of control. While he wasn't as bad as he used to be, he was still prone to setting himself off, his thoughts becoming nothing but static, his throat closing, vision tunneling. If he let it go too far, he'd end up with one of his headaches, which would knock him on his ass for a few hours at least.

The medicine he took—*Concentra! It'll help you concentrate!*— slowed the worst of the ADHD symptoms, but the headaches had increased in frequency. A side effect, he and Dad had been told, but one he'd have to deal with, given how Concentra was the best thing for him.

He breathed in through his nose and out through his mouth as Seth's grip tightened around his wrists, grounding him. "There you go," Seth said, brow furrowed in worry. "We're good, Nicky. Relax."

"Sorry," Nick muttered, feeling ridiculous. Of course he'd ruined the moment. Stupid, stupid, stupid. He couldn't even semi-seduce his willing boyfriend right.

"Nothing to apologize for," Seth said, letting Nick's wrists go and rubbing up and down his arms. "You good?"

Nick nodded. "Yeah. Just . . . you know how it is. I thought about your belly button and then I wondered if I have a kink for belly buttons." He frowned. "Or something. And then peanut butter got involved, and now here we are."

"I have no idea what to do with any of that," Seth said, "but here." He reached down between them and pulled up his sweater, revealing at least ten miles of taut skin. "How's the belly button?"

"So good," Nick breathed fervently. And because he couldn't *not*, he bent nearly in half and pressed his lips against Seth's stomach. When he felt Seth tense, he blew as hard as he could. The fart sound ripped through the room as Seth screeched, bucking his hips, knocking Nick off the side of the bed. Worth it.

"You *dick*!" Seth snapped at him. "What is wrong with you?"

Nick grinned up at the ceiling from his position on the floor. "I'm trying to blow you!"

"*Blow* me? You jerk, I'll show you *blow me*, just you watch. I'm going to blow you until you can't even remember your stupid name."

With that, Seth launched himself off the side of the bed, landing on top of Nick, knocking his breath from his chest. Nick managed to grunt before Seth pulled up his shirt and began to blow raspberries onto Nick's bare skin. Nick cackled as he tried to shove Seth off him, but Seth was too heavy. "Blow me!" Nick began to chant through his laughter. "Blow me, blow me, blow—"

"Ahem."

Once upon a time, Nick fell from the top of McManus Bridge, plummeting hundreds of feet toward the pavement in what was surely going to be his messy, awful death, all because of a douchebag Extraordinary named Shadow Star who'd taken Nick's fanfiction a bit too seriously.

And here, now, for the second time, Nick's life flashed before his eyes because he was sure this was the end. Only this time, it wasn't going to be because of impact trauma. No, he was going to die of mortification, because apparently his room had fantastic acoustics, seeing as how the words *blow me* echoed dully as he and Seth turned their heads at the same time to see Aaron Bell standing in the doorway, arms crossed over his chest, a grim look on his face.

"Um," Nick said. "It's not what it looks like?"

"Really," Dad said flatly. "Because it looks like my underage son is demanding oral sex from his underage boyfriend when they're both supposed to be in the kitchen doing homework."

Nick hadn't known that hearing his father say *oral sex* would be so emotionally devastating. He did now.

"Oh my god," Seth moaned, covering his face with his hands.

"*Dad!*" Nick yelped.

Dad rolled his eyes. "Seth, get off of Nick and get your things. I'm driving you home. Nicky, why don't you stay here and think about all the sex you're not going to have. In fact, when I get home, we'll discuss exactly that."

"What the hell," Nick muttered as Seth slid off him. Seth refused to meet either of their gazes as he stood from the floor, cheeks aflame. "Dad, you can't say things like that."

"And yet I did," Dad said, not moving from the doorway, even as Seth tried to push by him. In the end, Seth made himself as small as possible as he sidestepped Dad, back rubbing against the door frame. He didn't even say goodbye. "I live to make your life miserable. It's in the job description, kid. When you become a father, you get a manual called *How to Screw with Your Child*. It's very informative, and it's the only type of screwing that'll be happening in this household for the foreseeable future."

"I hate everything," Nick announced grandly as he glared at the ceiling.

No response. Nick turned his head to see an empty doorway. He groaned and sat up, glancing at the photograph sitting on his messy desk. In it, a young version of Nick stood with a beautiful woman, her hair blowing in the wind coming off the ocean as she laid her head on his shoulder. Jenny Bell, his mother, now three years gone.

"It was you, wasn't it?" he asked her picture. "You're the one who told him he had a sense of humor."

She didn't reply.

Nick looked away from the photograph when he heard the front door open. He jumped up from the floor and went to the window, sliding it open. The sounds of Nova City filtered through, loud and obnoxious and comforting. The air was frigid, causing goose-flesh to prickle along Nick's bare arms. They were supposed to get snow later, the clouds above an ominous gunmetal gray.

He looked down the stone path that led to the street. Seth and Dad were walking toward Dad's SUV parked in the space in front of the house. "He won't keep us apart!" Nick shouted, laughing when both Dad and Seth jumped, looking around wildly. "I'll find you, my beloved! No matter where you are, we will be together. Nothing will *ever* come between us!"

Dad glared up at him. "Kid, I'm warning you."

Nick blinked innocently as he leaned forward on his elbows, breath streaming from his mouth in a thick fog. "Why, Father! It's not *my* fault if the neighbors hear us and think you're trying to keep my boyfriend from me."

Dad slid a single finger pointedly across his throat as Seth looked as if he wished a sinkhole would open up underneath him and swallow him whole. Rude. Nick was being romantic.

But then Seth looked up at Nick and said, "We'll be together in this life or the next," and Nick knew it was quite possible they were meant to be.

Dad sighed dramatically before steering Seth toward the SUV.

Unfortunately, it was about this time that Nick realized two things: he was alone in the house and he was still thrumming with arousal.

He didn't think as he turned away from the window to reach for his phone. He typed in his passcode (Seth's birthday) and opened the internet browser. He created a new incognito tab just to be safe and typed in his favorite porn site. The screen filled with stills of men in quite a few different positions that should've been anatomically impossible. He swiped through until he found his favorite category, a recent addition gaining traction.

Extraordinary porn.

He sat on the edge of his bed, ready to make the most of his time alone. He clicked on the third video on the list, one he was intimately familiar with. In it, a skinny man in a ridiculous costume who went by the name Boner Boy saved a rough-and-tumble dude who worked at an oil derrick that had exploded. However, since the budget for this particular piece of cinema verité didn't allow for an actual explosion (or an actual oil derrick), it only showed the aftermath: the man covered in artfully placed smudges and most of his clothing ripped off as Boner Boy felt him up under the guise of tending to his fictitious wounds.

Nick hit play, already anticipating the first lines of dialogue.

"You're safe now," Boner Boy would say woodenly. "But I should check you for serious injury. Take off your pants."

"Yes," Rough-and-Tumble would reply. "You should check very closely as I take off my pants."

Except no sound came from his phone.

Oh, the actors were doing their acting, and the sex was most certainly happening on-screen, but he couldn't hear a single thing. Nick frowned, clicking the button on the side of his phone. The volume was already turned up all the way. It should've been loud.

He frowned. "Goddammit. I *just* got this phone."

A horn honked outside, but Nick ignored it as he lowered the volume and then turned it back up to no avail. Nick was about to throw his phone down and grab his laptop when his gaze darted to the upper right corner of the screen. A little symbol blinked at him—one he knew very well.

Bluetooth.

His phone was connected via Bluetooth to . . . to . . .

He raised his head slowly in abject terror. He stood slowly, as if in a dream, and drifted toward the open window as the horn honked again. He looked out to the street below.

The windows of Dad's SUV were rolled down. Seth's face was in his hands. Dad was leaning out the window. As soon as he saw

Nick, he waved up at him and reached over to the dashboard to turn up the volume of the sound system in the SUV.

"Yes!" Rough-and-Tumble shouted from the speakers, echoing in the street around them. "Superpound me with your Extraordinary penis! Fill me with your superqueero power! Yes! Yes!"

A neighbor looked over at the SUV before practically running away. That certainly wasn't necessary. What a disproportionate reaction.

Nick closed the tab. Rough-and-Tumble and Boner Boy's passionate love affair was silenced.

Nick looked back down. Seth was banging his head against the back of the seat. Nick would have felt bad if he wasn't already filled with fiery outrage. Before he could demand that his father apologize for ruining his life, Dad spoke first, shouting, "Get your coat, kid! You're coming with us. I think it's time we had a talk. You. Me. Seth." He grinned. "Bob and Martha Gray."

Seth snapped his head toward Dad, mouth hanging open, blood draining from his face.

Nick scoffed. How bad could it really be?

2

"And that's how you make a dental dam," Dad said at the end of a twenty-six-minute demonstration where he took scissors and cut multiple ziplock bags into large squares. Martha and Bob Gray sat on a couch in their living room, watching Dad with no small amount of interest. "I learned about it shortly after Nick came out and was saving it for a moment like this." He jerked his head toward Nick and Seth, who were sitting in kitchen chairs they'd dragged out to the living room with the pace of prisoners in a gulag. Nick didn't know what Seth was doing because his own mouth had dropped open, tiny sounds of pain pouring out.

Bob Gray—a barrel of a man with a devious twinkle in his eye and perpetual grime under his fingernails from his job as a super—leaned forward. "Dental dam, you say? And what's it used for?"

"No," Nick whispered. "No, no, no." Seth grabbed his hand, holding on tightly.

"Protection during oral sex," Dad said. "But not for penises. This is strictly for cunnilingus and anilingus." He frowned, stretching one of the squares in his hands. "Or, as the kids call it these days, rimming."

"Oh my," Martha said, picking up one of the squares. Normally a kindly older woman with fluffy white hair and a quick wit, she'd obviously decided in the past weeks that her mission in life was to make teenagers more miserable than they already were. "Rimming. So, you just . . . what, put this over the genitals and it makes it safer?" She lifted the plastic square up to her face, and Seth made a sound like his intestines were being removed through his nostrils.

"These will do in a pinch," Dad explained, as if he weren't ruining his only son's life. "Even cutting open a condom would work. But it's better to use dental dams made for that express purpose. They're usually latex or polyurethane. I don't know if you can buy them at the grocery store, but they're sold online."

"Or," Martha said, glancing at Bob, "we could shop local and support the community. There's that one shop down on Ninth. You know the one—it's always playing loud music and has those mannequins in the window with the fun little red balls that go in mouths and attach to the head with black straps. I bet they'd have all kinds of dental dams."

Nick had never seen a soul depart a body before, but it looked like that was exactly what was going on with Seth.

So, naturally, Bob decided to make it worse. Or better; Nick wasn't quite sure. Bob said, "Isn't Seth's Pyro Storm costume made of some sort of latex? If it comes down to it, he can put that on before he and Nick . . . you know."

Nick, forgetting where he was and who he was with, whispered, "Yes. That. For safety."

They all either ignored him or didn't hear him. Either way, it was for the best. "I suppose," Martha said. "Regardless, it's good knowledge to have. And you're not wrong, Aaron. It's a big step to take, and they both need to realize it's not something that can be taken back." She glanced at Nick and Seth and smiled warmly. "We get that your relationship is new and wonderful, but you need to think with your heads and not your bits."

"Easier said than done," Bob said, folding his hands over his stomach. "I remember being sixteen. I wanted to put myself in pretty much anything that would have me—men, women, didn't matter to me."

"Robert *Gray*," Martha said with a huff. "Honestly. We have company."

"Speaking of Seth's costume," Dad said.

Nick panicked. "Dad, *no*."

"Dad, *yes*," he said sternly. "I'm not talking about using the costume for . . . that." He shook his head as he set the mangled plastic bags on the coffee table before him. "Bob, Martha, when I came to you after what happened last year on the bridge, I told you I was happy for our kids. Seth seemed to know what he was getting involved with, so I'm not worried about that part, though I did question his judgment a little bit."

"Wow," Nick said loudly. "It's not like I'm sitting right here or anything."

Dad didn't react, almost as if he were used to having a child who could be irate about pretty much anything. "But Seth *is* an Extraordinary. He can do things most of us can't even begin to imagine, what with all the fire and the flying. And he told me he wasn't sure he still wanted to be Pyro Storm, not after everything that happened. I get that. I really do. I won't say I understand the weight of such a thing, but I know what it means to feel like you have a responsibility to protect those you care about."

Okay, maybe Dad wasn't so bad. Even if he was literally the most embarrassing person Nick had ever known, this was sort of sweet, in a way. He loved his kid, and Nick loved him too. Then he ruined it. "But if Seth and Nick take their relationship to the next level, how can we be sure that Seth won't burn him if he gets too . . . excited? Do we even know where the fire comes from? Could it come from *anywhere*?" He glanced pointedly down at his own crotch.

The silence that followed was absolute, and it was in this moment that Nick planned to find an attorney and file for emancipation.

He yelped, "Dad, what are you *talking* about?" just as Martha said, "Oh my, I never thought about that," just as Bob said, "We never tested that, for obvious reasons," all while Seth jerked his hand from Nick's grasp and groaned so loudly Nick thought he was dying. They all began to speak over one another, Nick louder than the rest because he knew that volume was the leading factor in winning arguments. He shouted about fire dicks and the sheer *audacity* of his father. Martha went on about the making of the costume and how she hadn't had plans in mind for it to be used as protection for anilingus. Bob picked up one of the discarded plastic squares and held it inches from his face, wondering aloud about elasticity of plastic and the human body. Dad said that while he didn't believe Seth's genitals could shoot fire, he wanted to make sure it was brought up because if that was the case, they needed to see if there was a flame-resistant material that could be used for condoms.

It wasn't until Seth shouted, "We're not having *sex*!" that they all shut their traps.

Everyone turned to look at him, including Nick. It was the first time Seth had spoken since Dad had begun ruining Nick's life with assistance from the elder Grays. In solidarity, Nick reached over and grabbed Seth's hand again. They were in this together. If they were going down, it'd be the both of them—just, apparently, not on each other.

"We're not," Seth said in a strangled voice. His face was red, his unicorn-print bow tie so askew it was almost vertical. He swallowed thickly, his Adam's apple bobbing up and down. "We . . ." He looked at Nick with wide eyes, begging silently for help.

Nick wasn't an Extraordinary, but he'd mostly accepted his lot in life as the sidekick/love interest to the hero. It wasn't ideal, but he made do because Seth needed someone like him.

Which is why Nick squared his shoulders, held his head high, and said, "Yes. We're *not* having sex. We like to make out and rub against each other without penetration of any kind. I haven't even stuck my hand down his pants, so you don't need to worry about that. Today was the first day I've even seen his belly button since we started dating. But if it makes you feel any better, should we decide to bone down, it's a decision we'll make together when we're both ready. And to be safe, we can get a fire extinguisher for my room and his in case he can orgasm fire. Now, if you'll excuse us, I'm going to take my boyfriend down to the basement so we can spar because he needs to keep up with his training and I'm still trying to see if I'm capable of getting an abdominal muscle. Father, I shall see myself home by curfew. I bid you good day." With that, he stood, pulling Seth up with him.

"But—"

Nick turned slowly, eyes narrowed. "I said *good day*."

Dad rolled his eyes fondly. "So you did. Funny how you think that means we won't be talking about this again, and in great detail."

Seth came willingly enough, only stopping when Nick did at the entryway to the living room. Nick looked back over his shoulder at his father, who watched him with a quiet smile. "Dad?"

"Yeah, kid?"

"I love you.

His smile widened. "Hey, I know. I love—"

"But you'll rue the day you decided to make dental dams in Bob and Martha's living room. Do you hear me? *Rue*." And with that, he pulled his boyfriend toward the stairs that led down to the basement.

Last autumn, Nick had knocked on the door to the Gray household and politely demanded to be let into the secret lair of the Extraordinary known as Pyro Storm. Nick was still reeling from his father lying injured in the hospital, his sort-of ex-boyfriend revealing himself to be Shadow Star—the supposed savior of Nova City—who'd offered Nick the powers he'd always dreamed about for the low, low price of getting addicted to mysterious pills. And then there was his best friend/potential love of his life turning out to be Pyro Storm, the villain who wasn't *actually* a villain, but was portrayed as such by said ex-boyfriend, Owen Burke, with help from a reporter whose very name spoken aloud caused children and small animals to flee in terror.

Nicholas Bell's life was extremely complicated.

In the intervening months since the Battle at McManus Bridge (something the news reports tended to capitalize to show the importance; Nick had no problem with this), not much had changed in the secret lair, much to Nick's displeasure. There were only two real differences that Nick could see: first, the pocket door now had a small sign hanging from it that read TEAM PYRO STORM in red letters with smoke rising off the top of them. He'd ordered it online.

Second was a gift from Nick's father: a police scanner, something he'd apparently stolen from work—all while telling his son that stealing was illegal, to which Nick had replied that Dad needed to work on his messaging. It had only been turned on a couple of times since Gibby had figured out how to make an app that did the same thing on their phones. Not only could people download a simpler version of the app to report situations in progress, but the app also acted as a tracker to show the others on Team Pyro Storm where Seth was when acting as Pyro Storm, just to be safe. Instead of sitting in the basement listening to the scanner or flying around the city looking for problems to solve, an alert would pop up on his phone for serious wrongdoings that might need Pyro Storm. They'd all downloaded it: Martha, Bob, and Dad included, even though Nick had wanted to keep it on the down low. How embarrassing would it be if Dad looked at the app and saw Seth in Nick's room when he wasn't supposed to be? Seth had looked horrified when Nick voiced this worry aloud, and they'd agreed to turn it off unless Seth was in costume.

Speaking of.

As Seth went to the punching bag hanging from the ceiling, Nick glanced at the Pyro Storm costume hanging behind the computer and police scanner. The costume had been repaired by Seth's aunt after the damage caused by Shadow Star. Pyro Storm's helmet was red and black with red lenses that acted as a sort of augmented reality when Seth wore it, information sent wirelessly from the lair. Nick was of the mind that since Seth had fought his first big battle, his costume needed a slight redesign to keep it fresh and exciting, but still recognizable. It happened in every superhero sequel he'd ever seen. Martha had invited him to sew Seth's new costume if he was so inclined. It took only two minutes before he'd stabbed himself with the sewing needle and decided the redesign could wait.

It was good. *They* were good. Sure, maybe he didn't see Seth as much as he'd like, given his responsibilities to the people of Nova City, but that was the trade-off with dating an Extraordinary. And *maybe* there was a bit of residual jealousy that Seth could do what he did while Nick was left with his feet firmly planted on the ground, but it was *fine*. That was the way things were.

Which was why Nick was careful about bringing up any of his

own petty complaints. Did he want more alone time with his boyfriend? Sure, but people trapped on the top floor of a burning building probably needed Pyro Storm more than Nick, and Seth had told him that his role as the leader of Team Pyro Storm was as important as his own. It was hard to be irritated with someone that selfless, so he kept his mouth shut. Besides, who else in the entire world could say they were the leader of Team Pyro Storm?

(There had been an election. Gibby voted for herself. Jazz voted for world peace because she hadn't understood what they were doing. Nick *also* voted for himself, but that was because he knew Seth would vote for him too. Seth didn't. He abstained. This led Nick on a twelve-minute rant that began with his qualifications and somehow ended up with him explaining the epistemological position of solipsism, the philosophical idea that one's self is the only thing that can be proven to exist, something he'd inexplicably found himself reading about the night before on Wikipedia. Seth, knowing that Nick wouldn't stop until he either died or someone stepped in, loudly proclaimed that Nick won the election. Democracy in action.)

It helped that Nova City had been somewhat quiet since the confrontation at McManus Bridge. So far, all the dire warnings from the pundits on the news that the contentious war between Pyro Storm and Shadow Star would lead to other Extraordinaries coming out of the woodwork in Nova City had proven false. With Owen Burke locked away in some facility (location unknown, much to Nick's frustration), no villain had risen to take his place. Owen had once said that a hero was only as good as their villain, but he turned out to be pure evil, so Nick tried not to take anything he'd said seriously.

It was fine now, here, in this moment. They were together, and yes, it was after watching Nick's dad make things to put on their buttholes, but still. Seth was laughing at Nick's antics, and Nick wanted to hear that sound forever.

"Badass Power Kick!" Nick shouted as he clumsily lashed at the punching bag, almost knocking himself over as Seth chuckled.

Seth had taken off his glasses and sweater and set them on top of the washing machine. He'd also loosened his bow tie and unbuttoned the top buttons of his shirt, something that caused Nick to be unable to form most words. Regardless of what had happened upstairs, Seth seemed softer, almost relaxed.

"You don't need to name every fighting move you have," Seth said, clutching the punching bag. "It's a waste of time."

"Says you," Nick muttered as he wiped sweat from his brow. "Everyone knows the best fighting styles all have names that you shout when doing them."

"Really," Seth said dryly. "Everyone knows that."

"Well, everyone except you." Nick lifted his shirt to see if he had abs yet. He did not. He'd been at it for close to twenty minutes. What was the point of exercising if you didn't see immediate results? He sighed as he dropped his shirt again. Maybe he was going about this all wrong. "Bear Hug of Destruction!" he bellowed and hurled himself at the punching bag, wrapping his arms and legs around it.

Seth grunted as he almost lost his footing but managed to stay upright. Nick grinned at him from his perch on the body bag. Seth rolled his eyes as he leaned forward, kissing him with a loud smack. Nick was still stunned that this was something they did now. They weren't just two bros anymore. They were bros who *kissed*. The best kind of bros.

"Let's try something a little different," Seth said, stepping around the punching bag. Nick dropped back down to his feet and cocked his head curiously. "Turn around."

"O . . . kay," Nick said. He faced away from Seth. He startled when Seth pressed up against his back, a line of heat that immediately caused Nick's heart to trip all over itself. He grunted when Seth wrapped an arm around his neck, though not hard enough to choke him. "I'm totally on board for this, whatever it is."

Seth snorted in his ear. "Yeah, I bet you are. Focus, Nick. I'm a villain. I've got you in my grasp. How do you get free?"

"Well, maybe I don't *want* to get free. I'm pretty good with this, if I'm being honest. Oh no, the villain won. Whatever shall I do?"

Seth jostled him a little, his chest bumping against Nick's back. "This is serious. You want to learn to fight, you've got to prepare for anything. Help won't always come. How do you get free?"

"I don't know," Nick admitted, having a hard time paying attention. He was distracted by the hairs on Seth's arms, tickling his chin.

Seth lowered his other hand to Nick's right elbow, gripping it tightly. Carefully, he pulled it back, pressing it against his side. "Here, a weak point. Use enough force . . ." He pushed Nick's elbow away before bringing it back against his side. "And you might be able to get them to loosen their grip on you."

Excited, Nick said, "And then I can flip them over me and send them flying! Whoa, this is frickin' *badass*."

"Uh," Seth said, "that might be a little advanced. Why don't we save that for—"

"Backflip of Chaos!" Nick shouted, jerking his body forward, ready to send Seth toppling over him. His back twinged painfully as Seth's grip loosened. Nick promptly fell flat on his face.

"Oh shit," Seth breathed. "Shit, shit, Nick, I'm sorry, I didn't—"

Nick shot to his feet, almost falling again. "I'm okay! I meant to do that. I wanted to see if you were paying attention. Ignore the way I'm hunched over. I'm standing like this because it's *my* choice. Again!"

Seth hesitated before nodding.

Ten minutes later, Seth groaned as he held his side, Nick's elbow apparently bonier than even he knew. And that didn't begin to cover that Nick had made friends with the floor seven more times.

Nick pulled himself up again, flinching as he poked at his nose. Didn't seem to be broken, though it hurt like hell. "Again!" he demanded.

Seth wheezed, grimacing. "Let's . . . hold off on that for a bit. I don't think my ribs can take it."

"I win!" Nick said, throwing his hands up in celebration. "All I have to do is make sure the bad guys keep grabbing me, and I'll wear them down eventually."

Seth winced as he went to the washing machine and hoisted himself up, legs dangling down. "Weirder things have worked. Don't tell your dad about this. He might try and make a dental dam that covers your entire body."

Nick groaned. "I don't know why he's hell-bent on making my life miserable, but that was bad, even for him. I'll make sure he knows that wasn't cool."

"Should we talk about it?"

"Furious Lightning Punch!" Nick cried instead of answering. His fist landed with a meaty thud against the bag, causing his knuckles to pop painfully. It was probably for the best that he never became an Extraordinary. Punching things hurt like crazy. If anything, at least he knew for sure now he wasn't into pain.

"Nicky."

Seth was onto him. Curse him for knowing Nick so well. "Yeah, yeah. I'd rather not, but a relationship isn't a one-way street. You have to give as much as you take to keep your man happy."

"You really should stop reading *Cosmo*."

Nick approached the washing machine, pleased when Seth parted his legs without question. He collapsed dramatically against him, his face on Seth's chest. He smelled good, like a fire burning on a cold winter day. It made much more sense now that Nick knew why. He shivered slightly as Seth reached up and scratched the back of his neck, fingers going into his hair.

"You need a haircut," Seth murmured.

"I'll get one," Nick said, voice muffled. "But thanks for giving me an out. We can talk about it." He lifted his head to meet Seth's gaze. "Probably should talk about a couple of things, you know?" Maybe now would be a good time to ask Seth to slow down a little, and not just for Nick's own selfish wants. Seth looked tired. He had dark lines under his eyes that never seemed to go away. He needed to take care of himself more.

Seth studied him for a moment before nodding slowly. He took a deep breath, exhaling through his nose. "So. Sex. Between you and me."

Nick immediately chuckled nervously. He coughed to cover it up, but Seth wasn't fooled. No matter what Nick had been through, no matter what he'd discovered lurking in the darkest corners of the internet, he was still a bit of a prude.

Seth let it go. Good guy, that Seth. "Is that something you want?"

Nick tapped his fingers on Seth's thighs, suddenly cognizant of how close his hands were to Seth's junk. He pulled away, crossing his arms to try to keep from fidgeting. "Yes? No. I mean, not right this second, obviously, because your aunt and uncle are still upstairs with my dad and that is *not* something I want to think about when we're going at it like rabbits in heat. Did you know there are furries who dress up like rabbits? That's so rad, right? *I* wouldn't be a rabbit if I was a furry, because little kids would think I was the Easter Bunny and I don't want kids accosting me for my eggs—"

"Nicky."

Nick deflated. "Thank you for stopping me. I have no idea where that was going."

Seth chuckled quietly. "I figured." He cleared his throat as he sobered. "I like the . . . stuff we do already."

Nick nodded so hard his neck cracked. "Me too. A-plus on the making-out thing. Go you. If I didn't know better, I'd think you'd've gotten a lot of practice with that secret boyfriend and/or girlfriend that you said you never had."

Seth poked him hard in the chest. "Or maybe I ordered a pillow online with a certain Extraordinary's face on it and made out with it."

"We agreed to never bring that up again," Nick hissed.

"Secret boyfriend and/or girlfriend," Seth reminded him.

"Yeah, yeah," Nick mumbled. "Fair's fair. I won't do it if you won't." He picked at a loose string on the hem of his hoodie. "Honest?"

"Honest," Seth agreed, and because it came from him, Nick knew he wouldn't be made fun of for the thoughts racing through his head. Ever since the day he'd met a boy eating pudding on the swings, Nick would do anything for Seth, even speak the hard truths.

"Sex sounds amazing," Nick said, hating how his voice broke in his nervousness. "If the porn I've watched is any indication, it feels good too."

"Porn isn't real life," Seth said, keeping his hands to himself, which Nick was grateful for.

"Right," Nick said. "But there has to be something to it, you know?" He looked away. "And, like, the making-out stuff we do is awesome."

Seth chuckled. "*So* awesome."

Relieved, Nick said, "So glad you agree. We're pretty good at it, if you ask me."

"Might even be the best at it."

"But it's more than that," Nick said, looking up at Seth and holding his gaze. It's . . ." Here, now, a chance. A chance to say some words he'd been thinking about lately, words that he couldn't quite get to unstick from his throat. Words that were enormous and terrifying and would change everything, even if everyone already knew they were true. Three little words about how much Nick cared for Seth.

He remembered standing in this very house, just upstairs, angry at all the lies Seth was telling him, only to have Bob flap his lips and reveal that Seth was in love with him. Love, like sex, was a vast, complicated thing that Nick didn't have a firm grasp on yet. He loved Seth. He *knew* that. He'd loved him since the moment he'd met him. Aside from his dad, there was nobody on Earth who Nick loved more. But what was the difference between love and being *in* love? Nick wasn't sure. Everything he felt for Seth was jumbled up in a complicated knot in his chest. It wasn't a bad thing, but Nick wasn't sure he was ready to parse through it yet. But no problem was ever solved by not talking about it, and Nick thought he might be ready to say . . . well. *Something.*

"What is it?" Seth asked, startling Nick out of his thoughts. "Hey, you all right?"

Nick smiled tightly. "Yeah, I'm good." He shook his head as he snorted. "Lost in my head a bit. You know how it is."

"I do," Seth said. "You can tell me anything, Nicky. You know that."

He opened his mouth to say this. To say all this and more.

Before Nick could, Seth's phone beeped, as did his own. Nick stepped back, pulling his phone from his pocket. He frowned when he saw a text from Jazz.

We have a problem.

He looked up, brow furrowed. Seth was holding out his own phone. He had a text from Gibby.

We have a problem.

"What the hell," Nick muttered. "What's trying to kill us now? You think it's some new Extraordinary villain bent on—"

He never got to finish. The door to the basement flew open, causing them both to jump. "Guys?" Dad called down. "You need to get up here. We have a problem."

"Why is everyone *saying* that?" Nick asked. "It'd better be a real problem, or I swear to god, I'm gonna do whatever I can to help because we need to take everyone's issues seriously, no matter how minor."

Nick grabbed Seth by the hand and pulled him toward the stairs, already formulating a plan in his mind that would involve Pyro Storm kicking ass and taking names with his Team Leader at his side. At the very least, he'd have new material for his fic.

And, if he was being honest with himself, wasn't he imagining fighting alongside Pyro Storm? Yes, he was. He wasn't an Extraordinary. He knew that. He'd never *be* an Extraordinary. He'd failed in that regard, but that didn't stop him from imagining standing back-to-back with Pyro Storm, brave and true, so Seth knew Nick would always have his back.

Underneath this funny little daydream was a pleasant itch, a tickle thin as a whisper, like a thought he couldn't quite grasp onto. Probably the beginnings of a headache. He hoped not. He needed to be able to focus.

Above them, the single bare light bulb flared brightly.

They ignored it.

It was nothing. Power surges happened all the time.

3

When they reached the living room, Martha and Bob were standing behind the couch, whispering furiously to each other. Dad stood at the window looking out at the street, peering out from behind the curtain like a creeper.

"What happened?" Seth asked, sounding breathless. "Do I need to suit up?"

"Whoa," Nick said. "Say that again, except slower and with feeling."

Dad sighed. "Nick, keep it in your pants. We're about to have guests."

The doorbell chimed, followed by a heavy pounding.

"Gibby and Jazz," Dad said, letting the curtain fall back in place.

Nick blinked. "What are they doing here? We weren't going to meet up with them until later." They'd planned a double date for Valentine's Day. He'd been unsure of what was expected of him now that he had a boyfriend, and he'd worked himself into a panic trying to plan the most romantic date he could think of, which involved a picnic in the park and a mariachi band. Gibby had saved him from himself ("It's *February* and you want to go on a picnic? Nicky, you're a disaster.") and had invited them out with her and Jazz, which Nick had accepted gratefully.

He headed for the door, Seth following closely behind him. When he opened it, he found his two favorite women standing on the porch, huddled close together, both glancing over their shoulders. Jasmine Kensington frowned as she adjusted her ridiculously expensive scarf, her dark hair falling on her shoulders in cascading waves.

"We have a problem," Lola Gibson muttered, looking grim.

"Hurray," Nick said. "What now?"

"That," Gibby said, jerking her head back out toward the street. She pushed by Nick, pulling her hood down to reveal her shorn head.

"Oh," Jazz said, turning to look out onto the street again. "Yeah. That. So, you're going to think this is funny. I hope. Then we'll all laugh about it and everything will be fine and nothing will be bad."

Nick frowned as he stepped out of the doorway onto the porch. His skin chilled almost immediately, but he ignored it. He looked out onto the street. Quiet—almost unnervingly so. The coming storm was keeping everyone inside. Cars lined both sides of the street, windows covered in a layer of frost. A panel van idled in front of the house, black exhaust streaming from the tailpipe. Faint laughter from somewhere, bright and happy. Other than that, nothing. No cackling villain cribbing Nick's fanfiction, no death and destruction raining down upon them from above.

"I don't get it," Nick said, scanning the street again in case he'd missed something. Seth came up behind him, hooking his chin over Nick's shoulder.

Jazz pointed toward the paneled van. "That's a delivery van."

"Okay," Nick said slowly. "And what are they delivering? Is it a Valentine's Day thing?" Oh, crap. Was he supposed to buy Seth a present? He hadn't even thought of that. Goddammit.

Jazz shook her head. "Remember how we talked about outfitting Team Pyro Storm with new tech?"

"Yeah," Nick said, looking at the van with renewed interest. "Did you actually do that?"

"Me and Gibby went a couple of weeks ago and picked a bunch of stuff out. We wanted it to be a surprise."

He squinted at Jazz as Seth said, "What's wrong? Did they forget part of the delivery?"

Jazz smiled beatifically. "So, here's the thing. Daddy gave me his credit card, right? And when I've used it in the past, I've always put in his phone number when placing orders in case they needed to call him to confirm the charges."

Nick shivered as Seth's breath warmed his ear. "What does that have to do with anything?"

"The delivery man is very good at his job," Jazz said. "So much so that he called the phone number on the order to confirm the delivery."

Seth made a strangled sound as he stepped back.

"And apparently," Jazz continued, "Daddy didn't know what the delivery man was talking about because the address the driver gave wasn't *our* house, but another address entirely."

Gibby leaned her head out the door. "Have you gotten to the good part yet, babe? I want to see the look on Nick's face."

"I'm about to," she said before turning back to Nick. "So, Nicky—oh my goodness, look how handsome you are today. Seth, you too! Is that a new bow tie? It suits you."

"Thank you," Nick said. "That's a nice thing to—you're about to say something bad, aren't you."

She winced. "Maybe? So Daddy and Mom were at lunch with Gibby's parents." She tapped a finger against her chin thoughtfully. "What were the odds that they'd all be together right when that phone call came? And even though I told Daddy there was nothing to be concerned with, they decided they're all going to come over and see what's being delivered."

"There it is," Gibby said. "That's the look I was hoping for: shock mixed with terror. Thanks for not letting me down, Nicky."

Dumbfounded, Nick turned back toward the street as Seth banged his head against the side of the house.

Two couples were hurrying up the street, the men huddled close with the women.

Miles and Joanna Kensington were in the lead, her arm looped through his. Miles was a charmingly chubby man with thinning blond hair and a devious glint to his eyes, dressed to the nines in a charcoal-gray suit and a red power tie. His long coat billowed around him as they approached the house, his expensive shoes smudged with street grime.

Jazz took after her mother almost completely, with dark hair and dark eyes. Joanna—Jo for short—was beautiful. She seemed to float wherever she went, with an ethereal air about her. She moved like a dancer, which made sense since she'd been one of Nova City's premier ballerinas in her younger years before retiring when pregnant with Jazz. She wore a suit of her own, tailored to her curves, expertly navigating the slick sidewalks in her heels. Her coat matched her husband's and was cinched at the waist.

They were followed closely by Terrence and Aysha Gibson, Gibby's parents, who'd earned the distinction of being the only accountants Nick knew who were also hippies. They weren't as formally dressed as Jazz's parents, but Nick had to admit they still looked amazing. Aysha's hair sat like a billowy crown upon her head, her Afro flecked with bits of snow. Her earrings dangled almost to her shoulders. The collar of her coat was popped up around her neck, and her jeans were bootcut and tight against her legs.

Terrence—or Trey, as he was called—had a shaved head, something he'd done when Gibby had shaved her own head, telling her he was so impressed by her that he had to emulate her style. He grinned widely, as he almost always seemed to do, a serene vibe emanating from him. Terrence was the most chill dude Nick had ever met. Most things didn't seem to ruffle him. In fact, the only time Nick had ever seen him angry was after some idiot douchebro at school had given Gibby shit for owning her butch identity, and the school had responded with, "Kids will be kids." Once Trey found out about it, he'd descended upon the school like a gathering storm. Fifteen minutes after walking into the main office alone, he'd emerged, followed by the principal, one of the guidance counselors, and the lead school resource officer. All three apologized profusely to Gibby while Trey watched, followed by Gibby receiving a letter from the douchebro the next day, a hasty yet thoroughly written apology saying that he would never again make fun of the hair decisions made by a person of color—or anyone, for that matter. No one messed with Trey's daughter.

Nick liked them all, simply because they had brought Jazz and Gibby into the world. And if that wasn't enough, the two sets of parents had become friends themselves after Jazz and Gibby started dating.

And here they were. Coming to the Gray house. To an unplanned meeting, all about Team Pyro Storm and upgrading the secret lair of an Extraordinary that they knew nothing of.

"Oh my god," Nick said fervently, feeling the blood drain from his face.

"Yeah," Jazz said. "Ha ha, funny, right? We have about fifteen seconds to come up with something that will explain why I spent thousands of dollars on electronics without making it look like we're doing something illegal. Nick, you have ADHD, which I've always said was a superpower. It's time to use that awesome brain for good instead of evil. And . . . go!"

Jazz was right. He might not be an Extraordinary, but he still had a brain that was different than most. On the cusp of panic, he said, "Team Pyro Storm, assemble! In Seth's room so we can come up with a plan that explains everything and doesn't look like we're drug kingpins laundering money or hackers planning on taking down the CIA!"

They never made it upstairs.

As soon as they got back inside, they were blocked by Nick's dad standing with his arms folded. "Are we good?"

No, no they weren't. "Dad! Just the man I was hoping to see. Funny thing happened outside. I need you to be my savior because *help*." Nick was not proud of the way the last word squeaked annoyingly.

Dad softened. "Hey, kid. We'll be all right. I've got your back."

Relieved, Nick didn't protest too much when Dad pushed by the four of them huddled in the entryway. Dad was here. It would all be okay.

Until Dad saw who was coming up the walkway to the Gray house.

The noise he made was one Nick had never heard him make before. It was the whine of a wounded animal. He froze in the doorway, hand squeezing the doorknob so tightly, Nick thought it'd break off in his hand.

"Trey!" Dad said, voice high-pitched and shocked. "Aysha." He swallowed thickly. "And Miles and Jo. And some random man I've never seen before."

"Hello!" Random Man said cheerfully, just out of sight. "I'm Geoffrey with Geoffrey's Wide World of Electronics, though the Geoffrey in Geoffrey's Wide World of Electronics is my father, not me. I'm only a delivery driver. But no worries, friend. I'm working my way up from the bottom, and one day, Geoffrey's Wide World of Electronics will be mine!"

"Great," Dad said weakly, frantically waving his hand behind him, as if he thought Nick and the others should get as far away as they could. "That's great. A delivery, you say? I don't know if anyone here was expecting a delivery."

"Uh, yes we were," Jazz said. "Surprise! Don't worry. I've got this." And then she underwent a transformation Nick had only seen a few times before. Her eyes widened to obscene Disney-princess levels, sparkling and wet. Her cheeks flushed as if she could control the blood in her body. She shook out her shoulders, her bottom lip trembling as she stepped next to Nick's father at the door. "Daddy," she said, her voice an odd coo. "You didn't have to come all this way. I told you I would handle it. I don't know what this is about, but I promise I can fix it."

"I know you can, sweetheart," Miles said jovially, climbing the porch stairs, his wife stepping forward and hugging Dad. "But I want to make sure that everything is all right. I didn't expect to receive a call today about a delivery of almost ten thousand dollars' worth of electronics to an address that wasn't our own. I'm sure it's just a mistake."

Nick turned slowly to look at Jazz. "Ten thousand *what* now?"

Jazz shrugged. "Blame Gibby. She's the one who picked everything out."

"Thanks," Gibby said wryly. "I appreciate that."

Seth was trying to make himself as small as possible, but since he was a beefy sex god, it wasn't going too well. It took a turn for the worse when Martha and Bob appeared behind him, Bob's thumbs hooked through the straps of his overalls, Martha holding a plate piled high with cookies. Seth bumped into them and whirled around. With a welcoming smile firmly fixed on her face, Martha muttered, "We'll get through this together. No one say a word about *anything*. We'll figure it—hel*lo*! Welcome, welcome! It's so lovely to see you all again. Please, come in. Have a cookie. Have *several* cookies. I've often found that when your mouth is full, you're unable to ask questions."

The new arrivals laughed as they came into the house. Miles kissed his daughter on the forehead before turning and shaking Gibby's hand furiously. "Gibby," he said as Joanna touched her cheek. "You're looking extremely queer. I approve. Gay rights!"

"Thank . . . you?" Gibby said, pulling her hand away before he could tear her arm from its socket, something Nick absolutely did not recommend. "Gay rights."

Miles beamed at her. "Exactly." He glanced at Seth and Nick before turning to Dad. "Aaron! I see you've joined the ranks of having your teenager in a queer relationship. If you have any questions, please give me a call. I've done extensive research on the matter."

Dad shook his head. "I've already made dental dams out of plastic baggies, so I think we're—"

"Mr. and Mrs. Gibson!" Nick bellowed. "I haven't seen you all since . . . I have no idea. I'm just talking to keep my dad from saying anything he'd regret." Nick would be *damned* if he'd let his father's evil infect the other parental units.

Dad snapped his mouth closed. Good man.

Trey grinned as he helped his wife out of her coat. Aysha stepped forward, her earrings bouncing as she hugged Dad tightly. "Aaron," she said, "it's been too long. I brought presents. You'd look good with the hemp choker I made. I opened my own Etsy shop. They're selling like you wouldn't believe. Mother Gaia gives only what we give her in return."

"Mother who?" Dad asked as Aysha let him go, whirling around and marching up to Nick and Seth.

She smiled warmly at them both. "I hear congratulations are in order. It's about time the two of you figured things out."

Nick gaped at her. "Did *everyone* know?"

"Only people with eyes," Aysha reassured him.

"Hello, folks!" Geoffrey said, appearing in the doorway. He was a slender man with spiky black hair and was rocking pink glasses. "Sorry to interrupt the reunion, but I've got a schedule to keep. Geoffrey Senior doesn't like it when I'm behind. I tried to tell him that something as ridiculous as a *schedule* shouldn't matter when dealing with our customers, especially those who spend so much on our products, but what do I know? Nothing, according to him. I have . . ." He looked down at the invoice in his hand. "Ten boxes for delivery. I see no setup was requested. Is that right?"

"Ten boxes?" Seth asked weakly.

"Setup," Miles said. "What is it you're supposed to be setting up?"

"Daddy," Jazz said, sticking out her bottom lip even further. "I *told* you I need it for school. You said it was all right, and that I should spare no expense when it came to my education."

"Right," Miles said. "Your education is the most important thing. But why isn't it being sent to our house? Martha! Bob! Look at the pair of you. Picture-perfect. Ooh, cookies."

Martha thrust the plate toward him as Jo twirled a strand of her daughter's hair. "Jasmine," she said, her voice smoky and sweet, "is there anything you're not telling us?"

Impossibly, Jazz's eyes grew wider. "Of course not. I tell you guys everything."

"Mm," Jo said. "Then why all the secrecy?"

"It's my fault," Nick said hastily. "I'm sorry. I thought it'd be best if it could all be sent here, since Seth's house is central for all of us. Makes it easier to get to. For . . . school . . . things."

Miles nodded, munching on an oatmeal chocolate chip cookie. "Makes sense. If it helps all of you, then we're all the better for it." He nodded at Geoffrey. "My good man, please bring in the boxes. I'll make sure you're adequately tipped after giving you a hand while also regaling you with the story about how I was once in your position, working my way up the corporate ladder until I owned my own company."

"Far out," Geoffrey said, suitably impressed. "Help is always appreciated."

Aysha, Jo, and Trey all followed Martha into the living room. Bob stayed in the entryway, whispering furiously with Dad, both glancing at the teenagers staring at them with wide eyes. They came to some sort of agreement, then turned and walked out of the house to help with the boxes.

"Ten thousand *dollars*?" Nick hissed at Jazz. "Are you out of your mind? How the hell did you think your dad wouldn't notice?"

Jazz's lips thinned to a bloodless line. "It's only money. If he hadn't been called, he wouldn't have even noticed. I'd appreciate a little more gratitude."

"Thank you for spending a ridiculous amount," Nick said quickly, not wanting to face her wrath. "And let's circle back to the whole 'it's only money' thing at a later date, because man, do I have thoughts on that. But what are we gonna do? We can't tell them what it's for."

"It'll be fine," Gibby said. "We gotta make them believe it's for school, like Jazz said."

"Exactly," Jazz said. "And if they ask about the night vision goggles, we'll say they're for science class."

They all stared at her.

"What?" she asked. "I had a coupon."

Nick shook his head. His brain was his superpower. *Think. Think.* "Okay," he said, pulling at one of his thoughts until it tugged loose. "Here's what we're going to do. We'll tell them we're thinking of our education, and that it's as your dad said: an investment in our future. We're planning not only for this year or next, but for college too. And beyond. We have an idea for . . . a project. Yeah, a *project*." He began to get excited. "Dad's the head of the Extraordinaries Division, right? We could say this project is about tracking Extraordinary activity in Nova City for the NCPD. That way, it's not *exactly* a lie, more just not . . . being truthful? I'm still working out the particulars, but I think it could work."

"Why would we help the police?" Gibby asked. "They already have more money than Jazz's parents. Didn't they give your dad a new SUV for no reason aside from his promotion?"

"Oof," Nick said. "That is absolutely correct. Shit." He glanced at the others. Jazz snapped her gum before blowing a pink bubble. Seth looked spooked, face pale, hands shaking. Nick went to him and grabbed him by the shoulders. "I know you're scared, but I'll protect you, okay? We've got this. I won't let anything happen to you."

Seth shook his head. "Nicky, I'm the one who's supposed to be protecting all of you."

Gibby snorted. "That's crap and you know it. Sure, you can do things that we can't, but we're a team, remember?"

"Team Pyro Storm," Jazz agreed. "The best team that's ever existed."

"We stand together," Nick reminded him, "so we don't have to struggle apart. You're not alone in this, okay?"

Seth gave him a shaky smile. "Really?"

Jazz nodded. "It's going to be fine."

It was not fine.

Because as soon as the last box was stacked in the living room around them, Geoffrey practically in tears at the tip Miles had given him, Trey said, "So, anyone want to tell us what's going on? I'm not worried, but I do have a few questions. What's with all the—"

And Nick—always and forever Nick—blurted, "I'm Pyro Storm!"

The only sound that followed came from the honking of horns out on the street. Then Dad put his face in his hands; Martha said, "Oh my"; Bob took out his handkerchief and blew his nose; Seth moaned quietly; Gibby said, "Nicky, I swear to god"; and Jazz laughed so hard, she started crying.

And that didn't even begin to cover the looks on the faces of the new arrivals. Trey's eyes were bulging from his head, Aysha's mouth had dropped open, Miles was squinting at Nick as if he didn't understand what he'd just said, and Jo said, "Come again?"

"Crap," Nick muttered. "Crap, crap, crap." He needed to fix this. Dig in or pretend it was a joke? He went with the easier route. "Okay. So. Um—here's the thing? I have superpowers. And I can fly. And create . . . fire? Yeah, fire. Like explosions and junk. And *yes*, I know the costume is *so* last year, but when I tried to make a new one, I stabbed myself and decided the old costume is fine." He glanced at Seth pointedly. "For now." There. Fixed. Sort of.

More silence. All the silence.

Then, Miles: "You're Pyro Storm. That Extraordinary from the bridge who fought against Smoky Guy."

"Shadow Star," Nick corrected automatically, even though he hated himself for it. "And yep! I fought against Shadow Star and saved the day." But since he wasn't selfish, he added, "But I didn't do it alone. Gibby and Jazz and Seth all helped because they are good people who you shouldn't be mad at for anything. It's all my fault. So. I'm . . . sorry?"

"Wait," Aysha said, holding up her hand. "I'm confused. We all saw the footage from the bridge, Nicky. You weren't the one in costume. You were standing next to Pyro Storm."

"You're so observant," Nick said through gritted teeth. "How fun. That was a . . . hologram. A hologram I created in order to confuse Shadow Star and gain the upper hand. It only *looked* like I was two different people because of the advanced tech that we somehow created that I won't bore you with the details about. *I* don't even understand it, for the most part. Story of my life."

Miles nodded slowly. "But didn't you—forgive me if this sounds a little forward—but didn't you maul Pyro Storm? It was very . . . wet. The wonders of high definition."

Dad sounded as if he were choking on his tongue.

"Maul?" Nick said, outraged. "I didn't *maul* anyone. It was a loving kiss that I placed . . . upon myself because I . . . deserved it?"

"Oh my," Martha said again. Bob folded his arms and grinned at Nick, as if he was enjoying the hell out of this. Nick made a mental note to plot serious yet harmless revenge against him.

Seth said, "Nick, what are you doing?"

He really had no idea. All that mattered was protecting Seth's secret identity, and if that meant throwing himself at the mercy of parental figures, then so be it. "Look," he said, trying to hold together the tatters of his completely plausible story, "I know it's shocking to hear that someone like me could be an Extraordinary—"

"Not that shocking," Trey said, rubbing a hand over his scalp. "If anyone was going to be an Extraordinary, I'd think it'd be you. It actually makes a lot of sense."

"It does?" Nick asked. He coughed. "I mean, of course it does, so there's no need to question anything else. Since you now know the big secret, we can all focus on the important things, like what is *up* with this weather? Global warming, am I right? Those poor polar bears with all that melting ice. We should be ashamed for treating our only home with such disregard."

Apparently not giving a crap about polar bears, Aysha turned to her daughter. "And you knew about this?"

"I don't know anything that's happening right now," Gibby said.

"Jasmine?" Jo asked. "Is this true?"

Jazz glanced at Nick before looking at her mom. "If I say yes, are you going to take my Alexander McQueen pumps away?"

Jo blinked. "No?"

Jazz breathed a sigh of relief. "Then, yes. Mostly. Nick is certainly capable of being Nick."

He didn't know if that was a compliment or not. He was about to ask for clarification when Seth said, "Nicky."

He looked over at him.

Seth shook his head. "You don't have to do this."

"Yeah," he said, "I do. Because Pyro Storm—*me*—needs to remember how important he is. And not . . ." He frowned. "Not just to me? Wait, that doesn't make sense."

Seth reached over and took his hand, squeezing gently. Nick studied his face, cataloguing the shadows under his eyes, the firm set of his jaw. He looked weary and resigned, something Nick never wanted him to be. "Nick," he said gently. "They deserve to know, especially since their kids are involved. It's only fair."

"Fair," Nick managed to say, that old, familiar feeling of his lungs constricting causing the word to come out choked. "How is it fair that you always have to clean up the messes I make? You only did what you did because—" *Because of me*, but he couldn't get the words out, couldn't finish because his throat had tightened, his breath whistling between clenched teeth.

Nick didn't see Dad move and flinched when his father knelt before him, gripping his knees, keeping them from bouncing. Nick's thoughts were caught in a storm, the knot in his head writhing, and that whisper, that caress in the back of his mind, grew claws, digging in. A headache bloomed quietly, and he couldn't focus, couldn't—

"Nicky," Dad said, sounding far away. "Kid, I need you to breathe. Deep breaths, okay? In. Hold. Out. Hold. You can do this. I know you can. Breathe, kid. Just—"

Nick snapped out of his spiral when the floor began to vibrate. The half-empty plate of cookies rattled across the coffee table. The windows shook. Pictures hanging on the walls swung crooked.

Then it stopped.

Everyone looked around. "What was that?" Trey asked. "An earthquake?"

"Maybe it was a train," Miles said, though he sounded dubious.

Martha and Bob looked just as confused. "Probably a garbage truck going by," Bob said. "You know how these old houses get."

Dad, though . . . Dad's hands shook as he reached up and cupped Nick's face. "Did you . . . you took your pill, right?"

Anger, then. Anger and embarrassment mixed together. He jerked his head back out of Dad's hands. "Yeah," he said, not meeting anyone's gaze. "I did. Like I always do. Every day. I'm sorry my brain makes me say stupid things, but I can't always control it." The bitterness in his words tasted like acid on his tongue.

Dad breathed in and let it out slow. "There's nothing wrong with your brain. There never has been. You're just . . . Nick. And that's a good thing," he added as Nick opened his mouth to retort. "I wouldn't want you to be any other way. We can go. We probably should get you some air."

Nick shook his head. "I can't. Dad, this is important."

"Nothing is more important than your health," Dad said, voice hard.

"He's right, Nicky," Seth said, and Nick couldn't bring himself to look at him. "There's nothing wrong with you." He sighed. "We have to trust them, especially since Gibby and Jazz are involved. They have a right to know what we're doing."

Nick finally worked up the courage to look at Seth.

Seth—wonderful, amazing Seth—nodded at him. He reached out and took his hand again. Dad watched the two of them, an inscrutable expression on his face.

Nick said, "I'm sorry."

Seth shrugged. "You don't need to be. You remember when I came out to you? You had my back then. I know you'll have it now."

"Please be my friend forever," Nick said, because it was the only thing he could think of.

Seth laughed quietly. "Forever is a long time."

"I know, but you're worth it."

Seth brought Nick's hand to his mouth, kissing the back of it sweetly.

"Oh my *god*," Gibby said, and they both jumped. They looked over to see her scowling, her eyes wet. "Stupid boys. I hate you so much. Incoming."

Nick squawked when she practically tackled him out of his chair, knocking Dad on his butt. He looked over her shoulder in time to see Jazz doing the same to Seth, though much more delicately, settling on his lap, pressing his face against her neck, petting his hair, cooing at him that he was the most precious thing in the universe and that she would destroy anything that tried to harm him. "Are you sure?" Nick heard Jazz ask.

"Yeah," Seth whispered back. "I think so."

"We're with you," Gibby said.

They were all brought back to reality when Miles cleared his throat. They looked at the adults in the room. Most were smiling, though they looked confused.

"Seth?" Martha asked. "This is what you want?"

Seth helped Jazz up off his lap, and she pulled Gibby along with her, sitting back down on the couch. "It is."

Bob said, "Whatever you need, kiddo. You want us to do it?"

Seth shook his head. "No. It's my responsibility." He glanced at Nick. "And I know I'm not alone."

"Damn right," Nick said.

"Team Pyro Storm," Gibby agreed. She looked at her parents. "Mom. Dad. I need you to listen to Seth, okay? Let him tell it how he wants to. Don't interrupt. You'll have questions—a *lot* of questions—but wait until he's done. And Seth, tell us if you need us to jump in."

"Same," Jazz told her parents.

Seth said, "Watch." He lifted his palm toward the ceiling. The skin around his eyes tightened briefly before twin flames bloomed above his hand. At first, they hung suspended, the fire crackling. Then they swirled together in the shape of a double helix. No matter how many times Nick had seen it, it still knocked the breath from his chest.

The flames rose up, beginning to spin in concentric circles above Seth's head.

As a stunned Miles, Jo, Trey, and Aysha looked up in wonder, Seth Gray lowered his hand and said, "I'm Pyro Storm. And this is my origin story."

By the time he finished speaking, Seth's voice was hoarse. Nick and Gibby and Jazz had helped as best they could, but it was Seth's story to tell. He told them of the train accident, the loss of his parents, how he'd figured out at a young age that he could create fire from nothing. There were many accidents, burning things that shouldn't have been burned. Bob stepped in once or twice, telling the rapt audience that Seth had gotten control of it far quicker than any of them had expected.

It wasn't until Seth reached the part about Owen and Simon Burke that anyone interrupted. Miles snarled angrily, his wife gripping his hand to keep him from rising. "Those assholes," he snapped. "If I'd known that they . . ." He shook his head angrily.

They allowed Seth to tell the rest of the story, ending with the Battle at McManus Bridge. The adults all looked shaken as Seth described fighting their former friend. "And Nick saved Rebecca

Firestone," Seth said. "If it wasn't for him, she could have gotten hurt. Or worse."

"Yeah, well," Nick muttered. "We can't all be heroes."

When Seth finished, everyone was quiet. Nick fidgeted, wanting to fill the silence, but he somehow managed to keep his mouth shut. This wasn't about him. It was about Seth and his endless well of bravery.

He let out a sharp exhalation when Aysha spoke first. "You're telling the truth; I know you are. But I . . ." She shook her head. "I'm having a hard time believing it." She rose from the couch and walked around the coffee table to Seth's chair. "Up," she said. "Up."

Seth stood and grunted when Aysha hugged him tightly, her face in his curly hair. For a moment, he just stood there, arms dangling at his sides. It wasn't until Aysha reminded him that's not how hugs worked that he clutched her tightly.

"You're a hero," she whispered to Seth, and Nick felt his bottom lip wobble. "You protected all those people. I'm so proud of you, Seth."

Seth blinked rapidly as Aysha took a step back. A tear trickled down his cheek when Aysha moved out of the way so her husband could hug him too, followed by Jo, and then Miles.

Once everyone sat back down, Seth still looking dazed, Jo glanced at her daughter and said, "You've been helping him?"

Jazz nodded. "We're Team Pyro Storm. We don't fight like Seth does, but we're there to make sure he has all the backup he needs." She pointed at the boxes. "That's what those are for. To make sure he has the best equipment. We call ourselves Lighthouse. It was Nicky's idea."

Dad made a small, wounded noise.

"I don't understand," Aysha admitted, looking around the room before settling her gaze on Bob and Martha. "You all knew about this? For how long?"

Bob shifted uncomfortably. "Martha and I have known for a while now. There was always something . . . different about Seth. We couldn't quite put our fingers on it. Not until . . ." He glanced at Martha, as if unsure.

Martha patted his leg. "Not until he accidentally lit his bed on fire. Luckily, it was a small fire that we were able to put out before anyone got hurt. We didn't know what had happened. It took a little bit longer to get the truth from Seth." She smiled at her nephew. "He was scared that we wouldn't want him anymore. As if pyrokinesis would make us love him any less."

Bob scratched the back of his neck. "We didn't want anyone else to know. Seemed safer that way. There wasn't much out there about Extraordinaries—at least, not enough to show us the best way to proceed. We had to figure things out on our own. It was . . . well, let's say the process was trial and error, with more error than anything else." He laughed quietly. "Quite a few singed eyebrows, but we got it under control, didn't we, Seth?"

Seth grinned at him, though it wasn't as bright as usual. He was still nervous, and Nick was in protective mode. Seth said, "They grew back, thankfully. There's a reason we evolved with eyebrows. You looked freaky without them."

"And you knew?" Trey asked Dad, and *now* he sounded angry. "You let our daughters get involved with this and didn't tell us? What the hell, Aaron—where's your damn head at?"

"*Dad,*" Gibby said, flushing slightly. "It's not like that. We knew before Mr. Bell did. In fact, out of everyone who knew before today, he was the last. If you're going to be pissed at anyone, be mad at me."

"Oh, I am," Trey said. "And when did you find out? Last fall at the bridge? Before? That was months ago, Gibster. I get that you were protecting your friend, but come on. You should've told us." He glared at Dad. "*Someone* should have told us. You say you weren't involved in any of the fighting, which—fine. But that doesn't mean you couldn't have gotten hurt." He closed his eyes. "Or worse."

Alarmed, Nick said, "Seth wouldn't hurt any of us. He's in control of—"

Trey's eyes flashed open, and Nick snapped his mouth closed. "I'm not talking about *Seth*, though, believe you me, we'll get to that in a moment." He glared at Dad. "What happens if my daughter gets pulled into a fight? What happens if the cops come and she doesn't raise her hands up quickly enough? Or too fast? What happens if a cop has an itchy trigger finger? You gonna tell me you did everything you could to keep her safe? That's bullshit, Aaron."

"Dad," Gibby said, sounding nervous. "Maybe we should—"

"Lola," Aysha said, and Gibby scowled down at her lap.

Dad didn't look away from Trey, and though Nick wanted to jump to his defense, he kept his silence. He wasn't sure if this was his fight, and he didn't want to make things worse. "I hear you, Trey," Dad said. "I swear I do."

Trey laughed, though it held no humor. "You say that, man—and oh, do I want to believe you. But then I remember I'm talking to the cop who assaulted someone in custody, and I don't know how to reconcile the man before me with the badge he wears."

"That wasn't his fault," Nick snapped. "The guy was talking crap about my *mother*—"

"Nick," Dad said, the warning in his voice clear. Nick deflated, picking at a small hole in the knee of his jeans. "Trey's right. It *was* my fault. It never should've happened. I messed up. That's on me and no one else. No matter what anyone says to me, I shouldn't have reacted the way I did." He looked back at Trey. "I am that man. I did hit someone in my custody, and I've regretted it every moment since. I can tell you it won't happen again, but I can't expect you to take me at my word. I have to prove that to you."

"Damn right you do," Trey told him, crossing his arms. "But that doesn't mean shit, given you're just one person. How many other cops have done the same thing you did and gotten away with it? Yeah, you were demoted, but that didn't last long, did it? Look where you are now. How much did the NCPD pay to settle the civil lawsuit against you?"

"A lot," Dad admitted. "It . . . a lot."

"And who paid for that?" Aysha asked. "It didn't come out of the police pension fund like it should've. It came from the taxpayers."

Nick turned his head slowly to look at his Dad. "People pay for police misconduct?"

"Oh, come on, Nick," Gibby said. "Where else would it come from?"

"I—I didn't know that." And wasn't that on him? He knew what his dad had done, knew that he'd been stripped of his detective rank, but why hadn't he asked more questions about the fallout? Why hadn't he pushed his father for more?

"And even with *all* of that," Aysha continued, "you still accepted that promotion."

"I thought it'd be better," Dad said, voice even. "I thought it'd help me be able to keep an eye on things, to make sure nothing happened to—"

"You should've *told* us," Trey snapped. He took a deep breath, letting it out slowly as Aysha took his hand in hers. "Look, I know you were trying to protect Seth. I get that; I really do. And I know down to my bones you'd do everything you can to keep the kids safe. But we're Black. Looking like me, looking like my wife, looking like my *daughter*, has gotten people killed for a whole lot less than you were promoted for."

"You're right," Dad said. "Everything you're saying is true. I won't try to tell you otherwise."

"Good," Aysha said, squeezing her husband's hand. She looked at Seth, then Nick, then Jazz. Her gaze lingered on Gibby for a long moment before she turned back to Dad. "We're not saying we're worried about Seth hurting anyone. But what about other people? Nick, *you* got hurt, remember? We came to see you in the hospital. We saw what happened with Pyro Storm and Shadow Star, along with everyone else. Who's to say that won't happen again? You know who he is, what he can do. And don't mistake what I'm saying—what Seth can do is magical. But what if someone comes after you because of what you know? Where's Owen now?" She looked wary. "I mean, my god. He *killed* people."

"Owen's not going to hurt anyone again," Dad said, and the steel in his voice sent a chill down Nick's spine. "He's locked away in a psychiatric hospital. And he's the only other Extraordinary that we know of. It's only Seth in Nova City now."

"But Simon Burke could," Miles pointed out. "If he's done half the things Seth said, then why hasn't he been arrested yet? At the very least, what he did to his own child should be enough to put him away."

"No proof," Dad said. "The secret floor in Burke Tower was vacant by the time we got inside. And Owen, as far as I know, isn't talking. I don't know if that's his choice or his father's, but that's the way it is."

"Either that, or Burke's got cops in his back pocket," Trey said. He held up his hand before anyone could protest. "Don't act like that's not a possibility. An extremely rich white man gets away with almost everything. Hell, he doesn't even need to be extremely rich for that to happen." He glanced at Dad. "How many of your colleagues are on his payroll? Moonlighting as security or some other bullshit?"

"I don't know," Dad said quietly. "More than a few, I'd expect."

Trey nodded. "You want to know why we talk about defunding the police? Because of this *exact* thing. They pick and choose who they protect, whether it's because they're racist dicks or because of who's lining their pockets—or both. If we have any hope for reform, you first gotta break everything down and start from scratch. And you can bitch and moan until you're blue in the face that we're talking about getting rid of police completely. It's not *just* about that. It's about holding cops accountable for everything they do." He scowled. "I'm not saying any of this to tell you how to fix your job, because that's not *my* job. It shouldn't have to be. And it shouldn't fall on Aysha, either, or Gibby. This isn't a game. Burke is powerful. If he's capable of making that evidence disappear in a matter of days, what could he do to our kids?"

Dad said, "This isn't something I've taken lightly. I've had the same thoughts about Nicky. And you're right; it was wrong to keep this from you. Don't be mad at them."

"Oh, I'm mad at you," Trey said. "And I know you feel guilty, but I can't help but think that it's guilt about getting caught more than anything else. If we hadn't come over here today, when would you have told us about any of this?"

"I don't know," Dad whispered. "I—"

"We're not stupid," Jazz muttered. "We've lasted this long, haven't we?"

"Of course you're not stupid," Miles said gently. "But you're only sixteen years old. All of you are, except for Gibby, and she's only a year older. I'm not going to speak for Trey and Aysha because I don't have the right to, but you, Jasmine? You're damn right I'm going to speak for you, because you're my daughter. Have you really thought this through? Any of you?"

"We have," Gibby said firmly. "And we'll do what we have to in order to protect our friend." She glanced at them before looking back at her parents. "We're Team Pyro Storm. We're Lighthouse. Seth needs us as much as we need him. You can try and break us apart, and maybe you'll succeed, but we're not playing around. We know this isn't a game. We take this as seriously as anything we have before. We need a new form of justice, and I want to be part of that change. I *am* part of that change, because it's what you taught me."

"Lighthouse," Aysha murmured. "And you—what, sit down in the basement on a computer, feeding him information about crimes in progress? That's all well and good, Gibby, but what happens next year? You're going to be leaving for school. You got into Howard, sweetheart. That's hundreds of miles away. Isn't it better to have a clean break now, so you can focus on your future?"

The air was sucked out of the room. Nick snapped his head toward Gibby.

"What?" Jazz whispered. "I thought—" She looked at her girl-friend. "You're leaving?"

"Dammit," Gibby muttered. "I wasn't going to—" She shook her head angrily. "I haven't made any decision yet."

Trey and Aysha exchanged a look that Nick couldn't decipher. "What do you mean you haven't made any decision yet?" Trey asked slowly. "Gibby, Howard is an amazing school. You've worked so hard getting the grades you have, and you're ranked first in your class."

"You're *what*?" Nick asked.

Gibby rolled her eyes. "It's not that big of a deal."

"It is," Jazz said in a hushed voice. "Just because you didn't want anyone else to know doesn't make it any less true. I'm proud of you. Everyone else should be too."

"You're leaving?" Seth asked, dumbfounded.

Gibby glared at the floor. "This isn't how I wanted this to come out. I'm still deciding what's best for me. And since it's *my* future, I get to make that decision." Her parents started sputtering, but she overrode them. "I know you think I need to go to an HBCU like you both did, but there's more to it than that. And it's not just about Jazz. Or Seth. Or Nick. Or even Lighthouse. It's about *me* and what I want." The fight went out of her voice, and she folded in on herself. "Doesn't that matter at all?"

"Of course it does," Aysha said. "And we'll support you no matter what you decide, but Gibby, I need you to think—really think. You say it's not *just* about Jazz or your friends. That plays a big part in it, though, doesn't it?"

For a moment, Nick thought Gibby wouldn't answer. She did. "It does. It's . . . we're making a difference. We're helping people. That counts for something, right?"

"It does," Trey said. "But so does your future. Say you stay in the city and go to school here. Are you going to be able to focus on your studies while still being part of Team Pyro Storm? And how long is that going to last? A year? Two years? Ten? Gibster, this isn't your system to fix."

"I know it's not," Gibby said. "But I want to. Because if anything is going to change, it has to start somewhere. Why can't it start with me?" She leaned forward, gaze leveled on her parents. "You told me the only reason change happens is because there are people willing to fight for it. I can't just sit by and let that fight go on without me, not when I can help make things better."

Trey looked stricken as he said, "I can't let anything happen to you, honey. I just can't. You are *everything* to me."

"I know, Dad," she whispered. "I love you too." She sat back in her chair, and when she spoke again, her voice was stronger. "I don't ask you for much. I never have. And I've never given you a reason to doubt me, which is why I'm asking you to trust me with this. We're young, yes, but we're doing good. We're making a difference."

Trey sighed, rubbing a hand over his face. "I want to trust you. I really do. But I've been around a hell of a lot longer than you have. I know how these things go. I'm not going to promise anything right now because that's not fair to any of us. I need time to think." He glanced at Aysha, who nodded. "We both do."

"She shouldn't make any decision based on this," Seth said. "Gibby, I—" He took a deep breath. "I don't know if this is even what *I* want. I can't be a hero forever."

Martha put her hand over her heart. "Seth? What are you talking about?"

He shrugged awkwardly, looking impossibly young. "I don't know. I just . . . There has to be more than this. I made the decision to become Pyro Storm because someone I cared about needed a hero. He didn't know that he was already *my* hero, and I wanted to do anything I could to make sure he never got hurt that way again. And it sort of steamrolled from there, because someone always needs saving, and if I could help them, then I had to. They were—are—my responsibility."

"You do what you need to do, Seth," Bob said gruffly. "And if that means hanging up the costume and just being a teenager, then so be it. The city survived long before you came into the world, and it'll be here well after we're all gone. Your aunt and I, we'll have your back, no matter what you decide."

"Let's take a step back for a moment," Miles said. "We need to think clearly about this, and I don't know if we can right now since we learned about all of it ten minutes ago." He jerked his head toward the boxes. "Jasmine, only the best, right?"

She nodded, though her face was pale. "Only the best."

Miles stood from the couch. "Well, let's see what we have, huh? Might as well make sure everything works like it's supposed to. What do you say, Trey? Feel up to helping me haul some boxes down to the basement?"

For a moment, Nick thought no one would move. He was surprised when Trey stood, sliding the sleeves of his thick sweater up his forearms. "Can do. I'm not much for computers and junk, but I know how to follow directions and plug things in."

"He does," Aysha said, pushing herself up from the couch. "It's one of the things I love most about him. Jo, let's go. We should probably make sure our husbands don't screw this up."

"Absolutely," Jo agreed. She followed the others as they began to hoist the boxes and carry them toward the basement stairs.

"I'll show you where the secret lair is," Bob said. "Built the pocket door myself, even though *some* people don't give it the appreciation it deserves." He looked pointedly at Nick, who rolled his eyes. After all, it wasn't *his* fault for having sky-high expectations when it came to something like a secret lair. At the very least, the door should've been outfitted with a retinal scan.

"And I have cookies!" Martha called after them, scooping up the plate from the table. "Everyone who helps will get as many as they want."

Dad jumped up at that, only pausing when Nick reminded him that he wasn't getting any younger, and that he'd already had four. Dad muttered under his breath that *he* was the adult and could decide how many cookies he could eat as he walked into the kitchen. Nick promised him if another cookie went into his mouth, he'd be eating only kale for the foreseeable future.

And then Team Pyro Storm was alone in the Gray living room, listening as the parents grunted and groaned as they descended the stairs to the basement.

Before anyone else could speak, Nick said, "Gibby, I know that look on your face. Do *not* apologize for anything."

Gibby sighed as she slumped in her chair. "He went after your dad hard."

"He did," Nick admitted. "But someone had to." He shook his head. "I just . . . I don't know, man. My dad isn't—" He stopped, thinking hard. He'd been about to say *My dad isn't like the other cops*, but that wasn't quite the truth, and it felt both familiar and gross to come to his defense so quickly. Instead, he said, "Your dad was right. About everything." He looked down at the floor. "And if anyone should be apologizing, it should be me for putting you in this position."

Gibby rolled her eyes. "I'm capable of thinking for myself, thanks."

Nick snorted. "Oh, don't I know it. But still. You deserve to hear it. I really am sorry."

"I know you are, Nicky."

"I do feel a bit better, though," Seth said, and they all looked at him. "Having them know. It takes a bit of the weight off our shoulders. We've survived this long, but I don't know how much longer we could have gone on without them finding out."

Nick glanced at Jazz, who had an expression on her face he'd never seen before. She looked almost . . . heartbroken. "Jazz?" he asked quietly. "You all right?"

But she only had eyes for Gibby. "You're thinking of leaving for school?" Jazz asked her, and Nick's heart ached at the hurt in her voice. "You never told me."

Gibby sighed, reaching out to take Jazz's hand. "I don't know what I want to do. I didn't say anything because I haven't decided yet, and with all that's happened today, I'm not going to make a decision right this second. But no matter what I decide, it won't be because I love you any less. No matter where I go, I'm not going to leave you all behind. We'll talk about it later." She jerked her head at Nick and Seth. "I promise."

Jazz nodded, though she still looked upset. Nick could only imagine what she was feeling. He didn't want to think of a time when Gibby wouldn't be there every day. And Seth was still thinking about hanging up the suit entirely? It felt like everything was changing, and he didn't know how to make it stop. And that didn't even begin to cover what had happened between Dad and Trey. He knew Trey was right, but he didn't know how to reconcile that with who he thought his dad was.

"Seth," Nick said suddenly. "Can I talk to you for a second?"

Seth nodded. "Yeah, of course. We can go up to my room and—"

"Stay here," Jazz said. "Gibby, we should go make sure our parents aren't messing up the secret lair. You know how I like having everything in the right place."

"That I do." She stood, pulling Jazz up with her. Gibby slung an arm around her shoulders, pulling her close. Nick watched as she whispered in Jazz's ear words only meant for them as they headed toward the stairs.

Only Seth and Nick remained. Nick gnawed on the inside of his cheek as he looked down at his hands. His heart was still racing, and he thought he might vibrate out of his skin.

"Nicky?"

He looked up. "You really don't want to be Pyro Storm anymore?"

Seth sighed, sounding frustrated. "I don't know. I have so much going on in my head, and I can't—"

His phone beeped a familiar sound that only meant one thing. Something was happening in the city.

Nick watched as the Seth he knew melted away. His eyes narrowed and darkened, his mouth stretched into a thin line, his jaw and shoulders tense. It wasn't Seth Gray who jumped up from the chair, pulling his phone from his pocket.

This was Pyro Storm.

"What is it?" Nick asked nervously.

"Accident," Seth said in a hardened voice. "On the Westfield River. A party barge crashed into a strut on a bridge. I need to get the people off the boat before it sinks."

Nick nodded as Seth started to get undressed. "Need help? Want me to go with?"

"No. It's fine, Nicky. I've got this. You'd just get in the way."

That stung more than Nick cared to admit. It wasn't like Seth was wrong, but it still hurt to hear. "Yeah. Okay."

Seth sighed, walking over to Nick and lifting his chin with a finger. "I didn't mean it like that." He looked so earnest. "I need you here to be my eyes and ears. There's no one I trust more to do that."

Nick smiled, and he barely had to force it. "I know. That I can do." He leaned forward, kissing Seth quickly. "Go. Do good, save lives, that whole thing."

Seth looked like he was going to argue, but before he could, footsteps pounded up the stairs. Dad appeared in full-on cop mode. This normally made Nick feel better, but didn't this time. He wondered if Gibby had ever felt . . . scared because of him. "Seth? We gotta go."

Seth nodded, stepping around Nick, charging down the stairs to suit up. Nick heard the surprise from the others below them, questions being asked and answered.

Dad was already on his phone, fingers flying across the screen. "You good to get yourself home? I'm going to see if I can help, though Harbor Patrol should already be on it."

He had to try. "I can go, too, if you want. I can help."

But Dad was already shaking his head. "We've got this. You'd just get in the way. And I . . . need some space to think. About a lot of things."

He forced a smile on his face. "Don't do anything stupid."

"Never, kid. I'll call you as soon as I can, okay?" He turned his head back toward the door and raised his voice. "Seth! We gotta go!"

Seth reappeared at the top of the stairs, cursing as he struggled into his costume. He tripped on the top stair, dropping his helmet as his cape fluttered around him. He bent over and picked it up before looking at Nick with wide eyes. "Gibby's and Jazz's parents just saw me get naked."

"Lucky," Nick muttered. "I mean, oh no. That's so bad. How dare they."

Seth gave him a quick kiss before joining Dad at the door. Dad leaned outside first, scanning the street. "Wait. Neighbor. Hold on—okay, they're inside. Streets are clear. Go."

In a bright flash of fire, Pyro Storm rocketed off into the sky, leaving a column of smoke behind him. Dad glanced back at Nick. "See ya." And then he slammed the door behind him as he left.

Nick turned and headed for the stairs. He descended quickly, scowling at the boxes in his way. Thankfully, they hadn't yet taken down the Systemax yet. Martha saw him coming and handed him the headset. He knew the others were watching him, but they faded into the background. "Pyro Storm, this is Lighthouse. Do you copy?"

"Receiving you loud and clear, Lighthouse," Pyro Storm said in his ear, his voice a deep rumble, modulated to disguise his identity.

He leaned toward the screen and took a deep breath. A moment later, Jazz and Gibby stood on either side of him. "Good, Pyro Storm. Let's go save some lives."

4

Nick was walking home, just blocks away from his street, with his attention on his phone, ignoring the people walking by him in the other direction. Footage from a news chopper flying high above the Westfield River showed a scene of chaos, the party barge half-sunken in the bay. Seth had been able to rescue everyone still trapped on the barge, carrying them all to safety before Harbor Patrol had shown up, late to respond to the call.

Nick's thoughts were thrumming like a live wire, exposed and crackling. He needed to do more, figure out a way to better help Seth. The news reports were cautious when it came to Pyro Storm, as if they didn't believe he was a hero, even though he'd saved countless people. Owen's shadow still stretched long over the city. There had to be a way to get people on their side. "Branding," Nick muttered to himself. "If Seth continues to be Pyro Storm, he needs to have brand recognition." He opened the notepad app on his phone and began to jot down ideas. A Twitter account from Pyro Storm's point of view? That'd be killer. Merch, definitely. Maybe even Instagram, which Jazz could run since her Insta was all black-and-white photos, and everyone knew black-and-white photos were tasteful as hell.

He wasn't paying attention to where he was going, lost in thought about how he could get the tide to turn in Pyro Storm's favor, all while grappling with what had happened at the Gray house. Trey's and Aysha's words rang in his ears.

Nick almost dropped his phone as he crashed into what felt like a solid wall. He stumbled back, ready—like a true citizen of Nova City—to snap at whoever had gotten in his way. The words died in his throat as he saw a man made purely of muscle standing in front of him in a dark suit, flecks of snow falling on his military crewcut.

"Nicholas Bell?" the man rumbled.

Nick eyed him warily. "Are you a fan wanting my autograph, or someone who wants to kidnap me? Either way, I'm going to need to reach into my bag to grab my pen for writing or stabbing."

The man didn't respond. He took a step toward the busy street, where a black limousine was parked against the curb. He opened one of the rear doors. "Get in."

"Wow," Nick said. "As much as I enjoy strange men asking me to get into their limos, I think I'm gonna pass. I'm sure whatever plot you have going on in that oversized head of yours would have been properly terrifying." He was about to turn and walk away when the man grabbed his arm, grip tight. Nick glared up at him. "Dude. Not cool. I didn't invite you to touch me. Seriously, back off before I literally stab your liver. I work out, okay?"

A low laugh came from the dark interior of the limo. Nick thought he recognized it, but he couldn't be sure.

"Get *in*," the man said, shoving him toward the open door.

"If you're kidnapping me, you're doing a shit job," Nick said, raising his voice. "There are a couple dozen witnesses. You, sir! Yes, you. Memorize our faces because—"

"Mr. Bell," a smooth voice came from inside the limo. "Enough with the theatrics. I'm not in the business of kidnapping. I only want a word. I'll even drop you off at home, if you'd like."

And oh, Nick knew that voice.

All the fight drained out of him. He didn't struggle as the man shoved him inside the limo. Nick stumbled, falling to his knees. He squinted against the low light as the door slammed shut behind him. It was warm in here. Too warm.

The rear of the limo had a row of leather seats against the driver's side, making an L-shape across the back. And sitting right in front of him was one of the few people Nick wished he'd never had to see again, for as long as he lived.

He was broad-shouldered, his suit black and expensive, his

tie blue. One of his legs was crossed over the other, the tip of his dress shoe bouncing slowly up and down. His hair was thick and wavy with streaks of gray. He smiled, and in it, Nick could see echoes of his son, cold and devastatingly handsome. The chill he felt had nothing to do with the cold winter day just outside the limo.

"Hello, Nicholas," Simon Burke said. "Have a seat. This won't take long."

Nick was about to tell him to go to hell when the limo pulled away from the curb, causing him to almost fall over again. He went to the back of the limo, trying to get as far away from Burke as possible. He settled on the seat, holding his backpack in his lap. "I have Mace," he announced. "And I know how to use it."

"Good to know," Burke said, his smile only growing. "I think you'll find it entirely unnecessary."

"What do you want?"

"I was driving by and I thought, oh my, that looks just like my son's former boyfriend. And I couldn't let the opportunity pass me by. We haven't had a chance to talk, you and I, and that simply won't do. We're tied together in ways you can't even begin to understand."

Nick scoffed. "Yeah, okay. Go, to hell, you weirdo."

Burke chuckled. "Feisty, aren't you? I bet your father has his hands full with you. How is he, by the way? I haven't had an opportunity to catch up with my old friend in a while. I heard about his new position as the head of the Extraordinaries Division. Good for him."

That stopped Nick cold. "'Old friend'? What are you talking about? You're not anyone's friend, much less my dad's."

Burke laughed, and Nick struggled not to flinch. He sounded just like his son. "Didn't you know? Why, I'm surprised he never told you, though I suppose recent . . . events would make him less likely to speak of it." He clucked his tongue. "Your parents and I used to be friends, back in the day. In fact, you could say we were more than friends."

And since Nick was Nick, he said, "You were in a three-way

relationship with my *parents*? Oh my god, why would you tell me that?"

Burke squinted at him. "No, though it's curious that's where your mind went. I'm afraid my tastes don't extend to the same sex." His smile softened, and for a moment, he almost looked . . . human. It only increased the alarm bells ringing in Nick's head. "I dated your mother for a time, while we were all at college. It wasn't long, but it was good. A lovely woman, Jenny Warren. But like some things, it wasn't meant to last. She met your father, and that was that. At the campus library, if I recall. She quite literally fell into his arms. Who was I to stand in their way, especially since I, too, came to care for Aaron? Their connection was undeniable, and they offered each other things I could not."

Nick's jaw ached as he ground his teeth together. Hearing his mother's name coming from Simon Burke set him on edge. "What did you do?"

Burke looked taken aback as the limo rolled over a couple of potholes. "Pardon?"

"I never heard them talk about you," Nick said coolly. "Not once. Not when she was alive, or after she died. You weren't at the service we had for her. And the only time I heard about you from Dad was after your psycho son tried to kill me and my friends, so you must have done something."

"Ah," Burke said. "Curious. I'm afraid I don't have a satisfactory answer for you, other than to say paths diverge. Perhaps that's something you should talk to your father about. I'm sure it would be enlightening."

Secrets. It always came back to secrets. They'd agreed to be honest with each other, but today had shown just how little Nick knew. Struggling to keep his expression blank, he looked out the window, recognizing the streets around them. They appeared to be heading toward his house, though Nick hadn't given them an address. He wasn't sure if he was relieved or not. "Uh-huh. Question: Do you know anybody on the Nobel Prize committee?"

Burke cocked his head. "I might. Why?"

Of course he did. What a pompous ass. "Good. Can you do me a favor and call them? I need you to let them know I've discovered that bullshit is genetic. I'm sure they'll want to give me an award."

The skin around Burke's eyes tightened, but other than that, he gave no reaction. "I can see why my son liked you. Quite the mouth you've got. I'd be careful if I were you. You could find yourself in trouble if you say the wrong thing to the wrong person."

"Riiiight," Nick said. He saw familiar houses outside the window. His street. "This is far enough. You can let me out here. I'll be sure to let Dad know you gave me a forcible ride and made vague threats, like you think we give two shits about anything you say."

Burke pressed a button on a panel near his seat. The divider lowered slightly, revealing the back of the driver's head. "Anthony," Burke said, never looking away from Nick. "Our guest is ready to leave."

The driver grunted, signaling as he pulled the limo to the curb a few houses down from Nick's. Nick waited until the vehicle came to a stop before reaching for the handle, the overhead light turning on as soon as he pushed the door open. He was partway out of the limo when Burke spoke again. "Owen asks about you."

Nick stopped.

He breathed in. He breathed out.

Then, through gritted teeth, he said, "What?"

"Owen," Burke said softly. "I'm told he asks about you. He doesn't speak much these days, especially not to me, but his medical team takes copious notes, and he's under constant surveillance. It's safer that way—for everyone. The room he's in is quite bright. Lights from all directions. No shadows, you see. They can't take the chance."

"I'm sure the drugs you forced on him have worn off by now," Nick snapped as he glared back over his shoulder.

Burke chuckled. "Forced? Is that what he told you?" He shook his head. "Always the victim, isn't he, never able to accept responsibility for his own actions. And you, swallowing it hook, line, and sinker. The sheer hubris of it all is staggering." He leaned forward, hands dangling between his legs. "Tell me, Mr. Bell. You knew him better than I ever could. Do you really think I could force him do to anything he didn't want to do?"

"Yes," Nick said. "Because I know I would do anything for my dad, even if it hurt me."

And though he tried to cover it up, that answer caught Burke off guard. His expression stuttered, there and gone in a flash, but Nick saw it clear as day. "Yes, well, I'm afraid Owen and I don't enjoy the relationship you and your father seem to have." And then he smiled again, and Nick had to keep from shuddering. "Though I do wonder if said relationship would remain intact if you knew everything there was to know about your father." He dropped his voice. "And your mother."

Bait. It was bait, and oh, did Nick want to take it. He was almost convinced that Burke was completely full of shit, but what if he wasn't? What if he was telling at least some version of the truth? If he'd known Nick's mother, that would mean he'd have stories about her Nick had never heard before. It'd be new information, and goddammit, he'd hoard every single word like gold.

But that was what Burke wanted. And even *if* he was telling the truth, it'd come with a price, and Nick wasn't about to play his games. This reeked of a setup. They hadn't heard a thing from Simon Burke after McManus Bridge, and now, out of the blue, here he was, dangling tidbits he knew Nick would want?

Nope. He wasn't going to dance, no matter what Burke said. And seriously, screw him for even bringing up Nick's mom. He had no right to say her *name*, much less—

The plastic covering on the overhead light cracked. A small piece of the cover fell to the carpeted floor of the limousine.

"Well now," Burke said quietly as he bent over and picked up the small chip. He held it in the palm of his gloved hand, bouncing it once, twice. "What have we here? I wonder how that happened?"

Nick was done with him. "As nice as this has been—and it's been

* 63 *

just lovely—I'm going to go home and pretend you don't exist. Have a nice life. Oh, and one more thing? A piece of advice: maybe don't pick up minors off the street. Not a good look, man."

"He's not the only one who's protective of you, is he?"

"What the hell is *that* supposed to mean?"

"Oh, Nick," Burke said. "Let's not do that. You and I both know who I'm talking about." He smiled that Owen smile again. Nick didn't like it one bit. "Since we're apparently in the position where we can offer each other advice, some for you." He held up the piece of plastic between two pinched fingers. "There are things at play here much greater than you know. If you want to know the truth, my door is always open." He pocketed the glass inside his coat. "Especially for one such as you."

Nick glared at him. "Dude, you are so not my type. And I'm taken, thank you."

"Yes," Burke said. "Because that's exactly what I was talking about." He sobered slightly. "You remind me of your mother. I see her in you. She . . ." He shook his head. "Phone."

"What?"

Burke held out his hand. "Give me your phone."

"No. Get your own. You can afford it."

"I'm not going to do anything untoward," Burke said patiently. "Please, Mr. Bell."

It was the *please* that got him. He didn't know why. He should've told Burke to piss off, but instead, he found himself reaching into his pocket, pulling out his phone, and handing it over. Burke didn't speak as he took it, fingers flying over the screen. Nick couldn't see what he was doing, but before he could ask, Burke handed his phone back. "There. You now have my contact information. When you're ready for the truth, you call me."

Nick snatched his phone back, already climbing out of the car. "Not gonna happen, dude. You can go back to your tower and be creepy there. Don't bother me again." Since the last word was Nick's greatest weapon, he slammed the door as hard as he could.

Except he didn't get the last word.

Because the tinted rear window rolled down, and Simon Burke

leaned forward. "Concentra, wasn't it? Yes, Concentra." He grinned. "Helps one concentrate, or so the slogan goes. One of the biggest breakthroughs of Burke Pharmaceuticals. I do hope you're reaping the benefits. Anthony, we're done."

Nick stood on the sidewalk, watching the limo as it pulled back into traffic and moved down the street until it turned a corner, out of sight.

Nick had his key in the door lock when he got a text from Dad saying he was on his way home, which surprised him. Dad's new job as the head of the Extraordinaries Division led to some odd hours, and Nick thought he'd have to stay at the harbor even if Pyro Storm had finished, to make sure everything was on the up-and-up.

Nick typed back a confirmation, saying he'd see him soon. And since he couldn't *not*, he asked Dad to describe in great detail the heroics Pyro Storm had shown in rescuing those from the sinking barge. Dad sent back an emoji wearing sunglasses. So aggravating.

Frustrated, Nick unlocked the front door and stepped inside, closing it behind him before heading toward the kitchen. He slapped together a cheese-and-ketchup sandwich, intending to spread out his homework and get back to it. He made it three minutes before he set down his pencil and picked up his phone. Gnawing on his lip, he searched *Concentra*.

Pages upon pages. Benefits. Side effects. Trials. Tests. FDA approval to be sold and distributed. Medical journals filled with incomprehensible jargon. Concentra, made by a company called Arc Medical Group.

Arc Medical Group, a subsidiary of Burke Pharmaceuticals.

"It's just a company," Nick muttered. "They probably make a billion things. Nothing to worry about."

He ran another search about Extraordinaries in Nova City to see if there'd been any hits he'd missed about any potential threats or new superheroes, something he'd done with increasing frequency over the past few months. Like most other people, he'd expected other Extraordinaries to appear after Pyro Storm and Shadow Star battled it out. Either there weren't any, or they were choosing to remain hidden.

No sightings, no speculations, nothing. Even on the message boards dedicated to Extraordinaries across the world, there was no mention in the Nova City boards about anyone other than Pyro Storm and Shadow Star, with the occasional reference to Guardian, the superhero who had patrolled the streets of Nova City back in the early aughts before disappearing. No one knew who they'd been, not even their gender—only that they'd been telekinetic. The few pictures that had been taken of Guardian were blurry, only catching flashes of their cerulean-blue costume. They had either quit, moved on, or died. Nick didn't know which was worse.

"If I was a hero, I'd never stop," he whispered to himself, throwing his phone down on the kitchen table. He scrubbed his hands over his face. He was irritated, but he didn't know at who. Seth, maybe, for saying he didn't know if he wanted to be Pyro Storm anymore, but was that fair? Once, before all the crap had come out about who Seth and Owen were, Seth had told Nick how lonely it must be being an Extraordinary, how you couldn't tell anyone about who you were or what you could do because they could become targets, or they might not understand and become scared. He'd practically given Nick a full confession, and Nick had responded by demanding they collaborate on a fic together.

Maybe he should clear his head by working on *A Pleasure to Burn.* He'd left Nash and Pyro Storm on a relatively sexy cliffhanger, and his readers would be demanding follow-through.

He was startled out of his fantasies of Pyro Storm whispering *I've never tried to use the costume for something so dirty* when the front door opened. "Kid, you here?" Dad called out.

"Kitchen," Nick said, looking down at his homework spread out before him. What a crappy Valentine's Day.

Nick listened as Dad went to the hall closet. He heard the familiar beeps of the gun safe Dad kept for his service weapon.

Dad appeared in the entryway, smiling tiredly as he glanced down at the textbooks and papers on the table. "You eat yet?"

Any appetite he might have had was long gone. His headache, a low simmer, pulsed behind his right eye. "We've got leftovers. I can nuke it in the microwave for you if you want."

Dad shook his head as he took off his coat, hanging it on the back of one of the kitchen chairs. He rounded the table, resting a heavy hand on the back of Nick's neck. He bent over and kissed the top of Nick's head before going to the fridge. "How's the homework coming?"

"Good. Fine. Almost done." Not really, but there wasn't anything due Monday. He had time.

Dad pulled Tupperware from the fridge. Lasagna from Mary Caplan. Mostly edible, but it had weird chunks of *something* in it that Nick never wanted to put in his mouth again. Mary was an awesome lady, but her cooking left something to be desired. Nick swiveled in his chair to watch Dad put the container in the microwave.

Dad turned, resting against the counter as the Tupperware spun in the microwave. He arched an eyebrow at his son. "So, more people know now." He looked uncomfortable when he added, "And I know you have questions about . . . a lot of things. What Trey said. And I want you to know he has a point, as hard as it was for me to hear. Whatever Gibby's and Jazz's parents decide, we need to respect their decisions because—"

"Simon Burke," Nick blurted.

Dad stiffened, eyes narrowing. He crossed his arms, the sleeves of his button-down straining against his biceps. "What about him?" He stared at Nick, and Nick didn't dare look away for fear he'd miss any sign Dad might accidentally let slip.

"You knew him." Saying those words was harder than Nick expected it to be. "Before." He pushed through it, even though it hurt. "You and Mom—you knew him."

Dad's expression gave nothing away. "Who told you that?"

Not a denial. And that made Nick feel worse, because it meant Burke hadn't necessarily been lying. It didn't mean *Dad* had lied, not quite. More that he'd kept something from Nick. And maybe that hadn't mattered before everything had come to light about Seth and Owen, but it sure as hell did now.

He could drop it. He could tell Dad that it didn't matter, that he was just happy he was home. He'd feign being tired, not that it'd be too much of a stretch. He'd go upstairs and put it out of his mind.

But Burke's voice was in his head, saying *Jenny Warren*, the words tinged with unmistakable affection.

Nick said, "He picked me up on the way home in his ridiculous car and said some stuff about you and Mom."

Whatever reaction he'd expected—outrage, denial, *something*—wasn't what he got. Dad's face twisted as he stepped forward, gripping Nick's chin, turning his head left and right before sliding his hands down Nick's arms as if checking for injuries. "Did he touch you? Did he hurt you?"

Nick pulled himself out of Dad's grip. "Chill. He didn't do anything to me, aside from basically kidnapping me. Except he was a bad kidnapper because he brought me straight home. It only lasted a few minutes."

That didn't seem to make Dad feel better. He crouched next to Nick as the microwave beeped at them. They ignored it. "Every word. Kid, tell me *everything* he said."

Nick hesitated before doing as he was told. He told Dad everything he could remember. He even thought about telling him about the broken light, but it was an ancillary detail.

By the time he'd finished, Dad was pale, eyes burning like hot coals. He'd rested one hand on Nick's knee, gripping tightly. "Did you take your medication?"

"What?"

"Your meds," Dad said. "When was the last time you took—"

"This morning," Nick said slowly. "Remember? You gave it to me at breakfast, just like always. We already talked about this at Seth's house." Weird. Why the hell would he bring that up now, of all things? Unless . . . "Did you know? That Concentra came from Burke Pharmaceuticals?"

No reaction, face stony. "They make everything, kid. I'm not surprised. But of course you took your pill. It must have slipped my mind. It's been a long day." He squeezed Nick's knee. "Yeah. We knew him. Your mother, she—" He closed his eyes. "I wouldn't call it dating. At least, that's what she said."

"Oh my god," Nick whispered. "They were friends with benefits?"

Dad's eyes flashed open. "Get your mind out of the gutter, Nicky. They went out a few times. It never turned into anything serious. By the time I met your mother, it was already on its last leg. And even though my opinion of Burke isn't the greatest, it has nothing to do with how he treated your mother. He didn't hurt her, didn't make her do anything she didn't want to do, so don't go down that road."

"Why didn't you tell me?" Nick asked. "After everything that happened?"

"This was years before you were even born. Your mom and I, we loved each other a lot. We got so wrapped up in each other those first couple of years, we sort of blocked anything else out. Burke just . . . drifted away. We weren't as good of friends as we could've been. He didn't seem to mind, at least not that we knew. He had his own thing going on, and then he met the woman who became his wife and moved on from us. It happens, okay? People change."

"Paths diverge," Nick said. Just as Burke had said.

Dad nodded. "That doesn't mean it's going to happen to you and Seth, or Jazz and Gibby. But even if it does, it's okay. What you want now might not be what you want in the future."

That alarmed Nick more than he expected. "I'm always going to want what I have now. Did their parents say something to you? I swear to god, if they try and—"

"Make decisions they feel are best for their kids?" Dad said. "Because if they do, you'll respect whatever choice they make. It's not up to you, Nicky. They have a right to protect Gibby and Jazz however they see fit."

"I know," Nick muttered. "But Gibby and Jazz are old enough to make up their own minds. We're practically adults."

"Oh boy," Dad said. "Let's talk about the *practically* part of that sentence."

"Did she love him?"

Dad was fluent in Nick, so he wasn't caught off guard by the conversational whiplash. "No, kid. Not in the way you're thinking. She cared about him. I did, too, but he wanted different things."

Nick nodded sagely. "I asked him if he was in a polyamorous relationship with you and Mom."

Dad gaped at him.

Seriously, what a drama queen. He was acting like that wasn't a plausible line of thinking. "What? We're very progressive in this household."

Dad managed to recover. "Really. That's what you think is progressive."

"Hey, I don't judge. For all I know, you and Mom were freaks in college." He grimaced. "I take that back; I don't want to know if you were. I'm pure and innocent and I can't have those images in my head."

"Uh-huh. I hate to break it to you, kid, but no one in our neighborhood will ever think you're pure and innocent again."

"You *monster*. You're lucky no one called child protective services on you."

"They can have you," Dad said. "No refunds."

"Bullshit," Nick growled. "You'd miss me too much. You need me to take care of you."

Dad softened as he stood, taking a step back. "Yeah, I suppose I do, huh?"

"You're not getting any younger," Nick reminded him. "You gotta watch your cholesterol levels. Don't make me call your doctor again."

"I still can't believe you did that," Dad muttered. "Can you make me a promise?"

And because he loved his father, Nick said, "Anything."

Dad looked down at him for a moment before nodding slowly. "Stay away from Simon Burke, okay? I don't want you having anything to do with him."

Nick said, "He picked *me* up. Why would I—"

"Promise me," Dad said. "This is important, kid. Given all

that's happened between you and Seth and Owen, we don't know what Burke wants. And until we find out, I want you to be careful. Can you do that for me?"

Nick hesitated, warming slightly at Dad's use of the word *we*. It meant they were a team. Of course he wouldn't have anything to do with Simon Burke. Why would he? Owen had made terrible choices, but how much of it was because of his father?

"What happened between you?" he asked finally. "What did he do that—"

Dad turned toward the microwave, but not before Nick saw his jaw set. "It's in the past, Nicky. Do what I'm asking, okay? And keep this between us. Don't tell the others about Burke or what he said. I don't want it being blown out of proportion."

"Okay," Nick said quietly, knowing the conversation was over. But he still had to try. "You'd tell me if something was wrong, right?"

"I would. Let's eat. We'll choke down the lasagna together in front of the TV. Sound good?"

It did.

It wouldn't be until later—much later, when everything had changed—that Nick would realize how neatly his father had deflected.

Dad went to bed earlier than usual after telling Nick not to stay up too late. Nick followed shortly after, trudging up the stairs to his room. He thought about trying to work on a new chapter of his fic, but when he sat down at his desk and opened his laptop, he found himself researching the best ways to launch a new brand. He wasn't surprised when he ended up on *Cosmo* again, reading an article about TEN CRITICAL SUCCESS FACTORS IN LAUNCHING A NEW BRAND IDENTITY FOR BUSINESSWOMEN. Damn his luck for being born male. He'd make an awesome businesswoman.

He'd only made it partially through the list, when he heard a tap at his bedroom window.

His window on the second floor.

He looked over slowly, heart rabbiting in his chest. The window was dark. Snow fell past it, catching the low light from the streetlamps below. *A bird*, he told himself. It was just a bird. Or flecks of ice. He turned back toward his laptop, trying to calm himself. Screw Simon Burke for messing with his head. He was making Nick paranoid.

The tapping came again.

Nick reached into his backpack, grimacing as his fingers slid through the remains of an exploded lip balm before finding what he was looking for, fingers closing around a cold metal canister. He hadn't yet had an opportunity to use the Mace, but if there was a villain outside his window, Nick was going to make them wish they'd never been born. And then he'd scream for his dad to save him. Solid plan.

He pressed himself against the wall with the window, inching over slowly. He stopped next to the window, just out of sight. He brought the Mace up, kissed the top of the canister, and said, "It's time to take out the trash."

Nick spun in front of the window, jerking it open with one hand, cold air washing over him as he thrust the Mace outside.

Nothing. There was no one there.

He leaned his head out the window, looking down at the street below. The sidewalk in front of his house was empty. He shivered as snow fell onto his hair.

"Yeah," a voice said from above him. "I knew it'd be a good idea to not stay in front of the window."

Nick yelped as he bumped his head hard against the windowsill. Frowning, he leaned back out the window, twisting at an awkward angle to look up. There, sitting on the edge of the roof, was a sight that set Nick's heart racing again.

Pyro Storm.

Except his helmet was removed, and it was Seth smiling down at him, cape fluttering around him, his feet dangling as he kicked them out.

"Texting is a thing," Nick told him. "You could have warned me you were coming over, so I didn't think I was about to be ambushed."

Seth laughed, a sound Nick dared anyone to try to say wasn't the best thing in the world. Nick gasped when Seth pushed himself off the roof, floating down until he was in front of him, the tips of his ears and nose pink from the cold. No matter what he'd seen in the last few months, Nick still wasn't used to the sight of Seth Gray being able to fly. He'd asked Seth repeatedly if he could carry him and fly around the city, to which Seth reminded him he didn't have superstrength, and Nick was heavier than he looked. That had led to an argument where Nick declared it wasn't *his* fault he liked shredded cheese on most things, to which Seth replied he didn't mean it like *that*, and then they'd somehow started making out and things had gotten a little hazy after that.

Still. A sight to see.

"At least you're prepared," Seth said, a few feet away from the window.

Nick glanced down at the Mace before shrugging. "Gotta be. It just so happens the hero of Nova City is my boo, and I—"

Seth groaned. "I told you not to call me that."

"Yeah, dude, not gonna happen. That's what you are. My boo. My superpowered love button. My—"

Seth said, "I got you a Valentine's Day present as a way of saying sorry we didn't make it to dinner."

Nick, knowing he was being distracted, said, "What? Give it to me now. Please."

Seth flew a little closer. Nick could feel the heat radiating off him. The snow hissed as it melted against Seth's costume, rivulets of water falling down his broad shoulders and strong arms and—

"I've had wet dreams that started just like this," Nick whispered.

Seth dropped a couple of feet.

"Um," Nick said. "Pretend I didn't say that."

"I don't know if I can," Seth said faintly as he rose back up.

"Present," Nick demanded, holding out his hand and wiggling his fingers.

Seth rolled his eyes but did as he was asked. He reached out with a gloved hand, setting a plastic package against Nick's palm. He looked down. Mango-flavored Skwinkles Salsagheti.

Nick—in a choked voice that he'd deny forever and ever—said, "This is the nicest thing anyone has ever gotten me. Thank you." He looked up at Seth, narrowing his eyes. "Are you trying to buy me off for leaving me behind to answer invasive questions by accountant hippies and rich parents?"

Seth grinned at him. "Maybe. Is it working?"

"Barely," Nick said. "And I'm not happy about how easy I apparently am, but that's another matter entirely." He batted his eyelashes. "Perhaps you'd like to come inside and see just how easy I am."

Seth stared at him. "Wow. That was . . . something."

Nick groaned. "It sounded sexier in my head. Let me try again. Hold on." He stood upright, puffing out his chest, hands on his hips, the candy wrapper crinkling. "Hey. Nice to see you. Let's discuss making out for the next thirty minutes and see where that—*oof.*"

His breath was knocked from his chest as Seth flew through the window, tackling him and knocking him off his feet. He braced himself for the hard impact on the floor but opened his eyes when no jarring crash came. Seth had wrapped his arms around him, holding them both a foot off the floor. They hung suspended for a moment before Seth lowered them down gently, settling on top of Nick, cape falling over them like a blanket.

"Hi," he whispered, brushing his nose against Nick's.

"Hi," Nick whispered back. "Not that I don't appreciate the late-night visit, but what're you doing here? Dad said you guys finished hours ago."

Seth shrugged, a thick curl hanging on his forehead. "I wanted to see you. I didn't like how our plans got ruined on top of everything else."

"It's okay," Nick said, letting him off the hook. "I kinda screwed up too, so let's just call it a wash."

Seth's smile faded. "It's not okay. I don't want you thinking I don't need your help. It's not like that at all."

"I didn't think that." He sighed when Seth arched an eyebrow. "Okay, maybe a little bit, but you're right. I can't do what you can."

Seth rolled off him, lying on his back next to Nick, their shoulders pressed together. He turned his head just as Nick did, their faces only inches apart. "I know. But I couldn't stop thinking about it. And then I had to go before we could work through it."

"That seems to be happening a lot lately," Nick admitted. Seth winced, and so Nick added quickly, "I know you have an important job to do. People need Pyro Storm; I get it. I'm not mad about that." And it was mostly the truth, though it was still wrapped up in that complicated knot in Nick's chest, tangled with love and jealousy and a thousand different things he didn't always understand.

"It's not fair," Seth muttered, taking Nick's hand in his own. Seth's glove was slightly wet from the snow, but it was warm. "You know I'd rather be with you than be anywhere else."

He did, but it helped to hear it said out loud. "I know," Nick said, squeezing Seth's hand.

Seth turned his head to look up at the ceiling. He raised his free hand above them and wiggled his fingers. Nick's eyes widened when a small bloom of fire appeared. Seth waved his hand slowly from side to side. The fire followed, elongating as it took the shape of a miniature comet. The heat of it was comforting, familiar. He closed his fist and the fire snuffed out, leaving behind a wisp of smoke and the subtle scent of burning air. He dropped his hand back to the floor. "Things are changing, Nicky. More people know now, but I can deal with that. It's everything else that scares the crap out of me. Pretty soon, we're going to start applying for college. I don't know where we'll all end up."

Alarmed, Nick said, "You still want to go to the same school, right? I mean, it's totally cool if you want to do something else." It wasn't cool at all. He should've texted Jazz to see how she was holding up.

"Yeah," Seth said. "You and me, okay?" He looked over at Nick again and kissed the tip of his nose. It tickled, and Nick squinted against it. "But I have to think about what I want too. Am I going to be doing this when I'm in my twenties? My thirties? Someone is always going to need saving. And who am I to turn my back on them, you know?"

"You're not alone," Nick said, leaning his head against Seth's shoulder. "We've all got your back."

Seth exhaled through his nose. "I know, but sometimes I want to be selfish. What about me? I don't know what my future is supposed to look like. There are days when I imagine I'm not Pyro Storm anymore. Where I get to do stupid things before I grow up and get a job and pay bills. Normal stuff. I want to be able to go out with you and our friends for Valentine's Day and not have to worry about being called away. Is that fair?"

"You're allowed to want things." Nick hesitated. "Being Pyro Storm isn't all of you, but it's a big part. Could you really let that go?"

"I don't know," Seth muttered. He sounded frustrated. "I won't know unless I try. That terrifies me. Because if I *did* try, there'll come a moment where someone will need Pyro Storm, and I'll have to decide whether or not to do anything about it." He rubbed his gloved hand over his face. "I don't know if I can choose to ignore someone who needs help. What kind of a person would that make me?"

"Human," Nick said. "It makes you human."

Seth laughed, though there was no humor in it. "But I can do things most people can't, whether or not it was because of the train accident or . . ." He trailed off, looking off into nothing.

Dangerous ground, this. Seth rarely talked about the deaths of his parents. He'd been too young to remember most of it, and he'd been one of the only survivors.

"Or?" Nick asked, unsure if he should be doing so.

Seth didn't speak for a long time. Finally, he said, "I wonder, sometimes. If I got this from them. My powers. If it was genetic. My aunt and uncle said they never saw my parents do anything like I can, but maybe they kept it secret. I did for a long time."

"Do you remember them?" Nick whispered.

Seth turned to look at him again, studying him—searching for what, Nick didn't know. "Bits and pieces," he whispered back. "Little things. Dad liked to sing. He had a good voice. Not the best, but good enough. And Mom, she—" He closed his eyes. "I remember her laughing. It was a big sound. She didn't try and hide it or cover it up. When she laughed, it was with her whole body. There's other stuff I can think of, but that's what I remember most." He sighed. "I don't remember what they sounded like when they spoke."

Here, in the safety of his room, while snow fell just outside the open window, Nick said, "That's one of the things that scares me most. That I'll forget what she sounds like."

Seth looked at him. "Your mom?"

Nick nodded. His eyes were starting to burn, but Seth would never make fun of him for crying, so he didn't try to shove it down. "It's only been a few years, and there are days when I think I'm okay, but then I panic because I can't remember what she sounded like when she was happy or sad or angry."

"What do you do?"

Nick sniffled as he shrugged awkwardly. "Sometimes I spiral until I can barely breathe. Other times, I feel stupid about it. I guess it depends on the day and how my brain is. In case you didn't know, I'm a little messed-up in the head."

"I like your head," Seth said seriously, and Nick grinned at him. "And you're not messed-up. You're just wired differently, like I'm wired differently."

Nick groaned. "If only ADHD could be a superpower."

"It is. You have the power to have a billion thoughts in the space of a few seconds. That's pretty cool, if you ask me—even if you also say those billion thoughts out loud. But that's okay, because you usually know what you're saying."

And because Nick was a sucker for reassuring compliments, he gave in kind. "I'm going to shove my tongue down your throat in a minute. Use the time I'm giving you to prepare yourself."

Seth laughed loudly, covering his mouth to try to keep as quiet as possible. Nick laughed along with him. Even though this Valentine's Day hadn't gone according to plan, it was ending on a good note. They'd be all right, Simon Burke and Rebecca Firestone be damned. In this moment, nothing else mattered, because Seth Gray was laughing like he didn't have a care in the world, and Nick had caused that. He'd have time to tell Seth about Burke later. He didn't want to ruin this, not for anything in the world.

He watched as Seth started hiccupping into his hand. Nick reached out and pulled Seth toward him and kissed him with everything he had. Seth was smiling against his mouth, and though he didn't shove his tongue down his throat (not for lack of trying), it was still good.

So good, in fact, that he rolled on top of Seth as they kissed, sliding his hands up Seth's chest to his arms, grinding his hips down. Seth groaned, and Nick's blood was rushing south. Seth seemed to be having the same problem. Seth wasn't Boner Boy, and Nick wasn't the rough-and-tumble oil worker, but Nick would be damned if he wasn't going to one day get that superqueero penis.

But maybe not today, because Seth yawned against Nick. He sat up, his butt on Seth's hips. He wiggled a little, causing Seth to gasp and grip his thighs, but he took it no further. Not only was Dad just down the hall, but Nick could see how tired Seth was. He needed sleep.

Nick stood above Seth, holding out his hand. "Come on. Bedtime. I'll set my alarm early so you have time to get home before Dad wakes up."

"Sleepover?" Seth asked, taking his hand and allowing him to be pulled up off the floor.

"Sleepover," Nick agreed. "I'll get you some sweats to sleep in. Sucks you won't be able to brush your teeth. We don't have a spare, and I like you, dude, but not enough to let you use mine. That's disgusting, so don't even ask."

"You're all heart, Nicky."

"Damn right I am."

They got ready for bed, talking about nothing of any real importance, which Nick appreciated. Too much had happened in such a short time, and he still needed to process all of it. By the time Nick returned from the bathroom, Seth was already in bed, pulling back the comforter in invitation. Nick gladly accepted, curling against Seth as he pulled the comforter up and over their heads, cocooning them in darkness.

And then it was like they were kids again, two kids who didn't have anyone but each other, whispering in the dark about how they would always be friends, no matter what. Pushing it further would be complicated. *Sex* was complicated, in all its forms. But this was Seth. This was his best friend. This was the person he thought of before he fell asleep and right when he woke up. This was the guy Nick would do anything for.

"I'll fix this," Nick said quietly when Seth slept. "I'll help make things easier for you. Promise. I've got an idea, and it'll all work out. You'll see. Things will stay the same, no matter what."

It was dark when he woke. He blinked blearily and heard Seth snoring. He turned his head, wondering what had awoken him. The clock on his nightstand showed it was just after four.

"Yeah," a voice said. "Tracker was right. He's here. You want me to send him home?"

Dad was standing in the open doorway, phone pressed against his ear.

Uh-oh.

Nick dropped his head quickly to the pillow, squeezing his eyes shut. Bob or Martha must have seen Seth wasn't home. Dammit. Dad was going to be pissed. Maybe he'd just let them be if he thought Nick was sleeping.

"Both zonked out. Must have tired Seth out more than we thought. All right. Yeah, talk soon."

The phone beeped.

The floor creaked as Dad stepped inside the room, muttering under his breath as he stepped over the clothes strewn about. Nick wanted to tell him it wasn't what it looked like, but decided pretending to sleep was the way to go.

He felt Dad standing over them.

He snored loudly to sell the ruse.

"Yeah, okay," Dad said, keeping his voice low. "Because *that* was believable."

Nick cracked open one eye. "Dammit."

"Explanation."

"We didn't do anything," Nick said, looking up at his father.

"Just . . . we needed to talk, and he came over and brought me Skwinkles Salsagheti for Valentine's Day, even though I didn't get him anything and who was *I* to turn him away, back out into the cold? No one, that's who."

"Do I need to make you dental dams?"

"Why are you *like* this?" Nick hissed at him.

Dad's eyes glittered in the dark. "Because your aggravation gives me life, kid. Ask, okay? The Grays were worried. I trust you, Nicky, but you and Seth still gotta think. We need to know where you are."

"Yeah. Sorry. We were talking and then fell asleep."

Dad shook his head. "It's still early. Go back to sleep. And then you and Seth can come down to breakfast. I'll be waiting."

He turned to walk out of the room but stopped after only a couple of steps. Nick followed his gaze to the photograph on the desk. Grief, Nick knew, could stay hidden for weeks and months. Just when you thought it was over, it sank its teeth back into you unexpectedly.

Shoulders hunched, Dad left the room without another word, closing the door behind him.

5

Fic: A Pleasure to Burn
Author: PyroStormIsBae
Chapter 37 of ?
138,225 words
Pairing: Pyro Storm/Original Male Character
Rated: R (Rating is finally going up!)
Tags: True Love, Pining, Gentle Pyro Storm, Happy Ending, First Kiss, More Than First Kiss, Fluffy like a Cloud, So Much Violence, Evil Shadow Star, Bakery AU, Private Investigator, Anti-Rebecca Firestone, Hands Going under Clothes, !!!, Naked Party and You're All Invited

....

Chapter 37: An Opportunity

Author Note: Another update so soon? Why yes, yes it is. You're so welcome! And while I know many of you were probably hoping for a continuation of the sexy times, I'm asking you to bear with me. It's important that these characters work toward the big event by talking about things that will bring them even closer together. Talking matters, and it's important to me that both Nash and Pyro Storm are on the same page. You, as well as our heroes, are about to be presented with an opportunity that will blow your mind! Also, this wasn't beta read because I wanted this to be a surprise for a certain . . . someone who does certain . . . things. Sorry if there are any mistakes! Thanks!!!

Nash gasped as Pyro Storm manhandled him up against the wall near the door to the roof, wearing only his mask and a tiny pair of underwear that was illegal in at least twenty-six states. The hero acted like Nash weighed nothing, even though his body was strong and heavy with muscle. He wanted to continue, to have Pyro Storm ravish him and fill him up with his fire of love, but something crossed his mind.

"Wait," he managed to say as Pyro Storm attacked his neck, biting down.

"What?" Pyro Storm murmured against his throat, hands roaming.

"We need to talk. But in a *good* way."

Pyro Storm took a step back, leaving Nash slumped against the wall. "Of course. We should definitely talk about what we're going to do before we do it. Safe, sane, and consensual, that's the best way to be."

"Exactly," Nash said. "Everyone on Reddit knows that, but that's not what I'm talking about."

"Oh?" Pyro Storm asked, muscles on full display. He had an eight-pack, and his thighs were like slabs of concrete. Nash had to look away to keep his thoughts in order. "Then what do you mean?"

Nash pulled out his phone, pulling up the presentation he'd worked so hard on. "I want to offer you an opportunity—one I think would help you to become a better hero. I'm talking, of course, about branding."

Pyro Storm nodded sagely. "Ah, I see. Yes, that *is* very important. Tell me more. I'm very excited to hear about this."

"Good," Nash said, "because every superhero worth his salt needs brand recognition. We need to be at the forefront of it so that no one steps in and tries to fill the void in the current market. I have a sixteen-slide PowerPoint presentation I'd like to show you, and I think by the end, you'll agree that Pyro Storm needs to have his own online presence: Twitter, TikTok, Instagram, the works. No Facebook because we're not elderly and don't post racist Minion memes. That will be part one. Part two entails the launching of the official Pyro Storm merchandise line. We will commission creators in the fandom to make art in their medium and sell them, with a portion going to nonprofit so people will feel good about paying for it. And it will be so much better than the cheap knockoff crap that's out there today."

"Wow," Pyro Storm said. "You've thought of everything. I can't believe how lucky I am to have you. But I've got a question, as everyone knows a good plan has three parts. What's part three?"

"You're so smart," Nash said. "Part three will be speaking engagements and/or photo ops. We can go to conventions together and charge people to take a photo with you while you say your catchphrase."

"My catchphrase?" Pyro Storm asked, adorably confused. "But I don't have a catchphrase."

"I know," Nash said. "Which is why I've made one for you. You ready?"

"I've never been more ready for anything in my life," Pyro Storm said, sweat trickling down his bare chest. "You're the best thing that's ever happened to me, and all your ideas are top-notch. And, I should say, you look hella good when you say them out loud."

"Thank you," Nash said. "You are hotter than" ***think of something to put here that's really sexy and don't forget before you post this.***

"Whoa," Pyro Storm said. "I can't believe you said that. What's my catchphrase, which I'll use without question because I know how hard you worked on it?"

Nash felt his heart trip in his chest. He'd never expected to have a boyfriend who was an Extraordinary and who also thought all his ideas were perfect. "Okay. Here goes. Ready? Your catchphrase is . . . *It's time to burn*."

"My *god*. Nash, did you really think of that all on your own?" Pyro Storm took an aggressive step toward him. "I'm going to put my hands on your butt and squeeze. It's time to burn."

"Awesome," Nash said. "I'm so happy that you like every one of my ideas and don't think any of them are dumb or a waste of time. I'll oversee your social media, and maybe the very people witnessing our love story blossom right before their eyes would like to take part in the merch store. There might even be a sign-up sheet available right now at Pyro Storm's official website, which will be linked below."

"You think of everything," Pyro Storm said. "So what if we're in the middle of solving a string of murders that have shaken Nova City to its core, or that we were about to have sexual relations for the first time? This is just as important. Thank you for bringing this up, and I hope everyone goes to the official website you created. Now, where were we? Because I have a mighty need to put myself inside yourself."

Nash's phone fell to the rooftop as Pyro Storm descended upon him. He brought his mouth close to Nash's ear, and whispered, "What's the name of the website where people can sign up?"

www.OfficialPyroStorm.novacity

....

Comments:

ImSoExtra(ordinaries) 09:19 Um. What.

PyroStormSuxx 10:14 WTF IS THIS? I HATE PYRO STORM BUT I CAME HERE FOR THE BUTT SEX. WHY DID YOU TURN THIS INTO A COMMERCIAL?

LetPyroStormSmash 11:02 I've signed up, thank you for the opportunity! Question: how explicit can we make the art? Because I have this idea, but it's going to show a lot of nudity, and possibly some tentacles. Please let me know!

ExtraordinaryGurl 11:16 This didn't go where I thought this was going. That's not cool. You must really be into edging.

ShadowStarIsBae 12:26 Okay, but this must be against the terms of service for the fic hosting site. You can't just turn your story into an advertisement. This is supposed to be fiction, not an infomercial. Can you please just get to the sex and the solving of the serial murders? In that order?

FireStoned 12:36 I SIGNED UP AT YOUR STUPID WEBSITE AND I'M ONLY GOING TO SEND REBECCA FIRESTONE FANART. I DON'T CARE WHAT YOU THINK BECAUSE REBECCA FIRESTONE DESERVES TO HAVE EVERYTHING GOOD IN THE WORLD. SHE IS THE BEST THING THAT'S EVER HAPPENED TO ANYONE AND THE FACT THAT YOU MAKE HER THE VILLAIN WHILE MAKING EVERYONE GAY IS UNREALISTIC.

SoundOfJazz 13:12 Wow, Nicky! This is certainly a way to go about it. Not what I would have picked or even considered, but I admire your follow through! Gibby said some stuff too, but I'm just going to leave this positive. Let me know how I can help!

When Nick had returned to Centennial High (Home of the Fighting Wombats!) last fall, his arm in a sling after he'd dislocated it saving Rebecca Firestone from certain death, he'd been something of a hero. Everyone had seen the footage from the *Action News* helicopter of him standing on McManus Bridge, the lights from dozens of police cars flashing, Shadow Star defeated and unconscious on the ground, the air filled with smoke.

But it was the kiss that had gotten everyone talking.

Pyro Storm—weathered and beaten, but not broken—kissing one Nicholas Bell for all the world to see before he rocketed into the sky in a bright flash of fire. There'd been others on the bridge then, too, people with their cell phones out, recording shaky videos from different perspectives. Someone had put them all together in a five-minute-long, multiangle video and posted it online. The last time Nick had checked, the YouTube video alone had racked up nearly four million views.

Nick had left the school a nobody, a queer kid who was loud and annoying and tended to give presentations on the mating habits of box turtles when he was supposed to be discussing Byronic heroes in English class.

He'd returned a celebrity.

Students who hadn't given him the time of day came up to talk to him: jocks ("So cool, bro, obviously no homo"); cheerleaders ("Like, I could not even *believe* you liked boys, but that is so *hot*"); the academics ("How exactly do Pyro Storm's powers work, and why did you not get burned when you engaged in mouth osculation?"); the stoners ("Whoaaaaaaa, dude, gnarly stuff—do you think Pyro Storm would come to my house and smoke us out?"); the theater kids ("So we don't have to do *Brigadoon* for the tenth time, we're putting on an original musical about you and Pyro

Storm"); the band geeks ("We're gonna do a concert in your honor for all that you—Nick, the trombone is not a toy for you to play with, put it *down*"); and the rich kids ("You poor waif, you can barely even tell your arm sling isn't Louis Vuitton").

Nick had basked in the attention, signing autographs for everyone who'd asked (six people). In the week he'd missed while recovering, his infamy had grown to near-mythical levels, especially when Rebecca Firestone had unmasked him as *ShadowStar744*, the most popular fanfic writer in the Extraordinaries fandom. She'd called his masturbatory ode to Shadow Star a manifesto and publicly questioned whether Nick had been working with Shadow Star, her own history with the villainous Extraordinary be damned. But it'd backfired on her, only adding to Nick's mystique. By the time he returned to school, rumors were flung about without evidence to back them up, especially when the truth came out that their fellow classmate and Nick's ex-boyfriend, Owen Burke, was Shadow Star.

Nick's favorite rumors included:

Nick was an Extraordinary himself—either a hero or a villain, or possibly both . . . or . . . neither;

Nick and Owen were murder-husbands and had killed thirty-six people;

Nick was a sociopathic black widow/femme fatale (how *that* worked, he didn't know) who'd seduced Owen and Pyro Storm and pitted them against each other in a fight to prove their loyalty; and

Nick, Owen, and Pyro Storm were in a polyamorous relationship that had gone sour when Nick and Pyro Storm wanted to break up with Owen.

Sure, Nick had failed to become an Extraordinary himself, but this was the next best thing. Nick let the attention wash over him with no small amount of glee, knowing changes such as this, while rare, lasted a lifetime. He wouldn't be going back to the life he'd once lived. This was forever.

It lasted four days, six hours, and seven minutes.

Nick had relished the attention, retelling the Battle of McManus

Bridge over and over and barely embellishing any of the details, but it soon grew tiresome when he declined to answer the biggest question on everyone's mind:

Who was Pyro Storm really?

With Nick's refusal to answer this simple question came an unexpected side effect: a fresh wave of speculation. Owen Burke had been Shadow Star, ergo it was possible that Pyro Storm was also a student at Centennial High. A list was made and circulated of the most likely suspects, and Nick was outraged when Seth hadn't made said list. It was mostly filled with douchebros who did nothing to dispel the rumors, cockily saying that even if they *were* Pyro Storm, they'd never tell. Even a few girls made the list, which offended Nick greatly—not because of their gender, of course, but because he would never be caught dead making out with a girl. The very idea was homophobic.

It didn't help that he knew everyone had *seen* him kissing Pyro Storm after the Battle of McManus Bridge. To keep anyone from connecting the dots to Seth, he'd started a rumor that Pyro Storm had broken up with him when he realized Nick's heart would always belong to Seth. This had backfired quite spectacularly as it'd spread like wildfire, most believing that Nick had cheated on Pyro Storm with Seth. Pyro Storm was better-off, they all agreed. He needed someone who would appreciate him for all that he was. Nick obviously couldn't do that, so it was for the best.

With that, Nick's popularity went as quickly as it'd come. It'd hurt a little, but he'd gotten over it.

That being said, he was a *little* (read: a lot) irritated when everyone suddenly became fixated on Extraordinaries. They showed up to school with graphic T-shirts with Shadow Star's face on them and backpacks with a terrible likeness of Pyro Storm printed on it. They shared pictures of sightings of Extraordinaries from all over the world:

Eis Augen, a German man who could shoot ice from his eyes, his name literally translating to Ice Eyes. He was suave and coldly handsome and lived in a frozen palace outside of Berlin.

Valve, the man in Oregon who could create portals to travel long distances in the space of seconds and was revolutionizing the travel infrastructure of Portland. He'd also accidentally on-purpose opened a portal on the marchers in a Straight Pride Parade. No one quite knew where the second portal had opened, and the problematic heterosexuals hadn't been seen since.

Florida Man, the dude in Tallahassee whose skin was the color and texture of an alligator, his teeth terribly sharp. He was currently going through a name rebranding, given that most search results for "Florida Man" brought up stories of people eating bath salts and going through a KFC drive-through on an alpaca.

The Sheep Herder, a woman in New Zealand who could control the minds of sheep to get them to do whatever she wanted. Her popularity had spiked when she'd sent seven hundred sheep after a group of twelve white nationalists who had been holding a rally in Wellington. Last anyone heard, they still hadn't stopped running from the herd of sheep chasing after them.

And dozens and dozens of others, some with powers small, some with powers great. He'd even heard of an Extraordinary capable of changing their appearance to mimic anyone they wanted, including getting the powers of those they copied. That sounded cool as hell, but Nick thought it was a little far-fetched, and he hadn't been able to confirm it after spending hours online, only to hit dead end after dead end. Everyone at Centennial High (and throughout the rest of Nova City) waited with bated breath to see if any other Extraordinaries would rise in their fair city, along with Pyro Storm.

It was quiet without Shadow Star, which was good. It was fine. They didn't *need* a villain. Quiet meant easy. Quiet and easy meant Seth would always come back to Nick.

But the problem with things being quiet and easy was that Nicholas Bell had never been quiet *or* easy. Loud and complicated was Nick through and through, and he couldn't help but wonder if things were a little *too* quiet, a little *too* easy.

But everything can change in an instant. A snowflake can lead to an avalanche.

And on a cold February morning, it began to snow.

W e're going to be late," Jazz said, eyeing Nick with mild disdain and curiosity. She frowned as she readjusted her Hermès scarf, as if it were Nick's fault it had gone slightly askew.

"I know, I know," Nick muttered. He set his backpack on a bench in the Franklin Street Metro Station and began to riffle through it. "I swear my phone was in here. I don't know where the hell it went." He wasn't panicking—not yet—but he was close. He needed his phone. It was his lifeline to Dad, just in case.

"Did you drop it?" Gibby asked. "I'll do it." She shoved his hands out of the way and pulled the bag into her lap. He didn't protest; Gibby seemed like she was in a foul mood.

"I didn't drop it," Nick said, glancing up at the crowd moving around them. "I had it on the train when Seth texted and said he was running late and was probably going to fly to school. I swear I put it back in my bag."

"Yikes," Jazz said. "I'm apparently not used to hearing stuff like that yet."

"*Thank* you," Nick said. "I mean, objectively, we know he can do it, but still, hearing about it trips me out. He doesn't get why."

"Gross," Gibby said, grimacing as she pulled out a busted lip balm that'd exploded and was now covered in hair. "What the hell, Nicky. Clean your damn backpack." She tossed the lip balm in the trash can next to the bench before resuming the search. "You're a gay boy. You're supposed to be neat and tidy."

"Don't listen to her," Jazz said, squeezing his arm. "That's stereotyping. You can be however you want to be, so long as it doesn't involve you jumping into the Westfield River again. I still have nightmares about the way you smelled."

"We all do," Gibby said. "I'm glad you've moved on from— A*ha*! Got it." She pulled out his phone and tossed it at him.

Nick was too grateful to argue. He glanced down at the screen—
no messages—before sliding it into his pocket and taking his backpack from Gibby. "How're things going with your parents?"

Gibby shrugged. "Slow going, I guess. I mean, Dad is still pissed
off. Mom too. They haven't said I can't hang out with you, so I'm
counting that as a win. We'll see where it goes, I guess."

"Daddy and Mom had a billion questions," Jazz said. "I
didn't know the answer to most of them, so they're probably still
confused—though Mom did have to tell Daddy that he can't just
ask Seth to light things on fire."

Nick sighed. "I don't know what it says about me that I think
the way your Dad does."

"It's good," Jazz said. "Or really bad. One of those two."

"Uh, yeah," Nick said. "Sure. Let's go with that." He glanced at
Gibby nervously. "Can I ask you a question?"

Gibby frowned at him. "When have you ever asked instead of
going for it?"

Shrugging awkwardly, Nick said, "First time for everything, I
guess. I—" He steeled himself, knowing this was important but
fearing the answer. "Has—has my dad ever scared you? Like,
not . . . ugh. Not like he was coming after you, but—"

Gibby stared at him for a long moment before saying, "Are you
asking *for* me or to make yourself feel better?"

"Probably a bit of both," Nick admitted. "But I know it's not
about me. And seriously, tell me the truth, okay? Or don't, if you
don't feel comfortable. You're important to me, Gibby."

Gibby groaned. "It's too early for feelings. What the hell,
Nicky." She gnawed on her bottom lip before squaring her shoulders and looking at Nick dead-on. "Okay. Honest?"

"Honest," Nick agreed.

"No. Your dad has never done anything *to me* to make me uncomfortable."

Sagging in relief, Nick said, "That's—"

But she wasn't finished. "Not *directly*. But Nick, he's—he's a
cop. And even though I know him, that still doesn't change what
that means. You see a badge and the uniform, and you think of

safety. *I* see the badge and uniform and think about how often people like him have failed people like me. It's not just about your dad; it's about *all* of them. And it doesn't help that your dad did what he did. I know it was a few years back and it was a white guy, but if he assaulted someone once, who's to say he won't do it again?"

"Yeah," Nick muttered. "I get that now. I'm not going to pretend that what Dad did was justified. It wasn't. And I think I kind of . . . I don't know."

"Glossed over it?" Jazz asked quietly.

"Maybe," Nick said with a wince. Someone bumped into him on the way toward the stairs, and he scowled over his shoulder before looking back at his friends. "No, *not* maybe. I did." All he'd been thinking about was how he'd act if someone was talking shit about his mother like that. He had to find a way to reconcile that with who he knew his dad to be. At least, who he *thought* his dad was. Now, he wasn't so sure.

Gibby shrugged. "I get that your dad was grieving, but that doesn't give him an excuse."

Nick shook his head. "I know. Thanks for being honest with me."

Gibby snorted. "When have I ever not? We'll figure it out. Just . . . think. Really think. Can you do that?"

"Yeah," Nick said. "Of course. For what it's worth, I'm sorry."

She rolled her eyes fondly. "Gee, Nick. Thanks."

Jazz laughed as Nick scowled. "Yeah, yeah. Laugh it up. Oh hey, I have an idea I wanted to float by the both of you."

"Uh-oh," Jazz said as Gibby took her by the hand, pulling her toward the stairs that led to the streets above. "I get chills when you say stuff like that."

Nick trailed after them, pulling his hoodie up and over his head to keep his ears warm. They reached street level as the sky began to spit flurries. "This is a good idea. I've thought this through."

"For how long?" Gibby asked. "Because your idea of thinking things through usually means you just thought of it two seconds ago and didn't think it through at all."

Nick rolled his eyes. "I'll have you know I first thought of it on Saturday, so that's almost two whole days of percolation." Gibby was about to speak, but he cut her off. "And *no*, this doesn't involve me becoming an Extraordinary. I've given up on that. This is about Team Pyro Storm." He bopped his head and wiggled his hips as they passed a group of buskers on the street, banging on plastic buckets. One grinned at him and flashed a thumbs-up, which he returned in kind. God, he loved the people in this city. He pulled out a few crumpled dollar bills and tossed them into a small box set before them and then moved on, blowing into his hands to warm them up.

"Does this have anything to do with the abrupt left turn your fic took?" Jazz asked. "Because I was a little disappointed I didn't get to read about you and Seth—oh, I'm sorry, *Nash* and *Pyro Storm*—getting down."

"Gross," Gibby muttered. "I told you not to read that stuff. There's no looking away once you see what goes on in Nick's head."

"I'll pretend that was a compliment. Thank you, Gibby. And Jazz, I appreciate you reading my work and leaving a comment. Comments are life."

"You're welcome," Jazz said. "Even if it didn't go like I was expecting it to—though, if you think about it, it's a really weird way to tell Seth you love him."

Nick almost walked into a pole. "Say *what* now?"

Jazz squinted at him. "That's the whole point of the fic, right? It's a love letter to Seth."

This . . . this was news to Nick. "It is not! I don't *love* him. Oh my god, we've only been dating for like four months, seven days, and sixteen hours!"

"Nope," Gibby said. "Nope, nope, nope. I sat through the cluelessness, the pining, the longing looks that made me want to yell at the both of you. I don't have the strength to listen to *this* now."

"But—"

"No. You're a boy, you're stupid, and I don't care." Gibby pulled Jazz further down the sidewalk, leaving a dumbfounded Nick staring after them.

"She cares," Jazz called over her shoulder as Nick jogged to catch up with them. "She has a funny way of showing it. I also care, but I just tell you so you'll know instead of wondering."

"It's not a love letter," Nick said, chasing after them. "And you *know* it, you jerk."

"Keep telling yourself that, Bell," Gibby said. "Branding?"

Right. Focus. "Think about it," Nick said as they rounded a corner, Centennial High appearing in the distance. "What does an Extraordinary need in the twenty-first century? Brand recognition."

He waited for them to be suitably impressed.

Jazz popped a bubble with her gum. Gibby yawned, covering her mouth with the back of her hand. He was losing them. Time to bring out the big guns.

"Okay," he said. "I can see you're interested but need to know more. I've got you." He hurried around the front of them to face them, walking backward. "Picture this: What's better than having a superhero protecting the streets of our fair city? Having a super-hero with *global brand recognition*."

They looked dubious at best. Time to bring out the bigger guns. It was a good thing Nick had had two whole days to mastermind his plan.

Ready to blow their minds, he said, "We'll have a Twitter account, which I'll run and get hashtags trending on—something like hashtag #ReturnOfTheFire or hashtag #TheHeroOfThe-People. And we'll even have some tweets from Pyro Storm's per-spective, saying things like *On Twelfth and Liberty Ave, crime in process, stay away, citizens.* Hashtag #SafetyFirst, hashtag #FriendlyNeighborhoodPyroStorm." He frowned. "We'll have to work on that last one, so we don't get sued for cribbing intellectual property, but still." He shook his head. "And merchandise! We'll commission artists in the Extraordinaries fandom to create art we can plaster on bags and shirts and coffee mugs and sell them in a merch store."

"Who gets to keep the money?" Gibby asked, pulling Nick to the side before he backed into a pole.

"We do," Nick said promptly. "We'll each get a cut, but maybe a bigger one for Seth since he's the Extraordinary doing all the heavy lifting. It'll help that we don't need to upgrade the secret lair anymore. Which, by the way, thank you—I hadn't thought of night vision goggles, but now that we have them, I can't live without them. Also, we'll donate a percentage to a LGBTQIA non-profit because it's the right thing to do."

"Only the best," Jazz said. "And Daddy didn't even threaten to take it all back, even though he said he and Mom wouldn't let me spend any more money until they've had time to think things through. I think part of them wonders if we all have superpowers and didn't tell them." She laughed. "Can you imagine? Me with powers. I'd make heroes look good." As if to prove her point, she lifted one of her heels to show them her Alexander McQueen, skull-embellished pumps. "Mom was fine with it after she got a couple of glasses of wine in her. Once that happens, she agrees with pretty much anything and tells you things you don't want to hear, like what she thinks about the shorts her tennis instructor wears. I've never met him, but I know more about his anatomy than I've ever wanted to, because apparently his shorts are *really* short."

They stared at her.

She shrugged. "What? She likes tennis and wine and her tennis instructor. I don't judge, and neither should you."

"Have you talked to Seth about any of this?" Gibby asked Nick as they continued toward school. "Or is this one of those times where you make plans without telling one of us and then hope for the best when you try and enact it?"

"He knows," Nick said defensively. "He read about it in the fic. Team Pyro Storm, ready to tweet and sell overpriced signed posters!" He smiled. They did not. He added, "And also save lives."

Gibby shook her head. "I don't know, Nicky. It sounds all well and good, but he said he wasn't sure about what he wanted anymore. It's taking a toll on him. He's tired all the time, and even though Shadow Star isn't around now, there's always something that has to be done."

Gibby wasn't wrong, but what could they do about it? Even Seth had said Nova City would always need someone like Pyro Storm. Nick was trying to help as best he could, hence the branding. The logic was a bit faulty, the equation not quite equaling the answer, but he'd get there. "I know, but all we can do is support him with—"

For the second time in a few days, he crashed into someone. His fault this time. He whirled around, the words *I'm so sorry* on the tip of his tongue, but then he saw who he'd hit, and his apology died screaming.

Her hair was a little longer than it'd been when they'd last stood face-to-face, and it was bleached an alarming shade of blond. But her shark's grin was the same, her makeup on point, her eyes sparkling as she raised a microphone to her lips, turning toward the man standing behind her with a camera on his shoulder and pointing directly at Nick. Nick had only seen her once in person since they'd both been trapped on top of McManus Bridge. She'd shown up at his house a few weeks after the battle, crew in tow, demanding that Nick give her an interview. Dad had told her in no uncertain terms that if she ever stepped foot on his property again, he was going to shove his own foot so far up her ass, she'd be gargling toes. After he'd slammed the door in her face, he'd turned and told Nick that violence was never the answer, and that violence against women was a pandemic that needed to be stopped. Nick had laughed it off at the time, but after hearing more clearly what Dad had done to the witness years before and the fallout that came after, he didn't think there was anything funny about it now. He'd never thought of his father as violent, but he had evidence to the contrary. He didn't know what that made his dad—or himself, for not asking the questions he should've. Gibby and Jazz were right. He'd just . . . glossed over it.

That night, she'd gone on live television and reported that she'd been verbally threatened by Aaron Bell, the former detective who'd been demoted after physically assaulting a witness and the father of one Nick Bell, who had been at the center of the fight between Shadow Star and Pyro Storm. "But I will persist," she said. "Nova City deserves answers, and no man will keep me from getting them." Even though he despised every fiber of her being, he wondered if she'd been scared of his father. He didn't know if he wanted her to be or not.

Regardless, Nick was not a fan.

"Rebecca Firestone," he snarled as she looked directly into the camera.

"We're standing on the streets of Nova City," she said as if he wasn't staring daggers at the back of her head. "And, by happenstance, we have come across Nicholas Bell. If you'll recall, Mr. Bell is the author of *This is Where We Scorch the Earth*, a lengthy manifesto disguised as poorly plotted fanfiction regarding the Extraordinary Shadow Star."

"Happenstance?" Jazz asked loudly. "You're standing in front of our school."

Nick, focusing on what was really important, exclaimed, "Poorly plotted? It was a goddamn *masterpiece*. Yes, in retrospect, it was extremely misguided, but still!"

She ignored them, even as students heading toward the front doors stopped and turned to stare at them.

"Shadow Star," she continued, "who turned out to be sixteen-year-old Owen Burke, a student at Centennial High and the son of Simon Burke of Burke Pharmaceuticals."

"And who you had a crush on, even though you're, like, fifty," Gibby said. "That's gross. And illegal."

"I am *thirty-two*," Rebecca Firestone snapped, façade of the plucky reporter shattering. "And he presented himself as someone far, far older, so—"

The cameraman coughed pointedly.

Rebecca Firestone schooled her face. "Right. Edit that out in post. Three, two, one." She smiled. "Nicholas Bell has been a central figure in the ongoing mystery of the Nova City Extraordinaries. On McManus Bridge, dozens of witnesses, including myself, saw him kissing the Extraordinary known as Pyro Storm, who was considered—and, potentially, rightly so—the villain of Nova—"

"Hell yes, I did," Nick said, leering at the camera. "Go gays!"

"—*who was considered the villain of Nova City*," Rebecca Firestone said through gritted teeth. She turned to Nick, eyes narrowed. "Mr. Bell, would you care to comment?"

"I would," Nick said as Gibby groaned behind him.

"You would?" Rebecca Firestone asked, momentarily shocked. "Of course you would. What do you know about Pyro Storm? Did you know Owen Burke was Shadow Star? What is your relationship with both of them? Emotional? Physical?" She thrust the microphone in his face.

His moment to shine. Rebecca Firestone would regret ever being born. "My comment is this: I'm a minor, and Rebecca Firestone is attempting to speak to me without my guardian present." He let his bottom lip tremble as he shook his head. "I wish there was an adult who would help save me from Rebecca Firestone's incessant questioning. I was a victim, and she's making me relive my trauma of a night I wish I could forget, even though I was the one who saved *her* from—"

"You little *shit*," Rebecca Firestone growled before composing herself.

The whispers from those standing in front of the school grew louder, a few of them laughing. Rebecca Firestone glared at Nick before that evil grin returned, her eyes alight in a way that made Nick uneasy. Without looking away from Nick, she held out her hand toward her cameraman and snapped her fingers. The cameraman reached down to a large duffel bag at his feet. He muttered under his breath that he wasn't paid enough for this shit before he pulled out a tablet and handed it to Rebecca Firestone.

She tapped the edge of her microphone against the screen. "Tell us, Mr. Bell, have you seen Pyro Storm since the events on the bridge?"

He shrugged, knowing he had an audience of his peers and that it was best to keep them guessing. There was a chance he could turn this around in his favor. "Maybe I have, maybe I haven't."

"Mm," she said. "And your boyfriend—Seth Gray, right? What did he think about you kissing another man?"

Uh-oh. That wasn't good. "We didn't get together until after that." Total lie, but she didn't know that. "Seth is the best," he added quickly, because he was of the mind that Seth Gray deserved to be complimented publicly. "His smile is like sunshine, and his bow ties give me life."

"Right," Rebecca Firestone said. "Young love. How precious. I would ask, however, what your boyfriend would think about you as you continue to fraternize with Pyro Storm."

Nick squinted at her. "I'm doing what now?"

Her smiled widened, her teeth bared. She turned the tablet around, showing Nick the screen. He felt Jazz and Gibby crowding his back, peering over his shoulder.

On the tablet was a picture. Nick knew exactly when it'd been taken. New Year's Eve. He'd had plans to go out with Gibby and Jazz and Seth, but they'd been forced into action when Seth had been alerted about a break-in at the history museum, where a display of priceless jewels on loan from India had been shown for almost a month. Pyro Storm had foiled the heist, and all the jewels had been accounted for. Their night out had been shot, but Nick figured it was worth it to keep relations between India and the US on the level. He was nothing if not diplomatic.

After, he'd met up with Pyro Storm in the streets of Nova City, hidden away in the shadows of an alley. Right at midnight, Seth had kissed him sweetly, promising that the New Year was going to be awesome.

Apparently, they hadn't been alone. Because here, on the screen, was a picture of Nick wearing ridiculous gag glasses covered in glitter that showed the numbers for the New Year, pressed up against the brickwork of an old building, Pyro Storm kissing him, Nick's hands hidden under his cape. The picture was blurry and had been taken from across the street, but it was obviously Nick, head tilted as he kissed an Extraordinary.

"What the hell?" Nick asked furiously, trying to swipe to see if there were any other photos. There weren't, but one was enough. "What is this?"

"An exclusive," Rebecca Firestone said as she plucked the tablet from Nick's hands. "Care to comment as to why you, someone who says he's in a healthy relationship, would be playing with fire?"

"Wow," Jazz said. "Did you really think of that all on your own? You're *so* impressive."

Rebecca Firestone ignored her. "Mr. Bell? Thoughts? I'd hate to come between young love, but this is something that should be addressed. Anyone can see what you were doing. In fact, someone did, which is why this picture was sent to me from an anonymous— yet concerned—citizen of Nova City."

"No comment," Gibby snapped, grabbing Nick by the hand and attempting to pull him away. "Lady, you don't want to piss us off more than you already have. I'll sic my girlfriend on you, and you don't want that. You haven't seen scary until you've seen Jazz-scary."

Rebecca Firestone scoffed as she looked over at Jazz in time to see her step out of her heels, flip them expertly in her hands, and advance with them raised like weapons. "Try me," Jazz said primly as she cocked her head.

"What are you doing here, Firestone?" Nick jerked his head to find his boyfriend pushing his way through the crowd, his dress pants perfectly creased, his black sweater lint-free as if freshly rolled, and a goddamn paisley *cravat*. Ascots and cravats were almost the same thing, but ascots were more informal, which Nick only knew because of Seth, and while it was mostly useless information, it still made him slightly weak in the knees, current situation be damned. Who the hell did Seth think he was, walking in here to save the day, looking so stupidly adorable that Nick thought he would just *die*?

Seth stepped between his friends and Rebecca Firestone, whose smile faded, brow furrowing as she looked him up and down.

"Leave now," Seth said coldly, and the growing crowd around them tittered. They'd never seen Seth so assertive, and Nick wouldn't be surprised if half of them weren't immediately and irrevocably lusting after him. If they weren't, then they should've been. Seth was pretty much the hottest thing in existence when he wore a cravat and spoke forcefully. "Don't make me tell you again."

"Uh," the cameraman said. "Yeah, I'm getting out of here." He lowered his camera, pointing the lens toward the ground. "I was already worried about this assignment, seeing as how your last cameraman died, but that young lady is scary, and I don't want to die or go back to prison."

Jazz feinted toward him, heel raised, and he stumbled backward, almost tripping over his duffel bag.

Rebecca Firestone snarled as she shoved the tablet back at him so hard, he almost dropped it. "Goddammit, *fine*." She whirled on them, poking Seth in the chest with a perfectly manicured finger-nail while glancing over his shoulder at Nick. "This isn't over. I know you're involved with the Extraordinaries, Bell, and no matter how connected you are to the NCPD, no matter how many people try to cover for you, you know it and I know it. And I *will* find the truth. We all deserve to know who hides behind masks." She turned around, glaring up at the students gathered on the stairs. "Stay in school!" she barked up at them before storming down the sidewalk, her cameraman trailing after her.

Seth stared after her until she disappeared into the crowd before he sighed, shoulders slumping. When he turned, gone was the steel. All that remained was Seth: tired, wonderful, *lying* Seth. "What did she want?" he asked as the students began to head inside the school.

"To cause trouble," Gibby muttered. "She's got a picture of you as Pyro Storm eating Nick's face. Good job, both of you. That's not going to help with rumors around here." She jerked her head toward the school, where everyone still stood whispering as they glanced at Team Pyro Storm.

"So they'll think we're in an open relationship," Nick said. "We're progressive that way."

Seth rolled his eyes. "Noted." He looked off to where Rebecca Firestone had disappeared. "What's her angle, though? She's not my favorite person by a long shot, but is she really just asking about who you're kissing? That seems beneath her."

"The only thing beneath her is the ground," Nick snapped. "She's a pain in the ass, and we have to figure out what to do if she tries to make trouble."

"Is that—is that his angry face?" Jazz whispered to Gibby as she put her heels back on.

"I . . . don't know?" Gibby said, squinting at Nick. "It looks like he has a nervous tic or he's holding in a fart. You never can tell with boys. It's what makes them so ridiculous."

Seth shook his head. "We don't need to worry about it now. There are bigger things to focus on." He looked at Nick. "Such as the latest chapter of your fic. Nick, I say this with nothing but admiration for you as a person, okay?"

Good start. Nick loved being admired. "I approve. You may proceed."

Seth said, "What the *hell* are you talking about with this branding thing? And a website? When did you have time to make a website? And why was there a tab to sign up for a meet and greet?"

Ah, time for the sales pitch! "I'm so glad you asked. Prepare to have your mind blown. It—"

The bell rang.

"—will have to wait," Nick said quickly. "Because we can't be late for class, as our education is important, and Dad will send me off to boarding school if the school calls him again. An empty threat, but I don't want to risk it because the boarding school is in New Hampshire and I don't even know where that is, which is a damning indictment of the state of our school system. But Seth, you're going to love it, I promise. And I'll let your mind run with the possibilities until lunch. Also, you look amazing and your cravat gives me life." He smacked a kiss against Seth's lips before stomping off toward school. "Good talk, team!" he bellowed over his shoulder.

Always leave them wanting. *Cosmo.*

6

On a good day, Nick had to push himself to focus. It wasn't as bad as it used to be, and he had hope he'd eventually become one of those lucky adults whose symptoms of attention-deficit hyperactivity disorder lessened with age. But he wasn't kidding himself in thinking he'd ever be free of it: a kid with ADHD became a teenager with ADHD who turned into an adult with ADHD. That was his lot in life. It sucked, but it wasn't a death sentence. He'd been on Concentra long enough now that it had evened out, and his mind was clearer and sharper than it'd been in a long time. He dutifully took his pills as instructed, knowing they were meant to help him, even if the source of the pills was now something he questioned.

And yet, no matter what it came down to, no matter how old he got or if he was finally on the right meds, his brain was wired differently. And though the bad days were few and far between, he still had them. *Those* days were when his thoughts were a jumbled knot in his head, and no matter how much he tugged on individual strands, it only made the knot tighter. *Those* days were when he felt like he was vibrating out of his skin, unable to sit still for any length of time. He fidgeted. He tapped his foot. He rapped his fingers against his thighs and the top of his desk. He clicked his pen again and again. It wasn't quite spiraling, not like when he had panic attacks and he couldn't breathe.

But it still sucked, especially on this particular Monday morning in February. He *knew* he was escalating, the battery that was his brain overloaded by a power surge. He tried to stop it, tried to calm himself by doing what he'd been taught: clearing his mind to the best of his ability, picking one thing to focus on, and breathing in through his nose and out through his mouth.

It didn't work.

All he could think about was the invasion of his privacy—Rebecca Firestone using an intimate moment against him, like she had any right.

"She can kiss my ass," Nick muttered as he scribbled circles in his notebook. "She's lucky I don't have powers and just *bam*. *Pow!*"

It was about this time that he became aware of his surroundings to discover that he was in the middle of second period (American Lit) and the teacher (a frizzy lady named Mrs. Werner) and his classmates were staring at him, some already whispering.

Nick blinked. Second period? What the hell had happened in first? Oh man, he hoped there hadn't been a pop quiz. He'd boffed it for sure if there was. And it'd be exactly like Hanson to give a trig pop quiz first thing on a Monday morning. He slumped lower in his chair, smiling widely to let Mrs. Werner know he was here and ready to listen to her drone on and on about allegory and blah, blah, blah.

It must have worked, because she resumed and everyone turned back toward the front of the class.

A moment later, he was lost in his thoughts again, picking through the knot in his head, tugging, tugging, tugging on the loose strands, trying to find one that would pull free. It was all *Dad* and *Seth* and *Burke, Burke, Burke,* which caused a low wave of anger to wash over him. The lights in the room buzzed loudly. In the corner, one shorted out completely with a low pop. No one paid it any mind. They were in a public school, after all. Things broke all the time.

We need to put on a united front before Seth gets here," he announced as soon as he sat down at their lunch table. The cafeteria was loud today, since most students were indoors, given how cold it was outside. The flurries were supposed to switch to full-on snow at some point, but so far, it was holding off. It didn't help that a group of the most popular kids in school were hanging banners for an event he'd totally spaced on. The biggest banner read: CENTENNIAL HIGH PROM COMING SOON! A NIGHT TO REMEMBER!

This was the first year they'd get to go, given that it was only for juniors and seniors. Gibby could've gone last year with Jazz, but they'd ended up watching terrible monster movies with Nick and Seth instead. Gibby hadn't seemed to mind at all, but when Jazz had asked her to the prom this year, she'd rolled her eyes, all while fighting a smile. She wasn't fooling anyone.

Nick hadn't asked Seth yet, nor had Seth asked him. *Cosmo* had taught him he should never assume, so he needed to plan the biggest, most elaborate promposal ever, making every other promposal look like crap.

They looked at him quizzically, Gibby arching an eyebrow and Jazz giving Nick a little wave. He set his backpack on the table next to him, digging around until he found the brown paper bag that held his lunch: a smashed sandwich, pulverized chips, and a bruised banana. The feast of kings.

Gibby had a basket filled with french fries, something Nick longed for but didn't dare. Ever since Seth had revealed his muscles, Nick had paid closer attention to what he ate. Seth assured him time and time again that he'd like Nick no matter what shape or size he was, and while that filled Nick with so much joy he'd thought he'd burst, Seth also had at least three abs whereas Nick had none.

Jazz had what looked to be pineapple chicken over shredded cabbage. He briefly wondered if her parents loved her before shaking his head. Bigger things to focus on.

"Still on that, huh?" Gibby asked. "Thinking about it all morning?"

"Of course I have," Nick hissed as he leaned forward. He looked around suspiciously. No one seemed to be trying to listen in, but that didn't mean they *weren't* either. "Who does Rebecca Firestone think she is? *No one*, that's who. And that bullshit about an anonymous source? Lie. All lies. She's obviously stalking me, and I'm going to get her so fired."

"Why is she stalking you?" Jazz asked, daintily wiping her

mouth with a cloth napkin. "And can't you say that Seth was cos-playing or something?"

Nick stared at her. "Cosplaying? In January? It's not even Extraordinaries Con season! You *know* that doesn't happen until October."

"So? My parents go to parties all the time that I'm not supposed to know about where they're in costumes." She smiled. "They call them 'Eyes Wide Shut' parties, whatever that means."

"What do they do there?" Gibby asked.

Jazz shrugged. "I don't know. Probably talk about market shares and yachts. I think it's like a slumber party for adults."

"I don't get rich people," Nick lamented. "Like, why would you—no, you know what? Focus. Stalking."

Gibby looked troubled. She reached over and took Nick's jittery hand in her own, squeezing tightly. "You need to be careful. All of us do, but especially you and Seth. Even if it wasn't Firestone who took the picture, she's not going to let this go."

"Oh, I know," Nick said. "Like a dog with a bone, that one." He sighed. "You know what? That's mean, even if it's Rebecca Firestone. She's a woman who's worked hard to get where she's at in a male-dominated industry that— What the hell am I saying? Screw her!"

Gibby and Jazz exchanged a glance. "I think you're allowed this one," Gibby said.

"Damn right I am," Nick said, pulling his hand back to open his lunch. "You know what? I should've seen this coming. They have to be working together. It's the only thing that makes sense. After Burke kidnapped me over the weekend and—"

"What?" Gibby asked sharply.

Nick blanched. *Crap.* He hadn't meant to say that. Rebecca Firestone had thrown him off his game. "Uh, I was speaking . . . metaphorically?"

"Nick," Gibby growled.

He shook his head. "Forget I said anything. We have bigger things to worry about. Seth—"

"—is coming up to the table, looking like he's about to go into battle," Jazz said. Then she raised her voice, a sunny smile on her face as she said, "Hi, Seth! We weren't talking about you at all! Come, sit, sit!"

"Good one, babe," Gibby said. "That was believable."

"I can hear you," Seth muttered as he sat next to Nick. He glanced cautiously at him, and Nick grinned rather maniacally in response. "Hi."

"Hello, boyfriend of mine," Nick said, and because he could, he leaned forward and kissed Seth right on the mouth. He hoped a homophobe had been watching and was now filled with so much heterosexual rage, they were choking on it. When he pulled back, Seth's glasses were slightly askew and his cheeks were pink, but he didn't look around as if embarrassed. Instead, he leaned forward and kissed Nick again. It was one of the things Nick loved most about him, seeing as how it was about damn time queer people were able to claim public displays of affection for their own without being worried about being harassed for it.

"You seem like you're in a good mood," Seth said, bumping his shoulder against Nick's. "I almost don't want to ask why."

"But—" Nick said.

"But," Seth said, "I feel like I have to ask in case it means you're going to do something that could end in the destruction of public property."

"That's only happened a few times!"

Seth snorted. "Oh, my bad. Only a few times."

And because Gibby was evil, she said, "Yeah, Nick was just telling us how he'd been kidnapped by Simon Burke."

Seth turned slowly to look at Nick, who decided that his lunch needed his immediate attention. The sandwich was salvageable. The chips, not so much. Maybe if he poured the remains onto the sandwich? Was that gross? Probably. Whatever. And that still left the banana, which Nick *knew* was his father messing with him, given the way he'd once given Nick the safe-sex talk involving a banana, a condom, and lube. Nick still hadn't recovered. He didn't think he ever would.

"Nick."

He groaned and wondered why no one else was as easily distracted as him. "It wasn't that big of a deal. And I wouldn't call it *kidnapping*," he added, shooting a withering glance at Gibby.

"You used that exact word," Jazz reminded him.

"Semantics," Nick muttered. "Okay, fine. Yes, Simon Burke made me get into his limo against my will, and *yes*, he made vague threats without them actually being threats—which, if you think about it, is a really impressive talent to have."

"Nick," Seth said through gritted teeth. "Every detail. Now. Leave nothing out."

"Ooh," Jazz said. "I got chills. Seth, don't move. Hold on." She held up her phone and took a picture. "Okay, there—I wanted to capture this moment for posterity. Nick, you may continue."

Nick didn't like the expression on Seth's face. It was cold and angry, and someone wearing a cravat should never look that way. "Hey, Seth?"

Seth stared at him.

And because Nick was nothing if not a gentleman (and a big fan of romantic callbacks), he said, "You make my heart so full, I think I'll die."

Manipulative? Maybe, but oh-so-worth-it, because the smile Seth gave him was Nick's favorite. It was slow to bloom, the corners of his mouth tugging upward, a hint of teeth between his lips, the skin around his eyes crinkling slightly. Nick didn't know what to do with himself that didn't involve potentially being arrested for public indecency.

"Ditto," Seth said quietly.

"Aw," Gibby said, "now I know what a diabetic coma feels like. Nick, get on with it. We only have twenty minutes."

Quickly, he told them about his jaunt with Simon Burke. They stayed quiet as he talked in a rushed, low voice, Gibby scowling, Jazz's eyes widening, and Seth looking more and more perturbed. He finished by saying, "And Dad didn't want me to say anything. I think he was embarrassed by all of it, so don't tell him you know." His voice cracked, but he powered through it. "It's important to me."

"Sure, Nicky," Jazz said, sounding shaken. "We won't say anything."

"The pills," Seth said suddenly. "Your Concentra. Did you look into it?"

Nick nodded. "The label on the bottle doesn't say anything about Burke Pharmaceuticals, but I was able to track the medicine back to them. He wasn't lying. His company developed Concentra. Dad says he'd have nothing to do with the pills, so he doesn't think there's any reason for me to stop taking them." He looked away. He didn't like to talk about being medicated. "They . . . help."

"I know they do," Seth said quietly.

Nick sighed. "I think if they were the same kind Burke gave Owen, we'd know it by now." He swiveled in his chair, raising his hand toward the prom banner. "Explosive Destruction!"

The cafeteria quieted as everyone turned to stare at them.

Nick glared right back. "Eavesdropping is rude. This has nothing to do with you. Return to your silly, inconsequential lives." He turned toward the table once more. "See? Normal, like always."

"I wouldn't go that far," Gibby mumbled.

"It's weird, though," Jazz said, spearing a piece of chicken. "Burke comes out of nowhere, and then a couple of days later, Rebecca Firestone shows up in front of our school?"

A thought struck Nick—one he should've had sooner. "Oh, crap. Can she use the footage she took today? I need to tell my dad before he sees it on TV and grounds me forever, even though I was the victim." He typed a text: Daddio, no cause for panic, but RF showed up b4 school asking questions re: our fire friend. Don't know what she wanted but can she use footage of me without ur permission?

He was about to set his phone down when it immediately started vibrating. Nick sighed. "Such a drama queen, I swear to god." He connected the call. "Hey, pops. How's your day going?"

"She *what*?" Dad snarled.

Nick had the best dad, no contest. "She was asking about me and Pyro Storm. She had a photo of me and Seth and kept saying

I knew more than I was saying. Said NCPD was covering for me, which is pretty much bullshit."

"Language," Dad said. "She recorded you?"

"She did, but then Jazz threatened to stab the cameraman with her heels, and that was pretty much that."

Jazz preened as Dad groaned. "Kid, I'm not even going to touch that one. Jazz is terrifying when she needs to be. And no, she can't use footage of you without the permission of a guard—parent." Weird. Dad's voice caught on the word *guardian*. "And if she tries, we're going to sue the hell out of her, *Action News*, and anyone else I can think of."

"I respect that and you," Nick said seriously. "Thanks, Dad."

"You let me know if you see her again," Dad said. "If anything, I'll get a restraining order filed against her. She's pushing her luck as it is."

"Will do. Lunch is almost over, so I gotta go. See you tonight?"

"Tonight," Dad said, already sounding distracted. "Love you."

"Love you t—and you're already gone." He set his phone down on the table. "Dad's on it. Whatever Rebecca Firestone and Simon Burke are cooking up, they won't get far. He'll make sure of it."

"It could be a coincidence," Seth said, though he didn't sound convinced. "We need to proceed carefully, just in case it's not. Nicky, if something ever seems off about your meds, you need to let us know. We can't take any chances, not with Burke."

"I will," Nick said.

"How did he know you take Concentra at all?" Gibby asked.

That gave Nick pause. "I don't know. That's gotta be a HIPAA violation. Maybe they have a list of everyone who takes the pills the company makes. And that's some kind of Orwellian nightmare I don't even want to consider."

"I'll look into it," Seth said. "Dig around, see what I can find. But as much as I hate to say it, we have other things that need our attention." He dug his phone out of his pocket and began to type. When he found what he was looking for, he set the phone on the table in front of Nick. "Explain."

Nick looked down. The screen displayed the official Pyro Storm website, complete with shifting flames that rose off the letters, the smoke curling into little hearts. Nick was proud of it. He admired his handiwork until he realized everyone was waiting on him. Showtime. "Now, I know what you're thinking."

"I really doubt that," Gibby said.

Nick ignored her. "It's a central hub for all things Pyro Storm. Want to know what Nova City's premier hero is up to? Want to find the links to Pyro Storm's favorite eateries? Need to find links to all of Pyro Storm's social media? Well, have I got good news for you! There's even a FAQ section where the most important questions are answered, like *what is Pyro Storm's favorite kind of dog*, and *can Pyro Storm shoot fire out of his junk?* Huskies, and no. No, he cannot." He frowned. "That last one is courtesy of my father, which I won't ever forgive him for."

Gibby's eyes bulged. "He asked *what*?"

"So," Jazz said, "I really want to know why you thought that was necessary for your FAQ section, but I can see you're on a roll, so we'll come back to that. Because *what*."

"We're not here to talk about it!" Nick said loudly as Seth groaned into his hands. "We're here to talk about how I've launched the new branding initiative for our favorite superhero. Everyone will now finally be able to support Pyro Storm and all his hard work by buying officially licensed merch, with twenty-five percent of the proceeds going to Pyro Storm, fifteen percent for the three of us, fifteen percent to the artist, and the remainder going to a queer nonprofit, because Pyro Storm is giving and kind."

Gibby grabbed Seth's phone and pulled it across the table so she and Jazz could look at it. She scrolled down the page. Nick waited for feedback.

"Is that—" Gibby said, squinting down at the screen. "You really made a Twitter account."

"And we already have over two hundred followers," Nick said excitedly.

"No," Seth moaned, rocking back and forth. "No, no, no."

Nick pulled out his own phone, opening Twitter before he shoved it at Seth. "See?"

"'Hello,'" Seth read as Nick mouthed along silently. "'This is Pyro Storm. Villains, run in fear! It's time to burn.'" He looked up at Nick. "It's time to *burn*? Isn't that in your fic? You called it a—"

"—catchphrase," Nick said promptly. "The more Pyro Storm says it, the better the chance it'll catch on. I workshopped it, and that was the best one. Which means I'll need you to say it as often as possible."

"Workshopped it with *who*?" Seth asked.

"Myself in my room." *Duh.*

"And what's this all for?" Jazz asked. "Why does Pyro Storm need this?"

"Ah! I'm so glad you asked. Thank you, Jazz. The reason is simple: Seth deserves to be compensated for his time. He's done years of service for the people of Nova City; it's time he's appreciated for everything he's done. I was also thinking about a dedicated YouTube channel where we could get Pyro Storm to attach a GoPro camera to his helmet and take people on a virtual tour of Nova City, but that's still in the planning stages. And, as his brand manager, I'll make it my mission to—"

"*Brand* manager?" Seth growled, and Nick did *not* swoon at the Pyro Storm in his voice. "I don't need a brand manager."

"You do," Nick said. "You just don't know it yet. Trust me, okay? I won't let anything bad get tweeted at you or about you. I've already got a new hashtag in mind to help promote fairness and equality. Ready? Hashtag #WWPSD—What Would Pyro Storm Do. Get it? It's like you're Jesus, but you can light things on fire, when he only did stuff with fish and wine or whatever."

"That's blasphemy," Seth reminded him.

Nick waved dismissively. "He'll forgive me. I have a feeling he likes gay people, so. And look! I haven't even told you about the Instagram account, which Jazz will oversee, since she's artistic AF."

"I am," Jazz said. "It's one of my gifts."

"It is," Nick agreed. "And since we all seem to be on the same page with this, I'll—"

"We're not," Seth said.

"We're . . . not?" Nick looked at his phone, then back at Seth. "Is something wrong? I can go through it again, if you want."

Seth shook his head. "I don't need you to do that, Nick. What I want you to do is *listen* to me."

"I am," Nick assured him. "I always—"

"You don't," Seth retorted. Nick tried to hide his flinch, but he wasn't sure how successful he was. "You guys don't get what it's like. You think it's all fun and heroics and saving the day. It's not. It's barely *even* that. I'm tired all the time, my back hurts, my grades are slipping. All I want to do some days is stay in bed and not move for as long as possible. You could never understand what I'm going through because you all get to be normal, whether you want to be or not."

That stung. It didn't feel like it was supposed to be a dig at him, but there it was all the same.

Seth's voice hardened as he continued. "Do you know what I would give to be like you? To be able to go one day without worrying if someone is going to get hurt on my watch?" He snatched his phone back from Gibby. "I'd give anything to only care about shit like this."

"That's not fair," Jazz said. "Because we *do* know what it's like to worry. We worry about you getting hurt every time you suit up."

Seth shook his head. "It's not the same. I'm just one person you care about. But I have to worry about *thousands* of people I don't even know." His hands curled into fists, and Nick thought the temperature at their table rose a few degrees. "I know you're trying to help, Nick, but this isn't it."

Seth was right. Part of Nick—the calm, rational part that he *did* have, no matter what anyone said to the contrary—knew this. But this part of Nick was still a tiny part of him, crying out in the dark, its voice almost completely buried by a swell of irrational anger. "You could talk to us about this," he said. "You could try and tell us what you're going through. You don't have to cut us out of part of your life because you don't think we'd get it. Maybe we won't, but we'd at least *try*." He glanced at Gibby and Jazz. "We've been here for years, Seth. Yeah, we've only known about what you can do for a few months, but we've had your back even before we knew what you could do. Why would you think you couldn't talk to us or come to us for help if you needed it?"

"Or," Gibby said, "we could give Seth the chance to work things out on his own. Some of us need that, Nick. Just because we don't tell you everything doesn't mean we don't know we can come to you on our terms, when we're ready."

"But how're we supposed to help if we don't know what's going on?" Jazz asked.

Nick looked at Seth, sure he was about to smile and say, *Yeah, Nicky, I know.* He didn't. He glared at Nick, eyes ablaze.

"You could get hurt," he said hotly. "Why don't you ever seem to get that? Do you know how many times I've had to—" He grunted, looking away. "This isn't a game."

Nick bristled. "I know it's not a game; I never thought it was. I'm trying to—"

Seth deflated, curling in on himself. If Nick didn't already feel awful, this would have clinched it. "I know you're trying, Nicky. I get that. But what about the real world? We can't keep this up forever. I mean, we haven't even asked how Gibby's doing with her whole college thing, or how Jazz feels about it."

"That's between Gibby and me," Jazz said as Gibby slumped lower on the bench. "And while I appreciate your concern, you don't get to weaponize that against Nick to try and win an argument."

Yep, apparently Nick could feel worse. He looked apologetically at Jazz and Gibby. "I'm sorry, I should've—"

The bell rang.

Nick startled, looking around to see everyone standing up from their tables. By the time he turned back, Seth was gone. Nick saw him disappearing into the crowd, shoulders stiff. "Shit," he muttered.

"Not one of your best moves, Nicky," Gibby said quietly.

Not what he needed to hear. He was hurt and more than a little angry, but he didn't quite know at who. He thought it was mostly at himself. "Yeah, well, maybe if he trusted us as much as we trust him, we could've heard this already."

"That's not fair," Jazz said, gathering up the remains of her lunch. "He has a point. We don't know what it's like for him."

Nick lowered his forehead against the table. "I screwed up, huh?"

Gibby reached across the table and punched him lightly on the shoulder. "Remember what we talked about this morning? You gotta think things through, Nick. Not everything is easy, just because you want it to be. You say you want to be better; part of that is listening without overreacting. I know you can do it. Seth does, too, but you have to show him that. Don't you think he's earned that right?"

Nick didn't see Seth for the rest of the day. They didn't share any classes this semester, much to Dad's relief and Nick's dismay. They usually found each other in the halls between classes, a couple of minutes where they'd lean against their lockers and grin stupidly at each other.

But he couldn't find Seth at all after lunch. And the more the afternoon wore on, the more annoyed Nick got, though it was mostly at himself. Sure, maybe he could've listened better, but couldn't Seth see the good in what he was trying to do?

When the final bell rang, Nick was up and out of the classroom before most had even started putting their things away. He ran across the school, dodging students spilling out the doors, apologizing when he bumped into a guy and almost sent him sprawling. He managed to reach Seth's last class (AP History) before the room had completely emptied, but Seth was nowhere in sight.

Cursing, he headed for the front doors. He stood at the top of the steps, looking around for that familiar mop of curls as a student hung another banner about prom above him. He was about to give up when he saw Seth out of the corner of his eye, trudging down the sidewalk, head bowed as flurries swirled around him.

"Go get your man," Nick muttered to himself.

He hurried down the steps, jumping the last few and almost losing his footing on the slick concrete. Someone shouted his name, but he ignored them. He reached the sidewalk and turned right. Seth was halfway down the block, heading toward the metro stop.

He caught up to him a moment later, barely out of breath thanks to their workouts. They may not have given him muscles yet, but at least he could now run for a couple of minutes without feeling like he was dying. Small victories.

He hooked his arm through Seth's, the chill of the winter air around them chased away by Seth's body heat. He burned a little warmer than most, and usually didn't mind being Nick's personal space heater. He startled and looked over at Nick, glasses slightly askew.

"So," Nick said, "I was thinking."

"That usually ends in disaster," Seth said, but there was a hint of a smile on his face. Good sign.

"Usually," Nick agreed. "But hear me out. Picture this: you. Me. Casa de Bell. Homework because we're required to. But after that, we watch a bad movie with explosions and spies, and we'll make fun of all the stupid decisions made on-screen while we eat popcorn. And *then* we'll tell Dad we're gonna go do more homework, but in actuality, we'll be pre-fornicating."

Seth's nose wrinkled. "You really have a way with words."

"It's a gift," Nick said. "And in the middle of all of that, I'll find somewhere to stick in an awkward apology about how I shouldn't have—"

"It's okay."

"It's really not," Nick said. "I—hold on." He pulled Seth into a shuttered storefront, the awning above them torn and hanging limply. Seth leaned against the wooden door, which creaked under his weight. Nick moved until he stood right in front of Seth, their knees bumping together. People moved behind them on the sidewalk and the sounds of busy traffic was irritating, but for a moment, Nick could pretend it was just the two of them. He studied Seth, cataloguing the tense set of his shoulders. "You told me you weren't sure about wanting to be Pyro Storm, and I didn't listen. I did what I always do and made it about me." He laughed hollowly. "I made a stupid *Twitter* account without thinking about what you wanted."

"That's okay." Seth took his hand, squeezing gently. He leaned forward, pressing his forehead against Nick's. "I'm lucky to have you in my corner."

Simple, but it was a string of words Nick had never heard directed at him before. It was humbling. "I'm trying to help. Pull my weight, you know? I can't do what you can. I'm not as smart as Gibby or as aware as Jazz." Certainly not something he'd ever expected to say, but they'd earned it. "I wanted to show you I could help."

"You do," Seth said, breath warm against Nick's face. "Whatever happens, we're going to do it together, okay?"

That sounded good to Nick. "Yeah. Okay."

Seth grinned. "Show it to me again."

Nick blinked. "What?"

"The Twitter account, you dork. Might as well get familiar with it, especially if you're going to be posting as me and—" He stopped when his own phone beeped, a familiar chime that sent a chill down Nick's spine.

Seth pulled out his phone and glanced down, eyes narrowed. He grunted and swiped the notification away before Nick could see it. "Don't worry about it," he said to Nick's unasked question. He smiled again, though it wasn't as bright. "It's nothing important."

Nick hesitated. He'd never known Seth to ignore the notifications. "You sure?"

"Yeah, Nicky. I'm sure. Let's see what you did."

He moved over until Nick had space to lean against the door with him, both huddling around his phone. They stayed there for a little while, the two of them, and by the time they left, Nick felt a bit better. Maybe he'd gone too far, but Seth was ready and waiting to help reel him back. He needed to figure out how to respond in kind. Seth needed someone to be his rock, and who better than Nick?

By the time they'd stepped back out onto the street, a new tweet had been sent—and by Pyro Storm himself, for the first time.

It read: Pyro Storm here with a message: the people of Nova City are under my watch, and I will do everything to protect them. It's time to burn! #NoVillainsWelcome

And as they walked hand-in-hand toward Nick's house, something unexpected occurred. Seth's first tweet was quoted by a verified account. The profile picture of this account showed a woman standing with a microphone on the windswept streets of Nova City, her hair billowing around her head.

Rebecca Firestone's own tweet read: Looking into if this is actually Pyro Storm. If it is, what does he mean by "everything"?? I promise my followers I'll get to the bottom of this, one way or another! #OnlyTheTruthIsExtraordinary

By the end of the day, the Official Pyro Storm account had six thousand new followers.

And counting.

7

As February wore on, winter descended on Nova City with a vengeance. Back-to-back storms locked the city down, dumping almost a foot of snow over a period of three days, beginning, unfortunately, on a Friday afternoon. The students of Centennial High were released an hour early and were told that classes were set to resume on Monday, unless the storms worsened.

Having snowstorms on the weekend with no school cancellation was, in Nick's opinion, like getting punched in the junk and being told to be happy about it. Dad didn't agree, but then, he seemed to be of the mind that things like education were important.

Nick frowned when he saw Dad dressed as if he were going out. It was a Saturday, and though there had been a break in the snow, he should have been in sweats like Nick and parked in front of the television. "Are you leaving?"

Dad nodded. "Meeting up with Gibby's and Jazz's parents for lunch."

Nick froze. He hadn't heard much about them since they'd all convened at the Gray house—at least, not from Dad. "Is that a good thing?" he asked carefully.

"I don't know," Dad said, wrapping his scarf around his neck. "But I'm going anyway, because it's the right thing to do. The very least I can do is make myself available to answer any questions they have. And even if they tear me a new one, I'm going to listen. Doesn't matter what age you are, you still need to own up to your mistakes. It can help make you a better person."

Nick sighed. "That's very mature of you. Still, it sounds like a weird support group for people whose kids—"

"—continually put themselves in danger?"

"We do *not*—"

"Nick." Dad reached down and poked his cheek. "I'm going to stop by the station after to catch up on paperwork, but I'll be home before too late. And get your butt off the couch, kiddo. I want all the Christmas decorations taken down by the time I get back. No excuses. It's February. It's starting to get embarrassing." He headed for the door.

"*What*?" Nick bellowed after him. "Do you have any idea how much crap we put up? That'll take forever!"

"Then you better get started," Dad called back. "I don't want to see anything holiday-related when I get home. Boxes and plastic tubs are in the attic."

Nick groaned as the front door closed. He was starting to see why people had kids: child labor. That was the only reason. He looked forlornly at the television, his plans of mindless entertainment evaporating. His promising Saturday was turning to shit.

He picked up his phone and texted Seth about the prison conditions of his current living situation. Seth responded almost immediately, saying that he was working with Gibby to figure out how to use all the new equipment in the lair. Nick was supposed to go over later, but Dad apparently thought Nick didn't deserve to have anything resembling a life.

He was about to throw down his phone when he got another text. Jazz.

> U up?
>> It's eleven in the morning. It sounds like ur hitting on me.
> Gross. U would know if I was. Can I come over?
> Need a friend.

Nick frowned. He hadn't had much of a chance to talk with her since finding out that Gibby might be leaving. Howard University was in Washington, DC. Planes were expensive. The train was cheaper, but it would take hours to get there. He didn't know if she'd made any decisions, but he'd been too scared to ask. He should've talked to Jazz sooner about it. This affected them all, but her the most.

> Yep! Come over. Need me to meet u and walk with u?

Already here.

He jerked his head up when a knock came at the door. Oof. Must have been worse than he thought. He climbed over the back of the couch, almost falling but managing to stay upright. The Concentra made him a little tired today. At least he didn't have a headache.

He opened the door, a wave of cold air washing over him. Jazz stood on the porch, her scarf wrapped around the lower half of her face. Her eyes crinkled slightly as she obviously smiled beneath the scarf. He hoped that was a good sign.

He pulled her in, closing the door behind them. Jazz unraveled her scarf as he brushed the flecks of snow from her coat. "Hey," she said. "Sorry for dropping by all of a sudden."

"No worries. Your timing is impeccable. I've been given the Herculean task of taking down the Christmas decorations. You can help if you want."

"Lucky me," she murmured, hanging her coat on the hook near the door. "Your dad's gone, right?"

Nick eyed her suspiciously. "You knew about the whole support group thing?"

"Found out about it this morning. I'm choosing to believe it's a good sign."

"Or they're all plotting our doom."

She waved him off. "Either way, at least they're all talking. Could be worse. They could've said I wasn't allowed to hang out with all of you anymore."

Nick winced as he led her into the kitchen. "They'd really do that?" He began to prepare her a cup of tea, using the tea bags he kept only for her.

She hopped up onto the counter, swinging her feet. "No. I don't think so. Daddy was too excited about the secret lair. Bob sold him with the pocket door. Mom was less impressed, but I think she's coming around. Might be some changes, but we'll have to wait and see."

"We'll figure it out," Nick told her, watching the water heat in the microwave. "It's not as if anyone has tried to kill us since Owen."

"Maybe leave that part of the argument out," she suggested. "Just in case."

He took the mug from the microwave, dropping the tea bag inside and handing it to her. She thanked him as he jumped up onto the counter beside her, their shoulders bumping together. "Everything else all right?"

She blinked rapidly as she looked down at the tea. She shrugged but didn't speak.

Nope. Not all right. Nick wrapped an arm around her, tugging her close. She laid her head on his shoulder. "Gibby, huh?"

"Yeah," she said softly. "Gibby."

Nick thought hard. She deserved his all. "Remember what you told me back in the hospital?"

She sniffled as she shook her head.

"No matter what happens in the future, she loves you here, in this moment. You gotta have faith, because she has faith in you."

"I said that?"

"You did. And it's exactly what I needed to hear. There was a bunch of other stuff I'm leaving out, but that stuck with me. You were right then, and you're right now. You're awesome, Jazz. You helped me when I needed you most, even if I didn't realize it then."

"We're pretty great, aren't we?"

He laughed. "Yeah, I think we are. And Seth and Gibby know it too. It's why they picked us."

"Things are changing," she whispered.

Oh, man. He *really* should've talked to her sooner. "Maybe. And it might suck, but it doesn't make us matter any less." He watched as she took a small sip of her tea, ignoring the twinge in his head.

"She's gonna do what she has to, and if she goes to Howard or stays here, it'll be okay. I promise."

"How do you know?"

Because if it wasn't okay for them, then it might not be okay for him and Seth, and that was something he didn't even want to consider. "I have to hope it will be. We can't know what's going to happen tomorrow, but if we spend all our time focusing on what *might* happen, we could end up missing what *does* happen."

She wiped her eyes. Nick, ever the gentleman, ripped off a paper towel and handed it over. "Sorry. We're out of Kleenex."

She was quiet for a long moment, clutching her mug in one hand, the paper towel crumpled in the other. Then, "What about you? You doing all right?"

He shrugged. "I think so. Seth seems to be coming around, but I'm not going to force him into doing anything he doesn't want to do. It's a give-and-take, you know? As long as you give only as much as you take, it'll be all right. *Cosmo* taught me that."

She bumped his shoulder, tea sloshing in the mug. "You tell Seth you love him yet?"

Nick's mouth went instantly dry. No. No, he hadn't. It felt too big, too wild. He wasn't even sure what it meant.

"Yeah," Jazz said. "I'll take that gaping fish look you've got going on as a *no*. What about prom?"

Nick, still in the process of rebooting his frazzled brain, said, "What *about* prom?"

"It's next month," she said. "Think about it: a romantic night, you and Seth slow dancing. It'd be the perfect time to tell him."

Nick turned slowly to stare at her, eyes bulging. "Oh my god, I didn't even think about that. What if he's expecting something big? Like, a declaration? A *love* declaration?" He began to panic. "I haven't even made a reservation! Wait—hold on. How in the hell do I make reservations?"

"Have you even asked him yet?"

"*No*," Nick whispered feverishly.

Jazz sighed. "We've got a lot of work to do. Don't worry, I'll take care of the reservation. You still want to do a double date?"

"Do I have to buy him a present on top of paying for dinner?" Nick demanded. "I have, like, twelve dollars. How the hell am I supposed to pay for a present *and* dinner? Unless we go to McDonald's and get sad little hamburgers. That's romantic, right? I think we have candles somewhere. I could bring those." He groaned. "Relationships are expensive. What am I supposed to buy my boyfriend who can fly?"

"I think you're probably the first person to ever say that sentence."

"Damn right I am," he muttered. "Gay freakin' rights."

"Come on," she said, jumping down from the counter. "I'll help you with the decorations, and we can plan something that'll be the most romantic thing anyone has ever done. How do you feel about flash mobs?"

"Badly," Nick said, "as everyone should."

"Well, we've got time. And since it's up to me to plan everything, we're all going to coordinate our outfits, and I won't take no for an answer."

"Why do *I* have to be the one to ask *him*?" Nick asked, following her toward the stairs. "That sounds sexist. Okay, not really because we're both dudes, but still. Down with the patriarchy!"

She laughed, looking startled as she did so, and Nick grinned at her.

Nick would remember this moment, here, right before everything changed. Jazz was still a little down, but he had her laughing again before too long. He couldn't fly or shoot lasers out of his eyes, but he could help people when they were feeling low. It might not be as impressive as a superhero, but the little things mattered too.

And that line of thinking was what he'd remember most.

Once they had a pile of decorations ready to be boxed up and stored away, Nick went to the small hatch in the ceiling of the hallway. He reached up and pulled the thin string to lower the lid to the hatch and the rickety ladder hidden therein. He jumped back as the ladder slid down and clunked against the floor.

"I'll go up first," he said, "in case there are spiders."

Jazz snorted. "Yeah, because the last time there was supposed to be a spider, you acted like a knight in shining armor."

He climbed the ladder into semidarkness, weak light coming in from a circular window at the front of the house. Boxes and plastic tubs lined the attic. He rubbed his hand against the wall until he found the light switch. He flipped it on, listening in case anything alive scurried around. Nothing did. The house creaked and settled, but nothing seemed to be crawling in his direction.

"Okay," he called down as he scanned the attic. "Bunch of boxes up here. I'll hand them down to you. Cool?"

"Cool," she said at the bottom of the ladder.

He grunted as he pulled himself up. The ceiling was vaulted, coming together like the top of a triangle. He could stand at full height, but only in the middle of the room. Thankfully, Dad hadn't pushed the boxes too far back when they'd finished decorating. Nick made quick work of it, picking up a box or tub and handing it down the ladder to Jazz, who stacked them on the floor. She'd turned on music on her phone, and by the time he picked up the last box, they were both singing at the tops of their lungs, Nick going falsetto, causing Jazz to wrinkle her nose and tell him to keep his day job. It was good.

He was about to turn around and climb down the ladder when something caught his eye. In the back corner of the attic, a low glint flashed from the light of the bare bulb. He frowned, letting go of the ladder.

"Is that it?" Jazz called up.

"Hold on a second. There's something up here."

"That's how horror movies start. Don't be the stupid white guy who needs to check things out."

Nick scoffed as he pushed his way further into the attic, moving dusty boxes to give him room. "I'm queer. That means I'd at *least* survive until halfway through the movie."

"I have questions about your logic."

"Most do," he muttered. He grunted as he lifted a heavy box marked RECORDS, a memory flitting about in the back of his mind like a little bird: his mother, pulling a black record from its sleeve and telling Nick there wasn't anything quite like the Rat Pack, lowering the needle to the record and Frank beginning to sing about how the best was yet to come.

Without realizing it, Nick began to hum along with the ghost in his head. He only stopped when he saw what had caught his attention.

An old, gray television was plugged into the only outlet in the attic. The top of it was covered in a thin layer of dust, though the screen looked as if it'd been wiped clean recently. Below the screen was a rectangular slot. It took Nick a moment to realize what it was for. A tape player. A VCR. He crouched down in front of the TV, pushing back the flap of the VCR.

Inside was a tape.

"How did people live without streaming?" Nick wondered aloud as he dropped the flap, looking around. Next to the TV was a cardboard box, unmarked. He lifted the lid. Inside were stacks of tapes without labels. He turned back to the TV and pressed the power button, blinking against the blue wash that covered the screen.

"I swear to god, if this is one of Dad's pornos, I'm going to be scarred forever," he mumbled.

He pressed play.

The VCR whirred and clicked as the tape began to play.

A park. The sun was shining. Summer, maybe? The trees were green, and the sky was so blue it looked fake. Clouds, thick and fluffy, hung suspended in the sky. And then the camera swung down to show a blanket spread out on the grass, the remains of a meal lying discarded—and a woman sitting on the blanket, her hair pulled back in a loose ponytail.

Nick fell back against the floor, mouth open but no sound coming out.

Jennifer Bell said, "What are you doing? Are you filming me?" She shook her head as she smiled. "Stop it. I'm not wearing any makeup."

And then Dad said, "You're beautiful. The camera loves you, baby."

She laughed, and Nick couldn't breathe. He couldn't get air into his lungs, because he'd never seen this before. He'd never known these memories existed. Anger, quick and bright, roared through him, but he shoved it away as he continued to watch.

The bottom of the screen showed the date in white letters and numbers. A few years before he'd been born.

The camera zoomed in on her face as she blushed. "There it is," Dad said, and he sounded so happy—so free—that Nick had to rub the ache in his chest. "Hello, wife."

She rolled her eyes. "Hello, husband. You still say it like it's a new thing. We've been married for four years."

"I want everyone to know," Dad said. He raised his voice to a shout. "This is my wife and I love her!" The screen shook as Dad spun the camera. "Do you hear me, world? This is my *wife* and she's the best thing that's ever happened to me!"

"Oh my god, *stop*," Mom said, though she didn't seem like she meant it. "You're such a dork."

"Nah," Dad said easily as he focused on her again. "I want everyone in the park to know I love you."

"I think they get it," she said, and she gave the camera a funny little smile, one that Nick recognized from the mirror. He looked like her. He *sounded* like her. How the hell could Dad stand to be in his presence when Before had become After? "You're going to get us in trouble. What are you going to do when the police come and ask about the crazy man with the camera?"

"Noted," Dad said. "Wouldn't want the police. They'd just put you to work again."

Her smile faded. "I told you, Aaron. Today isn't about that. I'm here, okay? You and me."

Dad sighed. "Yeah, I know. That was a shitty thing to say. Hey, I'm sorry."

Mom looked relieved. "And I accept your apology. Come on. Lie down with me. Let's look at the clouds and see what we see."

And they did, though the camera shot never really left Mom's face. They were speaking in low tones, saying *that* cloud looked like a dog, and *that* cloud looked like a dragon, see? There's the tail. The wings. The head with the horns.

"Nick?"

He jerked his head back toward the hatch. Jazz was climbing up into the attic, a concerned expression on her face. They both startled when a box near her suddenly *jumped* and fell over against the wall. "Uh," she said, "that was weird. How did— Oh, Nicky. What's wrong? Why are you crying?"

He reached up and touched his cheeks. His fingers came away wet. "Look," he said in a choked voice. He turned back to the TV as Jazz moved toward him.

She settled next to him on her knees just as Mom turned her face toward the camera. Her eyes were bright and knowing. "This is a good day," she whispered.

"The best," Dad whispered back.

"Is that—" Jazz leaned forward, face inches from the screen. "That's your mom."

Nick nodded dumbly.

"She looks like I remember," Jazz said quietly as she sat back on her legs. "Maybe a little younger, but almost the same."

"I've never seen this before," Nick said dully. "Dad never told me."

Jazz took his hand in hers. "Maybe he forgot."

Nick shook his head. "The screen was recently cleaned. I think—I think he comes up here and watches this." He waved his hand toward the box next to the TV. "There are more tapes in there."

She frowned as Nick's mom and dad whispered back and forth. "Why wouldn't he tell you about these?"

"I don't know."

She squeezed his hand.

Secrets. It felt like more secrets.

The video lasted a few minutes more before the screen once again turned blue. He hit the fast-forward button, but nothing else came up.

He could've left it there. He could've turned off the television and gone back down the ladder and done what Dad had asked him to do. Later, when Dad came home, he'd tell him what he'd found, and maybe he'd be a little pissed off, but he'd give Dad the benefit of the doubt. This tape was innocent. Maybe the rest weren't, and Nick didn't want to see things he shouldn't. If they were private, then Nick needed to respect that. Dad was allowed to have his own way of coping with his grief.

Except . . .

This was his mother.

Nick ejected the tape and set it on top of the TV. He grabbed the box, pulling it toward him as Jazz peered over his shoulder. He riffled through the tapes, not knowing what he was looking for. Unmarked. Unmarked. Unmarked. All of them were unmarked. He was about to pick one off the stack he'd made next to them when he saw a flash of white near the bottom of the box. He pulled the tape out.

There, across the front, was a label. And on this label, written in her familiar messy scrawl, were two words:

the truth

A little voice in the back of his head whispered he should stop while he still could, that whatever was on this tape could only lead to him hurting more than he already was. He barely noticed when the bulb above them flared, Jazz tilting her head back and murmuring, "These power surges. I don't know why they keep happening in your neighborhood."

He pushed the tape into the TV.

Mom appeared on-screen, her face close as she adjusted the

camera. The date blinked at the bottom. It took Nick a moment to place when this was. She and Dad would have still been in school. Their last year, maybe. Or second to last. Not married yet. It'd be a few more years before that happened.

He didn't recognize where she was. It looked like the living room of a small apartment. She frowned as she fiddled with the camera again, her light hair falling on her shoulders. She huffed out a breath of air, causing her bangs to flutter. She stood upright, taking steps back until she was standing in front of the camera. She wore jeans and a white shirt covered in cerulean blue stars. Her feet were bare.

"Okay," she said. "It's time. I've thought this through. I hope." She shook her head. "They'll be here in a minute, so I've got to be sure." She wiggled her shoulders as she took a deep breath. "I don't know why I'm so scared. I hope they see past that for what this is." She gnawed a thumbnail before wringing her hands. "I can't do this on my own anymore."

"What's she talking about?" Jazz whispered.

"I don't know," Nick said. "Maybe she's—"

On the television, a doorbell chimed. "Coming!" Mom shouted, stepping off-screen. An awful paisley couch lined the wall behind her, and Nick laughed wetly at the Backstreet Boys poster hanging above it. At least he knew where he got his taste for terrible music.

Other voices spoke, but they were low and Nick couldn't pick out the words. Shadows played along the walls and floor from the afternoon sunlight. Nick thought there were two more people coming into the apartment.

Mom reappeared first, looking nervous. She was smiling, but the edges of it curled down, as if her mouth couldn't support the weight of it. "Stop it with that look. I'm not pregnant, if that's what you're thinking."

"I wasn't," Dad said, and Nick *knew* that tone. Dad had been thinking exactly that. "But even if you were, we'd deal with it together." Dad moved into view, shoulders stiff, a worried look on his face. His hair was longer, hanging almost to his shoulders. He looked barely older than Nick did, skinny and awkward.

Mom snorted as she shoved him onto the couch. "'Deal with it.' Just what every girl wants to hear."

"I didn't mean it like that," Dad protested feebly. He looked off-screen. "Tell her."

Another voice spoke, causing Nick's blood to turn to ice. "He didn't mean it like that. But I'll admit I was thinking it, too, and I didn't want to be here for that conversation. I get that we're best friends, but I don't think I'm ready to be an uncle yet."

"That's how it works, man," Dad said as Simon Burke appeared on-screen. He moved through the room as if he'd been there countless times, kicking off his shoes and settling on the couch next to Dad, slinging an arm over his shoulders. He looked so much like Owen that Nick couldn't do anything but breathe through the storm in his head.

"Nicky," Jazz whispered. "Maybe we shouldn't be watching this."

Nick ignored her, glaring at Burke as he smiled at Mom. "Okay, you're not pregnant. That's good. It means Aaron remembered to wrap it, like I told him to. Still doesn't explain why we're here." His gaze drifted until it settled on the camera. He squinted at it. "Are you recording this?"

Mom nodded as Dad craned his neck around her to see what Burke was looking at. "For posterity. And I have a feeling you're going to want to watch it after I'm done."

"Done with what?" Dad asked, pushing Burke's arm off him. "What's going on, Jenny? You're starting to freak me out."

She fidgeted, moving like she didn't know how to stop. Nick was struck once again by how he took after her. She couldn't keep still, and Nick thought it was more than just nerves. What if she'd been like him? ADHD was genetic, right?

"Okay," Mom said. "I'm going to show you something, and you'll have a billion questions, but I ask that you . . . wait until I'm done. I don't have anyone else I trust that I can show this to. I didn't get a chance to talk about it with Mom before she died, and Dad's been gone for years, so no help there."

Dad paled. "Are you sick?"

She laughed, but it wasn't like the day in the park in their future. It was fragile and soft, like she was scared. "No. Not—not in the way you're thinking. It's nothing *bad*, but some might see it that way, which is why I've kept this to myself for as long as I have."

"What is it?" Burke asked. "Jenny, you can tell us anything. We're here for you."

"I know," Mom said, glancing over her shoulder at the camera. "And that's why I asked you both to come here today. Aaron, because I love you and this might affect you, too, one day, if we decide to have a family. Simon, because I need your brain. You're smart, and if anyone can figure this out, it's you."

Burke arched an eyebrow, and Nick wanted to smash his face in. "Consider my interest piqued."

"Okay," she said. "Just . . . hold on." She stepped off-screen once more, Dad's and Burke's gazes following her. She reappeared only a moment later, holding a clear plastic cup filled with what looked like water. She set it down on the cheap coffee table in front of the couch. The two men leaned forward with interest, Burke's gaze narrowing as he stared at the cup, Dad looking up from the table at Mom, confused. Mom took a step back from the table so the camera had a clear view. She said, "You might want to sit back," as she raised her right hand, palm outstretched toward the cup.

Dad did so immediately. Burke hesitated but followed suit.

"What's she doing?" Jazz asked as a buzzing noise began to fill Nick's ears.

"I don't know," he mumbled. "Like, a magic trick? She's—"

The cup shook slightly as if someone had kicked the table, the water rippling.

Dad's eyes bulged. "What was that? An earthquake? I felt it in the couch. Jenny, you—"

"Hush," she said. "I need to focus." She crooked her fingers like little claws before taking a deep breath, letting it out slow. The cup twitched before rising off the table in midair, spinning end over end without spilling any water. It lowered back to the table. Her fingers twitched as her brow furrowed. Instead of the cup lifting off the table once more, the *water* did, rising like it was sentient, limbs reaching out and gripping the edge of the cup. The water— the goddamn *water*—pulled itself out of the cup, quivering but holding together. The glass toppled over, but the water didn't spill and splash out. It formed a small translucent ball, glittering in the sunlight pouring in from a window out of sight.

The water ball began to stretch until it was at least a foot long, a thin strand whose surface rippled like a rock thrown into a pond.

"Oh my god," Dad and Nick breathed at the same time.

Mom glanced back at the camera again, a trickle of sweat sliding down her cheek. When she looked back at the water, the ends of the strand connected, forming a circle. It widened as it moved above her. She lowered her hand, the circle descending until it passed her head, her shoulders, her arms, her chest to her waist. She shimmied her hips a little, and the water bounced back and forth, wetting her shirt slightly when it touched her.

"A hula hoop," she said. "Funny, right?"

Dad gaped at her. "Funny? *Funny?* Jenny, what the hell? How are you doing this?"

Burke didn't look away from the sight in front of him. "Isn't it obvious?" he murmured. Nick didn't like the expression on his face. It was off, somehow, and hungry. "Psychokinesis. Telekinesis. The same thing, for all intents and purposes."

The water burst apart and fell onto the carpet, splashing against her feet. She grimaced, raising each foot and shaking the droplets off. "That's what I need you for. I don't understand what this is. It's always been with me, for as long as I could remember. This is the least of what I can do." Her voice cracked when she said, "Aaron. Please. Say something. I wasn't trying to keep this from you. I didn't know how to tell you."

"Tell me *what*?" Dad demanded.

Burke put his hand on Dad's arm. "Aaron, don't you know what this means?" He smiled as he looked back at Mom. "She's an Extraordinary."

The lightbulb hanging in the attic exploded with an electrical snarl, glass falling onto the floor. Nick and Jazz screamed as the television began rocking back and forth, the screen cracking as the picture from years before went black. The TV fell over, the cord pulling from the socket and whipping around, almost hitting Nick in the face. He stumbled back on his butt, crab-walking as the TV fell forward, something inside breaking.

Silence fell.

And it was in this silence that Nick realized he couldn't breathe. He couldn't focus. The knot in his head and chest writhed as the fractured bulb swung back and forth on its chain. He was nearly blind with panic, his breath whistling out his nose. Flashes of light burst across his vision. The walls began to close in around him.

He flinched when he felt hands on him, rubbing up and down his back. Through the storm in his head, he heard Jazz's worried voice. "Breathe, Nicky. Come on. You can do this. Breathe, just breathe. In. *In*, Nick."

He couldn't do what she was asking. His lungs didn't work. They were dead in his chest, his skin clammy. He was *cold*. He'd never been so cold in his life. He tried to inhale. It didn't work. The attic became hazy around him, the shadows bled together, and Jazz was *demanding* that he take a breath right this second or she was going to call 911.

He gasped in a breath. His chest expanded to the point he thought his ribs would crack. He exhaled explosively before drawing another breath, holding it as best he could.

"Good," Jazz said. "Again. In, Nick."

He did. In. Hold. Out. Hold. In. Out. In out in out in—

And then he began to cry, choked, weak sobs that echoed in the attic around them.

Jazz lifted his head while she scooted underneath him, letting him rest against her legs. She put her hands in his hair, whispering that he was all right, they were all right, let it out, Nicky, let it out.

He did. A hole opened in his chest, and from it crawled the ugly monster of grief.

He didn't know how long it took for him to come back to himself. All he knew was that when his vision finally cleared, the light from the attic window was off, as if it were late afternoon. Jazz was humming quietly, staring off into nothing as she stroked his hair.

"Sorry," he said, closing his eyes against the embarrassment that roared through him.

"Yeah," she said. "I kind of think that's not something you need to apologize for." Her hand paused in his hair. "Better?"

"I have no idea." He scrubbed a hand over his face, grimacing at his leaking nose.

"Good answer," she said, tracing a fingernail over his eyebrows. "You want to know what I think?"

He nodded tiredly.

She said, "I think your mother loved you very much, and if she kept things from you, then she had her reasons. Same with your dad. There isn't anything he wouldn't do for you."

"Except tell me the truth," Nick said bitterly.

"Yeah, there is that. But what if . . ." She trailed off, looking at the broken television. She stiffened, turning back slowly toward Nick, her eyes wide. "The TV." There was something in her voice, something Nick couldn't quite place. "The light bulb." She paled. "The bridge. Oh my god, Nick. The *bridge*."

Nick struggled to follow her line of thinking, his own thoughts a chaotic mess. "What are you— *McManus* Bridge?"

"You fell, Nick. You should've died. But you didn't. Everything collapsed around you, all that metal, and it should've crushed you flat onto the pavement. But it just . . . stopped. Like you did. Floating. Like a cup. Like . . . water." She sucked in a sharp breath. "Nick. *Nick.* Don't you see?"

Gooseflesh prickled along his arms, skin thrumming. "See what?"

And Jasmine Kensington said, "What if it's genetic? What if you have what she had? Nicky, what if you've been an Extraordinary all along?"

And that's why I asked you both to come here today. Aaron, because I love you and this might affect you, too, one day, if we decide to have a family.

Nick gaped at her as his mind shorted out in a furious burst of sparks. "What in the actual fu—"

8

"Cups. Make them move."

Nick looked down at the glass cups she'd brought up from the kitchen. Jazz had set them down in a line on the attic floor. All were empty. Jazz said she didn't get water because knowing Nick, if it worked, they'd both get wet and her sweater was dry-clean only. He had to hand it to her for having her priorities straight (at least for Jazz) in the middle of . . . well. Whatever this was.

"Okay, okay." He shook out his shoulders, wiggling his arms and hands. "Cups. I can do this. They're just cups. Little glass cups. Focus. Focus." He took a deep breath, letting it out slow. And like his mother had, he raised his hand up, palm facing the glasses lining the floor. He crooked his fingers as he began to strain, teeth grinding together.

Nothing happened.

"Powers activate!"

Nothing.

"Invisible Glass Smash!"

Jazz started laughing. "What? Why did you say that?"

He glared at her, hand still outstretched. "The name of the move I'm trying to do. Everyone knows that when you perform a move, you say the name of it."

"Oh, if everyone knows that, then keep going."

"I would if you'd stop laughing. Hurling Cup of Death!"

She did not stop laughing. If anything, she laughed harder. "Oh my god, this is *amazing*. Say something else. Wait, I've got one. Flying Cup of Eternity!"

"Flying Cup of Eternity!" Nick bellowed, curling his hand into a fist.

The cups didn't move.

Nick dropped his hand. "This is stupid. I don't have powers, Jazz. You were right when you said we'd have seen something by now." He was getting angry, but he didn't know at whom. Maybe everybody. Dad, for keeping their shared history from him. Mom, for doing what she could and not being here to tell him why. Burke, for existing. Owen, for trying to kill him and his friends. Seth, for . . . well, for nothing, because Seth was perfect.

Jazz wasn't laughing anymore. "Nick, calm down, okay? You're starting to breathe fast again." She placed her hand on his arm. "You're okay. We don't have to do anything now if you're not ready. It might be better if we pump the brakes and think."

He shook his head. "I need to talk to Dad. I gotta hear this from him. If he's—" He swallowed past the lump in his throat. "If he kept this from me, I need to know why." And *there* was his anger, bright and glassy. They should've told him. Secrets. It always came down to secrets, and Nick was sick of it.

A lance of pain burst through his head, and Nick groaned, bending over and wrapping his arms around his waist. The whisper in the back of his mind—that low, unintelligible voice—began to roar, and he *felt* it. He felt it down to his bones, a strangeness he couldn't escape. He heard Jazz's worried voice near him, but he couldn't focus on what she was saying. He gritted his teeth as the headache came for him with a vengeance, pulsing slickly, causing his gorge to rise. He tasted bile in the back of his throat, and just when he thought he couldn't take it anymore, just when he expected to be consumed by it, he grabbed hold of it. It wriggled furiously like it was alive, and Nick whispered, "*No.*"

His headache disappeared as quickly as it came. He blinked slowly as his head cleared, back popping as he pulled himself to his full height. He turned to Jazz, an apology on the tip of his tongue, but it died at the look on her face.

Her eyes were wide, her jaw dropped, bottom lip quivering. But she wasn't staring at him.

"What?" he asked. "What's wrong?"

She reached up and took his chin in her hand, turning his head toward the hatch.

The four cups were floating in midair. The one on the right spun in slow circles. The one on the left moved up and down, up and down. The middle two clinked together gently, the sound dull in the attic.

"You're doing it," Jazz whispered.

He watched as the cups began to spin in concentric circles, wider and faster. He took a step back when one of the cups passed right in front of him, whistling as it sliced through the air. "Ha, ha," he said weakly. "Okay, I'm done now. Cups, fall down. Cease and desist! Cups, *stop*."

They didn't stop. They moved faster, but he managed to grab Jazz in time and pull her down as one of the cups rocketed toward them. Jazz gasped as it shattered against the wall. "Turn it off!"

"I don't know *how*!" Nick shouted at her as another cup shot toward them. Jazz shoved him out of the way as the glass smashed against the ground where Nick had been standing only a second before. He fell to his knees as the boxes around him began to shudder and shake. A plastic tub flipped on its side, spilling out old books and papers. The books rose from the floor, the pages fluttering and snapping. He flinched when the broken television righted itself, the power cord whipping back and forth.

He pushed himself up, grabbing Jazz by the hand as the attic began to rumble. She moved quickly, following him as he pulled her toward the ladder. He looked back over his shoulder as he made her go down first.

Every single box and tub in the attic was floating inches off the floor.

He fell down the ladder to avoid getting hit in the face by the two remaining glasses. He landed on his back at the bottom of the ladder, Jazz standing over him, her hair hanging down around her face.

A loud crash came from above them, and he barely had time to recover when Jazz hooked her hands in his armpits from behind, pulling him away as the pile of Christmas decorations they'd gathered began to rise from the floor. The garland swirled. The lights blinked green and red and blue. The photographs hanging on the wall began to rattle.

"We need to get out of here," Jazz breathed in his ear as a box fell down the ladder and split apart before its contents, too, began to move. "Go, go, *go*!"

They went, flying down the stairs even as the railing creaked and groaned, the wooden slats of the steps shaking. It felt like an earthquake, the very floor vibrating beneath their feet. Jazz jumped from the last few steps, and almost fell over when the rug leading toward the front door slid out from underneath her feet, twisting like a snake. He grabbed her before she could fall, and they both hit the door at the same time. She grabbed her coat off the hook, throwing one of Nick's hoodies at him as he gripped the doorknob.

Outside, the cold air was a punch in the face. Nick immediately began to shiver as he slammed the door behind them. Through the frosted glass, he could see things still moving inside. He backed away slowly.

"We're good," Jazz panted. "We're safe. It's over."

They both screamed when the rug from the hallway smashed against the inside of the door, causing it to rattle in its frame.

"Run!" Nick cried.

They ran.

They made it to the sidewalk as Nick struggled to pull the hoodie up and over him. He got his head through, ready to tell Jazz she was never allowed to have ideas again, when the alarm of the car closest to them began to blare. As did the SUV behind it. And another car. And another. And another.

And then one of the cars covered in a thin crust of snow began to bounce on its tires, the frame squealing. Nick's next-door neighbor—a man with the amazing name of Percival Axworthy—came onto the porch, his car keys in hand. He frowned as he repeatedly hit the button to turn the alarm off. Instead of silencing it, the car—a 1982 Chevy Citation that Percival had lovingly restored for reasons Nick didn't understand, given how ugly it was—launched ten feet into the air before crashing back down onto the road, the windows blowing out, glass spraying in glittering arcs.

"I'm sorry!" Nick shouted as Jazz pulled him down the sidewalk. "Call your insurance company and file a claim!"

Percival didn't seem to hear him, staring, dumbfounded, as one of the tires of his beloved car deflated with a comical wheeze.

"Gibby," Jazz was saying into her phone. "We have a—would you *listen* to me? Yes, I'm yelling! This is a perfect time for yelling! Where's Seth?" They both almost slipped when the meters began spewing coins onto the sidewalk, people already taking out their phones and beginning to record the mayhem. "What do you mean he went out? Dammit, fine. No, don't. Stay where you are. We're going to go find Nick's—" The phone flew from her hands. They watched as it flew up into the air and landed on the roof of the apartment building across the street.

"Um," Nick said. "My bad?"

"Yeah," Jazz said faintly. "That's your bad. Daddy's going to be pissed that I lost another phone."

They began to push through the crowd that had stopped to stare at the destruction that seemed to follow in their wake. Too many people. Too many people, and they were stuck, they were *stuck* and—

A woman screamed as she began to slide *backward*, the tips of her shoes dragging along the cement. She stopped a few feet away on wobbly legs, looking around wildly, people running over to make sure she was all right.

"Train," Nick gasped as they burst through the back of the crowd. "We gotta get to the train. Dad's gotta be at the station by now."

"Are you out of your mind?" Jazz asked. "I'm not going in a metal tube with you while you're on the fritz. If you want to take the chance of getting stuck in one of the tunnels, then go for it. But

I have too much respect for myself to have to wait to be rescued. We'll walk."

"That's twenty blocks!"

"Then we better get moving," she said grimly.

They did, even as more car alarms began to shriek.

By the time they reached the block the precinct was on, they were worn out and frazzled, Nick's face covered in red marks after the strings of his hoodie began to slap against his face like they were alive. He'd pulled the string out and thrown it on the ground. It didn't move again. They stopped in the alcove of a shuttered shop with boards on the windows and graffiti covering the wood in bright colors. Nick bent over, hands on his knees, panting.

"Did you see the guitar explode?" Jazz managed to say, sweat trickling down her cheek. "That poor busker. Who knew such a big man could scream like that?"

Nick grimaced as he stood upright. His body felt weak, and he was more tired than he'd ever been in his life. His thoughts were sluggish as he leaned out of the alcove, looking up and down the sidewalk to see if anything else would happen. Or explode.

Nothing. Just people hurrying by, paying them no mind, the street filled with backed-up traffic, horns honking as construction workers yelled back at them.

"Oh, thank god," Nick muttered. "I think it's over."

"Are you sure?" Jazz asked. "Because that wasn't exactly what I was hoping for when I brought up the cups."

Nick groaned as he rubbed a hand over his face. "Stupid cups. Stupid powers." He laughed hollowly as he looked up the street toward the precinct. "Why would—"

But he never got the chance to finish. Because the double doors of the police station swung open, and Nick's father stepped out, mouth twisted into a scowl as he glanced down at his phone. Nick jerked his head back as Dad looked in his direction. He didn't know if he'd been seen. He waited a moment before leaning back out. He saw his father's back facing him as he walked in the opposite direction through the crowd. Jazz stood on her tiptoes, looking over his shoulder. "Where's he going?"

Thinking quickly, Nick said, "Jazz, go home—or—go to Seth and Gibby. I gotta talk to my dad."

She gripped his arm. "You don't have to do this by yourself."

He gave her what he hoped was a reassuring smile. By the look on her face, he'd failed. "I know, but I—I don't know what's going to happen, and I don't want you caught in the middle of it."

She dropped her hand. Looking perturbed, she said, "Are you sure?"

"I am," he said firmly. "I'll catch up with you after, okay? You good with getting out of here on your own?"

She rolled her eyes. "I can handle myself."

"Don't I know it," he muttered. He laughed quietly when she stood on her tiptoes, kissing his cheek. "Thanks, Jazz."

"Go," she said, shoving him out of the alcove. "Do what you need to do, but be careful, Nicky. You don't know what you're walking into."

"That's what I'm worried about," he said. "Later."

He hurried down the sidewalk, glancing into the windows of the precinct as he passed it. He remembered what Gibby had told him—how he saw a badge and uniform and thought *safety*, something so ingrained in him that he took it as gospel truth when perhaps he should've asked questions. He ducked his head when he saw Officer Rookie inside, wearing an ill-fitting suit, holding a folder in his hands. Since Nick had last seen him, he'd apparently decided that a beard was the right thing to do for his face, which, okay.

He made it by the station without the Rook seeing him, and he continued on, keeping an eye on Dad so he didn't lose him in the crowd. He thought about calling after him, but the look on Dad's face when he'd exited the precinct rubbed him the wrong way. He didn't know why, but he didn't exactly feel like giving Dad the benefit of the doubt at the moment. He wanted to see where he was going, what he was doing. He wasn't headed toward home. Maybe he was going back to Jazz's and Gibby's parents, though Nick didn't think that was the case. It'd been hours since Dad had left, and he'd said he was going to work when he finished with them.

Nick flinched when a car's brakes squealed on the street, sure his powers were coming back. He balled his hands into fists. Nothing happened. Everything was normal. Everything was fine.

Or, at least, that's what he kept telling himself.

Dad crossed the street with the light, and Nick began to jog to catch up so he wouldn't have to wait until it was safe to cross again. He made it across just as the walk symbol changed back into a red hand. Where was Dad going? And why were his shoulders hunched nearly to his ears? He looked stressed, angry. Was it because of the meeting with his friends' parents, or something else? What the hell was he hiding this time?

A memory, then, unbidden but rising like a rocket in his head. Dad in the hospital, Nick next to his bed, both of them watching Pyro Storm and Shadow Star battle it out on the television that hung on the wall.

If someone who loved you lied to you, kept things from you, hurt you, but they needed your help, would you do it?

I would. Because I can never turn my back on someone who needs me. If I was lied to, if I was kept in the dark and my heart was breaking, I would still do everything I could. Sometimes, we lie to the ones we love most to keep them safe.

Nick brushed his hand angrily against the burning in his eyes. He would get answers, one way or another.

Ten minutes later, Dad turned into a small park Nick wasn't familiar with. Bare trees reached up toward a gunmetal sky and a pavilion with empty wooden tables sat on a cracked cement slab. The ground was covered in dirty snow. The only other people in the park were a kid on a swing, laughing as a woman pushed her, causing the chains to creak as the girl shouted *Higher, higher!*

Nick hid behind a tree, watching his father go to the pavilion. Dad looked down at his phone, a furious expression on his face.

He tapped the screen a couple of times before bringing it to his ear. Whoever answered, Dad didn't greet. Instead, his mouth twisted into a snarl, teeth bared. Nick was too far away to hear what was being said. Dad began to pace, his back to Nick, his footsteps echoing dully in the pavilion.

Nick took a deep breath and stepped out from behind the tree, moving closer. He froze when Dad turned toward him, but he was looking down at his feet, shoulders stiff. He paced the other direction, and Nick rushed forward, heart in his throat as he reached a thick pillar at the edge of the pavilion.

He could hear his father now.

He wished he couldn't.

—and where do you get off?" Dad snarled. "Who the hell do you think you are? I told you I'd do what you wanted. I *told* you I'd handle it. You can't—"

Nick covered his mouth with his hand, his hot breath stinging his palm. The woman pushing the kid on the swing stared at him for a moment before pulling the girl off and walking away, glancing over her shoulder, eyes narrowed.

"I don't give two shits what you're doing," Dad said coldly. "He's not your son. He's *mine*, and I'll be the one to decide what he does and doesn't know. You're in no position to give me parenting advice, Simon. Not after what you did to Owen."

Nick's blood turned into icy sludge as he gasped against his hand.

Dad laughed bitterly. "That's not what we agreed to. I told you I'd keep you in the loop when it came to the Extraordinaries, and I've *done* that. You know everything I do about Pyro Storm's movements. And there aren't any other Extraordinaries. I would know if there—what? No. Of course I don't know who he is. He wears a *mask*. How the hell am I—no. He doesn't know either. I don't *care* what you saw on the bridge, he doesn't know who Pyro Storm is. Listen to me, Simon, because I won't say this again. Leave my son out of this. All the Concentra in the world doesn't matter if you're screwing with my child, and I'm telling you right here and right now: if you try to speak to my son again, I'll kill you myself. Just because you found a way to suppress what's inside Nick doesn't give you the right to involve yourself in his life."

Nick tried to move, but his feet were rooted in place. He couldn't make his legs work, couldn't do anything but struggle to breathe as his father broke his heart.

He'd known. Dad had known about all of it. Mom. Nick. The pills. The Concentra made by Burke Pharmaceuticals.

Have you taken your pill, Nick?

Don't forget your meds, kid.

Did you take your pill, Nicky?

"I *know*," Dad said. "But I'll keep it going for as long as I can. I know what happens to people like them. I've seen it. And you did too; you saw how much it weighed on Jenny. I won't let the same thing happened to Nick." A beat of silence. Then, furiously, "She was targeted. They knew who she was the day they followed her into that bank, even though it'd been *years*. They killed her because of what she meant to the people of this city. If I'd known where that would lead, I would have *begged* her to never put on that suit. The city didn't need her to be Guardian, *we* needed her to be alive and—"

Guardian.

Guardian.

The Extraordinary who'd watched over Nova City.

The hero who'd disappeared before Nick was born.

Nick's phone rang in his pocket, startlingly loud in the quiet of the park.

Nick panicked, muttering, "Oh my god, no, no, *no*," as he stepped away from the pillar, trying to pull his phone out, trying to make it stop. He didn't even see who was calling as he jerked it from his pocket, hissing as his knuckles popped. He swiped his thumb across the screen, sending the call to voicemail.

"Nicky?"

Nick whirled around. Dad stood there, all the blood having drained from his face. His mouth hung open, the phone falling from his hand and bouncing on the floor of the pavilion.

Dad recovered first. "Nick? Hey, hey. What are you doing here?" He tried to smile, but it crumbled as he took a step toward his son. "Kid, what's—what's going on?"

Nick picked up his phone and took an answering step back, his mind viciously blank. He couldn't form a single coherent thought, and the sound that fell from his open mouth was a high-pitched whine, broken and weak.

"No," Dad said, hands shaking as he reached for his son. "Oh, Nicky. I didn't—" His chest heaved, his breath pouring from his mouth in a thick cloud. "Please. Listen to me, okay? I need you to listen. We're okay. We're all right, I swear it. Let me explain. Oh my god, please don't—Nick, *no!*"

Nick, yes.

He didn't look back as he ran out of the park, his heart thundering in his chest, head spinning. He slid on a slick patch of ice hidden under the snow but managed to keep his footing with a few hard steps that jolted his knees. A thin tree limb slapped against his cheek, causing it to go numb as he picked up speed. He heard his father shouting his name, begging for him to stop, but he didn't. He couldn't.

Nearly blind with panic, he ran.

9

The sky had darkened considerably. Flurries fell, catching the light from the streetlamps. It was freezing, but Nick barely felt it as his feet pounded pavement, pushing through the people on the sidewalk.

He didn't know how long he ran for, only that by the time he stopped, he had a painful stitch in his side. He was hot. He was cold. He couldn't focus, couldn't latch onto a single clear thought that would help pull him through the storm in his head. He couldn't pull enough air into his lungs.

He lifted his head, his neck stiff and sore. In an alley. He was in an alley a few feet off the sidewalk, hidden in the encroaching dark. Nick pressed his forehead against the side of a building, the brick cold against his skin. Before he could stop himself, he punched the brick. The pain was fierce and immediate, the knuckles of his skin splitting, blood welling. It was enough to clear his head a little, and he sucked in a breath that burned his throat.

"Think," he muttered, shaking his hand, blood falling to the ground. "Think. You can do this. Focus. Next step."

He couldn't call Dad. He didn't know where Jazz had gone. Last he heard, Gibby was still at the Grays' house, working on—

Seth.

Seth, Seth, Seth.

He would know what to do.

Nick pulled his phone from his pocket, wincing when his injured hand rubbed against rough denim. He ignored it, grunting as his fingers flew over the screen.

The phone rang once. Twice. Three times.

"You've reached Seth's voicemail. I'm probably busy. And nobody calls anyone anymore unless it's an emergency. Send a text. Unless it's an emergency."

"It *is* an emergency," Nick hissed into the phone after it beeped. "Pick up your damn phone! I can move things with my *mind*."

He tried again.

Voicemail.

Like last year, when he thought Seth had been ignoring his calls, because if his phone was off, it would have rung once before going to voicemail. If he hadn't heard, it'd ring at least six times.

Three times meant Seth silenced the call.

Seth—for whatever reason—couldn't talk right then. Before he could get pissed off, he remembered vaguely that earlier, Gibby had said that Seth suited up, meaning something had happened.

Just busy. That's all it was. Seth was saving the day.

Again.

But then, why hadn't Dad known? Unless he'd been distracted by his call with Simon Burke, Dad should've been where Seth was, or at least monitoring the situation remotely.

Nick swallowed thickly, unable to comprehend that level of betrayal. Simon Burke was the enemy. And Dad was helping him.

Nick was alone. No one to call. No one to help him. No one he could trust.

"Oh, come on," he mumbled to himself. "You're not *that* much of a drama queen. Call Gibby. Call Jazz. Call Martha or Bob. Be smart about this. Figure out. My superpower is my brain, so *think*, goddammit!"

Before he could get anywhere, his phone beeped.

A text from Seth, as if he knew Nick needed him. Saw u called. Long day, heading home. Talk tomorrow? xx

Kiss kiss. It should have made Nick flush to the roots of his hair.

Except his phone beeped again, this time from the Team Pyro Storm app, the alert with an 8-bit cartoon of Pyro Storm's face with a word bubble proclaiming PYRO STORM IS NEARBY! He clicked on Pyro Storm's face, which opened a map of Nova City on his screen. Gibby had integrated Google Maps to show every street, complete with the names of buildings, parks, and neighborhoods. A green dot blinked on the screen as it moved. The dot showed Seth about twenty minutes away from where he now stood. The green blip moved toward what Nick thought was an alley behind a row of restaurants and a bodega with a particularly mean cat the size of a small horse.

The opposite way of his house.

Nick frowned as he went back to the text thread. Hesitating a moment, he tapped a reply.

> Going to bed?

Yep! Exhausted. Easy stuff, no worries. Even sent a new tweet on the account!

Playful. Fun. Their usual banter.

And a lie, because he switched back to the app and saw that Seth still wasn't going home. The dot was stopped in the alley.

He was about to text back that he could *see* that Seth wasn't going home. His thumb hovered over the screen. But that wasn't cool, right? The app wasn't made for Nick to track his boyfriend. It'd be an invasion of privacy if Nick called him out for it. He trusted Seth as much as he did his . . . well, as much as he *had* trusted his father. So what if Seth was lying about where he was? He didn't need Nick's permission to do anything.

He switched back to the app, planning on shutting it down, when the green blip disappeared.

It only did that when Seth turned off the tracker himself.

Like he realized he wasn't where he said he was.

But . . .

Nick's gorge rose, his mouth flooding with saliva. What if Seth had been captured by a new villain? What if this new villain had taken Seth's phone from him to respond to Nick's messages while ordering his lackeys to torture Pyro Storm? What if Seth was screaming for help and no one was there to save him? That was more likely than Seth Gray *lying* about where he was. Seth never lied. Sure, he'd kept his alter-ego from Nick for years, but there'd been a good reason for that.

Doubt crept in. Seth *would* be the type to keep things from Nick if he thought it'd put him in danger. He gnawed on the inside of his cheek as he stared down at his phone.

He typed back a response. Glad ur using the Twitter. Remember that candy I gave u last year? What was it called again?

No one outside of their friend group would know the answer. If this wasn't Seth on the other end, then they wouldn't be able to tell him.

Skwinkles Salsagheti. Good night <3

"Oh no," Nick breathed. "You're lying."

He left the alley behind.

Nick tried to run the entire way but he'd already run more today than he'd probably done in his entire life, and the stitch in his side grew teeth.

He made it to the cross streets he'd seen on the map. The snow flurries had lessened, the sky now spitting a few flakes that swirled around him. People laughed and smiled as they hurried by him. Though the streetlamps lit the sidewalks, the shadows of night seemed to reach toward him, and he felt colder than he had in his life.

The alley was as he thought: in between a bodega and an apartment building at the forefront of gentrification, sleek and made of steel and glass.

Nick crossed the street as soon as the light gave him the go-ahead, hurrying as he pulled his hood up and over his head. It wasn't a costume, but it'd have to do until he could change that. He reached the alley, hoping Seth hadn't left. No lights, only darkness. He couldn't even see how far back the alley went. "Okay. You can do this. Furious Lightning Punch. Make sure they know you mean business. Move silently. Don't let them hear you."

With that, he stepped into the alley.

And immediately tripped over a bag of trash lying on the ground. The bag was apparently filled with at least five hundred pounds of glass; it shattered so loudly, Nick was sure the sound registered as a seismic event on the Richter scale. He managed to stay upright, but only because he stepped down hard onto the bag, breaking even more glass.

He froze, waiting to see if anyone called out to him.

No one did.

He took another step forward. More glass broke. And then more. "Are you kidding me?" he whispered angrily. "Come *on*."

He took an exaggerated step forward, clearing the glass. Relieved, he hurried further into the alley, keeping close to the building on his left.

He was halfway down the alley when he heard Seth's voice.

Scratch that.

Pyro Storm's voice, modulated and deep.

He didn't sound hurt.

He sounded *fine*.

Nick pressed himself flat against the building as he inched closer.

"—and we'll have to be careful," Pyro Storm was saying. "They'll figure out something is up before too long. I don't like keeping things from them, my boyfriend especially. People don't give him the credit he deserves. He's smart. He'll figure it out eventually. We need to get ahead of that."

Before Nick could puff out his chest (because compliments he wasn't supposed to hear were his favorite kind of compliments), another voice spoke, breathy and deep. "I get that, honeybunch, but I'd remind you this isn't about him. It's about you and me."

Pyro Storm sighed. "I know. And I'm not going to force you to do something you're not ready for, but I don't like lying to people I care about. I've had enough of that to last me a lifetime."

"Don't I know it," the voice replied. "There may come a time when I'll change my mind, but it's not today. I gotta watch out for me, because I'm the only one who will."

"We're in this together," Pyro Storm said. "I promise."

Nick stopped moving, his back against a wall that ended a couple of feet away, turning inward at a ninety-degree angle. An alcove. Pyro Storm and whoever he was talking to were in an alcove.

"I wish I could believe you," the voice said. "But I've seen what happens to people like us. We're different. It's like coming out. I went through that once already. I don't know if I'm capable of doing it again. I don't even know who you are behind the mask."

"Just like I don't know who *you* are outside of your costume," Pyro Storm said. "It's safer this way, at least for now. We're Extraordinaries. You need to get used to keeping your identity a secret."

Nick's heart thudded painfully in his chest. Extraordinaries? As in *plural*? There was no way there were others he didn't know about, right? Seth wouldn't . . . he would never keep something like that secret.

"You're breaking my heart," the voice said. "Look at you. You can mope with the best of them. Come here. Let me make it better."

Nick heard movement, and then the voice said, "There. That's it. Tighter, fire boy. I'm not gonna break. Put your back into it."

Nick trusted Seth with his life. He trusted Seth with his heart. Seth would never do anything to hurt him, at least not intentionally. But today hadn't been a normal day, even in the life of one Nicholas Bell, which was filled with many abnormal days. Nick was tired, hurt, and more than a little angry.

So Nick didn't think he could be blamed for jumping out of the shadows into the alcove, a thunderous expression on his face. He blinked against the bare bulb hanging over a rusty door at the back of the alcove.

And there, standing in a pool of light, was Pyro Storm, hugging a spectacularly tall woman with brown skin who had to hunch over to wrap her arms around Nick's boyfriend. Her hair, which hung in shockingly blue curls, bounced as she swayed Pyro Storm back and forth. She wore a leotard of sorts, covered in black sparkly sequins, and killer white boots that rose up to her knees. Her arms were covered in thin metal bangles, and if Nick wasn't extremely confused, he'd think this stranger had the best costume he'd ever seen.

Perhaps, then, he could be forgiven for blurting out, "Oh my god, you look amazing. Bangles? I could *never* pull that off."

The effect was instantaneous. Pyro Storm yelped and stumbled back, the lenses covering his eyes flashing brightly. The other figure whirled around, and Nick could see she (he? they? Nick needed to get their pronouns before he made a fool of himself) wore a white mask that covered their eyes, the tips of which curled up into spiky points like old-fashioned glasses. The mask had tiny, electric-blue rhinestones on it that sparkled when they caught the light from the bulb.

"*Nick?*" Pyro Storm said in a strangled voice.

Nick ignored him in favor of this new Extraordinary. He rushed forward, and as he approached, he thought he heard the snarl of electricity, the air around him thickening with the stench of ozone. He stopped in his tracks when what appeared to be blue lightning crawled along the Extraordinary's arms, down to their fingers. They raised one hand, the lightning collecting in a ball above their palm.

"No, *wait*," Pyro Storm cried, jumping forward and knocking their hand down. The ball of lightning fell from their hand, hitting the ground and bursting, sending arcs of electricity along the dirty pavement. Nick managed to hop over it, but not before what felt like every single hair on his body stood on end. He came to a stop a foot away from the two people gaping at him.

"Whoa," Nick breathed, staring up in awe at the Extraordinary towering over him. "You have *lightning* powers? Holy shit, that's freaking rad. Please don't electrocute me, but if you still feel the need to, at least I'll go out knowing my murderer wears the hell out of those boots. I bet they're good for kicking people in the junk." He blanched and took a step back. "Uh, not that I'd like to find that out for myself or anything."

"Pyro Storm," the Extraordinary said, squinting down at Nick. "Who is this little twink who won't stop talking?"

"Hi!" Nick said, thrusting out his hand, hoping he wasn't about to get fried. The Extraordinary hesitated before taking it. Nick pumped their hands up and down three times before letting go. "I'm Nick. I'm Pyro Storm's biggest fan. Also, his boyfriend. Also, I'm the leader of Team Pyro Storm. Also, I run Lighthouse." He paused, considering. "Well, not by myself. Gibby and Jazz help, too, but *still*." He struck what he hoped looked like a heroic pose, hands on his hips, gazing off into the distance as if contemplating the road that still lay ahead.

"What," the Extraordinary said flatly, and Nick had to admire someone who could put so much into a single word.

The moment was broken when Pyro Storm rushed forward, cape billowing behind him. He grabbed Nick by the arm, pulling him back out of the alcove. "What are you doing here?" he whisper-shouted. "I told you I'd see you tomorrow!"

"Right," Nick said. "And I respect that, but I needed to see you as soon as possible." He craned his neck back toward the Extraordinary, who stood staring at them with narrowed eyes. "Who is that and why do I want to be like them when I grow up?"

Pyro Storm groaned. "Nick, you can't be here."

Nick blinked. "What do you mean I can't be here? That certainly doesn't seem true, because I *am* here. Weird how that works."

Pyro Storm jostled him. "Nicky, focus. Look at me."

Nick did. He leaned forward, kissing the bump in Pyro Storm's mask where his nose was. "Hi. Nice to see you."

Pyro Storm sighed, though he was fighting a smile. "How did you find me?"

Nick winced. "Uh, the tracker? But I swear I wasn't being creepy or that I don't trust you, even though you lied when you said you were going home and going to bed. I forgive you for that, by the way. Who is that? Why didn't you tell me there was another Extraordinary?"

"Go home," Pyro Storm said. "We can talk about this tomorrow, okay? I swear, it's not what it looks like."

"What does it look like?" Nick asked, confused.

Pyro Storm looked over his shoulder at the other Extraordinary before turning back to Nick. "I'm not—*we're* not doing anything. With each other. I wouldn't do that to you."

Nick gaped at him before bending over, wrapping his arms around his waist as he laughed.

Pyro Storm frowned. "It's not funny!"

"It is," Nick gasped, wiping his eyes. "Dude, I know you, okay? You would never cheat on me."

"You didn't think that?" Pyro Storm asked, sounding small and unsure.

And Nick couldn't have that. He leaned his forehead against Pyro Storm's, the heat from him chasing away the chill in the air. "Of course not. I trust you not to mess around on me. That's pretty mature, if you think about it."

Pyro Storm shook his head. "You dork."

"Introduce me," Nick said, stepping back. But instead of waiting, Nick pushed by Pyro Storm and marched toward the new Extraordinary. "Sorry about that. He's really protective of me. I'm cool with it. Hey! Hi, hello. I'm Nicholas Bell, and you are . . . ma'am? Sir? Some other pronoun you would have me use?"

The Extraordinary looked past him at Pyro Storm. "He's loud."

Nick nodded furiously. "That's my default setting. Sorry about that. So—about that electricity you almost fried me with. I have questions."

The Extraordinary looked him up and down. "Seems like you have your hands full with this one."

"Not yet," Nick said. "Just because we're dating doesn't mean we're ready to take our relationship to the next level. We're waiting until the time is right, even if it means blue balls."

Pyro Storm groaned as the Extraordinary snorted. "I certainly wasn't talking about that."

Nick blanched. "Oh. Uh—right. My bad. I can see now that you weren't inquiring about our sex life. Let's start again. I'm Nick. And you are . . ."

"*Wait*," Pyro Storm said as the Extraordinary opened their mouth. "Don't."

Nick and the Extraordinary both glared at Pyro Storm. "Honey-bunch, he just asked my name. If I don't want to tell him, I won't."

Pyro Storm shook his head. "It's not that. You need to work up to it slowly with him. Trust me. Watch. Nick?"

"Yes," Nick said promptly.

"I'm going to tell you her name in a moment, but first, I have to give you some information. I want you to breathe, okay? Easy breaths, in and out. Can you do that for me?"

Nick could. He sucked in a breath, held it, then let it out. He did it again. And again.

"Okay," Pyro Storm said, taking his hand. "I'm going to tell you two things. I don't want you to speak until I'm finished. Can you do that?"

Pffft. Easy.

Pyro Storm squeezed his hand. "First, she's a drag queen. When she's in costume, she uses she/her pronouns. When she's not, she uses he/him."

"A Puerto Rican drag queen," the Extraordinary said, a seductive curl to her lips. "The best in Nova City."

Nick opened his mouth, but the only sound that came out was—for lack of a better word—a squeak.

"Yes, yes, I know," Pyro Storm said in a soothing voice. "I'm going to tell you her name now, and I need you to stay calm, okay?"

"What's with all the theatrics?" the Extraordinary asked. "And when a drag queen asks you that question, you know shit's getting weird."

"Your name is a double entendre," Pyro Storm explained, never looking away from Nick. "If there's one thing Nick can't handle, it's a double entendre. Which is why I want to make sure he's warned beforehand. Nicky, I believe in you. Hold back your reaction, okay?"

Nick nodded. He could do this.

"Nick, I'd like to introduce you to . . . Miss Conduct."

Nick couldn't do it. He slapped his hands over his mouth and screamed into them, the sound mostly muffled in the alcove. Miss Conduct? As in a *conduct* of electricity with a cheeky implication of bad behavior? Holy shit, it was literally the greatest thing Nick had ever heard. But—he didn't want to embarrass Pyro Storm, especially in front of a drag queen. He had to maintain control. He dropped his hands, clasped them in front of him, and blurted, "Hello, Miss Conduct. I like your name. And your costume. And the fact that you exist."

"Of course you do," she said. "How old are you, twinkie?"

"Seventeen," Nick said. "Well, almost. My birthday is in April. And I don't know if I'm a twink or a furry. Being queer is very confusing. So many labels. Did you know there's something called a twunk? *Cosmo* taught me that."

Miss Conduct gaped at him before looking at Pyro Storm. "Are you seventeen too?"

"He is," Nick said. "His birthday is in December. I bought him flame-retardant sheets so he didn't burn his bed if he had sexy dreams about me. I give excellent gifts."

"You're *children*?" Miss Conduct asked. "What in the flying fu—"

Nick bristled. "We're not children. Thank you for noticing that we're young and attractive—"

"I never said *anything* about—"

"—but we're more than capable of handling ourselves. We took down Shadow Star, didn't we? Sure, my shoulder got dislocated and Pyro Storm almost died, but we *won*." He stared defiantly up at Miss Conduct. "Don't you dare give Pyro Storm shit over his age. He's good at what he does. The best, even. If anyone tries to say otherwise, they have to go through me."

"You look like you weigh a hundred pounds soaking wet," Miss Conduct said, flicking his forehead. "I've eaten bigger men than you for breakfast."

"Oh my god," Nick mumbled. "So unfair. Your catchphrase is already better than mine."

Pyro Storm shook his head. "Nick, what are you doing here? Did something happen?"

And with that, the weight of the day crashed back down upon Nick's shoulders. He slumped inwardly, looking down at the ground, defeated. He flinched when a hand came under his chin, lifting his head. Pyro Storm cupped his face, thumbs brushing over his cheeks. "What's wrong?"

Nick tried to smile, but it cracked right down the middle. "I should probably just show you."

"Show me what?"

Nick took a step back away from Pyro Storm and Miss Conduct. Turning, he saw a metal trash can, dented and lying on its side on the ground. He closed his eyes, shaking out his shoulders and arms, trying to rid himself of the heavy tension that flooded his body. He opened his eyes, determined. He raised his hands in front of him, palms facing the trash can and prepared for the extraordinary. And because he could, he said, "It's time to take out the trash."

Nothing happened.

Nick wiggled his fingers.

Still nothing.

"Okay, uh, hold on a second. It worked earlier." He curled his hands into fists before opening them again. "Flying Trash Can of Doom!"

Nothing.

"Levitating Metal Smash!"

The trash didn't even twitch.

"Come on. Do it. Move! Furious Garbage Annihilation!"

The trash can shook. Nick's eyes widened, sure he was about to show Pyro Storm and Miss Conduct that he absolutely deserved to be at their secret Extraordinary meeting. Then a cat ran out from the inside of the trash can, ears flattened as it hissed at them. It took off, disappearing into the darkness of the alley.

Nick dropped his hands. "Well, shit. It worked earlier. I don't know how to turn it on."

"Turn *what* on?" Pyro Storm asked.

Nick looked back over his shoulder. "Dude. I'm an Extraordinary."

Pyro Storm shook his head. "Nick, we've been through this, remember? You're perfect the way you are. You're already—"

"It's not *like* that," Nick snapped. "I swear. I—look, I found out some stuff today, things my dad kept from me." He swallowed thickly. "My mom, she—she was—"

He never got to finish. That moment, the temperature plummeted at least thirty degrees as the air around them crystalized, small snowflakes hanging suspended around them. Miss Conduct reached out to touch the closest snowflake. It broke apart, the minute ice crystals spinning slowly. She gasped as smoke began to billow around them, thick and noxious as it rose from the concrete. Nick started to cough roughly when Pyro Storm grabbed him by the wrist, jerking Nick back behind him. Nick crowded against him, peering over his shoulder.

"Something's coming," Pyro Storm growled. "Stay behind me, no matter what. Miss Conduct, either get out of here or get ready."

"I'm not leaving you," Miss Conduct said, coming to stand next to them. Nick looked over to see lightning arcing across her fingers. He gasped when her exposed skin turned almost translucent, electricity running along the entire length of her body. Her eyes began to glow an ethereal blue, as if the electricity was coming from within.

A crackling sound from above.

Nick lifted his head to see a figure *skating* down the side of the apartment building on a sheet of ice. Ten feet above the ground, they launched themselves off the building, landing in the alley in a crouch, the ground beneath them freezing instantly, shards of ice sprouting around their legs. They were clothed in white from head to toe. The only skin exposed was around their eyes, glittering darkly.

Before the team could react, smoke rose near the ice Extraordinary, taking on a vague shape that looked like arms and legs attached to a body. As they watched, the smoke parted, and from its center stepped another person, this one dressed similarly to their ice counterpart, except their costume was entirely black.

"Please tell me they are also friends you didn't want me to know about," Nick muttered in Pyro Storm's ear.

"They're not," Pyro Storm snarled.

The two figures looked at each other and nodded before turning toward the others. As one, they took a step forward, their movements almost choreographed.

Ice said, "Hello." A man, his voice deep and rough.

Smoke said, "We've found you." A woman, her voice light and happy, almost like she was singing.

"What do you want?" Pyro Storm asked, pushing back against Nick.

Ice cocked his head, the movement staccato like a bird. "You."

"The spare?" Smoke singsonged.

Ice glanced at Miss Conduct. "Leave her. We're here for the others."

Smoke nodded. "Pyro Storm, Nicholas Bell—Mr. Burke sends his regards."

Chaos, then, an explosion of noise and movement. Nick shouted as Pyro Storm shoved him back with one hand, the other raised in front, a wave of fire rising from the ground in front of him. The heat was immense, melting the ice that had swallowed the alley. Nick reached for Pyro Storm, but his fingers only managed to graze his cape as the Extraordinary darted forward. Ice and Smoke parted, and Pyro Storm flew right between them, slamming into the brick behind them with a terrifying crash.

Nick yelled for Pyro Storm, but even as the words echoed in the alley around them, Miss Conduct said, "You bitches picked the wrong queen to mess with." Her entire body transformed into electricity, her costume staying perfectly in place. She moved like a current, quicker than Nick could follow. The air sizzled around her as she launched herself forward, going for Smoke. Smoke saw her coming and right before they collided, Smoke dissipated into a black cloud. Miss Conduct flew *through* the smoke, hitting the building alongside Pyro Storm. She snarled as she turned, electricity arcing around her, even her *hair* turning into blue energy.

Smoke re-formed between them, facing Miss Conduct and Pyro Storm, her back to Nick. Ice stood and came to Smoke's side. "The spare," he said. "He doesn't know about the spare."

"Kill her," Smoke said. "Kill her, and he'll never know."

They advanced, one step at a time.

Nick looked at his hands. "Come on," he muttered, shaking them out. "Come on. *Work*."

Pyro Storm threw a vicious punch, hand alight with fire, but his fist flew right through Smoke, sending a black cloud swirling into the air. The force of his movement caused Pyro Storm to over-correct, spinning toward Miss Conduct. He grunted when smoke curled up around his legs, almost like shadows. It crawled up his body, holding him in place. He struggled against it to no avail.

Ice advanced on Miss Conduct, the flurries around his head crashing together and solidifying, forming needle-sharp icicles. They floated above Ice's head, growing bigger and bigger until they were the size of railroad spikes.

"Work," Nick demanded. "Turn *on*. Powers activate!"

"Nick!" Pyro Storm shouted as he struggled against the smoke, bursts of fire crackling the air around him. "Get out of here! Run—you need to *run*."

He should have. If he was smarter, he'd have taken off down the alley into the street, where he could see crowds still moving on the sidewalk. Even though he was scared out of his mind, he couldn't leave Pyro Storm and Miss Conduct.

Without thinking, he rushed forward, but not toward Ice and Smoke and Miss Conduct and Pyro Storm. Instead, he went left, picking up the trash can that he'd tried to move with his mind. He grunted as he lifted it above his head, and he knew then and there that he'd probably never have a moment like this again.

So he said, "It's time to take out the trash."

Like a *badass*.

He hurled the trash can at the villains who dared to try to hurt Pyro Storm. Smoke saw it coming and dissipated again, the binds holding Pyro Storm in place falling away. But Ice didn't move as fast, and the trash can broke a few of the icicles before smashing into his back, knocking him forward. Miss Conduct was ready and waiting, reaching up and grabbing Ice by the throat, electricity arcing off her arm. She pulled Ice close, their faces inches apart. "Ice, huh? Which is water. And we all know what happens when water meets electricity."

Ice screamed as electricity coursed through him, snapping furiously, causing the spikes above him to shatter into powder and rain down around them. Miss Conduct lifted him off the ground, Ice's legs kicking uselessly. "Get out of my face," Miss Conduct hissed before throwing him as hard as she could. Nick managed to duck in time as Ice flew over him, smashing against the rusted door in the alcove.

Pyro Storm surged forward, leaving a trail of fire in his wake as Smoke re-formed, turning to look for Ice. Smoke grunted when Pyro Storm collided with her back, knocking her off her feet. Nick crouched low, and just when Smoke was about to hit him, he pushed himself up as hard as he could. Nick's shoulder hit Smoke in the chest, and he pushed Smoke up and *over* him. Smoke hit the ground hard behind Nick, rolling until she stopped at Ice's feet. He helped her up as Miss Conduct and Pyro Storm appeared on either side of Nick.

"Better than we thought," Ice said, voice cold.

"Underestimated," Smoke panted as she stood. "We will not make that mistake again. Finish this." She took Ice's hand in hers, raising them both toward the others. And though Nick couldn't see their mouths, he thought they were both smiling.

Black clouds mixed with particles of ice as the alley rumbled around them. The door rattled and the lightbulb burst, sparks raining down as darkness fell. Nick took a step back as Ice and Smoke rushed toward them, hands still joined, the black cloud mixing with the ice and forming a gigantic wall in front of them, scraping along the ground, streams of black trailing behind it. He raised his hands in front of his face and screamed. A sharp pain lanced through his head, a pressure, as he waited for impact.

It never came. He cracked open an eye, wondering if he was already dead. He wasn't.

Smoke and Ice were frozen mid-step, eyes darting wildly from side to side, still holding hands behind the wall of ice and smoke.

"What the hell?" Pyro Storm whispered. He looked around and raised his voice. "Who's doing that? Show yourself!"

"Uh," Nick said, grimacing. "I think it's . . . me?"

Pyro Storm jerked his head toward him. "*What?*"

"Maybe," Nick said, looking down at his hands. He raised them again, pointing them toward Ice and Smoke. He flexed his fingers, and the wall cracked furiously before shattering, ice turning to powder as the smoke blew away. "Holy shit, it *is* me! Suck it, you dicks! I'm an Extraordinary, and I'm going to kick you in the freaking *balls*."

The pressure in his head released, the pain falling away. Ice and Smoke stumbled forward, both gasping.

"Oh crap," Nick said, eyes growing wide. "No, come back! Turn on again! Powers, if you don't activate, I'm going to—*urk*!"

His arm was almost torn from his socket as Pyro Storm pulled him at a run, heading for the mouth of the alley. "Miss Conduct, *go*!" he cried over his shoulder.

"I'm not *leaving* you to—"

"We'll draw them out into the street, but you'll be seen! Get out of here!"

Nick looked back in time to see Miss Conduct turn completely into electricity, her body morphing into arcs of blue. One moment she stood in the alley, and the next, she flashed like lightning, rising off the ground and hitting the cord that held the broken light bulb. Her body *shrank* as she hit the filament of the bulb, and then she disappeared, the cord shaking as if . . .

As if she'd turned her entire body into a current and was riding the power line.

"I love drag queens," Nick managed to say as they ran toward the street. Ice and Smoke chased after them, Ice jumping to the side of the building and running along it, Smoke turning into just that, a gigantic cloud that roiled toward them.

"Move!" Pyro Storm shouted, and Nick turned his head to see a crowd of people gathering near the mouth of the alley. "Get out of the way!"

People screamed and jumped as Pyro Storm raised his hand in front of him, fire bursting from his palm and forming a rail of sorts that snapped and crackled along the street. "Hang on!" Pyro Storm bellowed at Nick.

"To *what*?" Nick screamed back.

"To me," Pyro Storm snarled, and then jumped even as he hurled Nick forward. He didn't let Nick's hand go, and the momentum caused Nick to fly in front of Pyro Storm, his shoulder protesting angrily as Nick snapped back against Pyro Storm's front, an arm wrapped around his waist, holding him tightly. Pyro Storm landed on top of the fire covering the ground, and like Ice had done, began to *skate* along it. Wind whipped around them as they flew by the crowd of people, their faces pale, eyes wide, many of them shouting in warning, even as they held up their phones to record.

"How are you doing this?" Nick demanded.

"Practice," Pyro Storm said, and Nick did *not* swoon.

He looked back over Pyro Storm's shoulder to see Ice and Smoke chasing after them, ignoring the people on the street. Horns honked as Pyro Storm deftly weaved between stopped cars, riding the rail of fire. Faces pressed against windows as they flew by, quick flashes of wide eyes and open mouths.

They had half a block's distance on Smoke and Ice when a taxi-cab's door flew open right in front of them. "Oh shit," Pyro Storm had time to breathe, but it was already too late. Pyro Storm spun around in an apparent attempt to lessen the impact, but it did little as they crashed into the door. The breath was knocked from Nick's chest as Pyro Storm grunted painfully, the door snapping off in a metallic shriek, the cab spinning and colliding with another car. The cab driver managed to pull his legs back in at the last second, and his sneakers were the last thing Nick saw before he was flying.

He hit the ground hard, rolling until he crashed into a parked delivery truck. He blinked slowly, his body coming back online and cataloguing the scrapes on his knees and arms. Nothing seemed broken or dislocated, and he groaned as he lifted his head in a daze.

Pyro Storm was a few feet away, already climbing to his feet. He looked toward Nick, shouting something that Nick couldn't hear above the thick buzzing in his ears. Waving him off, Nick pushed himself up, grimacing at the bits of road embedded in his skin. His hood managed to stay up on his head, but his jeans were torn, and his Chucks were scuffed beyond recognition. All in all, Nick wasn't having the best *Holy Crap, I'm An Extraordinary!* day.

Fire burst near him, and he looked up in time to see Ice descending on Pyro Storm, glittering spikes hitting a wall of flame, causing them to melt instantly. Pyro Storm *pushed* the fire toward Ice, who backflipped off the top of a car, the fire slicing the air underneath him. He landed on the ground, eyes narrowed as people screamed around them but made no move to leave, their phones up and recording.

God, people could be so damn stupid. Why weren't they *running*? Nick rushed toward the closest crowd, waving his hands above his head, shouting at them to get back. He was almost to the sidewalk when a black cloud bloomed in front of him, and Smoke stepped out of its center. Nick skidded to a stop.

"You," Smoke said. "I don't like you."

"Feeling's mutual," Nick snapped, sounding braver than he felt. He froze when Smoke brought her right arm up against her chest before snapping it back down to her side. A thin column of black coiled from her hand, almost like a whip, the end curling on the ground at her feet.

"Well, shit," Nick said weakly.

"Indeed," Smoke said, and then she snapped the whip directly at Nick's head.

He yelped and ducked, hearing the whip carving the air, missing the top of his head by inches. Nick panted as he stood upright. "Is that all you've got? Who do you think you're messing with? Goddamn amateurs. You don't come into *our* city and—"

Smoke swung the whip above her head before lashing out again. This time, Nick wasn't quick enough. The whip struck him in the chest, knocking him back against a parked car. The whip slithered around him before he could recover, pinning his arms at his sides.

He struggled to break free, but it was too strong. It was like shadows. Like Owen. Like Nick was on a bridge, his father screaming from below in terror, Shadow Star cackling as he lifted large sections of Nick's fanfiction wholesale.

Nick bellowed as the smoke band tightened around his chest, his ribs creaking. He was barely able to turn his head toward Pyro Storm, only to see Ice standing with a terrified man in his grasp, Pyro Storm's cape billowing as he pulled himself to his full height.

And Nick knew, then, what this would mean. He found himself in a position Seth Gray had nightmares about. A choice. Pyro Storm had to make a choice about who to save.

"Please," the man pleaded, struggling against Ice's grip around him. "Help me."

Pyro Storm looked back at Nick, Smoke's cloud making it hard for Nick to breathe.

"No," Nick gasped. "Save him. Save him, you hear me? Don't worry about—" He gagged as the pressure in his chest increased tenfold.

Pyro Storm made his decision. He came for Nick, leaving the man trapped in Ice's hold.

Smoke didn't see him coming. In a burst of fire, Pyro Storm charged, shoulder dropped low as he collided with Smoke, knocking her down. Before she hit the ground, her body evaporated into a black cloud, and when the smoke cleared, she was gone.

Nick stumbled forward, falling to his knees against the sidewalk.

"Nicky. Nicky!" Pyro Storm was there, crouching next to Nick, helping him to his feet. "Are you all right?"

But Nick never got the chance to answer. The man in Ice's grasp tried to break free, elbowing Ice in the stomach. Ice repaid him in kind by backhanding him across the face. The man fell to the ground and landed on his arm, which broke with an audible *snap*. Ice raised his hand toward Pyro Storm and Nick. But instead of blasting them with ice, he wiggled his fingers in a sick approximation of a wave. Then he turned and ran, people scattering in fear as he reached the sidewalk and disappeared down an alley.

Others rushed forward toward the injured man, helping him to his feet, his broken arm clutched against his chest.

Sirens in the distance, though already far too late.

Nick grabbed Pyro Storm's hand. "We have to get out of here. We gotta go *now*."

Pyro Storm didn't move.

"*Seth*."

Pyro Storm turned his head. Nick couldn't see his eyes, but his bottom lip was trembling. "We'll figure it out," Nick muttered. "Come on. We need to leave."

And so they went, leaving the destruction in the streets behind them.

10

By the time they reached the familiar neighborhood where the Gray brownstone stood, Nick was lagging, his body exhausted, and he'd never been more relieved to see a familiar place.

Seth pulled him up the stairs, looking around to make sure they weren't being watched. Nothing. He pushed the door open, shoving Nick through before shutting the door behind them as Nick collapsed to the floor.

"Seth?" Nick heard Martha call. "That you? You're home late. I was down in the secret lair earlier, but I didn't pick anything up. What—oh no. Bob! *Bob!*"

Nick rolled over on his back and blinked slowly up at the ceiling. A worried face appeared above him. "Hi," he said dully. "Sorry about bleeding on your floors. I know you hate that."

"How bad is it?" Martha asked him in a no-nonsense voice. The nurse was here. "Anything broken?" She gingerly rubbed her hands along his arms and chest.

He shook his head. "Don't think so. Just scraped up."

Bob appeared in the foyer. "Why are you yelling? I was in the living—oh, hell. What happened?"

"Bad guys," Nick said. "Tried to kick our asses, but we gave them the ol' what for."

Bob pushed by Martha as she asked Nick if he could breathe without pain. Bob helped pick Seth up off the floor and pulled his helmet off, Seth's curls springing free and falling messily on his head.

"Who did this?" Bob muttered, running his hands over Seth. "Was it an Extraordinary?"

Seth pushed him off. "I'm fine." He shook his head angrily.

"I—" He turned around and punched the door. The wood cracked as the door rattled in its frame. "I couldn't—"

Guilt bled through Nick's rib cage, vast and complicated. On one hand, he was happy to be alive. On the other, a man was out there somewhere, probably on his way to the hospital, his arm broken.

"He saved me," Nick said quietly. "He didn't have to, but he did."

Seth whirled around, eyes ablaze. "Of course I saved you. But I shouldn't have had to. What the hell were you thinking, Nick? I told you to *run*."

Nick flinched at the censure in Seth's voice. Martha tried to keep him still, but he pushed her hands off, rising to his feet. He glared at Seth. "I wasn't going to leave you."

"You should have," Seth snapped at him. "I can't always be there to save you. You should have stayed away, Nick. Why were you even *there*? That wasn't for you to see. That was *private*, and now it's—it's—" He sagged, shoulders hunched near his ears. "Dammit. That wasn't supposed to happen. This isn't how it's supposed to be." He shrugged Bob off when he reached for his nephew. He stormed out of the foyer, heading for the basement door. Nick winced as it slammed against the wall, Seth stomping down the stairs.

"What happened?" Bob asked as the sounds of Seth's anger faded.

Nick blinked rapidly against the sting in his eyes. "Nothing much," he said in a cracked voice. "Attacked by two Extraordinaries made of ice and smoke. Oh, and Seth was meeting with a drag queen Extraordinary named Miss Conduct, and I have superpowers. My dad lied to me and gave me pills that messed with my head, my mom was the telekinetic Extraordinary called Guardian, and at one point, I thought she and my dad were in a polyamorous relationship with Simon Burke—which, now that I think about it, is really freaking awful. Poly people are valid, but Simon Burke sent Smoke and Ice after us." He sighed. "It's been a very trying Saturday."

Bob and Martha gaped at him.

Nick shrugged awkwardly. "It is what it is. Can I stay here for a few days? I can't go home. Not yet."

Martha recovered first. "Of course you can. You—you take all the time you need. And let's get those cuts cleaned up so they don't get infected."

"Great," Nick said weakly. "Fantastic."

The doorbell rang as Martha was finishing up with Nick. All in all, it looked worse than it was. He'd gotten away with minor scrapes and bruises, the worst of which were across his chest, where Smoke had held him in place. Already, the skin between his nipples was mottled blue and purple.

While she worked, he told her everything that had happened. It felt almost like betrayal, telling Martha how Dad seemed to be working with or for Burke. The only reaction he got from Martha was the slight tightening around her eyes. She went to the sink, washing up as Nick struggled to put his shirt back on.

"We have a lot to talk about," she finally said, turning off the faucet. "You can't avoid your father forever, Nick."

"I know," he muttered. "But at least for a couple of days. I need time to think."

"He's still your father," Martha said. "If he wants you home, you have to go, okay?" She turned from the sink and crouched next to Nick, her knees popping. She put her hands on his thighs, squeezing gently. "You're safe here, I promise. Whatever's happening, whatever you're becoming, you're safe here."

Nick sniffled, hanging his head. "I could really use a hug right now."

She hugged him without hesitation, cupping the back of his head, pressing him against her chest. His shoulder shook, his eyes burned, and he hung on for dear life.

Until the doorbell rang again.

Martha pulled back, cocking her head. From below, Bob opened the door, and voices filled the Gray house. Nick sagged in relief when he recognized the voices. Gibby. Jazz.

"Go into Seth's room," Martha said, standing up quickly. "Change out of these clothes. I'll fix you all something to eat."

"Not hungry."

"I don't care," Martha said. "You will eat, and you will say thank you."

"Thank you," he said.

She bent over, kissing his forehead. "You're welcome."

When he opened Seth's bedroom door again, now clad in fuzzy pajama pants and an old, oversized shirt, Gibby and Jazz were waiting for him in the hall. Gibby was gnawing on her hoodie string, her wallet chain dangling against her side. Jazz was wearing the same clothes she'd been in when she'd come over to Nick's house earlier that afternoon. Nick couldn't believe it'd only been a few hours since he'd been staring at the TV in the attic, watching his mother move things with her mind.

"You all right?" he asked Jazz. "I shouldn't have left you like I did."

"Stupid boys," she said with a sniff. "Scaring the crap out of me, like you have any right to." And then Nick found himself with an armful of Jazz, his face in her hair. She smelled of blooming flowers, and Nick calmed a bit more. He held an arm out for Gibby, who rolled her eyes for show but came willingly. She hugged them both, and they swayed back and forth.

"So, Extraordinary, huh?" Gibby muttered against his throat, her lips on his skin. "Jazz told me."

"Seems like," Nick whispered back. "Though I feel really stupid now about the whole cricket-in-the-microwave thing. And the meteor thing. And the breaking into a power plant. And jumping into the river."

"What about the *Cosmo* idea board? You should probably feel stupid about that too."

Nick reared back. "That was an amazing idea board, and don't you *dare* talk shit about it. I worked really freaking hard on it, and look! It worked, sort of. Hurray."

Gibby snorted as Jazz wiped her eyes. "Jazz is right. Stupid boys."

"Seth?" Nick asked.

Gibby and Jazz exchanged a glance. "Downstairs beating up the punching bag. We figured it was best to leave him for now."

"He—yeah, I guess he's pissed."

Jazz took his hand, tugging him toward the stairs, Gibby trailing after them. "We're gonna fix this. We'll talk it through, and everything will be all right. You'll see."

"What if it's not?" Nick asked.

To that, she had no answer.

Martha was in the kitchen, phone in her hand. She brought a finger to her lips as they peered in from the entryway. "I understand that, Aaron," she said into the phone, and Nick closed his eyes. "But you have to see where he's coming from. It's just for a day or two, okay? I'll make sure he gets to school on Monday if he's still here." She paused, brow furrowing. "Well, sure, if you want to drop them by, I'll make sure he gets his medicine." Nick's eyes popped open, but Martha continued. "But that doesn't mean I'll force him to take it, especially if he's right about where the Concentra came from and what it does. Seems to me as if you have some explaining to do. To all of us." Dad said something else. Martha shook her head. "Regardless, if he doesn't trust what you're giving him—and, potentially, rightly so—why would he take it?" She flapped a dish towel at them, mouthing the word *Seth*.

They left the kitchen behind, heading for the basement.

Bob stood at the top of the stairs, leaning against the wall. He turned his head as they approached, nodding toward the basement. From below came the sounds of dull thuds as Seth worked out whatever was going on in his head.

"Tread lightly," Bob said. "I've never seen him this keyed up. He's angry, but I don't think he knows at who. When we're that upset, we lash out at whoever's closest, even if they don't deserve it."

"We can handle it," Gibby told him. "Trust me, we're experts in the minds of idiots."

"It comes with the territory," Jazz agreed, and Nick couldn't even find a reason to complain. "We won't be weird, promise."

"It's only weird if you make it weird," Nick reminded her.

"Yeah, no," Gibby said. "It's weird. What are the chances that three people we know personally ended up being Extraordinaries?"

"And they're all gay," Jazz said with a frown.

"Seth's bisexual," Nick said, because he'd be *damned* if he'd allow bi erasure, even in the face of all the ridiculousness.

"Yeah," Bob said, patting him on the arm. "You'll be all right. Gibby, Jazz—your parents know where you're at?"

"They do," Jazz said, already pulling Gibby down the stairs. "We called them on our way over. We'll let them know if it's going to take longer than we think."

"Make sure you do," Bob called after them, shaking his head. He looked at Nick. "You doing all right?"

No. Not at all. "I don't know."

Bob huffed, as if that was the answer he expected. "Can I give you some advice?"

"About how to not make Seth mad at me anymore? Yes, please."

Bob chuckled. "He'll come around. This has to do with you, Nick."

Nick blinked. "What about me?"

"You serious about the whole being-an-Extraordinary thing?"

Nick raised his hands, wiggling his fingers. Nothing happened, but he didn't expect it to. "I think so. I don't know how to turn it on. Or off, when it gets going."

Bob shrugged. "That's how it was with Seth, at least at first. It took time for him to learn control. It takes patience and hard work. You'll make mistakes, some bigger than others. If you're able to forgive yourself, then you'll be on the right path. Know your limitations, Nick. And never, ever use them against someone who doesn't deserve it. I'll help as best I can—as will Martha— but there's someone more important than the two of us who needs to see and hear it from you."

"Dad," Nick said dully. "How can I trust him again?"

"Patience," Bob said again. "And talking it through. If there's two people who can do it, it's the pair of you. You're allowed to be furious. I'm a little pissed myself, and I can't promise your dad and I won't have words. But I don't think for a minute that your dad was working for Simon Burke. He may have been allowing Burke to think so, but if Aaron told him who Pyro Storm really was, we would've known by now. Remember that, okay? It'll all work out."

Nick hoped so, but he couldn't see how it was possible. Too many secrets, too many lies. Bob hugged him roughly before letting him go. Nick watched as he ambled toward the kitchen, where Martha was still having her say to Dad.

Taking a deep breath, he descended the stairs.

Jazz sat on the washing machine, Gibby leaning back between her legs. They both watched Seth as he attacked the punching bag, sweat dripping down his face in rivulets. He'd changed out of his Pyro Storm suit, wearing a pair of sweats and a white shirt, the back already soaked through. Seth didn't look at Nick as he reached the bottom of the stairs, continuing to punch again and again, his fists a blur.

The room was muggy. Heat poured off Seth, though there was a distinct absence of fire.

He kept to the edges of the basement, working his way over to Gibby and Jazz. He nodded toward Seth. "He say anything?"

"Not yet," Jazz said, snapping her gum. "Seems like he's more interested in hitting than talking."

Nick didn't blame him. He also wanted to punch things, but figured it was better to keep that to himself. "Great. Super. Just what we need." He leaned against the dryer. "How did you know to come here?"

"Got a news alert on my phone," Gibby said. "Extraordinary activity."

"Told her everything after you ditched me," Jazz said primly.

Nick winced as he pulled his phone from his pocket. "Yeah,

sorry about that. I—" His phone was in one piece, somehow. The screen wasn't even cracked. He panicked at the number of notifications he had: missed calls from Gibby and Dad, Dad, Dad, and Dad, followed by at least a dozen text messages from him, each sounding more frantic than the last, if the number of exclamation points indicated anything. Nick ignored them with a twinge of guilt, shoving his phone back in his pocket. "I had to get out of there."

"What happened?" Gibby asked. "Jazz said you could . . ." She wiggled her fingers.

"Yeah," Nick said, frowning. "Apparently I'm telekinetic. Who would have thought?" As quickly as he could, he filled them in on what he'd overheard, voice hardening. He'd gotten to the part about finding Pyro Storm in the alley with Miss Conduct when Seth stopped attacking the punching bag. He grabbed a towel hanging off the back of the chair and wiped his face. He didn't look at them as he began to pace back and forth, towel trailing behind him.

"So, another Extraordinary," Gibby said, clearing her throat. "Care to fill us in?"

Seth stopped moving and dropped the towel onto the ground. He rubbed his face with his hands, exhaling sharply. He gnawed his bottom lip—something he did when he was thinking hard. Finally, he said, "Look, I . . . know I should have told you all. But it wasn't my place to tell. She found me a few weeks back. She saw what happened on the bridge with Owen. She sought me out because she didn't want to be alone anymore. It took her a while to work up the courage, and then even longer to track me down."

"Does she know who you are?" Jazz asked quietly.

Seth shook his head. "I don't know her real name, or even her drag name. I'm sure I could find it, but I'm not going to. I have to respect her privacy, and I need you all to do the same." His expression hardened. "But I don't know how much longer that's going to last after what happened. If the footage hasn't made its way onto the news yet, it will soon. I'm sure Rebecca Firestone will get her hands on it."

Nick sighed. "I'm so disappointed in all of you."

"What?" Gibby asked, sounding offended. "What the hell did *we* do? We're not the ones who kept this secret. Seth did!"

"Thanks," Seth mumbled. "I've always wanted to be thrown under a bus."

"You didn't ask the most important questions," Nick said, letting his displeasure fill his voice. "When one finds out about a new Extraordinary, one must ask two questions that matter above all else."

"Are they good or evil?" Jazz asked.

"Do they want to kill us?" Gibby asked.

"Is their costume better than mine?" Seth asked, and didn't even have the gall to look affronted when they all stared at him.

"Oh my god," Nick muttered. "I'm constantly surrounded by incompetence. You should all be on your knees, thanking me for holding Team Pyro Storm together." He paused, considering. "We'll probably have to come up with a new team name now, seeing as how I can do shit now too."

"Only one of us is gonna get on our knees for you," Gibby said. "And I'll give you a single guess as to who that'll be." She high-fived Jazz over her shoulder without even looking at her. Nick would have been impressed if she wasn't so annoying.

He exhaled through his nose. "No. The most important questions are as follows: What is their superhero name, and what is their power? Have some self-respect."

They all looked at Seth expectantly, even though Nick knew the answers. It was better if it came from Seth, who hesitated only for a moment. "She can turn her body into electricity. Her entire body. If there's an electric current around, she can conduct it. But what's more is that she can *ride* it. Power lines, subway rails, all of it. She can travel from one side of the city to the other in a matter of seconds."

And that was enough of the conversation not having Nick's input. "And her name is Miss Conduct. Get it? Because of the electricity and the drag queen. It's *genius*. God, I love double entendres."

"Yeah," Gibby muttered, "screw whatever Nick said before about only two questions being important. I have at least a dozen more."

Seth shook his head. "I haven't really asked for specifics beyond that. I don't *want* specifics beyond that. I still don't know if I trust her."

That stopped Nick cold, all the goodwill he had toward Miss Conduct flying out the window. "You think she could be"—he swallowed thickly—"like Owen? Or Smoke and Ice?"

Seth sighed. "I don't think so." He looked at Nick, and for a brief and shining moment, Nick felt his heart swell uncomfortably. Here was this guy, this awesome dude, obviously scared out of his mind but pushing through it. If Seth could do it, so could Nick. "I should have told you. I'm sorry. I just—I wanted to make sure of what I was dealing with before I said anything." He took a deep breath and let it out slow. "And she—uh. She might not be the only one? There's another Extraordinary, too, who we've met up with, but only recently."

Nick wasn't quite sure how it happened. One moment, he was leaning against the dryer, Jazz's hand playing with his hair, and the next, he was flat on his back on the floor, staring up at the ceiling. He blinked slowly as three faces appeared above him: exasperated Gibby, laughing Jazz, and concerned Seth. "What happened?" he asked weakly as Seth pulled him up.

"Who's this other Extraordinary?" Jazz asked.

"I don't know," Seth said, sounding frustrated. He hadn't let go of Nick's hand, for which Nick was profoundly grateful, not only because it kept him upright but because it meant Seth wasn't *too* pissed off at him. "I can't even tell you their gender, though I think they're a man because of their lack of . . . you know."

"Because they don't have boobs?" Jazz asked, amused. "You can say that, Seth. It's not a dirty word."

Seth flushed, and Nick did *not* find it adorable because the situation was serious, and he didn't want to derail it by telling Seth he was the most perfect being who had ever existed. "Right, but that doesn't necessarily mean anything. You don't need . . . boobs to be a woman. Their voice is disguised, and their costume is like mine in that it covers their entire body. I can't see their face at all because they wear a full mask. They found me and Miss Conduct a week ago. They appeared on a rooftop above us." He shivered. "I thought they were going to attack us."

This morning, Nick had thought Seth was the only Extraordinary left in Nova City. Now, there were at least five more, including himself. He tried to keep his excitement in check, but it was a losing battle, especially when he had the wonderfully terrible (and not at all practical) thought that he could write them into his fanfiction. He really needed to work on his priorities.

Seth frowned. "I don't know. They're intimidating, I guess. They didn't say much beyond finding me for the same reason Miss Conduct did. I don't even know how old they are. Miss Conduct is probably mid-to-late twenties, but this other Extraordinary is . . . I get the feeling they're older than us."

"What can they do?" Gibby asked. Good question. Nick would keep her around.

Seth stared at Nick unnervingly. "Since they won't give me a name, I've been calling them TK because they're telekinetic. Like you." He hesitated. Then, "Nick, that—that wasn't you, right?"

Nick burst out laughing. He stopped when no one else joined in. "Oh, crap. You're *serious*? Hell no. Do you really think I'd be able to keep that a secret from you? I found you in a dark alley with a stranger, and I immediately blurted that I could move things with my mind! Just because they're telekinetic, too, doesn't . . . mean . . . oh no."

Owen Burke's voice filled his head. What had he said in Burke Tower in his attempted seduction of Nick? It'd been about the white pill, the one that—

The white one is off-limits. Even for you, Nicky. It's the most unstable. It's telekinesis. The power to move things with your mind. We can't touch that one. According to my father's tests, the last person who was given the white pill lost their mind.

"What is it?" Seth asked.

Nick shook his head. "It's something Owen said about the pills his dad made. The telekinetic one was bad news." A thought struck him, terrible and quick. "What if Simon Burke did this to them like he did to Owen? You heard Smoke and Ice. *'Mr. Burke sends his regards.'*"

"I thought of that too," Seth said grimly. "But Miss Conduct and TK have never met Burke. Miss Conduct didn't even know who he was."

Nick scoffed. "Of course that's what they'd say. They wouldn't just come out and *tell* you they know each other. They'd be pretty shitty villains if they did."

"I'm kind of with Nick on this one," Gibby said, sounding apologetic. "Where have they been this whole time? Why come around now? You gotta admit, Seth, the timing is a little weird."

"It's not like that," Seth said, jaw tightening. "We're not teaming up or anything, and it's not like I trust them completely." He looked down at his hands. He had a scratch on the back of his right hand, red and slightly irritated. "They saw what happened on the bridge, like everyone else. Miss Conduct said it gave her the courage to try and find me. Same with TK."

"Well, *yeah*," Nick said. "They could be telling you what you want to hear."

Seth jerked his head up. "Like Owen did to you? Because that sure worked, didn't it?"

Nick flinched. He tried to tamp down on the quick flash of anger thrumming through his veins. When he spoke, he kept his words even. "You're right. It did work, which is why I'm asking you to be careful."

"Do they know about us?" Jazz asked. "About Lighthouse?"

"Well, Miss Conduct does because Nick told her. TK doesn't. I was trying to keep everything compartmentalized until I could figure out what the plans was. If it wasn't for tonight, we wouldn't even be having this conversation."

"You wouldn't have told us?" Nick asked incredulously.

"No," Seth said, the line of his jaw twitching. "I wouldn't have because *they* weren't ready for me to. And I wasn't either. Again, Nick, not everything is about you. We're still feeling each other out—"

"You seemed to be feeling Miss Conduct just fine," Nick muttered before he could stop himself.

Seth gaped at him.

Nick groaned. "Goddammit. That's not what I meant. I don't think—ugh, I suck. That was a stupid thing to say, I'm sorry. Ignore me. I'm being a dick."

Seth deflated. "A little, but I can't blame you for that, especially since I was about to tell you again that you don't know what it's like being this—this *thing*, but that's not true anymore, is it? Because you're part of this now, Nicky, more than you were before." His expression softened. "Your mom, huh?"

Nick swallowed thickly. "Yeah." It took him a moment to be able to get the next word out. "Guardian. She was *Guardian*."

"And your dad knew?"

Nick nodded. "He did. And the Concentra . . . it was doing something to me." A thought struck him, terrible and wonderful in equal measure. "What if I don't have ADHD at all? What if it was only my powers manifesting themselves against the drugs?"

"Hey, Nicky?" Gibby asked. "Don't take this the wrong way—"

"Because *that's* not an ominous start or anything," Nick mumbled.

"Yeah, well, I know you," she said dryly. "You need a disclaimer." She sobered, bumping her shoulder against his. "Even if you can do what you say you can, that doesn't necessarily explain everything else. No one thinks like you do, and I mean that in the best way possible. You can have both, okay? Superpowers and ADHD."

"You're pretty great," Jazz whispered into the top of Gibby's head.

"She is," Nick agreed, bumping Gibby's shoulder back. "Thanks, Gibby. Maybe you're right, but the only way I'll know for sure is to—"

"—is to talk to your dad," Seth finished for him.

Nick shook his head. "We need to figure out what Burke thinks he's doing, sending Extraordinaries after us." He looked down at the ground. "And if my dad is part of it, we need to be careful with what we say and who we trust." He grimaced. "He went out with Gibby's and Jazz's parents this afternoon. Said it was just a meeting, but I know it's really a type of support group for parents whose kids get involved in the mess we're in. Do you think . . . do you think they're in on it too?"

"No," Jazz said immediately. "I would know. Daddy tells me almost everything, whether I want to hear it or not. If he thought your dad was doing something wrong, he'd say something. I don't think they know anything other than what we've already told them."

Nick felt a little better hearing that. But then, *a little better* wasn't much in the face of betrayal. "Gibby? What about your parents?" He didn't think for a minute Trey and Aysha would be involved in this, given how angry they were at Nick's dad, but today had been a stupidly awful day, and he had to make sure.

Gibby didn't answer. Nick raised his head to look at her. She was staring off into nothing, eyes slightly glazed over. Jazz rubbed the top of her smooth head. "Gibby?"

Gibby shook her head. "No, I don't think they know anything. But—"

"But what?" Seth asked.

"We're going to be busier than usual," she said, as if he hadn't spoken at all. "How long is it going to be before Nick suits up himself? And with all the new tech we have, it's going to be more important than ever to have someone here. Multiple someones. Jazz can't handle it on her own. Martha and Bob have done it for years. They deserve a break."

"What are you saying?" Jazz asked.

She tilted her head back, looking up at her girlfriend. Jazz smiled down at her, confused. Gibby grinned back. "I'm saying that you all can't do this without me. You'll probably end up dead or captured or arrested, and I can't have that." She looked at Seth, then Nick. "I'm going to stay in the city next year for school. Howard is a good school. A *great* school. But I want to help change things here in Nova City, and I can't do that if I'm hundreds of miles away. This isn't just about Extraordinaries. It's about making sure people have a voice, someone fighting for them who doesn't have to wear a mask. And I can be that someone. I know I can."

Guilt rolled through Nick, grating and harsh. Even as Jazz squealed and Seth squeezed Gibby's hand, Nick said, "Gibby, you can't make decisions about your future based on us. That's not fair to you."

Gibby frowned. "That was uncharacteristically mature of you, Nicky. I don't like it."

Jazz didn't either, if the way she glared at Nick was any indication, but he had to get this out, even if he couldn't believe what he was saying. "I love you. Nothing would make me happier than if you stayed in the city next year. But is this what you really want?" He shook his head. "Paths diverge. Seth, remember when you said you didn't know if you wanted to do this forever?"

Seth nodded slowly. "I still haven't made up my mind."

"I know," Nick said. "And whatever you decide, I'll support it. But we don't even know what I can do, and Seth doesn't know what he *will* do. What if I'm just a fluke, and Seth decides to hang up his suit? What if Team Pyro Storm disbands, and Lighthouse isn't needed anymore?" He was getting worked up again, but he couldn't stop. "Won't you hate us for taking this opportunity away from you?"

She didn't say anything for a long moment, giving Nick enough time to squirm uncomfortably. He was about to push more when she lunged at him, wrapping him in a tight hug and lifting him off the ground, feet dangling. His back cracked, and he laughed as she spun him around. She set him back down, hands on his shoulders. They were almost eye-level, and Nick was hit square in the chest by how much he cared for these ridiculous people. They were his, and no one could take that away from him. Maybe things would change in the future, but here, now, they were together.

Gibby said, "I could never hate you. I've been thinking about this for a long time, longer than any of you know. I'm doing it for me. We're growing up. We need to start making decisions for ourselves. It's what I want, and no matter what happens, I know I'm making the right choice. I can help. And more than that, I can be a voice for change. Besides, my parents always wanted Howard more than I ever did. I'm doing this for me."

Jazz sniffled. "I love us. We're the best."

"We really are," Seth said quietly.

And because she was Gibby, she punched Nick gently on the shoulder. "And seriously, you really think I'm gonna leave right when you're becoming an Extraordinary? Like I would miss you doing stupid shit like exploding streetlights or getting attacked by cups."

"It wasn't *that* funny," Nick muttered.

"It was," Jazz said. "You and I were running screaming down the street. I'm sure it was hysterical to many, many people. Including me." She jumped down from the washing machine and pushed her way between Gibby and Nick. She cupped Gibby's face, thumbs brushing the skin underneath Gibby's eyes. "You sure?"

"Completely," Gibby said.

Jazz kissed her sweetly. Well, it *started* sweet, and then Gibby grunted and lifted Jazz, who wrapped her legs around her waist without breaking the kiss, and Nick groaned. He loved his girls, but he really didn't need to hear the way Jazz gasped as Gibby mauled her face.

"What do we do now?" Seth asked him, sounding amused.

"Now?" Nick said. "Research. We need to find out everything we can about Smoke and Ice, and what Burke is up to." He also needed to find out as much as he could about Miss Conduct and the Extraordinary only known as TK, but he kept that to himself. He couldn't take the chance they were villains.

And then there was the matter of Guardian . . .

One thing at a time.

"Sounds like a plan," Seth said as Gibby did this thing with her tongue that looked wet and disgusting, but that Jazz apparently found quite agreeable. "We also need to see what you can do."

Nick nodded. "I like the way you think, Gray. Especially since it'll most likely involve a montage in which I attempt to use my powers in increasingly hysterical set pieces where I try to lift a Buick or jump from the top of a building to see if I can catch myself before I hit the ground."

Seth sighed. "That's not what I meant at all. I swear to god, if you try and jump from a building, I'm going to—"

The basement door opened. Gibby set Jazz on her feet as Bob called down, "We have a problem."

Martha stood in the living room, hand pressed against her throat. She looked up at them as they filed in, crowding around her, Bob bringing up the rear.

Steve Davis of *Action News* smiled aggressively at them from the television. "And now, to our top story tonight. A short time ago, violence erupted in the streets of Nova City with the Extraordinary known as Pyro Storm at its center. We go to Rebecca Firestone, live at the scene. Rebecca, what can you tell us about this latest attack?"

The screen switched to Rebecca Firestone standing on a sidewalk, flurries falling around her. Behind her, police vehicles lined the street, lights flashing. Beyond them, a familiar alley. Rebecca Firestone nodded solemnly. "Thank you, Steve. Earlier tonight, Pyro Storm found himself in the middle of yet another brawl that caused thousands of dollars in property damage, as well as injuries to people in Nova City. We have exclusive footage of what took place, provided to us by a concerned citizen who wishes to remain anonymous, fearing reprisal from the superpowered denizens that stalk our streets."

Rebecca Firestone disappeared, her high-definition evil replaced by grainy cell phone video. It'd been taken from the mouth of the alley. Bright flashes of fire and ice burst across the screen, followed by billowing smoke. Pyro Storm was clear. Smoke and Ice were clear. The fourth figure, hood raised over his head, wasn't.

Not until he raised a trash can above his head, preparing to hurl it.

The screen froze. Though it was still a bit fuzzy, it was obviously Nick.

"Oh no," Nick whispered.

"Look at you," Gibby said, sounding impressed. "Your workout routine finally showing some results, huh?"

Before he could answer, Rebecca Firestone said, "While we at *Action News* don't typically name minors, tonight we're making an exception. Since I know him personally, I can say without any hesitation that one Nicholas Bell was once again involved in the fray. If you'll recall, Mr. Bell took part in the Battle of McManus Bridge, where the Extraordinary known as Shadow Star fought valiantly against Pyro Storm last fall. Many are still convinced that Shadow Star was set up by Pyro Storm, and Owen Burke, the now-seventeen-year-old behind Shadow Star's mask, has not been seen since, nor have any charges been filed against him *or* Pyro Storm relating to the deaths of two *Action News* team members. While Pyro Storm's motivations remain unclear even to this day, the central figure in this ongoing mystery has always been Mr. Bell. What does he know? When did he know it? What is the purpose of his inane manifesto disguised as fanfiction?"

"*Inane?*" Nick growled, outraged. "I don't even know what that means!"

The screen, still stuck on Nick, zoomed in. Nick's face was twisted in an ugly sneer, making him look like a monster. Rebecca Firestone continued. "Our attempts to speak with him over the last few months have been repeatedly stonewalled by his father, Nova City police detective Aaron Bell. Aaron Bell, who three years ago was demoted after assaulting a witness, was recently promoted to head the Extraordinaries Division, a top-secret faction of the NCPD, whose budgetary information has not been released. A spokesperson for the NCPD told us earlier this year that the funding didn't come from taxpayers but declined to elaborate further."

The screen cut again to a man eating a burrito, Rebecca Firestone standing next to him, microphone at the ready. "Sir, could you tell us what you saw?"

The man had guacamole on his lip. "Oh yeah. There I was, minding my own business. Just doing my thing, you know? Got off work, thinking about what to get for dinner. I was going to get Chinese, but then I saw this new Mexican place opened, and I haven't had a burrito in a long time. I thought, *You know what, Jerry? You deserve a burrito.* So then I got one." He held it up to the camera. "But it's cold now because of *Pyro Storm.*"

"Exactly," Rebecca Firestone said, ever the despicable professional. "But not only did Pyro Storm let your dinner get cold, he also destroyed cars and hurt people."

The man nodded, crumpling the tinfoil around his burrito. "I don't know much about that. Jerry does what Jerry does, you know? Anyway, I was walking down the street, burrito in hand, when I heard fighting. I don't normally get involved in such things, especially when I'm hungry, but then there was fire and ice and smoke and explosions."

"Explosions?" Rebecca Firestone asked as a chyron appeared on-screen, proclaiming PYRO STORM RUINS MAN'S DINNER WITH EXPLOSIONS. "How big were the explosions?"

"Gigantic," Burrito Jerry said. "It sounded like bombs were going off. Things were exploding, and I thought, *Jerry, you know what? You gotta get out of here.* I tried to run, but then that Pyro Storm dude started riding fire, and then the others came after him, and I hid behind a 1967 Mustang. Good car. Good year."

"What are your thoughts on Pyro Storm?" she asked.

Burrito Jerry shrugged. "Don't know much about him. I think he's like me, out there trying to live his best life. I get burritos; he gets to burn things. Don't make no difference to me."

The screen switched again, Burrito Jerry disappearing as Rebecca Firestone appeared alone in a close-up shot, looking into the camera. "An innocent bystander named Ronald Ronaldson was injured in the attack. He was taken from the scene to Nova City Memorial, where I'm told he's currently being treated.

"I conducted a flash poll earlier tonight, asking ten people their opinions on Pyro Storm. Seventy percent said that he's a menace on par with a domestic terrorist. Twenty percent said that he's doing good work, but I believe there was a chance they misunderstood what I was asking. The remaining ten percent only wanted to discuss his burrito, obviously too frightened by what he'd witnessed. Troubling times for our fair city. It appears the court of public opinion has reached a verdict on Pyro Storm and found him guilty. And with me now is someone who has firsthand experience in dealing with the Extraordinary menace."

The camera pulled back into a wide shot. And there, standing next to Rebecca Firestone, looking dapper and severe, was Simon Burke.

"Mother*fu*—" Nick began to snarl, only to be silenced by a glare from Martha.

"Simon Burke," Rebecca Firestone said, "thank you for joining us."

"It's my pleasure," Burke said gravely, "though I wish it was under different circumstances."

Rebecca Firestone nodded, eyes sparkling. "Your son, Owen, was revealed by this reporter last year to be Shadow Star. Is that correct?"

"Parenting is difficult," Burke said, breath pouring from his mouth in a white cloud. "You try to do your best for your children, but sometimes they find themselves on a path that they can't be diverted from." He bowed his head, as if in grief. Quite the show. "I wish I could've done more. Hindsight can be a terrible thing."

"No one blames you," Rebecca Firestone said, reaching out and squeezing his arm.

"Thank you, Rebecca," Burke said, smiling softly. He looked directly into the camera. "Last year, I announced a new initiative in order to better understand our Extraordinary brethren. While we haven't yet gotten the results that we'd hoped for, we're slowly moving forward. Tonight's events are a clear indicator of the need to know who these people are and what they can do—which is why tonight, I'm announcing a new phase in our plan, one that I hope will help other parents who may find themselves in a position like mine. I was too late to help my son, but I need to learn from his and my mistakes in order to create a better future for us all. Burke Pharmaceuticals is launching the Save Our Children campaign. If you believe that your child is exhibiting signs of abilities beyond what humans are capable of, or if they might know someone who is, you can visit SaveOurChildren.novacity and fill out the form you'll find there. It asks for comprehensive information, which will be kept confidential. Our goal is not to curtail the superpowered, but to help them explore options that will ensure their safety and the safety of their families. Our children are our most precious resource, and we must do all that we can to help them in this newfound existence we find ourselves in. It's becoming abundantly clear that the NCPD won't help us, so we must do it on our own."

Rebecca Firestone said, "Quite the impressive announcement—one I'm sure will help parents sleep better at night, knowing someone in your position cares. And while you're here, Mr. Burke, I do have to ask: Is there any truth to the rumor you're considering a bid to become mayor of Nova City in the next general election?"

Burke chuckled and Nick's skin crawled. "Ah, rumors. I have nothing to announce at this current time. But when and if I do, you'll be the first to know. Consider it an exclusive, for all the tribulations you've been through."

"Wonderful," Rebecca Firestone gushed. "Before we let you go, is there anything else you'd like to say?"

"There is," Burke said. "I have a message for Pyro Storm and anyone who might be helping him." His smile widened. "You think you're doing the right thing. You think you can turn the tide. But things are already changing. I don't blame you for what happened with Owen and Shadow Star. If anything, I'm grateful you stopped him before he could hurt anyone else. But tonight has shown me that you're no more in control than my son was. Meet with me before someone else gets hurt. I promise you, I'll listen and do whatever I can to help you. Come forward before it's too late."

"Wise words from a wise man," Rebecca Firestone said as the

camera focused back on her. "For *Action News*, I'm Rebecca Firestone. Back to you, Steve."

"A damning indictment of the current state of affairs," Steve said in the studio. "Why do people eat pickles from a barrel? The answer may shock you. Stay tuned."

11

Monday morning was cold and dark, like the depths of Nick's heart.

"I guess I could be the brooding kind of hero," he muttered. "Filled with rage and a lack of self-preservation, unable to stop fighting because it's the only thing that makes me feel alive."

"Yeah, let me know how that works out for you," Gibby said, and he jerked his head up to find his friends staring at him in various stages of amusement. They were on their way to school, but Nick had been lost in thought, trying to figure out the type of superhero he was going to be. He hadn't spoken to his dad since Saturday, ignoring the increasingly intense texts and voicemails he'd left. Nick hadn't been home, either, and now wore chinos and a cardigan—the only thing Seth had that fit him, much to his dismay. Seth made it look good. Nick looked like a defeated professor who hadn't gotten tenure.

They'd spent Sunday researching the far corners of the internet, searching for any sign of the new Extraordinaries. While Seth and Gibby and Jazz had been all about Smoke and Ice and Burke, Nick had huddled over his phone, logging into his fic before dismissing it. If there was ever a time he didn't feel like writing, it was now. Closing it (and disappointing his legions of fans), he'd turned toward looking for anything about Miss Conduct and TK. The internet failed him once again, and though he almost looked up the queer bars in the city to see if he could find where Miss Conduct performed, he left it alone. Seth was right. She deserved her anonymity, if that's what she wanted. And now that Burke was chasing after them via Smoke and Ice, it was better that Miss Conduct stay hidden for now.

The searches for Guardian hadn't yielded anything that Nick didn't already know. There weren't any clear pictures of her, cell phone cameras nowhere near as ubiquitous as they were today. Nick read through multiple news stories about her, but they were old and mostly archived. Nothing about her identity, only that she had appeared one day out of nowhere, foiling a kidnapping of an ambassador's husband by a gang of radical separatists. From there, it was stopping bank robbers, assaults, and that time the large globe in the Financial District had broken free from its moorings, rolling down the street and nearly crushing a group of nuns on holiday from their convent in Lithuania. Guardian had saved them at the last second.

And that was it.

It didn't help that Nick had neither taken Concentra in two days, nor been able to use his powers. No matter what he did, he couldn't so much as move another cup. He'd spent Sunday afternoon in the Gray house under the watchful eye of Seth, Martha, and Bob, straining to no avail. He was frustrated, his thoughts jumbled and roiling.

All in all, not a great start to the week. He couldn't even relish in the fact that he'd slept over at his boyfriend's house, given that Bob had set him up in the spare room with the stern warning that Nick and Seth were *not* allowed to sleep in the same bed. "I was a teenager once," he'd said, arms folded. "I know what goes on in your minds. Oh, it'll start off innocent, but then there's Vaseline on the ceiling and where will we be then?"

So, no. Not a good Monday in the slightest.

"You'll figure it out," Jazz said. "And I'm totally on board with the montage idea. I even downloaded a soundtrack for it so it feels like a movie. Fair warning, it's mostly Gregorian chanting because I have wide and varied tastes. You'll get used to it."

"My soul is withered," Nick said in a growl, trying to sound like the hero he was meant to be. "I want to reach out for help, yet I don't know how. I've always been a loner, but I use that as an excuse to not let anybody get close, scared that they might see me for who I really am." He looked off into the distance, contemplating the despair that fueled him. "I want someone to love me for who I am, darkness and all."

"Oh boy," Seth said. "It's a good thing I already do, then."

"Yeah," Nick said. "But you could get hurt because I let you in, and I don't—don't—" His throat closed. His eyes bulged. He tried to talk but could only squeak.

"What's wrong?" Seth asked, looking worried. He ran his hands up and down Nick's arms. "What happened? Is it your powers?" He looked up as if he expected to see something floating above them. Nothing was.

"Holy crap," Gibby breathed. "Is this happening right in front of us? Yesssss."

"*Quiet*," Jazz hissed at her. "We can't interfere. We can only observe. We talked about this. You know how queer boys are in the wild. If they know they're being watched, they get skittish and run for the forest."

Seth blinked. "We run *where*? What're you talking about?"

"You—" Nick managed to say. "You just told me you loved me."

"Oh," Seth said. "*Oh*. Uh, shits. Right. Um, okay, so—" He exhaled explosively, cheeks expanding. "Wow. Yikes. Okay. Hoo boy." His face turned red, and Nick didn't know what to do that didn't involve lying on top of Seth and gyrating obscenely. They were in public, and Nick's dad had made sure when Nick had started dating Owen that he knew the ins and outs of indecency laws. That was a conversation on par with lubed bananas, something Nick never wanted to think about again. "I didn't mean . . ." Then Seth clenched his jaw and squared his shoulders. "No, you know what? Screw it. I did mean it." He turned on the street and tilted his head back, shouting, "I love Nicholas Bell, and I don't care who knows! He's my boyfriend, and I am in *love* with him!"

Nick gaped at him, brain misfiring as it collapsed into catastrophic shut-down mode. But through the storm, he saw a small ray of light, warm and sweet and kind. He watched as Seth spun around, announcing to everyone on the street that Nick was the best boyfriend in the world, and that Seth loved him. A man walking by high-fived him, telling him to get down with his bad self before continuing down the street.

Seth dropped his arms, cheeks flushed, grinning widely as he looked at Nick.

And Nick said, "I—" He didn't know what to say.

Seth's expression softened as he took Nick's hand. "I know, Nicky. You don't have to say it back, okay? Not until you're ready. It's for you, yeah, but it's also for me."

Nick didn't know if he was ready to say it or not, which seemed to be answer enough. He loved Seth, almost more than anything in the world. And since they'd turned from bros to bros who kissed and junk, that feeling had grown exponentially, new facets to it that Nick couldn't completely understand. He felt something for Seth, something grand and exciting, but he couldn't quite parse through it, not with any clarity.

So he blurted the only thing that came to mind. "Will you go to prom with me?" Then, "*Dammit*. It wasn't supposed to happen this way. There was going to be a flash mob and everything!"

"Good," Jazz said sagely. "Good."

Seth laughed, and Nick's heart was so full, he actually thought he'd die. "Yeah. Yes, I'll go to prom with you." And with that, he threw his arms around Nick, kissing him hard right in the middle of the sidewalk. Gabby and Jazz cheered behind them.

"Huzzah!" someone on the street shouted. "Get your man!"

Seth pulled away but only just, pressing his forehead against Nick's. They breathed each other in. "See?" Seth whispered. "It's not all bad. We've still got good things, Nick. No matter what, okay? You and me. Always."

Nick nodded dumbly, unable to speak.

"I love love," Gibby said with a sigh. "If you tell anybody I said that, I'll get Jazz to stab you with her shoes."

"I haven't stabbed anyone in a long time," Jazz said. "Feel free to tell anyone we don't like."

"Not all bad," Nick choked out.

Not all bad?

Ha.

The moment they stepped into Centennial High, things were much, much worse. Because it seemed *everyone* had seen the news over the weekend. Not only were a good quarter of the students wearing unsanctioned Extraordinaries gear, they had also apparently decided that Nick was cool again.

"I followed the Twitter account," a douchebro in a letterman jacket told him, slinging an arm around Nick's shoulder and pulling him toward the front doors while Gibby, Jazz, and Seth glared behind him. "You think you could set up a meeting? You're Pyro Storm's spokesperson, right? Can you see if he'll come to my house party next weekend? My dad will pay for him to come and light some stuff on fire."

Before Nick could respond, he was pulled away by Megan Ross, one of the most popular girls in school. She was a senior and absolutely terrifying. "Ignore them," she said, all business. "Hyenas, all of them, scavenging for meat. You need someone like me, Ned."

"My name is Nick."

She smiled sweetly. "You look like a Nick. It's the eyebrows."

He didn't know what to do with that. "I need to get to class—"

She hooked her arm through his. "Here's what I'm thinking. I'm in charge of the prom committee. The theme is Starry Night, which is stupid, but I was outvoted by heathens. However, if I go to them and tell them *Pyro Storm* is coming to prom, we could get the theme changed. Think about it, Niles: all of us dressed in our best, music and lights and dancing, and then *Pyro Storm* descends from the ceiling, fire flying around him. Starry Nights? Who needs Starry Nights when we could have Fiery Nights?"

"I don't—"

She pressed a finger against his lips. "Shh. Shh, shh, shh. Think about it. Talk it over with Pyro Storm. And I'm his biggest fan. If he needs a date, I'd be more than willing to put out—I mean, put myself out there as a volunteer."

"Don't you have a boyfriend?" Nick asked. "In fact, isn't he the douchebro you just stole me from?"

"Pyro Storm is on my celebrity list," she said. "Jason and I both have them. If we ever get the chance to get with someone on our list, it doesn't count as cheating."

"I don't understand heterosexuals," Nick mumbled.

She ignored him. "So it's settled; you'll talk to Pyro Storm about coming to prom. Thank you, Nelson. You're a sweetheart. I'll never forget this. Erica, that better not be how you're leaving the prom banner. It's crooked. It *is*. I can—you know what? I'll handle it myself. Move. I said *move*."

"They've all lost their damn minds," Nick said as Megan practically shoved a girl out a window to fix the banner.

"It'll blow over," Gibby said. "It did last time, and it will again. Trust me. By the end of the day, people are going to forget all about you and Pyro Storm."

Oh, Gibby.

Lunch—their refuge, where everyone usually ignored them—turned into a free-for-all. A line formed at their table with students asking for everything from autographs to wanting to know what Pyro Storm smelled like when he was angry. One enterprising girl asked if Nick would give Pyro Storm a package, telling him he shouldn't open it because it was only meant for Pyro Storm. "It's my underwear," she whispered aggressively as she thrust a wrapped box (complete with a comical red bow) into Nick's hands.

Nick yelped and threw the box across the cafeteria.

Unperturbed, the girl said, "It's the thought that counts."

"Your thoughts need *Jesus*," Nick bellowed after her as she left. He looked back at the line, hoping to see it starting to thin out. It wasn't. If anything, more people were joining, and Nick couldn't even enjoy the bologna sandwich Martha had made for him.

"Still think it's a good idea to promote Pyro Storm?"

"Seth, I swear to god if you don't—what? No, I'm not going to ask Pyro Storm to sign your purse, strange woman! I don't even know who you—wait. Don't you work in the front office? What the hell is wrong with you?"

By the time the final bell rang, Nick was convinced that Extraordinaries were the worst thing to happen to the world and that he never wanted to hear anything about them again. He hoped none of the fandom was hoping for an update on his fic anytime soon, because he'd most likely do something drastic, like update the tags with the dreaded Major Character Death so he could kill off Pyro Storm or, at the very least, make him lose his powers so that he and Nash could live a normal life away from the spotlight.

Which sucked balls, seeing as how an Extraordinary was in love with him and was going to prom with him. It should have been one of the best days of his life, instead of him wishing for a meteor to hit the earth and destroy everyone in a wave of fire. At least then they'd leave him alone. Because they'd be dead.

They stepped out of school and into the cold air.

"It'll blow over," Gibby said. "Give it a few days. By the end of the week, everyone will have forgotten about it. We'll—uh-oh."

Nick groaned. "What? No uh-oh! I am *done* with uh-oh!" He followed Gibby's gaze and found what she was looking at. "Uh-oh."

There, standing in front of the school next to the idling SUV, was his dad, arms crossed, his expression unreadable as he looked directly at Nick.

"Shit," Nick muttered. "Any chance someone can create a diversion so I can escape? Seth, how do you feel about lighting something on fire? Good, I hope."

Seth rolled his eyes fondly. He glanced around quickly before dropping his voice barely above a whisper. "Part of being an Extraordinary is facing things, even when you don't want to. You have the power, Nick. Now you need to figure out what to do with it." He nodded toward Dad. "This could be a start. It'll be hard, but the Nick I love doesn't ever back down, even when it'd be easier to do so."

Nick scowled at him. "That is blatant manipulation, and I'll allow it because of the whole you-love-me-thing. But this is the *only* time, Gray. You hear me? Don't get used to it. Also, you are the best boyfriend in the world."

Seth laughed quietly. "Ditto."

"You want us to go with you?" Gibby asked.

Nick sighed and shook his head. "Nah, Seth's right. I have to deal with it at some point. Might as well be now."

"I like Extraordinary you," Jazz said, reaching out and squeezing his hand. "I mean, I like you no matter how you are, but this Nick? This is a good Nick. Just . . . go easy, okay? Listen. Don't overreact. Use your words."

"When have I *ever* overreacted?" Nick demanded. Then, before anyone could speak, he added, "Yeah, okay. All the time. Whatever." He squared his shoulders as Jazz let go of his hand. "I can do this."

"You can," Gibby said. "Because you deserve answers, Nicky. And your dad is the only one who can give them to you. Text us later, all right?"

"Thank you," he said. "I know I probably don't say that enough, but I really mean it. You guys are the best, even when you're making me go talk to my dad." He looked away. "I'm a little scared."

He laughed when they all hugged him at the same time, other students milling around them, a few staring. Nick glared at them, daring them to speak. They moved on without comment. His friends stepped back, and Nick nodded at them before turning back toward his father.

Each step toward him was harder than the last, but Nick felt the eyes of his friends watching his every movement and knew they were right. It was time to deal with this, to get the answers to all his questions.

Dad dropped his arms as Nick approached.

"Father," Nick said stiffly.

"Nicholas," Dad said with a nod, his expression giving nothing away. He opened the passenger door for Nick. Hesitating briefly, Nick climbed inside as Dad shut the door behind him. Dad stared at him through the window for a moment before circling the front of the SUV.

Whatever happened, he wasn't going to make this easy for his dad. He glanced out the window, seeing his friends watching him from the top of the stairs. Before he could stop himself, he reached into his pocket and pulled out his phone, which had already synced up with the SUV, the little Bluetooth symbol bright in the top right corner. Fingers flying over the screen, he found what he was looking for. He grinned as Extraordinary porn began to blare from the speakers. He rolled down the window, letting everyone hear Boner Boy give the oil worker the dicking of his life. Seth's face was in his hands as Jazz patted his shoulder. Gibby gave Nick a thumbs-up. Everyone else around looked mostly horrified.

The moment shattered when Dad climbed into the SUV and slammed his hand against the dash, silencing the porn. Without so much as a glance at Nick, he pulled out onto the street, leaving the school behind.

12

The ride home was, in a word, excruciating.

Dad didn't talk. Nick didn't either. He wanted to, but he didn't know what to say that wouldn't come out in fierce accusations that he'd later regret. Regardless of what some people thought, Nick *did* have the presence of mind to know that some things said aloud—even if he didn't mean them—could never be taken back. He couldn't sit still. His leg jumped. He tapped his fingers against his thigh. He looked at his phone and set it down, only to pick it up again a few seconds later. He glanced out the window, watching the city pass them by, careful to only look at his father out of the corner of his eye. A headache was coming on, but that only made him more furious. Was it because he was stressed? Or because he hadn't taken his pill? Or was it his telekinesis, struggling to break free?

Nick opened his mouth more than once but closed it before he could speak. He wasn't going to go first. He'd done nothing wrong. It was Dad who needed to explain himself. And it'd better be good, or Nick was going to make him wish he'd never been born.

I'm a drama queen, he texted to Seth.

> I know <3 Need help?
>> Thanks, boo, but I've got this.
> Jfc Nicky. Don't call me that.
>> Nah. You told me u luuuuv me so it's official.
> I did. And I do.

* * *

When they got home Dad went in the kitchen. He never looked back, expecting Nick to follow. The Christmas decorations were gone. Dad must have packed them away. He and Jazz had left a mess when they'd fled the house, but most everything looked back in order. He wondered if the tapes were still in the attic.

A rectangular box sat on the kitchen table. Nick eyed it warily as Dad leaned against the counter, chin against his chest as he breathed in, held it, breathed out, held it. Just like he'd told Nick to do time and time again when things got bad. It struck Nick, then, that he might not be the only one on the verge of panic. He didn't know why he'd never seen it before. Did Dad have panic attacks too? What if he'd gotten that from his father, like he'd gotten his abilities from his mother?

Nick stood in the entryway to the kitchen, unsure of what to do. He waited. He wouldn't be the first to break. Stubborn, both of them, through and through.

Dad spoke first. Without looking at Nick, he said, "Open the box."

Nick stiffened, overwarm and uncomfortable. "What is it?"

"Do it, kid. Please."

Nick approached the table slowly. His mind whirred, the knot in his head writhing. Each step felt as if he were walking underwater, movements slow and lethargic, even as he thought he would buzz right out of his skin. The box was big, white, and made of cardboard. He settled his hands on the lid but didn't pull it off. "Dad, I—"

Dad shook his head. "Box first, then we'll talk. I swear. I'll tell you everything, but you need to see what's inside."

"I've never seen this before," Nick said, stalling for time, trying to figure out what the box could contain.

Dad laughed hollowly. "That's because I kept it in a storage facility. Same with most of the tapes you found. I brought them home because I was—" He sounded like he was breaking into pieces. "Because I was missing her. I needed to hear her voice, and I—you weren't supposed to find them. I forgot they were there when I—" He shook his head, blinking rapidly. "Open the box, Nicky."

He did as he was asked. He pulled the lid off. And froze.

There, resting in the box, was a cerulean-blue Extraordinary costume, complete with a mask with white lenses. He recognized it almost immediately, even if he'd only seen glimpses of it caught in grainy photographs.

Guardian. It was the costume that had belonged to Guardian. To his *mother*.

"She wore that," Dad said, words coming out forcefully, as if they pained him, "when she went out. Said it always made her feel safer, because hiding her identity meant keeping those she loved safe while still being able to help those who needed it. It made her feel . . . powerful. I told her that it was her powers that made her feel that way, but she said I didn't understand. That it wasn't about what she could do, but what she could do *with* it. And that costume was a symbol of it. She said that, in a way, it was like the uniform I wore when I was a street cop. It meant something." He looked away. "Or at least, I thought it did. I'm not so sure anymore."

Nick touched the helmet. It was harder than he expected it to be, the material dense. He grappled with the thought that this was something Mom had touched, something she'd held in her hands, something she'd *worn*, and he had to stop himself from tearing through, trying to find out if it still smelled like her, like sunshine on a warm day, like wildflowers and something so distinctly Jenny Bell that Nick couldn't find the words to explain it.

He didn't. "You kept this," he said in a hushed, reverent voice.

Dad looked up, eyes swollen. "I did."

"Why?" A slow wave of anger rose in his chest, and he didn't try to stop it. "You got rid of everything else she wore, so why keep this?"

Dad scrubbed a hand over his face. "Because she—*I* couldn't bear to part with it. I hated it, Nick. I hated everything it stood for because it terrified the hell out of me. Every time she put it on, I wondered if that would be the last time I saw her—that one day, late at night, I'd get a phone call saying she'd been killed trying to protect the city. I didn't want her doing what she did. We fought over it constantly. She said I wasn't being fair, that she had a gift and that meant she needed to do what she could with it." He made a pained noise, low and harsh. "Stubborn. So stubborn, like you. She was right, of course. She didn't know—at least, at first—that the only reason I became a cop was to try to help her as best I could. I told myself that putting on the uniform meant I was doing the same thing she was."

"That makes you a hypocrite," Nick said.

"Don't you think I know that?" Dad snapped. "But it was the only thing I could think of to do, because she wasn't going to stop. No matter how hurt she got, no matter how many times she came home bloodied and bruised."

Nick curled his hands into fists, a headache pulsing behind his right eye. He tried to focus on his father, but it felt as if his vision was frenetic, jumping, always jumping. "Do you know what it did to me?" Nick said, voice cracking. "When I got the call that you were in the hospital? That you'd been hurt when an entire *building* collapsed on top of you? It killed me. It killed me because I thought you were gone and I was going to be alone. That you left me, just like she did."

Dad hung his head. "I'm fine, Nick. I'm okay. I'm always going to be okay. I'm always going to come home to you."

"You can't promise that," Nick said. "No one can. You go out there every single day, and there are people who don't give two shits about your stupid promises." Dad took a step toward him. "Don't. No. Don't come near me. You stay right where you are."

Dad fisted his hair. "That's not fair, Nick. I have a *job* to do."

"So did she," Nick said coldly. "Yeah, it scared you, but she did it anyway—not because she didn't love you, but because she knew it was the right thing to do."

"I know," Dad spat. "Believe me, I know that better than anybody."

"Do you?" Nick asked. "Because she eventually stopped, didn't she? You must have worn her down until she couldn't—"

"She stopped because she found out she was pregnant with you."

The lightbulb above them flared. Dad looked up, eyes wide and spooked. Nick ignored it, staring at his father. "What?"

"You," Dad said in a low voice. "We lived in a shitty apartment on the East Side, a hole with faulty wiring and never enough hot water for a shower. But it was ours, and we didn't care. We were out of school and making the most of our lives. I was a cop, and she was a lawyer during the day and Guardian at night." He began to pace, the cracked linoleum creaking under his feet. "I came home late one night. I expected her to be gone already. There was this group of people—we didn't know who they were. They were robbing banks all over the city, but it wasn't about protecting banks. People were getting hurt, and she couldn't stand for that. She never could. She'd been getting close to figuring it out, and I thought she'd be on their trail. She wasn't. She was sitting at the kitchen table. She looked up at me as I walked in, and she was crying. I thought someone had died."

Nick swayed back and forth, his heart in his throat.

"I rushed over to her," Dad continued, still looking up at the light. "I asked her what was wrong—*just tell me what's wrong and I'll fix it, I swear I'll fix it*. It took me a bit to see that while she *was* crying, she was also laughing. And when she looked up at me, she smiled and said that she'd taken three different pregnancy tests, and all of them showed the same thing. You, Nicky. They showed you." He lowered his gaze to Nick. "Eight weeks. She was eight weeks pregnant with you. You weren't planned. You weren't something we'd done on purpose, but *oh*, there was this light in her eyes that I hadn't seen before. You changed everything for us, Nick."

"She stopped because of me?" Nick asked dully.

"She didn't want to take the chance," Dad said, "that something could happen to you while she was acting as Guardian. She said that at least for the length of the pregnancy, she wouldn't go out anymore. It hurt her, even though she tried to hide it. But I never made that choice for her. I never told her she couldn't still be Guardian."

"I bet you didn't try and stop her," Nick said bitterly.

"You're damn right I didn't," Dad snarled. "Because I wanted to be selfish. I wanted us to be more important to her than other people. If that makes me the asshole, fine. I accept that. But I won't apologize for it."

"It didn't matter though, did it?" Nick said. "Because they still found her. Eventually. It wasn't random, was it? Who are they? Did you lie to me about them too?"

"They don't matter," Dad said. "They're locked up, Nicky, and they won't ever be getting out. They can't hurt anyone again."

"And I'm supposed to take your word on that?"

"It's the truth. It's over, Nick. It's been over for a long time. But that's the reason for all of this, okay? That's the reason we—*I*—made the decisions that I did. You . . . it was little things, at first. You were a kid, just a baby, and I'd come to your crib, and the mobile—this cheap plastic thing the guys at the precinct chipped in for—would be spinning, even though it was turned off. You were kicking your legs and watching it as it turned and turned and turned. We didn't know that what she could do was genetic. We knew *nothing* about Extraordinaries because there was no one to ask."

"You knew," Nick whispered, "even then?"

Dad hung his head, slumping in on himself. "We didn't know what was going on. But the older you got, the more things . . . happened around you. Stuffed animals floating in midair. Your little toy cars racing around the room. Your blocks, little wooden blocks with numbers and letters painted on them, would spell out words even before you could spell. They'd say things like DADDY and MOMMY and LOVE and HOME and she was so scared for you, Nick. We both were. We knew what she'd been through, knew there were people out there who, if they knew who she was, would stop at nothing to destroy everything she loved."

"What did you do?" Nick asked, and the bulb began to blink slowly, light and dark, light and dark. The pain in Nick's head lessened slightly, but it was a *good* ache, a *good* pain.

"We went to the only person we thought we could trust. The only person who knew what she could do."

"Burke," Nick said. "Simon Burke."

Dad nodded, looking at the floor. "You were . . . four, maybe five. We told him that we were worried that her abilities had passed on to you. That we wanted to—not stop it, but suppress it, if we could." He held up his hand as Nick started to sputter angrily. "You were diagnosed with ADHD, Nicky. Do you have any idea what could have happened, since you had ADHD"—he exhaled explosively—"and telekinesis? We didn't make the decisions we did to stop you from being who you are but to try to keep you safe until the time was right. When we could help you figure things out."

"I'm sixteen years old," Nick said. "When the hell were you planning on—"

"You're still a minor," Dad snapped. "I don't care if you're six *or* sixteen, you're a kid. You should be focusing on school and boys and thinking about what comes next, not worrying about exploding shit with your mind."

"I can do both," Nick retorted. "I *have* been doing both. What were you thinking when you found out about Owen and Seth? That I was going to walk away from everything? That I wasn't going to get involved? If that's what you thought, then you don't know me at all."

"I know you better than anyone," Dad said, taking another step toward him. The table stood between them, and Nick thought if he pushed, if he really pushed, he could send it flying. He could probably destroy the entire kitchen if he wanted to. The entire *house*. "I've watched over you every day of your life. Everything I've done—everything I am—is because of you."

Nick laughed, the sound harsh. "Don't put the blame on me. You did this. You took this—this part of me and tried to keep it from me. You went to Simon fucking Burke—and why the hell don't I remember that?—and found a way to take something from me that you had no right to."

"We wanted to keep you—"

"Safe? By crushing me? By shoving this *thing* so far down behind a wave of pills that I wouldn't be able to find it? Do you have any idea the kind of violation that is? What if you'd been a homophobic dick, on top of everything else? Would you have tried to find a way to kill that too?"

"No, Nicky—oh god, no, it's not like that. It's not—"

"And what about after she died?" Nick demanded. "After everything we went through, didn't you ever stop to think that I had a right to know about her? About myself?"

"*I couldn't lose you too!*" Dad cried, and Nick flinched, heart shattering. Tears were falling freely now. Dad, too, his face twisting as his chest heaved. "Oh my god, I couldn't lose you too. All I ever wanted was to have you grow into the man I knew you could be, kind and loving and so damn brave. Did I make mistakes? Yeah, Nicky. Many, many mistakes. But I couldn't have the same thing happen to you. Hate me all you want, but I did what I did because I love you more than anything on this earth. I would do *anything* for you, even if that meant squashing the part of you that you think makes you extraordinary. You were already extraordinary. Every single piece of you. Every single part." He moved around the table. Nick couldn't make his feet do what he wanted them to do. He was rooted in place, and his father stopped before him, shaking, shaking as he gripped Nick by the elbows. "Nick, please. Okay? Please try to understand—"

Nick took a step back, shoving Dad's hands away. "Burke knew. And you did. When I started dating Owen, you both knew. When I found out about Pyro Storm and Shadow Star, you knew. When I was fighting for my *life*, you knew."

Dad scowled. "Burke. Goddamn Simon Burke. If he hadn't—"

No. No, no, no. "Don't. This has nothing to do with him. This is on *you*. At least he had the balls to tell me the truth, in his own way."

"He's trying to tear us apart. Can't you see that? This is exactly what he wants. He's never forgiven me for what happened to Jenny, and I—"

"We don't need Burke to tear us apart," Nick said, his words clipped. "You're doing that just fine on your own. How am I supposed to ever trust you again?"

Dad was shaking his head even before he finished. "That's not— I don't know, Nick. I don't know what I was thinking."

Nick tasted bile in the back of his throat. Even as angry as he was, he couldn't stand to see his father so beaten down. He startled when Dad slumped to the floor, wrapping his arms around his knees, pulling his legs to his chest.

Part of Nick's anger—a small part—dissolved as he took a step forward. He stood next to his father, racked with indecision before putting his hand on the top of Dad's head, fingers curling into his hair. "I can be both," Nick said softly. "I can be a kid and still do what I can. You taught me to be brave and selfless, and while the whole selfless thing is probably up for debate, I still listened to you. I always have."

"I know," Dad said, wrapping an arm around the back of Nick's knees, anchoring him in place.

Nick took a deep breath and let it out slow. "I'm going to ask you something, and you can't lie to me."

Dad nodded against his leg.

Nick hesitated. Then, "Did you tell Simon Burke about Seth? About who he is and what he can do?"

Dad lifted his head, looking up at Nick. His eyes were watery, but he seemed as if he was in control. "I never told him who Seth is. I never told him what he could do. The only thing I did was keep him apprised of Pyro Storm's movements, and even then, I kept it vague. I never gave him even a *hint* about Pyro Storm's true identity."

Nick glared at him. "That's still pretty messed up. Burke could've used the information you gave him and done something to Seth. If that'd happened and I'd found out, you really think I would've forgiven you?"

"No," Dad whispered. He let Nick go, hands resting in his lap. "I know you wouldn't have. And you would've been right."

Nick nodded slowly, parsing the words, trying to find any hint of deception. Dad was good, but Nick had spent far too much time clicking through Wikipedia and knew what to look for. Dad's eyes never darted away; he didn't try to embellish by filling in the blanks. It struck Nick, then, that he was trying to see if his father was lying to him. Dad, the one person he never thought he'd have to think that way about. "You'll need to talk to Bob and Martha," Nick finally said. "They deserve to hear all this from you. Seth is their kid, and since you were giving Burke information, they need to do what they can to make sure Seth is protected. And I'm going to do the same."

"What are you talking about? Nick, you need to stay the hell away from Burke. I don't know what he's doing, but you can't get involved."

Nick swallowed thickly. "A little late for that. I don't know what's going to happen, but I won't let the stupidity of adults get in the way. You screwed up. We're not going to pay for your mistakes."

Dad looked at him for a long moment before finally nodding. He reached for Nick but aborted the movement at the last second, hands falling back to his sides. "Where do we go from here?"

"I don't know," Nick admitted. "I love you, but I don't like you very much right now. I'm probably going to feel that way for a while. And I'm not taking the Concentra again," he said, reaching out and touching the costume on the table in front of him. The material was soft. No cape, as far as he could see. He approved. He'd gotten his good taste from her. "That's not up for debate."

Dad looked like he was about to argue but deflated instead. "Okay, Nick. We'll—we'll figure it out. No more Concentra, but you have to get something to help you out. It's not a bad thing, but if it can be managed, then we need to make sure it's done so you can focus. I'll make an appointment. We'll get it sorted."

"Nothing from Burke Pharmaceuticals."

Dad's jaw tightened. "No. Nothing from Burke Pharmaceuticals. I'll make sure of it."

Nick relaxed incrementally. "Sorry about the light bulb."

Dad chuckled. "Don't worry about it. It's the reason we got a Costco card—to buy them in bulk. Your mom did the same thing whenever she got upset."

He couldn't let this moment pass him by. "Will you tell me about her? I want to know everything."

For a moment, Nick thought he'd refuse. Instead, he said, "Yeah, kid. Everything."

13

Fic: A Pleasure to Burn
Author: PyroStormIsBae
Chapter 36 of ?
138,225 words
Pairing: Pyro Storm/Original Male Character
Rated: R (Rating is finally going up!)
Tags: True Love, Pining, Gentle Pyro Storm, Happy Ending, First Kiss, More Than First Kiss, Fluffy Like a Cloud, So Much Violence, Evil Shadow Star, Bakery AU, Private Investigator, Anti-Rebecca Firestone, Hands Going Under Clothes, !!!, Naked Party and You're All Invited

....

Chapter 36: NOT A CHAPTER

Author Note: Sorry for the delay! Things have been . . . weird lately. I wish I had a new chapter for you, but I don't. I tried to sit down and write, but I can't focus on this right now, not when it seems so . . . trivial? I know that probably doesn't make sense, but things are happening that are bigger than me. This was a place where I could not worry about what others thought about me (though I love all your comments!! THANK YOU SO MUCH!!!). It doesn't feel the same now. I'm going to take a bit of a break. It's not going to last forever because I refuse to let another fic go unfinished, but I need to step away for a bit.

Extraordinaries can do incredible things, but I think we forget that no matter what powers they have, they're still human.

Anyways, the Extraordinaries fandom is the best fandom there is, especially since the K-pop fandom likes to spam the fancams EVERY SINGLE PLACE I LOOK. SERIOUSLY. STOP IT. WHAT IS WRONG WITH ALL OF YOU. That being said, thank you for going after idiot politicians and making their lives miserable, as they so rightly deserve. I love you. But stop spamming.

I'll be back! I promise. After all, Nash and Pyro Storm are still about to get down and dirty, and I'd hate to leave them (and you!) with blue balls.

See you soon,

PyroStormIsBae

March came to Nova City with an icy grip, temperatures plummeting, though the worst storms stayed up north. Nick was of the mind that if it was going to be this cold, then the city should be blanketed with snow so he could stay in bed until spring with his own personal space heater in the form of Seth.

But it was probably for the best, especially since he found himself standing on the roof of a building on the first Saturday of the month, peering over the edge, trying to convince himself that if he fell, it wouldn't be *that* big of a drop. If anything, he could probably grab onto the metal stairs that lined the outside of the building. Thirty feet, max. Maybe forty. But he could do this.

"I don't think you can do this," Jazz said, standing next to him and peering over the edge. "I mean, I'm all for a montage, but I thought we'd start a little smaller. Maybe some cappuccinos in a cozy coffee shop while we discussed what your potential Extraordinary name could be."

Now that he was here, Jazz's idea sounded much better than what he had planned, but he couldn't back down just because of something as inconsequential as becoming a smear on the pavement.

"I'd really appreciate it if you all backed away from the edge of the roof slowly."

They turned to see Gibby looking pale, her mouth curved down. She was wringing her hands, her breath pouring from her mouth in a thick cloud.

"What's wrong?" Nick asked.

"She's afraid of heights," Jazz told him. "It's cute."

"I'm *not* afraid of heights," Gibby snapped. "I'm not afraid of anything. Just because I don't want to watch Nick splatter on the ground doesn't mean I'm scared."

"So cute," Jazz breathed.

Nick shook his head, not wanting to get caught up in their flirting, even though it was ridiculously endearing. "I don't know what my Extraordinary name will be. I can't decide that until I know what I can do."

"Which is why you want to jump off a building," Jazz said. "That doesn't make any sense and actually might make things worse. Please don't take this the wrong way, but this is objectively a dumb idea."

Nick rolled his eyes. "We tried jumping off the porch for the first part of the montage. It didn't work because it was too small. We tried jumping from the roof of my house, but before I could climb the ladder, Seth threw a snowball at my head, and I couldn't let *that* go without an appropriate response."

"Why do you have to jump off *anything*?" Gibby asked in a strangled voice. "Why can't you move cups again?"

Patience, Nick knew, was a virtue and a sign of a good Extraordinary. If he had any hope to become just that, then he needed to listen to the concerns of his friends and not make them feel lesser for sharing. "Because my powers seem to come out only when I'm super pissed off or scared or some other heightened emotion yet to be discovered. And since I don't want to be mad today, I figure it's better to be scared by jumping off a building."

"This is why men don't live as long as women," Jazz said. "It's not your fault. It's your penis that's making you do this."

"Not all men have penises," Nick reminded her.

"True, but you don't see them up here trying to jump off a building, do you?"

"But they also can't move stuff with their minds," he said. He paused, considering. "Well, not that we know of. Oh my god, wait. There *have* to be trans Extraordinaries! Do you think we'll get to meet them?"

"Probably," Jazz said. "I've personally met an absurd number of queer Extraordinaries. Poor straight people. They really don't get to have much, aside from fake-white Jesus, do they?"

They took a moment of silence for the heterosexuals of the world. When enough time had passed (six seconds—straights didn't need *that* much sympathy), Nick clapped his hands and said, "Okay! I think I'm ready to do this. Once Seth gets into position, I'll . . ." He peered over the edge again. Had the building gotten taller? It sure seemed like the ground was further away. "Jump, I guess."

"I feel like we should talk about this more," Gibby said quickly. "Like, a lot more. Weigh the pros and cons. Make a list! Yes, a *list*. Nicky, you love making lists."

"I do," Nick agreed. "But I know what you're doing, and I won't be distracted."

"Seth agreed to this?" Jazz asked.

"Sort of?" Nick said. "I mean, there might have been some yelling and also some crying, but then I remembered that tears can be manipulative, so I said he could catch me if it looked like it wasn't going to work. It pays to have a boyfriend who can fly."

"Yeah," Jazz said. "Still not used to hearing that." She glanced at Nick, expression softening. "How're things with your dad?"

Nick groaned. He'd been waiting for that question. After his confrontation with Dad, things had been weird. They were walking on eggshells around each other, Dad trying too hard to make up for all the shit he'd kept a secret. Every morning, a full breakfast. Every night, dinner that didn't need to be heated in the microwave. "Weird," Nick said. "It's getting better but it's going to take time. Just when I think we might be on the mend, I have to do things like vet the new doctor he found to make sure they're not connected to Burke at all."

"New meds?" Jazz asked gently.

Nick scratched the back of his neck, uncomfortable. "New

meds. I'm still getting used to them, but they don't seem to be too bad. I can think without my brain exploding, so that's good."

"Speaking of brains exploding," Gibby said. "I will *not* go to your funeral if that happens, closed casket or not."

"Her parents aren't happy," Jazz told him.

"About the school thing?" Nick asked, watching Gibby rant about the idiocy of queer teenage boys. He knew it was probably a whole hell of a lot more than just the *school thing*, but he didn't know what else to ask without making it sound like he was protecting his father and his job.

Jazz shook her head. "No, they're mostly okay with that. They went on a campus tour of NCU, and I think they're coming around. It's what she wants, and she's managed to convince them it's her idea and has nothing to do with us, which is somewhat true. It helps that she's gonna be valedictorian."

And even though Gibby was insulting him in the background, a swell of pride roared through Nick's chest. "Damn right she is. Smarter than anyone we know. Her speech is going to be epic. But it's not just about school, is it?"

Jazz sighed. "Your dad. And the NCPD in general."

"Yeah," Nick muttered. "I thought as much. They're right, you know."

"I know. My parents aren't very happy, either, but I've managed to talk them down from sending me to private school in Switzerland, which is good because I don't even know where that is."

Nick scowled. "Yeah, that doesn't surprise me. He's got a lot of shit to make up for, if he even can. You should have seen the look on his face when he came back from meeting with Martha and Bob. He said she didn't even offer him any cookies."

"Whoa," Jazz whispered. "She gives cookies to *everyone*."

He was about to say that was how he knew she meant business when he heard a voice shout up at them. He looked over the edge of the roof again to see Seth standing in the alley below them. Nick gulped at how tiny he looked. He was at least six thousand feet down.

Nick waved back, ignoring how panicked Seth looked. He

needed to be in the right headspace. He couldn't let doubt seed in his head. If it did, he wouldn't be able to jump off the roof of what had to be the tallest building in Nova City.

Nick took a step back, tilting his head side to side, popping his neck. He shook himself out, wiggling his entire body from his shoulders down to his toes. He looked across from them at the other building, pausing when he thought he saw a flash of movement. Probably a pigeon.

"Okay," he said, taking a deep breath. "Okay, let's do this. One time—that's all it takes. And when I do it and *live*"—he shot a glare at Gibby, who rolled her eyes—"we'll go celebrate by getting our fancy clothes for prom, which is not the best way to celebrate, but I agreed to it anyway because that's the only way you said you'd come."

Jazz sniffed. "I won't have you looking like crap when we make our entrance. It's going to be the biggest night of our lives." She leaned forward, dropping her voice. "And don't forget, we need to go buy condoms in case you and Seth decide to . . . you know."

The sound Nick made was one he wasn't proud of, a low wheeze that was better suited for the brakes on a city bus. She was right. *Always be prepared.* The measuring tape he'd used cemented the fact that he didn't need Magnums, much to his consternation, but he was sure they made condoms for someone who was . . . well, average. For his age. *Cosmo* told him there was a chance he'd get bigger as he got older, but he needed to learn to work with what he had. After all, it wasn't the size that mattered, but what you could do with it. That also came from *Cosmo*, in an article titled "So You're Average? Guess What? That's Okay!" He'd read it enthusiastically, nodding along with the carefully placed platitudes that assuaged his ego, all the while wondering if *Seth* would be in the same boat, or if he was hiding some kind of monster that probably only existed in fics and porn—which then, of course, sparked a bit of inspiration: Nash Bellin and Pyro Storm, trapped in a mountain cabin in the middle of a snowstorm, and wouldn't you know? *There was only one bed*, and then Pyro Storm would take off his pants, and underneath, there'd be . . . he'd have a . . .

"Right," he choked out. "The condoms. How could I forget?"

Jazz shook her head. "If you can't even talk about rubbers without blushing, you aren't ready. Don't do anything you don't want to do, Nick. You only get your first time once."

"Did you—do you and Gibby—"

"Have sex? Yes, but we talked about it a lot before we ever decided to do it. There was some trial and error, but Gibby can do this thing with her tongue that is . . . absolutely not helping this conversation, by the look on your face."

"Congratulations on all the sex," Nick managed to say before coughing roughly.

"Thank you," Jazz said primly. "We're very good at it."

"One thing at a time," he said. "First, I'll jump off a building, and then we can go buy condoms."

"And lube," Jazz said. "You'll need lots and lots of lube. Like an entire *vat* of lube."

"Stop saying *lube*!" he bellowed at her as he backed away from the edge of the roof, bouncing on his feet. One jump. That's all it would take. One jump, and if it didn't work, Seth would be there to catch him. Do it. Just do it and get it over with.

Raising his hands above his head, he yelled, "It's time to take out the trash!"

"Nicky, *no*!" Gibby moaned.

"Nicky, *yes*!"

And then he ran for the edge of the roof.

He stopped right before the edge. "Okay, that was a practice one to get me in the groove. Only seventeen more of those, and we'll be in business."

Gibby sighed. "I can't believe I'm wasting another Saturday with this."

Ten minutes later, he'd run to the edge sixteen more times. Gibby had given up on him and was watching cat videos on her phone. Jazz, ever the cheerleader, stood next to Nick, rubbing his shoulders, saying *You got this, champ; I believe in you, sport; you're golden, bud.* And while Nick appreciated her support, he stopped her when she began telling him that she always thought of him as a son.

What he *didn't* tell her—or any of them, for that matter—was that this very building was one his father had told him about. That his mother had come here with the same idea in mind after she'd revealed what she could do. Dad had been terrified, standing on the ground below, waiting for her to jump. She hadn't stalled like Nick was currently doing; Dad had told him that she was fearless to the point of lunacy. She'd vaulted off the roof of the building and fallen so fast that Dad had thought she was going to die right in front of him.

She hadn't. It hadn't even been close.

Halfway down, she'd just . . . stopped.

"Brave," he whispered. "Be brave."

Everything else melted away. Jazz, Gibby, the birds screeching on the roof opposite them, the cold air, the honking of car horns from the street below—all of it was gone, and the only thing Nick could hear was the sound of his quick breaths, the thundering of his heart.

And in his head, a flash of pressure, a bit of pain.

Gibby said, "Maybe we should—*Nick*!"

She must have seen the moment indecision was replaced by conviction. Wind whipped through his hair as he pumped his arms and legs, teeth gritted, skin slick with sweat despite the winter chill.

The edge of the roof grew closer and closer.

He jumped.

And immediately regretted all his life's choices.

He began to fall, screaming, "Mistake! I've made a mistake, oh my god, what is *wrong with me*?" He plummeted toward the ground, Seth already at a crouch, licks of fire blooming around his feet, ready to rocket up and catch Nick so he didn't freaking *die* in an alley wearing underwear with buffalo printed on them. He hoped the coroner wouldn't make fun of him when performing the autopsy.

He closed his eyes—and there, in the darkness, was a little ball of light, a spark floating. He reached out and wrapped his fingers around it. It was warm and soft and he clutched it close, keeping it safe, holding it tight—

The wind stopped slamming into him.

"Holy shit," he heard Seth breathe, sounding much closer than he'd been before.

"Am I dead?" Nick asked in a quivering voice.

"Uh, no? You're . . . doing it."

Nick opened his eyes.

The ground was at least ten feet below him, Seth looking up at him, mouth forming an *O*. Nick tilted his head back to see Gibby and Jazz above him, staring down, eyes wide and shocked.

He was *floating*.

"Ha!" he cried. "I did it! Yes. *Yes*! Take that, Mr. Baker, who in fourth grade said that I lacked follow-through! Suck it, you bastard! I'm doing it because I'm—"

Extraordinary was how he would have finished, except he happened to look into the window of the building across from him. Inside, two children were staring out at him, jaws dropped. They had to be only six or seven years old.

He waved at them.

They screamed.

Startled, Nick tried to rear back, but he was floating in midair with nothing but the power of his mind. And said mind blanked out at the sound of overdramatic children.

He dropped a couple of feet in an instant, his stomach rising into his throat. "Abort! Abort!" he cried as he dropped again.

"I've got you!" Seth shouted from underneath him, but that did little to calm Nick, seeing as how he'd advanced from the five-pound barbells to the *seven*-pound barbells, meaning his body was much, much heavier than ever before.

The breath was knocked from his chest as he landed on top of Seth, both collapsing to the ground in a heap of limbs.

"Ow," Seth said.

Nick blinked down at him before grinning. "Hi."

"Hi," Seth said, fighting a smile. "That went better than I expected."

Nick leaned down and kissed the tip of his nose. "You make a very good landing pad."

Seth laughed. "You did it, Nicky. Oh my god, you *did it*!"

He'd done it.

He'd done it.

He didn't even realize he was crying until Seth said, "Hey, hey, Nicky, it's okay. You're okay."

"I know," he sobbed. "I'm pretty much the best thing ever. You're so lucky to have me."

"I really am," Seth said.

He raised his head once more, tears streaming down his face, looking up at the pale blue sky above them. Gibby and Jazz were gone, most likely on their way down to congratulate Nick for having the best ideas. He startled when he thought he saw someone looking down at them from the opposite building, their head backlit by the gray sky. But when he blinked, the shape was gone.

Nick sat slumped in a chair outside of a dressing room, making faces at a bank of mirrors on the wall next to him. Jazz was in the changing room with the door shut, trying on yet another dress, searching for the perfect one. Nick had told her she wore the hell out of every dress she'd shown him so far, and while she'd beamed at him, she said that he wasn't allowed to decide what she looked good in. Nick tried to argue but was immediately shot down when she reminded him the suit he'd decided on was an affront to fashion. Which, fair point.

Nick had tried on suit after suit, lamenting at how ridiculous he looked. He didn't see the point in getting so dressed up, especially when he'd most likely lose the tie and coat as prom night wore on.

He'd been about to give up—all while groaning that he didn't even know how to dance and Seth was going to dump him for stepping on his feet—when the clerk had reappeared, followed by Jazz, who looked like she was about to laugh. Nick wanted to know what was so funny, but the words died in his throat when he saw what the clerk was carrying.

"What the hell is *that*?" he breathed.

The clerk looked down at the suit he carried on a hanger. "This? The last time I rented this out, it was for a magician performing at a child's birthday party under the name The Tremendous Carl. He died. Lead in the face paint he used. Your friend seems to think this is more your style, and who I am to argue, so long as your credit card isn't declined?"

The pants were fine. They were black, nothing special. But the coat? Holy shit, the *coat* was the stuff technicolor dreams were made of. It, too, was black but sequined, the lapels a violent shade of purple that had to be a crime against humanity. The bow tie that hung from the hanger was also sequined, glittering in the recessed lighting.

Nick fell irrevocably in love. "I can wear this in public?" he demanded. "And you won't give me shit over it?"

"Maybe a little," Jazz said. "But I've already spoken with Gibby to make sure Seth has some similar colors so you two match."

"Give it," Nick said, snatching the suit from the clerk. "I've never wanted to wear anything so badly. My entire life has been building to this moment."

The clerk grimaced. "Really? I don't know what that says about you that—ahem, of course, sir. Please try it on, and let's see how it—sir, *sir*. Please get changed in the dressing room and stop throwing *pants*."

"I like your underwear!" Jazz called after him as he slammed the dressing room door behind him.

When he reappeared a few minutes later, he was transformed.

"Yesssss," he hissed as he looked at himself in the mirror, arms outstretched as he spun around slowly. "Look at that ass. That's an ass that says open for business. This—*this* is what we came for. I look like a dollar-store disco ball."

"Is that . . . a good thing?" the clerk asked.

"It is," Nick said.

He hadn't wanted to take it off, but the clerk had been starting to give him the evil eye, so he'd changed back into his street clothes and turned his attention to Jazz. He was impressed with how quickly she could change, disappearing into the changing room and reappearing only moments later in something new. She took his breath away every time she came back out, but Jazz frowned at herself in the mirror, muttering under her breath before heading back into the dressing room in a swirl of lace, her long hair trailing after her.

He never hurried her, knowing Jazz would finish on her own time. He was messing around on his phone when he heard Jazz say, "I think—I think this is it."

He looked up at the closed door. "Really? Oh man, let me see."

"Hold on a second. I need to . . . there. Okay. Close your eyes."

He shoved his phone back in his pocket and did as she asked. A moment later, the door opened, the sound of her footsteps soft on the carpeted floor. Fabric rustled, and then Jazz said, "Okay. You can look now."

He opened his eyes.

Jasmine Kensington stood before him, a vision he wasn't prepared for. The dress she wore was red, long, and flowing, chest covered in patterned lace, a red sash cinched around her waist. The dress extended down to the tops of her bare feet, surrounded by an exterior layer of white lace with red trim that billowed as she spun in a slow circle, eyes sparkling. Her shoulders were exposed, pale and lovely, and she smiled at him as she stopped spinning. "Well, what do you think?"

Nick swallowed thickly. "I think you're amazing. And the dress is pretty killer too."

She laughed as she turned back to the mirror. "Thanks, Nicky. I like it too." She turned back and forth in front of the mirror, looking at herself from all angles. "I think this is the right one. I hope Gibby likes it."

"Yeah," Nick said dryly. "I don't think you'll need to worry about that. She's not gonna know what hit her when she sees you. You want to show her now, or do you want to wait, like me and Seth?" Clichéd, perhaps, but he and Seth had decided to wait until prom night to see each other in their suits for the first time. He couldn't wait to see the look on Seth's face when he saw Nick's dead magician tux.

Jazz gnawed on her bottom lip as she pulled at the sash around her waist. "I think I want to see her now. She was nervous too. I want to show her she doesn't have to be."

Nick stood from his chair and bowed comically, one hand behind his back, the other extended toward her, fingers beckoning. "Then, if you would, please allow me the honor of escorting you out of the dressing room."

She smiled at him as she took his hand in hers. "Don't mind if I do, good sir."

Later, when all was said and done, Nick would think back to this moment, the one where Jazz and Gibby saw each other in their fancy dress clothes for the first time. This, he would tell himself, was worth fighting for. Moments like this where nothing else mattered but the happiness of the strong, beautiful women in his life.

"Close your eyes," Nick told her, pulling her down the hall. He nodded at the clerk who disappeared into the back storage room. "Let it be a surprise."

She played along, closing her eyes. "I can't wait to see her."

"Me too," Nick said, knowing Seth would've done his best for Gibby, like Nick had done for Jazz. Granted, neither of them probably needed the boys' help, but the fact that they got to be involved made Nick ridiculously happy.

"I'm a little nervous," Jazz admitted as they reached the door that led out to the front of the shop.

"Why?" Nick asked, looking back at her, hand on the doorknob.

Jazz laughed quietly. "I don't know. Isn't that funny?"

"You don't have anything to be nervous about," Nick promised her. "Trust me."

She cracked open one eye. "I do, Nicky."

He squeezed her hand. "I know. Close your eyes."

She did, and he pushed open the door.

Seth had his back to them, standing in front of Gibby, blocking him from seeing her as his boyfriend fiddled with something on Gibby's clothes. "Man," Seth said, not yet aware they were being watched. "You make this look good. Puts the rest of us to shame."

Nick heard her snort. "Damn right I do. Pants are a little tight, but I'm sure they can tailor them to make them—Nick, what are you—"

"Nope," Seth said, putting his hand over her eyes. "We're going to do this right." He glanced back over his shoulder, jaw dropping as he saw Jazz standing next to Nick. Then a slow smile bloomed on his face. "Whoa."

"Right?" Nick said. "That's what I said. And *whoa*, Gibby. You look fantastic."

"Keep your eyes closed," Seth told her, moving to her side and dropping his hand to hers. Gibby did as asked, and Nick took her in. She wore the hell out of an old-fashioned black tuxedo, the coat tails hanging down the back of her legs, her top hat sitting at a jaunty angle on her head. Her bow tie was red, as were her boots, which matched Jazz's dress perfectly. Separately, they looked amazing. But Nick couldn't wait to see them side by side. The world wasn't prepared for them.

Nick led Jazz to the center of the shop. Seth did the same with Gibby, stopping in front of them. "Okay," Nick said, letting Jazz's hand go. "Don't open your eyes yet. I want to record this for reasons that'll become immediately clear in just a moment. Hold on a second, and I'll count you down."

Jazz and Gibby nodded in unison as Seth moved behind Nick, wrapping his arms around Nick's waist as he looked over his shoulder. Nick held up his phone, hitting the record button. "You did good, Nicky," Seth whispered in his ear, sending a shiver down Nick's spine.

"I'm flattered you think I had anything to do with this," he whispered back. "Trust me, I didn't. This is all Jazz." He raised his voice. "Okay, you guys ready? I'm going to count to three, and then you can open your eyes, all right?"

"Get on with it," Gibby muttered. "These pants are going into places they shouldn't be."

"You're ruining the moment," Nick said. "Anticipation is the better part of—"

"*Nick*," Jazz and Gibby said at the same time.

Nick rolled his eyes. "Yeah, yeah. All right. Here we go. Ready? One. Two. *Three*."

He saw it the moment it happened, lifting his gaze from the screen to his friends. Jazz opened her eyes, and Gibby did too, and then it was as if they were the only two people in the entire world. Gibby's mouth dropped open, her eyes wide as she took in the sight of her girlfriend. She recovered quickly, shaking her head and holding out a trembling hand. Jazz took it in her own, smiling as wide as Nick had ever seen her.

"Jazz," Gibby said in a hushed voice, and Nick felt warm at the reverence in that one word. "You . . ." She glanced away, blinking rapidly. When she looked back, her eyes were wet, but her own smile rivaled Jazz's. "You look beautiful."

"Thank you," Jazz said with a sniffle. "You do too. That tux suits you." She eyed Gibby up and down. "*Really* suits you. Wow. Look at you." She let go of Gibby's hand and walked around her. Gibby winked at Nick and Seth before she turned her attention back to Jazz, who stopped in front of her once more. "I love it. All of it."

Gibby blew on her knuckles and rubbed them against her shoulder. "Oh, this old thing? It's nothing."

"Bullshit," Jazz said. "It's the exact opposite of nothing. It's everything."

Gibby leaned forward and kissed her sweetly. "You always know what to say."

"That's because I love you," Jazz said, cupping her face and kissing her again.

"I love you too," Gibby murmured against her lips.

"You sure you don't want to show me your suit now?" Seth asked him quietly, but Nick was lost in his head, watching his friends. It was so easy for them. It always had been. Why was Nick making this so hard for himself?

Especially because he knew what he felt. He loved Seth Gray. He was *in love* with him, and no matter what happened in the future, no matter where their roads took them, nothing could ever change that. Not now, not ever. Here, today, at this moment, he was in love with his best friend.

But he didn't want the first time he said these words to Seth to be in the middle of a shop, especially since this was about Gibby and Jazz. So he whispered, "We're really lucky, aren't we?"

Seth chuckled in his ear. "We are. And we're going to—"

Seth's phone went off, loud in the quiet. Seth frowned as he came to stand next to Nick, pulling his phone from his pocket. He looked down at the screen, brow furrowing as he swiped his thumb against it. Whatever he saw there caused his expression to harden. Nick knew that look. Something was wrong.

He leaned forward, trying to see what Seth saw. Jazz and Gibby came over to them, a question on both their faces. They crowded around them, looking down at Seth's phone. Gibby took off her hat, holding it at her side.

Simon Burke appeared on the screen, standing in front of a row of microphones. Cameras shuttered and flashed, casting dancing shadows behind him against a familiar glass building. Simon Burke was giving a press conference in front of Burke Tower. On his left stood a white man and to his right a white woman, so eerily similar in appearance that they had to be related. Perhaps they were twins. They both looked severe, wearing black suits and heavy coats, staring straight ahead, hands clasped behind them. The man's head was shaved. The woman's dark hair was cut short and slicked back. Nick felt a twinge of recognition, but he couldn't place when he'd seen them. Had he met them when he was dating Owen?

"Thank you for coming on such short notice," Burke said gravely. "When I announced our new initiative to Save Our Children a few weeks ago, we never anticipated the level of community involvement it would inspire. While many provided information on our website that turned out to be inaccurate, we were able to parse through the bluster and noise, and as of today's date, we have received at least seven credible reports of Extraordinary activity from concerned citizens. This list will not be disseminated, nor will it be exploited for nefarious purposes."

"You know," Gibby muttered, "when someone tells you they're *not* going to be nefarious, chances are they're going to be exactly that."

"—while it's a start, and it's my hope we can help these people, should they ask for it, we need to take care with how we proceed. Nothing is more important to the future of our city—and our country as a whole—than for us to understand what exactly these people are capable of. Which is why it's my pleasure to announce that we now have the support of the mayor's office, and that of the Nova City Police Department."

"*What?*" Nick growled. "Dad never said anything about—"

"With me now," Burke continued, "is Nova City Police Chief, Rodney Caplan. Chief Caplan, if you please."

Cap stepped into view, pushing by the man next to Burke, who didn't seem inclined to move. Cap was irritated, that much was clear; his mustache was twitching dangerously, a sure sign to anyone that knew him that he wasn't pleased. The cameras flashed again, Cap holding up his hands to ward off questions being shouted at him. "Quiet!" Cap barked, glaring out at the reporters gathered before him. "I won't be speaking for long, and I won't be taking any questions. I have been asked by Mayor Stephanie Carlson to provide resources to the Burke initiative. I have made my objections known, telling her that my officers shouldn't be at the beck and call of a private business owner to act as his personal guard dogs. Trust is paramount between the police and the communities they patrol. I will remind everyone watching and listening that I have zero tolerance for anything that causes harm to the people of Nova City, which includes Extraordinaries. We live with them. They are our friends. Our loved ones, even if we might not know what they're capable of. Remember that as you're anonymously submitting private information about your neighbors to the wealthiest local business owner in Nova City. And an additional reminder to every single officer who makes up the Nova City Police Department: you do *not* answer to Simon Burke. Any officer acting outside of my orders will immediately be suspended pending an investigation. Good day."

Cap stalked offstage, ignoring the reporters shouting after him.

Burke stepped forward once more, a hint of a smile on his face. "Thank you, Chief Caplan. Your years of service are appreciated, and we're lucky we have someone such as yourself on our side. And he's right: we *do* live with Extraordinaries, and they *could* be our friends and loved ones. But until there are protections in place for those of us who *don't* have superpowers, we must do what we have to in order to Save Our Children."

He glanced left, at the man. Right, at the woman. He faced forward once more, leaning down toward the microphones. "And to show you how serious I am, I'd like you to introduce you to two associates of mine. They are part of a new outreach program to help Extraordinaries come to terms with who they are. With the cooperation of the Nova City School District, we will be sending them out to all the schools in the city to meet with your children, acting as ambassadors to meet with anyone—with or without powers—who would like to discuss things they've seen or what they can do in a safe, nonjudgmental environment. See something, say something, because that is the only way we'll be able to understand our superpowered brethren. Christina, Christian—a demonstration, if you please."

The man and woman stepped forward. They raised their hands as one, palms toward the sky. From the hands of the woman rose a thick column of billowing smoke, moving as if it were sentient. From the hands of the man, ice, snapping the air around it until it froze. Frozen particles swirled around as the reporters gasped.

"It's them," Seth snarled, hands tightening around his phone so hard, Nick heard the case creak. "They're the ones who attacked us. Smoke. Ice. What the hell is going on?"

Burke stepped forward to the podium once more as Smoke

and Ice dropped their hands, clasping them behind themselves. "Christina and Christian were involved in the recent altercation with the Extraordinary known as Pyro Storm. Before that, they came to me, seeking my help. Given my extensive history of philanthropic endeavors, along with the fact that I was unknowingly raising a son with preternatural abilities, they knew I was and am in a position to offer assistance. At my request, they went to meet with Pyro Storm in the spirit of peace, to extend an invitation to meet and discuss participating in the Save Our Children initiative, only to be viciously attacked. They tried to deescalate the situation, but Pyro Storm would not listen to reason. People were hurt as a direct result of his actions. That cannot be allowed to happen again, which is why I am now offering one million dollars to anyone who can identify the Extraordinary known as Pyro Storm." His smile widened. "Please don't misunderstand me; this is *not* a call for vigilante justice. If you possess verifiable knowledge as to the identity of Pyro Storm, we're asking that you call the hotline number we've set up. Operators are standing by to take down all tips, which will be vetted until the truth comes out."

Across the screen, a chyron scrolled with the hotline number.

"Safety first," Burke said. "Because the emerging generation of extraordinary members of our society deserve to have better role models and options than Pyro Storm."

Burke pulled back slightly, cameras flashing, reporters once again shouting at him. He looked as if he were basking in the attention.

Burke leaned forward again, raising his voice above those of the reporters. "And finally, a message to Pyro Storm: You think yourself alone, but I can assure you that's far from the truth. I am here for you. Christina and Christian are here for you. Nova City is here for you, and together, we can make our home the shining jewel of this great country of ours. Make yourself known before someone does it for you. Thank you, and good day."

The video ended, Burke raising his hands above his head, as if in victory.

Nick looked at Seth. His jaw was twitching as he ground his teeth together. Seth lowered his phone, closing his eyes.

"What do we do now?" Jazz asked in a small voice.

Seth shook his head. "I don't know. Cap didn't seem too happy about it, but what can he really do if he's being ordered into this?"

Nick scowled. "Cap isn't the biggest fan of the Extraordinaries, but he wouldn't do anything that put us in jeopardy. Even if he's being told to do something, he's not going to make things easy for Burke." He wished he could believe that more than he did, but he didn't know what, if anything, they were holding over Cap. Maybe nothing. Maybe everything. "It's not like he knows about Seth."

Gibby looked perturbed. "Unless you think . . . Nick, could your dad have told him?"

Jazz and Seth turned their heads slowly to look at Nick.

Nick took a step back, suddenly unsure. "He—he said he didn't. I know he's been a jerk, but that's not him."

Seth nodded. He looked around at all three of them. "We have to be careful. Anything seems off, we'll deal with it together. As a team."

"Hell yes," Gibby said. "We're not gonna let something like a million-dollar bounty stop us from doing the right thing."

Nick wished he had their optimism. "What do we do now?"

"We need to meet with Miss Conduct and TK," Seth said. "Strength in numbers. I'll reach out, see if they'll talk to us."

"Are you sure about that?" Gibby asked. "We don't know them."

"I do," Seth said firmly. "At least, as well as someone *can* know them. I'm asking you to trust me on this. I wouldn't do anything if I thought it'd put any of you in danger. If we're as alone in this as I think we are, we need all the help we can get. I don't know if they'll agree, but we've got to try."

"Superhero team-up," Nick breathed. "It's like this is a sequel! Oh my god. Yes. *Yes.*"

"Uh," Seth said. "Sure. Why not. Let's go with that."

Gibby wasn't as thrilled. She frowned at Nick before looking back at Seth. "If you're sure. Be careful, all right? Things are crazy enough as it is. We can't take the chance that we'll have someone stabbing us in the back just because we want more people on our side."

Seth nodded. "I'll keep that in mind. Trust but verify, yeah? Nick, get in touch with your dad, find out what he knows. Gibby, go to my house and talk with my aunt and uncle. Jazz, go with her. I need you in the lair to—"

"Secret lair," Nick corrected automatically.

Seth snorted. "Yeah, the secret lair. Jazz, I need you on comms. You're the best at it."

"On it, boss," Jazz said. "Ooh, that gave me bad chills. I'm not going to call you that anymore."

"Please don't," Seth said. "All right, let's go. Nick and I will—"

The sound of a door swinging open followed by a voice startled them. "Are you guys going to just stand there wearing my clothing without paying for them? Because that's not how commerce works."

They all jumped, looking back behind them. The clerk stood with his arms crossed, glaring at them.

"Right," Nick said hastily. "We'll pay for them and then be on our way. And don't change a thing about my dead magician suit. If you even remove one sequin, I'll know, and the Yelp review I'll leave will be emotionally devastating but still have five stars because I shop and support local."

The clerk rolled his eyes. "Get into tuxedo rentals, they said. You'll love it, they said. Well, guess what? They *lied*."

"That sounds like a you problem," Nick said. "But since I'm not in the mood to destroy dreams right now, I'll let it slide. You did a good job. Thank you for your help."

The clerk blanched. "Oh—you're welcome. And please, tell your friends about my shop for all their prom needs."

"We don't have any other friends," Gibby said.

The clerk threw up his hands in disgust.

14

Later, as the sky began to darken, Nick and Seth hurried through the streets of Nova City, keeping their heads down. Nick had just gotten off the phone with Dad, who said he was as caught off guard as the rest of them, not having known about the press conference until it happened. He sounded upset, saying he'd been unable to get ahold of Cap.

"And before you ask," Dad said, "I haven't said a word about Seth to him or anyone. I'm not going to out him. I promise."

Nick believed him. He was still pissed, but Dad seemed to be trying. Perhaps a test was in order. "A million dollars is a lot of money."

Dad snorted. "Yeah, it is. But no amount of money will ever make me hurt Seth."

Nick gnawed on the inside of his cheek, thinking hard. "Can I send you something?"

"What?"

"Hold on." Nick pulled his phone away from his ear, opening the text thread he shared with his dad. He sent an attachment before saying, "Picture on its way to you."

"Okay. It's . . . I see it. Let me figure out how to . . . open . . . it . . ."

"Oh my god, Dad, you're such a Luddite. You have to click on it and it'll—"

"Yeah, yeah, I see that. It's . . . whoa."

"Whoa," Nick agreed. He'd sent a picture he'd taken of Jazz and Gibby in their dress clothes, standing next to each other, hands clasped between them, Jazz's head resting on Gibby's shoulder.

They had bigger things to focus on, but Seth said they needed to remember the little things, too, pushing Gibby and Jazz together and telling Nick to take their picture.

"That's real good, Nicky," Dad said quietly. "They look wonderful. Reminds me of . . . your mom. Ah, she had this . . . dress she liked to wear. Made her feel beautiful. She only wore it for special occasions, and she was just—"

Nick's heart broke a little more at the wistfulness in Dad's voice, but he knew what his father meant. "She was just."

Dad hesitated, and Nick listened to him breathing. Then, "I need you to know that—shit. The Rook's here. Kid, I gotta go. We're going to hunt down Cap and demand he tell us what the hell the mayor is thinking."

"And make sure you tell him that I'm not a fan of the people he's hanging out with," Nick said.

"Will do. Where are you? I won't be home until late."

Nick glanced at Seth, who didn't seem to be listening as he pulled him through the streets, making sure he didn't bump into anyone. Seth knew Nick and multitasking were not on the best terms. "Hanging out with friends. Probably not going to do much. Get something to eat, make plans for prom."

"Text me if you're going to be late. I'll call you when I know anything. I can't—I'm *coming*, Rook, stop honking the damn horn! Nick, love you, talk soon, don't do anything stupid."

The phone beeped as the call disconnected. Nick sighed as he shoved it into his pocket. Seth looked back at him. "All right?"

Nick nodded. "He says he didn't know this was going to happen. You get ahold of Miss Conduct and TK?"

"Miss Conduct, yeah. She'll be there. Nothing from TK, but that's not surprising. He shows up when he wants to."

"You think he'll come?"

Seth glanced back at him, narrowly avoiding a group of tourists following a guide as he extolled the virtues of Nova City's illustrious history. "I don't know. If he does, he does. Why?"

"He's the only one we know like me," Nick said. "Maybe he'll take pity on me and want to help me out a bit. I can't keep jumping off buildings to try and get my powers to work. What happens if we get into a fight? I'll tell the bad guys to hold on a minute so I can climb ten floors and jump down?"

"I don't know," Seth said slowly. "He doesn't seem like the type to want to take on a protégé, even though you'd be the best protégé anyone has ever had."

Yeah, it was love, all right. Seth could have said *sidekick*, but he didn't. If that wasn't enough to convince Nick, he didn't know what else he was waiting for. He opened his mouth, but before he could speak, someone screamed in front of them.

Seth stopped suddenly, Nick bumping into his back. He recovered, peering over Seth's shoulder to see what was wrong.

A woman stood in the middle of the sidewalk, holding a leash attached to a tiny dog that yipped over and over, tail whipping back and forth. With her other hand, the woman pointed at Seth and Nick, finger trembling. "It's *him*," she cried. "That's the kid they keep showing with Pyro Storm! He knows who Pyro Storm is!"

People around them began to whisper as Seth took a step back, crowding protectively against Nick. "Lady, you've got the wrong idea," Seth said, the warning clear in his voice.

She shook her head furiously. "No, I don't. He knows who Pyro Storm is." She raised her voice again. "He was on the bridge with him! They were *kissing*!"

The whispers became mutters as more and more people stopped to look at them.

"A million dollars," Nick heard someone say. "That kid has info worth a *million dollars*." Hands began to touch Nick's shoulders, his back. Someone grabbed his arm, fingers digging in, jerking him away from Seth, spinning him around until he collided with a sweaty man who smelled like week-old sushi.

"Tell me who he is," the man growled, face inches from Nick's.

"Let me go!" Nick snapped, struggling to pull free. "You've got the wrong dude, dude!"

"I saw him first!" the woman shrieked. "He's *mine*." She took a step toward them, dragging her dog behind her.

"Get your hands off of him," Seth snarled, pushing his way

between Nick and the sweaty man. "You try and touch him again, you'll have to go through me."

The man laughed. "*You?* Who the hell are you? I only want to talk to the kid. What's his name?"

"Nelly!" someone cried. "His name is Nelly Babbish!"

"No it's not," another person scoffed. "Who the hell names their kid Nelly Babbish, you moron. His name is Nicodemus Bracewell!"

"Oh, because *that's* a better name."

"It *is*. Nicodemus! Hey, Nicodemus!"

"What is *wrong* with you?" Nick demanded as the crowd began to close in around them.

"Yes, hello," the first woman said, phone pressed against her ear, trying to push her way through the people in front of her. "Did I dial the right number for the hotline? Yes? Good. I'd like to report that I've found Nigel Buckendorf. *Nigel Buckendorf.* The one who is always making out with Pyro Storm. I'd like my million dollars to be dispersed in rolls of quarters, and no, you don't get to ask why."

"Run!" Seth cried, grabbing Nick by the hand and shoving his way through the crowd. People tried to stop them, Nick ducking when hands reached for them. Someone grabbed the back of his hoodie and Nick thought it was going to tear, but the hand slipped as Nick stumbled. He looked back over his shoulder to see a few people chasing after them, the sweaty man and the woman with the dog leading the charge.

Seth ducked down an alley, grip tight on Nick's hand. They jumped over a trash can on its side and burst out the other side of the alley as Nick pulled his hood up over his head. They pushed into the crowd, blending in as best they could. Nick could hear the woman screaming behind them when Seth shoved him into a darkened storefront, pressing the length of his body against Nick's front. They were both panting as Nick held onto the straps of Seth's backpack, holding him close. Footsteps slapped against the pavement, coming closer, closer, and Nick held his breath. Seth reached up and cupped the back of his neck, squeezing gently. Their pursuers rushed by them by without so much as a glance in their direction.

"You all right?" Seth asked.

"People are so stupid," Nick mumbled.

Seth kissed him quickly, lips warm. "Yeah. They are. School is going to be a nightmare on Monday."

Nick groaned. "I didn't even think about that. I'm gonna get in trouble, and it's not even my fault for once."

"We'll figure it out." Seth leaned back out of the storefront, looking down the street. "I think they're gone. Come on. We're almost there."

Ten minutes later, they stood in yet another alley in a neighborhood Nick wasn't familiar with. Seth was stripping, and if they hadn't just run for their lives, Nick would be enjoying it a hell of a lot more. He watched as Seth pulled his Pyro Storm suit out of his backpack, grimacing as he toed off his loafers, glasses askew on his face. "Keep an eye out, would you?"

Nick nodded, looking toward either end of the alley, making sure no one was watching. Just as Seth fitted his helmet over his head, lenses flashing as they came online, the air thickened around them, making it hard to breathe. It smelled of ozone, and Nick looked around wildly. Before he could warn Seth, a power line out on the street lit up with familiar, bright-blue electricity. It shot toward the alley, arcing like lightning. Nick jumped back at the sharp *crack* as Miss Conduct appeared in front of them, electricity crawling along her costume, her blue curls bouncing as she pulled herself up to her full height.

"Honeybunch," she said in a stern voice. "If you weren't an adorable little queer, I'd strangle the shit out of you. But family's family, and we gotta watch out for each other."

Nick nodded knowingly. "Gay rights."

Miss Conduct scoffed. "And *you*—you're a brave little thing, aren't you? Figure things out yet?"

Nick sighed. "I jumped off a building and floated and then got scared and fell the rest of the way to the ground earlier today, but that's about it. I'm a work in progress."

"Aren't we all," Miss Conduct said. "Now. You tell Miss Conduct who she needs to kill, and I'll do it."

"Whoa," Nick breathed. "That was intense."

"I'm a drag queen who can turn into lightning. Everything I do is intense."

Nick had no argument there, so he wisely kept his mouth shut. Miss Conduct turned to face Seth, who appeared to be arguing with his helmet. "No, we're not. It wasn't our fault! What do you mean it's already on the news? It *just* happened! Who even— Rebecca Firestone?" He groaned. "Of course it was." He looked up at Nick and Miss Conduct. "Jazz says Firestone is already interviewing the woman with the dog."

"I hate her so damn much," Nick muttered and looked up at Miss Conduct. "You said you'd kill people for me because I'm an adorable queer and we're family, right? Can you start with her?"

"On it," Miss Conduct said, electricity beginning to arc from her fingertips.

"*No*," Seth said, stepping forward. "We don't kill. Ever."

"I never agreed to that," Miss Conduct said. "Just because you have a righteous moral compass doesn't mean the rest of us want one."

"He's right," Nick said as he deflated. "We can't kill her. Maybe we could only maim her or something instead."

Seth shook his head. "No maiming."

Miss Conduct rolled her eyes. "I'm not seriously going to murder anyone. Learn to have a little fun, yeah?" She shook her head. "Not that I don't appreciate you reaching out, but what's going on?"

"You saw the interview with Burke?" Seth asked.

Miss Conduct made a face. "That man. Nasty. Too bad he's an asshole. Otherwise, I'd ride him like a bronco."

Nick gaped at her.

She laughed at him. "What? It's not like I'm actually going to. Trust me when I say been there, done that. I have too much respect for myself to ever go through a headache like that again."

"I want to be you when I grow up," Nick breathed. "Even if your taste in men is suspect."

She patted his arm. "Not all of us like twinks. Two sticks banging together, that's what you are. Give me a roughrider any day."

Nick began to pull out his phone. "Oh man, you should see this video I found. It's got an oil worker who—right," he said quickly as Seth glared at him. "Not the time."

Seth waited a beat, as if to make sure Nick wasn't about to share porn with a drag queen before saying, "We need help. I don't know if we can do this on our own."

"Ah," Miss Conduct said. "I see. You want us to work together."

"Superhero team-up," Nick whispered to no one in particular, which was good, seeing as how he was ignored.

"I *want* us to survive this," Seth said. "Burke is much more dangerous than people think, and we have to do what we can to stop him."

Miss Conduct snorted. "I sure as shit won't end up on any list, you can bet on that."

Nick looked back and forth between them before settling his gaze on Miss Conduct. "You won't help us?"

"I didn't say that, twinkie," Miss Conduct said sharply. "While I don't like the idea of going up against someone like Burke, I refuse to live in fear forever. Life's too short to worry about the simpleminded people who hate us for who we are. I went through that the first time I put on makeup. I'll be damned if I'm going to let people make me feel bad because of who I am. Never again. And if they want to come for me—well, I think they're in for the shock of their life." She raised her hand, a little ball of electricity snapping and snarling before it disappeared as she closed her fist.

"Oh my god," Nick whispered. "That was a *catchphrase*. Why didn't you tell me you have multiple catchphrases?"

"Because I just met you the once," Miss Conduct said.

Nick nodded, puffing out his chest. "I'm going to tell you mine, Miss Conduct. Ready? It's gonna blow your mind." He cleared his throat, hands on his hips. "It's time to—"

"—take out the trash," Miss Conduct said. "Yeah, I heard it the first time."

"Oh," Nick said. "Right. Well, I can see you're impressed, so you're welcome for—"

Another figure landed in the alley.

Nick stumbled back, raising his hands to ward off whoever was attacking them now. He waited a beat, but nothing struck him. He lowered his hands.

There, standing in the alley in front of them, was another Extraordinary.

They pulled themselves up to their full height, which was still shorter than Nick, though they looked much, much stronger, the muscles in their legs and arms shifting as they prowled back and forth. Their costume was completely black and bulky, made up of what appeared to be thick armor that covered their torso and legs. The front of their helmet was an opaque sheet of what looked like thick plastic, not unlike a futuristic motorcycle helmet. They turned their head side to side, looking at the three of them in the alley. Nick felt a chill run down his spine as their gaze settled on Nick. They took a step toward him, and though Nick couldn't see their eyes, he knew they were looking directly at him.

"Nick," Seth said. "This is TK."

TK. The telekinetic Extraordinary. The hero who'd found Seth and Miss Conduct.

Before Nick could introduce himself (and possibly gush until everyone was supremely uncomfortable), TK held out his hand. "Phone," he said, voice heavily modulated.

Nick blinked. "Uh—what?"

"Phone," TK demanded.

"Okay?" Nick said. "But if you're gonna use the internet, anything you find on there isn't something you can use against me. I have . . . unique tastes."

Nick thought TK chuckled, but he couldn't be sure. TK snatched the phone out of his hand, and before Nick could stop him, he dropped it onto the ground and stepped on it with his boot, shattering it into pieces.

"Hey!" Nick cried. "Why the hell did you do that? My entire life was on that phone. How *dare* you!"

TK wasn't moved by Nick's protestations. He kicked the remains of the phone, spreading the broken pieces around. "You were being tracked. Burke knew every movement you were making. The alley where you were attacked? He knew where to send Smoke and Ice because he was tracking you."

Nick stared at him, dumbfounded. "What? No, he wasn't! I would've known if he'd . . . done . . . that. Oh, shit." The limo, when Burke had snatched him off the streets. He'd asked to look at Nick's phone, saying he'd given Nick his contact info. Nick hadn't even considered calling him. He'd planned on deleting Burke from his contact list, but he'd forgotten. "That *bastard*." Angry, Nick kicked the pieces of his phone, spreading them out further. "Seth, forget what I agreed to earlier. We kill. We kill so hard, and we're going to start with Burke. And then we can move on to Rebecca Firestone."

"And I've got a list of my own," Miss Conduct said. "TK, you're looking as mysterious as ever. How delightfully annoying."

Nick froze as TK moved forward, slowly circling him. TK didn't try to touch Nick, but he was far too close for comfort. When he'd finished his inspection, he stopped next to Pyro Storm, shaking his head. "Why is he here?"

Before Nick could snap at him, Pyro Storm said, "Because he's part of this. And I'm done keeping secrets from him."

Nick puffed out his chest. "Damn right. And besides, I'm an Extraordinary too. Sometimes. I haven't quite figured out how to make my powers work when I want them to, but I jumped off a building." He grinned smugly. "And *floated*. Can you even do something like that?"

TK cocked his head. Then, without another word, he raised both his hands and spread his arms like wings, palms toward the ground. Air began to whip around them, biting and cold, numbing the skin of Nick's face. Before he could ask what TK was doing, the dumpster against the building rose into the air, floating above them, the trash inside shifting as the dumpster started to spin.

Metal creaked and groaned as *another* dumpster further down the alley shot into the air, flipping end over end, the lid clapping furiously. Detritus flew into the air as if caught in a tornado, swirling around them, plastic bags and newspapers and a startled, squeaking rat, tail twitching as its mouth opened and closed.

TK lowered his hands, and everything crashed back down onto the ground. The rat landed on its feet, taking off and disappearing into the shadows.

"Right," Nick said weakly. "So you can do stuff. That's . . . so *cool*." He rushed forward, grabbing TK's gloved hand and pulling it close to his face, as if proximity would explain all that he needed to know. "Teach me everything you know. You can be my mentor, and I'll be your young and headstrong protégé who'll one day take up your mantle when you become way too old to continue fighting, and then you'll look at me and nod wisely and say, 'The world needs fresh blood to save her. It's up to you now, Nicholas Bell. I've taught you everything I know. Now, go forth and save the planet like the hero I know you are.' Holy shit, the fic practically writes itself. How do you feel about being memorialized in fanfiction? Good, I hope, because I'm sure as shit going to introduce a new character based on you. *Yes*, a hundred and thirty thousand–plus words is probably a little late to introduce a new major character, but that's the best part of writing fiction! I can make it up as I go along. My followers are going to eat it up when I—"

TK jerked his hand back. "Stop. *Talking*. I don't need a protégé, especially one like you."

Nick frowned. "You don't even know me."

"I know enough," TK growled. "You're a child." He glanced at Seth. "Both of you are children. This isn't a game."

"We know it's not," Pyro Storm said, shaking his head at Nick in warning. "We never thought it was. Nick gets excited, but his heart is in the right place and he could use your help. You're the only other telekinetic we know."

"I don't work with others," TK snapped.

"You're a loner, the weight of the world on your shoulders," Nick said. "I get that. You do you, my dude. But if you'd consider changing your mind, I promise I'd be the best protégé the world has ever known. I won't even betray you at some point in the distant future because being a villain sounds exhausting. Always making plans to ruin my day. God, I hate them so much."

"Is he always like this?" TK asked Pyro Storm.

"Sometimes," Pyro Storm said. "But it comes from a good place. You can trust him. I do."

"Do you trust me?" TK asked. Pyro Storm hesitated, which was all the answer TK needed. "I thought as much. You don't know me. I don't know any of you. And it's better if it stays that way. Knowing people means getting hurt. And I'm not going to put myself into that position. Not again." He turned as if meaning to leave.

And Nick couldn't have that. "We have to watch out for each other. We're all we have."

TK stopped, shoulders stiff. He didn't turn around. "What?"

"Something my dad taught me," Nick said quietly. "And while we're not . . . it doesn't matter what he and I are, at least not right now. We'll figure it out because he's my dad, and I'm not going to lose him. He taught me that we can't always do things alone. We need others to help us, even if it's scary letting someone in. I know you think it's better on your own, but you don't have to be. We're here. And we can be here for you, if you let us. It'll mean you never have to be alone again."

TK turned his head toward the sky, light glinting off his helmet. "Your father sounds like a wise man."

"He is," Nick agreed. "Even though he kept things from me, and even though I'm so mad at him I can barely think straight, he's still my dad. We all make mistakes. Some bigger than others, and while it might not seem forgivable, I'm all he has left. If I don't watch out for him, no one will."

TK turned back, looking at Nick once more. "He's very lucky to have someone like you."

Nick looked down at the ground, shuffling his feet. "I think so too."

TK nodded, glancing at Pyro Storm. "Talk. Now. I don't like being out in the open. Why did you call us?"

"We need to work together," Seth said. "It may be our only chance to get through this. Burke knows about Miss Conduct. Not who she is in her real life, but that she exists. It's only a matter of time before the rest of it gets out. And we need to be ready for that."

"The bounty isn't on *us*," TK snapped. "Burke's gunning for you."

"But that doesn't mean he won't try and get as many of us as possible," Seth countered.

TK scoffed in derision. "Don't worry about me. I can handle Burke. If he tries to come for me, it'll be the last thing he does."

"Whoa," Nick breathed. "That was *dark*. High five!" TK was apparently not in the mood to high five, so Nick dropped his hand awkwardly. "Or not, which is cool too."

"TK's right," Miss Conduct said, looking down the alley. Nick followed her gaze. Out on the street, people passed them by without looking at them. "We can handle Burke if it comes down to it. Wouldn't be the first time I've had to deal with a man who didn't understand what *no* means, and he won't be the last. But I'm worried about the two of you. A million-dollar bounty?" She shook her head, curls bouncing. "That kind of money makes people stupid."

"We know," Pyro Storm muttered. He filled Miss Conduct and TK in on what had happened on the way to the alley, all the people chasing after them.

"You need to watch out for each other," Miss Conduct said. "If we're lucky, maybe this will all blow over."

"I doubt it," Pyro Storm said grimly. "Burke has his sights set on us, and now that he knows what Nick can do, we have to—"

Nick didn't even see TK move. One moment, he was standing next to Pyro Storm, and the next, he had Nick by the hoodie, pulling him down so he had to hunch over until he was face-to-face with TK. "What the hell are you doing?" Nick gasped, struggling to break free. TK's helmet was inches from Nick's face, and he could see himself reflected off the opaque plastic.

"He told you he knows?" TK demanded. "What did he say?"

Nick slapped at TK's hands to no avail. "Let me go!"

"Release him," Pyro Storm said, taking a step toward them.

TK jostled Nick, causing his head to snap back and forth. "Tell me!"

"He's known longer than I have! He's the one who told me that his company manufactures Concentra, the pills I took for ADHD that were also apparently suppressing my powers for years," Nick said in a strangled voice as TK lifted him even higher. "He knew about my mom—she could do what we do. I guess her telekinesis passed on to me, and my parents decided it was too dangerous. They tried to suppress it, and Burke helped them." TK shoved him back and began to pace, ignoring Nick glaring at him. "Not cool, dude. You already broke my phone. You don't have to break me too. Not that I'm fragile or anything," he added quickly, needing TK to see how awesome he was, in case the Extraordinary might change his mind and allow Nick to be his protégé.

"He's getting too confident," TK said. "He's not trying to do things in secret, not anymore. And he managed to get the mayor in his pocket. And don't get me started on the police. They're probably just as involved."

"Do you know him?" Pyro Storm asked, head tilted to the side. "Because you're talking like you do."

"Whatever Burke's planning, you can bet it's only getting started," TK said. "If you're telling us to lie low, then you *both* need to do the same. If he knows about Nick, then it's only a matter of time before he figures out the rest." He shook his head angrily. "Don't underestimate Simon Burke."

"We've handled him so far," Nick retorted. "I know you think we're just kids, but we've already done more than most. We survived Shadow Star. We survived Smoke and Ice. We can deal with someone like Burke."

"This isn't one of your fics," TK growled at him. "This is real life. People could get hurt. You could *die*. And someone isn't always going to be there to catch you when you fall."

Nick stared at him, thinking hard. "What do you mean, *catch* me?"

"Nick can handle himself," Pyro Storm said. "And even if he couldn't, he has me to back him up. He's not alone in this. He never will be. I'll make sure of it."

"You can't always be there. No one can," TK said, folding his arms across his chest. "And what happens if they get to you first, and Nick's the only thing between you and death? Are you really going to tell me that you'd put your life in his hands? He doesn't even know how to use his powers."

"Being a hero isn't about powers," Pyro Storm said, reaching out and taking Nick's hand in his own. "Nick is braver than anyone else I know, and it's not because he's telekinetic. He was already that way. So, yes. If I'm taken out, and Nick is the only thing that stands between me and death, then I know I'll be okay because he's relentless. All of our friends are. If we don't trust each other and work together, then what the hell are we fighting for?"

"You're children."

"Who've handled themselves remarkably," Miss Conduct said. "You know that, TK. You saw what they did on the bridge. It's why you sought Pyro Storm out. You didn't want to be alone anymore. We have each other now. That means we watch each other's backs against shitheels like Simon Burke. And if the need should arise, we will do what we have to in order to protect each other."

TK slumped. "I'm not like you. I'm not like any of you. I've been fine on my own. I don't need a team to—"

"Bullshit," Nick said, and TK jerked his head up. "Miss Conduct's right. You found Pyro Storm because you wanted to connect to someone else who has amazing powers and is doing something good with them. And sure, I don't really know how to make my powers work when I want them to, but I helped to stop Shadow Star before I knew I could do anything like that. You already at least kind of trust Seth, or you wouldn't have sought him out. We'd be unstoppable if we're all working together, so why are you fighting this so hard?"

"Twink's got a point, TK," Miss Conduct said. "Maybe we don't trust each other completely yet, but Nick still came here without a disguise because he was willing to take the risk that we all want the same thing. Am I scared of risking increased exposure by teaming up with a public hero? Hell yes. But if we don't fight for ourselves and our future, then those who can do what we do won't have anyone to turn to. It's not just about us. It's about those who'll come after us. If I need to pick up a damn brick like our lord and savior Marsha P. Johnson, then that's what I'll do." She smiled sharply. "And if anyone gets in our way, then they'll have a fight on their hands."

"You're all out of your minds," TK said, though he sounded begrudgingly impressed. "Fine. We work together. For now. Don't do anything stupid that'll get yourselves killed."

Pyro Storm sounded relieved when he said, "Good. I'll send updates through the app. You can do the same."

"Is that it?" TK asked. "It's getting late. You need to get home."

Nick rolled his eyes. "It's Saturday night, and you're not my parent. I've already got one of those, and he's a pain in my ass."

"Keep telling yourself that, kid," TK said.

And then TK turned, leaping up to the wall of the building to the right. The brickwork bulged from the wall with a groan, giving TK purchase as he climbed swiftly, almost too fast to follow. The last Nick saw of him was the flash of his helmet catching the lights from the city as he reached the roof and disappeared.

"I do love a dramatic exit," Miss Conduct said, staring upward. She shook her head as she glanced back at them. "If there's nothing else, I'm going to get out of here too. Some of us have work in the morning. Pyro Storm, it's been real. I'll be in touch if I find out anything. Twinkie, keep on doing what you're doing. You'll figure it out."

And with that, electricity began to arc along her body until she became so bright, Nick had to look away. The electricity snapped and snarled, and when the light faded, she was gone, leaving Nick and Pyro Storm alone in the alley.

"Still think they're working with Burke?" Seth asked as he removed his helmet. His curls were a mess. He brushed them off his sweaty forehead.

"No," Nick said quietly, looking up again to where TK had

disappeared. "I don't think they are. But it would really suck if one or both of them ended up betraying us, so I reserve the right to complain dramatically if that happens."

"I would expect nothing less," Seth said, stripping quickly out of his costume. Nick didn't look away this time, watching as gooseflesh prickled along Seth's arms and bare back, the muscles shifting under his skin.

Seth complained only a little when Nick practically tackled him, kissing every part of him his mouth could reach. As Nick held Seth close, chin hooked over his shoulder, breathing him in, Nick promised himself that nothing would tear them apart. They were in this together, and no one—not Burke, not Dad, not any villains who'd come after them—could take that away from them.

15

Monday sucked.

Mondays usually did, but this was worse.

Nick thought they'd prepared for it, thought they'd covered all their bases, but the moment he stepped into Centennial High on that cold morning—Seth at his side, Gibby and Jazz ahead of them—Nick knew immediately they'd made a mistake.

"Oh no," he whispered as people turned to stare at them as they walked down the hall toward their lockers.

"He's here!" one person whispered furiously.

"Talk to him!"

"Find out what he knows!"

"A million dollars, a *million* dollars! My dad said that if we get that, we can finally go on vacation somewhere that doesn't involve a giant ball of yarn."

"Nick! Hey, Nick!"

"Nick, over here!"

"Nick! Just the guy I was looking for. Hey, man. How are you? Good weekend?"

Nick glared at the hand on his arm. The douchebro removed it slowly but didn't step back. People began to crowd around them, following them down the hall as they called Nick's name, trying to get his attention.

"Back *off*," Gibby snarled. "Don't make me sic Jazz on you."

"I'm dangerous," Jazz said sweetly. "I'll make you bleed, though I won't be happy about it. Do you know how hard it is to get blood out of cashmere?"

But they wouldn't be deterred.

For the first time in his life, Nick was relieved to see the rheumy gaze of Mr. Hanson, his trig teacher who thought Nick should constantly be in detention for having ideas. Hanson glared at the kids behind them. "You have classes to get to," he said, the warning in his voice clear. "I suggest you move before we have a problem."

"I'm Pyro Storm," Seth said.

The students who hadn't scattered all turned slowly to stare at him as Nick did the same, eyes bulging. Jazz's jaw dropped, and Gibby sighed as if she couldn't be bothered to deal with the idiocy of teenage boys.

Hanson snorted. "Gray, next time you tell a joke, try something that's funny—or even remotely believable. Otherwise, it's just sad." He shook his head and turned on his heels, marching down the hall toward his classroom as the warning bell rang around them, the other students whispering as they left.

Nick whirled on Seth. "What the *hell*, dude? We're blurting out your secret identity now? Maybe warn me next time. Like, I can totally back you up on it and stuff. I wasn't ready."

Seth sighed. "Sure, Nick. I'll remember that for next time."

"Come on," Jazz said. "Let's get through the day. If that's the worst of it, we'll be all right."

It wasn't the worst of it.

All day, people came up to Nick, some of them asking outright who Pyro Storm was, others trying to act like they were Nick's friend. Normally, Nick would've been extremely on board with all this attention, but when it came in the middle of class while he was pretending to pay attention? Yeah, that wasn't the best. Case in point: the girl at the desk next to his leaned over and whispered rather aggressively that she'd rock his world if he wanted, trailing a bright pink fingernail down his arm, biting her lip seductively.

"No thanks," Nick said. "I'm super gay, so."

She blinked. "Are you sure?"

"Yep. Like, full-on queer and junk."

"Oh," she said. "My brother's gay too, and apparently people think he's really hot—which, gross, but yay for you! I'll give you his phone number, and he'll—"

"We're in the middle of a *test*," Nick hissed at her. He looked around the class, finding that everyone was listening in, even if they were trying to hide it. Including the teacher. "Stop interrupting my learning by offering me your brother!"

"Ignore her," a boy whisper-shouted from two desks over. "I know *three* gay people, and they're my best friends. I could get them to help you, since you're just coming out." He looked earnest when he added, "Which is, like, *so* brave of you. I mean, no homo, but congrats."

Nick threw up his hands. "I've been out for years! I have a *boyfriend*."

The boy shrugged. "Good for you. It Gets Better or whatever. Anyway, my friends would love you, and they're all really gay. Their names are Gabby, Jizz and . . ." He frowned. "Oh!" he said as he brightened. "Serf. No, wait. That's an agricultural laborer bound under the feudal system to work on his lord's estate."

"That's exactly right," the teacher said. "I'm glad what I'm teaching you is sinking in. How wonderful to see young minds expanding with knowledge."

"Oh my god," Nick muttered. "It's Gibby and Jazz and Seth, and they're *my* best friends, not yours. In fact, who are you? I've never even seen you before! And Seth isn't *gay*. He's bisexual, so take your hetero nonsense somewhere else, because I won't allow my boyfriend's sexuality to be erased."

"Okay, that's enough," the teacher said. "Get back to your tests, everyone. Leave Nick alone and let him focus."

"Thank you," Nick said loudly.

Satisfied, Nick turned back to his test.

Only to be interrupted a minute later by the teacher passing by his desk, sliding a folded piece of paper underneath the test sheet. He waited until she left before he opened it.

You're doing great work! If you need to talk about anything, please don't hesitate to come to me. My door is always

open. Being a teenager can be hard, but I'm hip and cool and
willing to talk about <u>anything</u> you need. Some examples:
boys, relationships, academic futures, identities of super-
heroes, parental struggles, drug prevention, Pyro Storm, peer
pressure, self-confidence issues, Extraordinaries' real names
and addresses, and I make a mean quiche if you should ever
need the recipe!

Nick raised his head slowly to stare at the teacher.

She brought her finger to her lips and winked at him.

"I hate everything," Nick grumbled, slumping low in his seat.

By the time the lunch bell rang, the following had occurred:

- Nick had been asked to prom by nine different people: five boys (all straight) and three girls (all straight), and the lady who worked in the front office, who told him everyone would think he was the coolest for bringing an adult to prom, to which Nick replied she really didn't understand what it meant to be the *coolest*.
- Three teachers—two of which Nick didn't have a class with— pulled him into their rooms, all of them telling Nick he shouldn't have to carry the burden on his own, and that they were willing to listen to whatever he needed to get off his chest. One of the teachers, an older woman with perfect teeth that had to be fake, turned a chair around and sat down on it, hands dangling down the back, saying, "Man, teenagers, right? It's hard out there for a pimp. Let's chill, my dude. Say, I got a question for you, since you're here. What is *up* with all these Extraordinaries, am I right, my man? My guy? Bro? Bro, where are you going? Bro, you don't need to leave, I'm not—the door opens the other way. No, you have to pull, not—Nick. Seriously. Stop screaming and just *pull the door open*."
- Seventeen different students—including the guy who moved to Nova City from Venezuela named Santiago, who had the most

erotic jawline ever given to mankind—invited Nick to house parties. And birthday parties. A bar mitzvah. A quinceañera. An orgy, though Nick might have misheard that one. One enterprising girl even told Nick that she'd always wanted a gay best friend to take shopping, since all gays had the best tastes in clothes. He might have given her the benefit of the doubt had she not been glaring at his clothes, which consisted of his beat-up Chucks, frayed jeans, and a green hoodie missing the string around the neck. He then proceeded to explain to her how problematic her views on queer men were, and that he did *not* exist to feed into her terrible stereotypes. She nodded solemnly and said, "Thank you for educating me. I'm taking the time to listen and reflect on my biases to become a better person. So, shopping, or . . . ?"

By the time Nick collapsed onto a seat at the lunch table, he was convinced humanity was a mistake and that getting sent to a boarding school in Switzerland might not be a bad thing, even if he, like Jazz, had no idea where Switzerland was.

"That awful, huh?" Gibby asked, patting him on the top of the head.

"Everything is terrible," Nick mumbled. "I know now what it feels like to be used, and honestly? Not as big a fan as I thought I'd be."

"You thought it'd be a good thing to be used?" Jazz asked.

Nick lifted his head. "If it meant being popular, sure, but at what cost, Jazz? *At what cost?*"

"Popularity is overrated," Jazz said, opening her Tupperware, which was filled with beef cutlets over a bed of bone-marrow pasta. "Popularity in high school doesn't matter in the real world. People are fickle. What's important today won't be important tomorrow."

"Where's Seth?" He looked around, trying to find the familiar mop of curls.

"He was talking to a teacher when I saw him before lunch," Gibby said. "Didn't look like it was going well."

Nick blinked. "What? Why? He's almost as smart as you are."

"I dunno. I was going to wait for him, but he waved me off. He'll be here when—there he is."

Seth pushed his way through the crowd, scowling at everyone who bumped into him. He practically threw his backpack on the table as he sat down next to Nick. "What in the *hell*?" he growled. "I just spent ten minutes talking to Sewell, who told me that I needed to be a good boyfriend to Nick and listen to everything he says, and if he *happens* to talk about Pyro Storm, to let her know so she can—and I quote—'Make sure you two are safe and making good decisions, and if that leads to a financial windfall, remember how much I'm helping you because teachers are vastly underpaid.'"

"Money makes everyone stupid," Nick muttered.

Seth looked around to make sure no one was listening in. He dropped his voice and said, "It's getting worse. I got a notification on the app last night. Someone reported an incident in progress, and I—"

They all jerked their heads toward him. "What?" Nick asked. "What happened to lying low?"

Seth winced, pulling on the polka dot cravat hanging limply around his neck. "I was going to ignore it. I thought I could. But—" He shook his head tiredly. "I don't know. I was careful, but when I got to the scene, no one was in trouble. Three people were waiting for me. I overheard them talking about how when I showed up, they were going to use fire extinguishers to subdue me."

Nick gaped at him. "They *what*?"

Seth sighed. "Burke has turned this into a manhunt, and he won't stop until he gets what he wants."

"Maybe it's time for Pyro Storm to take a break," Jazz said. "Not permanently, but at least until this all goes away."

"What if it doesn't?" Gibby asked. "Is he not supposed to be Pyro Storm again?"

"It might not be such a bad thing," Jazz countered. "Last I checked, Seth wasn't even sure he wanted to be Pyro Storm anymore. Has that changed?"

"I don't know," Seth admitted. "This certainly isn't making things easier." He took off his glasses, pinching the bridge of his nose. "And I don't know if I could do it, not all the way. The first time a real call comes in, and I, what, pretend I didn't see it?"

"You can't save everyone," Gibby said, sounding troubled. "You're already stretched thin enough as it is."

"What else is new?" Seth asked. "That's how it's been for years."

"And look where it's gotten you," Jazz said. "I know you don't do this for the accolades or the press, but Seth, you really need to think of yourself here."

"Which is why I asked Miss Conduct and TK to help us," Seth reminded her. "We can't do this on our own."

An idea struck Nick. It wasn't anything grand, but at least it'd be a start. He reached into his pocket, meaning to get out his phone, only to remember that it had been crushed by TK in an alley. His life was so weird. "Gibby, can I see your phone?"

She didn't question him, just slid her phone across the table. He snorted at the picture of her and Jazz she'd saved as the background before opening the app he was looking for and logging himself in. "How about this? I delete the official Pyro Storm Twitter account, and I don't send the email I wrote to the creators who I wanted to make the art for the merch." He looked down at the phone again. "Well, crap."

"What?" Jazz asked through a mouthful of Wagyu.

"We're up to three hundred thousand Twitter followers," Nick said, "and there's a new hashtag trending worldwide." He squinted at the phone. "Hashtag #PyroStormMillion. Hold on, the mentions are through the—holy shit, we've been *verified*? Goddammit, Jack! There are freaking *Nazis* on your platform, and you're busy verifying Extraordinaries? Okay, you know what? That's pretty cool. I've never been verified for anything, and this might be the validation we— No. *No.* I will *not* let this go to my head." He looked up at the others. "Right? I shouldn't let this go to my head?"

"Right," Gibby said slowly.

"Right," Nick said. "I'll . . . okay, I really was going to delete this, but we've now been retweeted by two former presidents, one of whom quote-tweeted me and said, *Who is this fire guy and how can I meet him? Twitter, work your magic!*"

"Which president?" Jazz asked.

"The bad one," Nick said with a frown. "I feel gross."

"Don't delete it," Seth said as he pulled away. "Not yet. Too many things are up in the air. I don't want any of us making decisions right now. We'll figure it out. I don't need this turning into— Nick, did you just respond to the president?"

"Damn right, I did," Nick growled. "I told him you'd never meet with him, since he's a war criminal. Oh no. What if the Secret Service is going to come to my house now? Dad will make me mop the floors, and I hate mopping."

Gibby snapped in his face. "Focus, Nicky."

"Right," Nick said, shaking his head. "The Secret Service won't care if our floors are dirty. What was I thinking?"

"That's not what I—you know what? Let's go with that."

"We need to talk about other things," Jazz said. "Take our minds off all of this. Agreed?"

"Agreed," they all said as Nick slid Gibby's phone back to her.

"Good," Jazz said. "Prom. We all have our outfits, and I've made reservations at Austers for dinner."

"Austers?" Nick asked. "Isn't that the place that charges twenty bucks for a glass of water and is impossible to get a reservation for?"

"It is," Jazz said. "Daddy knows the owners, so they bumped a diplomat and gave us their table. It might create an international incident, but Daddy said Ireland will get over it."

"Great," Gibby said. "Because all we need is Ireland getting mad at us now too."

Jazz ignored her, focusing on Nick. "You'll be at my house by noon on Saturday. You need to learn how to dance, and I'm going to teach you. Topics that will *not* be discussed: Extraordinaries, fire, telekinesis, smoke, ice, Simon Burke, or parents who kept life-long secrets that are now out in the open. Are we clear?"

"Crystal," Nick said. "Also, why do *I* have to go and not Seth?"

"Because I already know how to dance," Seth said.

That was news to Nick. "Like, what kind of dancing?" He grinned as he waggled his eyebrows.

Seth rolled his eyes. "I'm not stripping for you." He paused, considering. "Well, not yet."

Nick's eyes bulged as his brain misfired. "Must . . . witness . . . this . . . now."

And to his amazement, Seth stood from the table and held out his hand for Nick, who hesitated only for a moment before taking what was offered. Seth pulled him up. They stood chest to chest. Nick allowed Seth to position his hands, one going to Seth's waist, the other on his shoulder. "Jazz, if you please."

"On it," Jazz said, and a moment later, Elvis Presley began to croon about wise men saying that only fools rush in.

But Nick barely heard the King as Seth began to sway them both slowly. It was awkward, but that was to be expected. He stepped on Seth's feet, blushing furiously as he apologized. Seth smiled at him and said, "It's okay, Nicky. Move with me."

And though Nick knew people were watching them, he only had eyes for Seth. Nick was stiff, unsure, but the longer it went on, the more he relaxed. He laughed when Seth sent him out for a spin, their hands twisting but never letting go. Seth pulled him back with a snap, their faces inches apart. Everything melted away around them, and for a moment, Nick could imagine they were two normal boys, dancing, dancing, dancing.

Three words.

Three little words on the tip of his tongue.

The song ended. Nick startled when exactly four people clapped, the rest of them staring with varying degrees of feigned interest.

"That was so great," one of the people clapping said as Nick took a step back from Seth. "Queer people are valid members of our society and should be allowed to dance in a cafeteria, just like everyone else."

Touched, Nick said, "Thank you. That's very—"

"You're *so* welcome. And if you're feeling generous about my allyship, I'd be happy to listen to you if you want to tell me who Pyro Storm is. Hurray for gays!"

"Gays! Gays! Gays!" someone else shouted. "Now help us get paid!"

"That didn't even *rhyme*," Nick snarled as Seth tried to hold him back. "You dumb shits, how dare you interrupt a beautiful moment between two people who are privately dancing in public! I'll make you pay! I'll make you *all pay*!"

And as I'm sure you can agree," the principal said to Dad, "we can't have Nick making threats like that. It isn't a good look."

Nick glared at him but wisely kept his mouth shut.

Dad, on the other hand, was having no part in it. "I see. And yet he's told me he's been accosted by not only other students but members of the faculty as well."

The principal winced. "I don't know if I would characterize it as *accosted*—"

Dad leaned forward. "How would you characterize it, then, when teachers are soliciting private information from my son for their own financial gain?"

"I—"

"It's funny how you think I was finished," Dad said coldly, and Nick felt a surge of affection for him. Their current situation be damned, Nick would never doubt for a moment his father would go to bat for him when it really mattered. "I don't know what kind of school you're running here, but when my child's learning is disrupted by both students and faculty, then you can bet I'm going to have a big problem with it. So unless the next words out of your mouth are a detailed plan to ensure this doesn't happen again, I don't want to hear it."

The principal held up his hands as if to placate Dad. "I hear you, Mr. Bell. Nicholas, I'm going to do everything in my power to make sure you don't see any further interruptions on school grounds."

"You do that," Nick snapped. "All I want to do is learn and be successful and go on to become a baker-slash-private-investigator who bakes scones and fights—"

Dad coughed pointedly.

"Right," Nick said. "No fighting. Just scones. All those delicious scones."

Dad laughed but did an admirable job at covering it up. "I expect you'll let your staff know that any discussion with Nick that doesn't pertain to school or homework will not be tolerated. Good day. Nick, let's go."

"But—"

"He said *good day*," Nick snapped over his shoulder as he followed his dad from the office. The last he saw of the principal was the man sitting stunned behind his desk, face pale, eyes wide.

Nick's plan to go upstairs as soon as he got home was thwarted by an unexpected guest waiting for them on the porch of their house.

"What's he doing here?" Nick said, glaring at the figure waving at them. "Traitor. You, too, since this is obviously an ambush."

Dad turned off the car and looked at his son. "He probably wants to make sure you're all right. I didn't explain much when I left the precinct, just that the school called about you. I didn't know he was going to be waiting for us."

"That's what phones are for. Speaking of, we need to get me a new one."

"Next weekend," Dad promised. "And notice how I didn't ask what really happened to your phone."

"I *told* you it was stolen on the train by a man who—"

"—who looked like a serial killer disguised as Santa Claus, I know. It was very descriptive. I expected no less."

"Good," Nick said. "Now that *that's* out of the way, you should tell Cap to leave. I don't want to talk to him."

"Get out of the car," Dad said.

Nick did, though he complained loudly. He slammed the door behind him, stalking up the walkway to their house. Cap's mustache twitched as Nick got closer.

"Hey, Nicky," Cap said. "All good?"

"Sure," Nick said brightly. "Everything is fine! You know how it is. Prom's coming up, my boyfriend is amazing, I have to start thinking about college soon, and what else? What . . . else? Oh! That's right! Your new boss, Simon Burke, put a bounty on Pyro Storm's head, and now everyone is after me because of it. How are *you*?"

"Oh boy," Cap said.

"Nicky, no," Dad said.

"Nicky, *yes*," Nick said savagely, fumbling with his keys. He managed to fit the key into the lock before throwing the door open, causing it to bounce off the wall. He dropped his backpack on the floor near the door before heading toward the kitchen.

"Come on in, Cap," he heard Dad say from the front entrance.

"I don't know if I should," Cap said. "He's scary when he wants to be."

"Damn right I am!" Nick bellowed as he slapped together a cheese-and-ketchup sandwich, pretending it was the blood of his enemies. He had quite a few now for a sixteen-year-old. While not ideal, it certainly added to the mystique of him being a brooding hero with a dangerous sneer that disguised his bruised heart of gold.

"Get in there," Dad said.

When Nick turned around, sandwich in hand, Dad and Cap were standing in the entryway, watching him.

Nick bit into his sandwich without looking away from Cap, chewing obnoxiously. Cap took off his service hat, holding it in front of him. "Nick."

"Cap," he said through a mouthful of ketchup cheese. "How are you? Betrayed anyone else lately?"

"Can't say that I have," Cap said easily as he sat at the table, service hat sitting in front of him. "Mary isn't fond of me betraying anyone, much less her favorite kid. She says hi, by the way. Wants you both over for dinner soon. We'll order takeout, I promise."

"You can tell her I said hi back, but also make sure she knows I'm not very happy with you."

Cap snorted. "I'll do that, Nicky." He sobered, glancing at Dad before looking back at Nick. "Sit down, the both of you. It's time we had a conversation."

Nick thought about telling him to piss off, but Dad jerked his head toward the table and Nick did as he was told. He made sure the chair scraped along the floor loudly to show he wasn't happy. He sat down, crossing his arms as Dad pulled out the chair next to his.

Once they were both seated, Cap sat back in his chair, stroking his mustache. "Your dad said you saw that press conference. Thought I might come over and explain so you didn't get the wrong idea. Seems like I'm a bit too late."

"Way too late," Nick agreed. "Why the hell were you standing with Burke?"

"Nick," Dad warned. "Watch the tone."

Nick rolled his eyes. "It's not as if Cap was with someone whose son tried to kill me and my friends, who you went to in order to make sure I—"

"—got on the proper medication for your ADHD," Dad said quickly. It was only then that Nick remembered that Cap wasn't in the know about him—or, it seemed, Pyro Storm. Nick's view of his father raised a notch or two.

Cap blinked. "Burke? He's not a doctor. What does he have to do with Nick's meds?"

"Burke Pharmaceuticals makes all sorts of things, don't they, father of mine?" Nick asked innocently. "But yes, it was just for my ADHD meds. Whatever else could he have gone to Burke for?"

Cap looked between them, brow furrowed. He had questions, but Nick saw the moment he let it go. "Right. For your ADHD meds. How's that going?"

"Great!" Nick said, ketchup on his chin. "I still have it, so."

Cap stared at Nick for a long moment. He finally nodded and said, "I'm not working with him."

"Oh, really? Because that press conference suggested otherwise."

"Nick," Dad said. "Let him talk. You need to hear this. I did, too, and it answered some of the questions I had."

"Good for you," Nick said. He winced as guilt burned in his chest. "Sorry. I'm being a dick."

"A little," Cap said, "but I get it. Can I trust you to keep this to yourself? And I mean that, Nick. No one outside of this room can know what I'm about to tell you."

It was as if Cap knew exactly how to play this. Nick was a sucker for cloak-and-dagger shit, but he needed to play it cool. Make it look like he wasn't interested, even though he was practically bouncing. "Sure. Whatevs, man. Ain't no thang." There. Better.

Cap's mustache twitched as if he were fighting a smile. "I'm investigating Burke."

Nick choked on the last bit of sandwich, coughing roughly. Dad started to rise, looking alarmed, but Nick waved him off. He managed not to die, swallowing until the piece sank like lead in his stomach. "For what?" he croaked out.

"Many things," Cap said seriously. "It's complicated, but I'll try to keep simple. In a few weeks, Burke is going to announce his plans to run for mayor. If that happens, he'll own the police outright, and there are members of the force who feel threatened by the emergence of Extraordinaries, so they're looking forward to seeing someone in charge who has a plan to document and track them." He looked exhausted and far older than his sixty-plus years suggested. "There's a wave of anti-Extraordinary propaganda rising through the force. I've done my best to stymie it, but it's getting bigger than even I can control. It's not helping that certain individuals think the police are being unfairly targeted and attacked for simply trying to do their jobs, which is crap. Our job isn't to pick and choose who to protect—or, at least, that's the way it should be. I'm not so sure about that anymore. I don't know what that means, or what role I've played to allow it to happen. I thought—" He scrubbed a hand over his face. "I thought my officers would see right through the noise to what's really going on. I was wrong. Very, very wrong, and I have to reconcile that with the reality of the situation. There's . . . excitement from some at the idea of Burke taking control."

Nick stared stupidly at him, trying to understand. "What? Why?"

"Because they feel that he's the only one who can bring the

NCPD back in control of Nova City," Cap said bitterly. He glanced at Dad, who remained stoic. "I was . . . well . . . not threatened, but it was made abundantly clear that if I didn't fall in line, I might not be in my position for much longer."

"They want to fire you?" Nick demanded. "How is that not a threat?"

Cap shrugged. "Or force me to resign. And it's not just about me either. There's . . . talk about shutting down the Extraordinaries Division. Or overhauling it to make it something else entirely."

Stunned, Nick choked out, "Like what?" He looked at his father. "You didn't tell me about this."

"I didn't want you to worry," Dad said. "And for now, it's all talk." He spread his hands out on the table, fingers flexed. "But talk can turn to action. I don't know what they have planned, but I doubt it's anything good."

Nick slumped in his chair, mind racing as he put his chin in his hands. "What the hell."

"I know," Cap said, reaching over and squeezing his elbow. "It's a lot, Nicky. And though I want to tell you not to worry because your dad and I can take care of ourselves, I know that's not fair to you. The reason I'm telling you about any of this is because I don't want there to be any secrets between us, especially since Burke isn't playing around. This Save Our Children initiative is horseshit. He's trying to make a comprehensive list of Extraordinaries in Nova City, and I don't know for what, but I plan on finding out while I still can. I had no idea about the bounty he was going to put on Pyro Storm." Cap looked at Dad again and then took a deep breath. "You can tell Seth that while I may not understand how he can do what he does, I'm going to do my best to watch out for him."

The air was sucked out of the kitchen. Nick's skin thrummed painfully as he stood, chair scraping along the floor. Panicking, he glanced at Dad, who looked as shocked as Nick felt. He tried to breathe through it, tried to maintain control, but it was a losing battle. His breath whistled in his throat as he bent over, wrapping his arms around his waist.

"Shit," Cap muttered. "I didn't mean to spring it on you like that." But then Dad was there, cupping Nick's face, telling him to *breathe, just breathe, kid. You got this. In. Hold, one, two, three. Out. Hold, one, two, three.* Again. Again. Again.

By the time Nick came back to himself, he felt cold and clammy, sweat trickling down the back of his neck. Dad asked if he was all right, and Nick nodded. Dad whirled around, his hands in fists at his sides, shielding Nick behind him. It was ridiculous, of course. This was *Cap*, of all people. Cap wouldn't—he couldn't—

"We have no idea what you're talking about," Dad said flatly.

Cap sighed. "Yes. You do. I haven't told anyone, not even Mary. And I won't. You have my word on that. Stand down, Aaron. We're just having a conversation. No need to get all riled up."

"No *need*?" Nick blurted, standing on his tiptoes to look at Cap over Dad's shoulder. "You can't come here and say something like that and not expect a reaction. It's like you don't even know me!"

"But I do," Cap said. "I know you both very well. And if we're laying all our cards on the table, I'll admit that for a time, I thought Nick was Pyro Storm." He held up his hand as both Nick and Dad started to sputter. "It made sense, at least at first. Nick kept showing up wherever Pyro Storm had been. He knew more than he should have for someone claiming not to be involved. And don't even get me started on the whole Shadow Star fiasco. I thought Nick's—uh, obsession was an act to throw people off the trail."

"Yeah," Nick muttered. "That would have made me so much cooler, but alas, I sucked instead. Not one of my better moves. And I wasn't obsessed. I was merely guided by hormones that ended up betraying me spectacularly."

"You're not the first person to have a crush on someone awful," Cap said seriously. "There was this girl who I'd have done anything for when I was younger, even after I found out she was a part of a gang that robbed retirement communities and zoos."

Nick and Dad gaped at him.

Cap shrugged. "We all do stupid things when we're young. Hell, we do stupid things no matter how old we get." He shot a pointed look at Dad. "It's part of being human. Thankfully, like

Nick, I realized that a life of crime wasn't exactly something I was looking for. Then I met Mary, and she put me on the straight and narrow, and here we are."

"You might have skipped over a detail or two," Nick said faintly as Dad began to relax.

"Just a few," Cap said. "But my point remains. I thought Nick was Pyro Storm. I didn't think he was evil, no matter how the news and Shadow Star tried to spin it. Then the bridge happened, and Pyro Storm and Nick were standing side by side, and I knew I'd been wrong." He grinned at Nick. "That kiss kind of put all of that to rest."

"But that doesn't explain how you got to Seth," Dad pointed out, slumping back into his chair. Nick stood behind him, hands resting on Dad's shoulders.

Cap rolled his eyes. "It wasn't that hard. The fact that no one else has picked up on it is ridiculous. No offense, but it's pretty obvious."

"It is?" Nick asked.

"It is," Cap agreed. "Nick, you're not exactly . . . subtle. And I don't mean that in a bad way; it's part of your charm. While you were kissing Pyro Storm, you were apparently *also* kissing Seth, and I sat down and had a hard think. The Nick I knew wouldn't do something as mean as two-timing the boy he's been in love with for years—"

"*Years?*" Nick gasped. "I haven't even said . . . okay. We'll come back to that part because *what*? You're telling me that you thought I'm such a good person that the only way for this to make any sense was for Pyro Storm and Seth to be the same person?"

Cap nodded.

"Well," Nick said, "that settles it. I'm pretty much the greatest queer ever to exist. Thank you, Cap."

"Uh, yeah," Cap said, eyes darting from side to side. "That's exactly what I meant." He shook his head. "From there, I looked back on all that had happened. Wherever Pyro Storm went, Nick was sure to follow. He wasn't always there, but more often than not, the road from Pyro Storm always led back to our Nick here. I told myself that you'd all tell me when you were ready, especially after I figured out that Aaron was in on it. Which was why I had no problem helping him create the Extraordinaries Division. If it meant keeping you *and* Pyro Storm safe, then I didn't see who it could harm. I may not understand what people like Seth can do, but I like to think I know Seth, at least a little bit. Nothing about him screams 'criminal.' I doubt that boy has ever done anything illegal in his life."

"Well," Nick said. "That's probably not true."

Cap stared at him as Dad groaned.

"Uh," Nick said. "Ignore that part. Go back to talking about how amazing you think I am and stuff."

"Right," Cap said slowly. "Then Burke reared his head again with all this Save Our Children bullshit, and I remembered how Aaron had gotten an anonymous tip about what was going on in the basement of Burke Tower. We found nothing, of course, but that didn't mean something *hadn't* been there. Burke thinks he's smart, and he is. But he also tends to underestimate those he sees as being beneath him. Do you think Owen told him about Seth? A last little *screw you* as he was sent off to whatever hospital he's in?"

Nick said, "Owen hates his dad even more than we do. He turned Owen into a bulldog, just to protect himself and his work."

"Be that as it may," Cap said, "the thing about dogs is that they love with their whole hearts, even when they're abused. Doesn't mean they won't bite back when pushed, but there is loyalty in fear. All it would take is Owen opening his mouth, and Burke would know who to target. And that's what I think this is all about. What Burke's doing. His plan."

Nick blinked. "What are you talking about?"

Cap shrugged. "Revenge, pure and simple. You took from him, Nick. You and Pyro Storm. Whatever he was doing, you both got in his way. And what's worse, you exposed his son for what he truly was. Burke may be powerful, and he may be out of his damn mind, but I think he loves his son, regardless of what he did to him. You took that away from him. Even before the bounty, he was trying to flush Pyro Storm out. I bet what may be my last paycheck that he hoped someone would call his hotline with information on Pyro Storm, or at least point him in the right direction. And if he could gather intel on other potential Extraordinaries in the meantime, then he'd be all the better for it. But I don't think he got what he wanted from it, which is why he announced the bounty on Pyro Storm."

"But—but that's so *stupid*."

"What?" Cap asked, startled. Even Dad tilted his head back to look at Nick, brow furrowed.

Nick began to pace. "It can't be that simple. We exposed Owen, but Burke came out of that whole debacle relatively unscathed. Yeah, people wondered how he couldn't have seen what Owen was, but Burke spun the story right. He painted himself as a victim of his troubled son's out-of-control powers, and everyone believed him. If he was that pissed off, why run the risk of letting people see who he really is? Especially with Smoke and Ice standing at his side."

"Money talks, kid," Dad said. "It's not fair, but there it is. So long as he can throw money at whatever problem he has, people tend to not ask questions."

"Except for us," Cap said. "Because I have many, many questions for Burke, but I don't have enough information yet to ask the right ones."

"You sure about this, Cap?" Dad asked. "You don't want to be in Burke's crosshairs. If he even gets a hint that you're working against him . . ."

"I'm already in his crosshairs," Cap said. "And it wouldn't be the first time someone in power was coming after me. I became a cop because I thought I could make a difference in the way justice was served, help reform how police operate. And while I like to think I've helped make a difference, it's spinning out of my control. There are too many cops who think they are the be-all and end-all when it comes to the law. Give a man a gun and a badge, and he believes he's the most powerful person in the world. That's not the way it should be, but unfortunately, that's the way it is." He looked at his hands.

"Then what are we supposed to do?" Nick asked helplessly.

"What we can," Cap said. "Burke may be powerful, and he may have more money than most folks will see in a hundred lifetimes, but that doesn't mean he gets to do whatever he wants. We have to draw the line somewhere."

Nick closed his eyes as he stopped behind Dad's chair. "Except it's not just about revenge. At least—not against Pyro Storm for what he did to stop Owen."

"Nick?" Dad asked.

Nick opened his eyes and smiled weakly down at Dad. "We have to tell him. He has to know if he's going up against Burke."

Dad paled. "No. Nick, *no*."

"It's not only about Owen," Nick whispered. "It's about us. You. Me." He looked away. "He . . . I think he loved her. More than you know. And I think he allowed his feelings to fester until they were rotten. He acted like it didn't matter, acted like it didn't hurt him, but what if it did? She was her own person and she made her own decisions, but what if he felt like you took her away from him?"

"Aaron?" Cap asked. "What's he talking about?"

Dad ignored him, eyes on Nick. "If we do this, we can't ever take it back."

"I know," Nick said. "But this is Cap. Him coming here and telling us what he did puts a target on his back, and he needs to know everything. We have to stand together because we're struggling apart."

Dad hung his head, hands curling into fists on the table. "I'm scared."

"I am too," Nick said gently.

"I just want you to be safe," Dad said in a choked voice. "I want you to be happy and free and not worry about any of this."

"I know. And you did what you thought was right," Nick said. "Whether or not it was is something else entirely, but I don't blame you for that. I'm mad because you tried to take away part of me that you had no right to. I'm mad because you lied to me. But I can never be mad that you tried to protect me. No one knows what it was like for us when Before became After. We're a team, and no one can stop us."

Dad wiped his eyes. "Team, huh?"

"Damn right we are. And if Burke thinks he can use that against us, then he's making his biggest mistake yet."

Dad stood, holding his arms open. "C'mere, kid."

Nick went. Of course he did. Dad hugged him tightly, Nick's face buried in his chest.

After a time, Dad pulled away, studying Nick's face. "If you're sure."

Nick nodded. "If it helps Cap figure out what Burke is up to while there's still time, then it helps us. And it's better he hears it from us. You know I'm right. It was never just about Owen, or even Seth. It was about Mom and you and him." He took a deep breath. "And me."

Dad hesitated before nodding slowly. He turned back toward Cap, but he wasn't going to do this alone. Nick was with him until the end. That's what Bell men did.

Cap arched an eyebrow at the pair of them. "Why do I have a feeling I'm not going to like what you're about to say?"

Nick laughed hysterically. "Cap, you have no idea. So—you were right, I'm not Pyro Storm, but I *am* an Extraordinary. Telekinetic, though my powers don't always work when I want them to unless I'm jumping off the roof of a building."

Dad stiffened and turned his head slowly to Nick. "You did *what*?"

Nick shrugged. "Oh, yeah. Sorry. But don't worry. I floated. Hooray!"

Dad's eyes bulged.

Cap sat forward, hands folded in front of him, his knuckles bloodless. "Perhaps you should start at the beginning."

And so they did.

By the time they finished, the sky outside had begun to darken. Nick had let his dad do most of the talking, only jumping in to provide color commentary that he knew was appreciated, even if Cap and Dad didn't say as much. In fact, Cap barely spoke at all, allowing the Bells to tell their story. When Nick got to the part about falling off the bridge, the metal struts floating above him, Cap made a wounded noise as if gut-punched, low and breathy. He closed his eyes as Nick filled him in on being pseudo-kidnapped by Burke. And though he was itching to tell them everything, Nick didn't say a word about Miss Conduct or TK. If he could keep them away from this mess, all the better. They didn't deserve to have this crap piled on top of them, especially since they wouldn't have been involved, had it not been for Nick. If he could keep them safe, then it was a small price to pay.

Thankfully, Cap looked too dazed to even question it. Nick almost felt bad, but then he remembered Cap had tried to enact a plan without telling them, leading them to believe he'd switched sides and joined Burke.

Nick and Dad fell silent, waiting for Cap's reaction, both fidgeting in their seats.

Cap closed his eyes, hands resting on his stomach as he leaned back in the chair. Nick opened his mouth, but Dad shook his head in warning. Nick sighed instead, picking at the edge of the table.

Finally, Cap opened his eyes, though they looked distant. He surprised the hell out of Nick when he said, "Thank you for telling me. I—" He laughed quietly, glancing at Dad. "You've got your work cut out for you."

Dad sighed. "You have no idea."

Cap sat forward in his chair, thumping his knuckles on the table. "All right. Now that that's out of the way, what's the most pressing issue we need to focus on first?"

Nick blinked. "That's it? That's all you have to say?"

Cap smiled at him. "Oh, I'm sure I'll have a million questions as soon as I can think straight, but that can wait. I know you, Nick, and this is—well, if anyone can do it, it'd be you. That being said, it seems to me we've got bigger things to worry about at the moment. Where do we begin?"

Good question. Simon Burke was after them. He had Smoke and Ice. Nick had powers that he couldn't properly use, and he had no idea what he was going to call himself *if* he figured out how to use them. Owen Burke was hidden away in some psychiatric hospital, probably seething and plotting revenge, not unlike his father. Nick's mom was dead, and while she could have told him how to do what she could, nothing was going to change the fact that she was gone. TK didn't want to help him and was hopefully in hiding, along with Miss Conduct. There was a bounty on Pyro Storm's head, causing the city to go mad with greed. Rebecca Firestone was hell-bent on stoking the flames of discontent.

It was too big. All of it.

So Nick started with the one thing bothering him the most. "I don't know how to dance, and prom is coming up. Jazz is supposed to help me, but I think I'm beyond saving because Seth made me dance with him in the cafeteria and I stepped all over him. I don't want to look like a dick when we're at prom. I mean, I'm wearing a dead magician's suit because of lead face paint. Wait, that sentence was confusing. *I* didn't have lead face paint. He did, which killed him and now his suit is mine, but I still don't know how to dance, and I can't embarrass Seth by moving like a three-legged hippo in front of everyone again."

Dad sighed. Cap stared.

Nick shrugged. "What? I'm sixteen; I have a lot going on. Just because we're all probably going to end up fighting for our lives in some epic showdown at the end of all this Burke stuff doesn't mean I can't also worry about wanting to impress my hot boyfriend. My god, have you seen him in an ascot? The things I want to do to him should probably not be described here, since I'm a virgin and will stay that way for a long, long time."

Dad looked toward the ceiling. "I don't even know what to do with any of that."

"I do," Cap said. He stood, unbuttoning his uniform, then pulling off his coat and hanging it on the back of the chair. He nodded toward the battered radio sitting on the counter next to the small television. Without waiting for an answer, he went to it, switching it on and fiddling with the dial until he found a station playing old music, the voice sweet, the horns wailing in the background. Cap turned and held his hand out for Nick.

Nick stared at it. "What are you doing?"

Cap rolled his eyes. "Showing you how to dance. Trust me when I say I've got a move or two. Mary says I've got hips that won't quit, and while I—would you stop gagging? Seriously, Nick. Focus. While I may not be the best, I still know what I'm doing. I can show your skinny white ass what to do."

"Yes," Nick breathed. "Yes to all of this, oh my god, *yes*." He jumped up from the table, rounding Dad's chair and taking Cap's hand in his. Nick looked over at Dad, who watched them with a quiet smile.

Things would be all right, Nick thought. One way or another, they'd be okay.

16

"Wow," Dad said, staring at Nick as he walked down the stairs, head held high. "Now I know why you didn't want me to see the suit until you were ready to go to prom."

"Right?" Nick said gleefully, jumping the last few steps. The dress shoes didn't have any traction, and his feet almost slid out from underneath him. He managed to stay upright, playing it off like he'd done it on purpose. Spreading his arms away from his body, Nick turned in a slow circle, hoping the overhead light was catching the sequins on his suit. "Isn't it awesome?"

"Ye-es?" Dad said. "You'll certainly stand out, that's for sure. I'll admit, when you told me that it once belonged to a dead magician, I thought you were overselling it a bit. I was wrong."

"It might even be haunted," Nick said as he stopped turning. Suddenly realizing he was about to go to prom with the boy of his dreams, Nick asked nervously, "Do you really think I look all right? It's not too much, is it?"

"Nah," Dad said. "It's you, through and through. And that's a good thing."

"Good," Nick said, slightly relieved. "At least I'll look devastatingly handsome, which will hopefully divert attention away from the fact that I still can't dance very well."

"I doubt Seth is going to care about that at all," Dad said, "looking like you do."

Nick narrowed his eyes. "Are you making fun of me?"

"I wouldn't dream of it," Dad said, eyes wet.

"Aw, Dad, come on. You don't need to cry. I know I'm redefining couture, but it's not *that* big of a deal."

"Yeah, yeah," Dad said as he sniffled. "I'm . . . you look happy, Nicky. Which makes me happy."

"I am," Nick said. "We've earned a night where we get to go be stupid and not worry about someone trying to punch us in the throat or freeze our innards." He paused. "Huh. Our lives are weird."

"That might be an understatement, kid." Dad lowered his phone. "You do deserve this. All of you do."

"Which is why I convinced Seth to ignore the app, at least for tonight." Nick had expected Seth to put up a bit of a fight, which is why he was surprised when Seth agreed almost immediately, saying that he wasn't going to answer any call, no matter how serious. Tonight was about them and Jazz and Gibby.

"Good," Dad said, taking a step back. "She'd love this, Nicky."

Nick flushed happily. It was getting easier now to bring her up. It still hurt and probably always would, but it wasn't like how it used to be. "I think so too. She'd say I looked kickass."

"Yeah, that sounds like her." Dad took a deep breath before shaking his head. "Okay, let's head out. I'll need to take at least a hundred pictures when we get there, and I don't want the restaurant to send the hit men after you."

"Five pictures."

"Ninety."

"Ten."

"Ninety-one."

Nick glared at him. "I hope you're never called to be a hostage negotiator because everyone will die, since you don't know anything about negotiating."

"Or do I know everything?" Dad said as he headed for the door. "Get your butt in gear."

Grumbling, Nick followed Dad toward the door.

On the ride over to the Gray house, Nick played with his new phone. It wasn't anything special, but so long as it got him online and could get him in touch with Dad, he really didn't care.

He pulled up the Pyro Storm Twitter account, staring, dumb-founded, as the number of followers now approached almost half a million. The mentions were a mess, so he mostly ignored them, trying to keep his excitement in check at the verified celebrities who'd started retweeting Pyro Storm's missives. Knowing this sort of popularity was part of the slippery slope of becoming evil itself (a social media influencer), Nick absolutely did not consider sliding into the DMs of one of the retweeters, the dude who played a superhero on the big screen with a costume so tight it was basically an advertisement for circumcisions. Nick already had a boyfriend, and he was a real superhero who also happened to wear a skintight costume. Granted, it didn't give away whether Seth was circumcised or not (and Nick did *not* pull up the many, many photos he found of Pyro Storm to look closely, no sir!) but that was okay. It'd be like a fun surprise when they got around to . . . doing stuff. Which they would, eventually, right? What if something happened tonight? What if Seth was ready for hand stuff or butt stuff and Nick hadn't even prepared? What did one *do* with another person's penis, anyway?

"What are you looking at?" Dad asked.

"Nothing!" Nick cried, shoving his phone back into his pocket. "And I definitely wasn't looking up the differences between circumcised and uncircumcised penises, if that's what you were asking!"

"No," Dad said slowly. "I wasn't asking that at all. But now I think I need to. Nick, why were you looking up the differences between—"

Nick was saved when Dad pulled up to the curb a couple of spaces down from the Gray house. He was already out of the car and running up the pathway before Dad had even come to a stop. Pounding on the door, he shifted from one foot to the other, glancing back at Dad, who was stepping out of the SUV and demanding Nick answer his question *right this second*, and that he shouldn't be looking up *anything* about penises.

"Oh my *god*, Dad!" Nick bellowed. "Would you stop shouting about penises in public?" What the hell was taking them so long to answer the goddamn door?

Dad reached him before anyone let them in. "You're wearing a dead magician's suit to prom. Nothing I could say could possibly embarrass you. I have something for you."

"Would you stop calling it—ooh. Present. Give it." He held out his hand, wiggling his fingers.

Dad reached into the pocket of his slacks, something plastic crinkling as he pulled his hand back out. Slacks. Weird. And a button-down. Nick frowned. Why was Dad so dressed up? When he wasn't at work, Dad was a jeans-and-shirt sort of man. Before Nick could ask (a brief thought, dangerous and bright: what if he had a *date*?) Dad dropped whatever he'd pulled from his pocket into Nick's hand.

For a second, Nick thought it was a wet wipe wrapped in plastic. Or candy. A mint to keep Nick's breath fresh? It certainly didn't feel like a mint. And there were . . . three of them? All squishy, almost wet, like it was . . . like it . . .

No. No, no, no.

Nick's eyes bulged as he stared down at the condoms in his hand. "What," he whispered, "in the fresh hell is *this*?"

"Just in case," Dad said as if he hadn't blown Nick's mind, and not in a good way. "I don't know what you and Seth are going to get up to, but it's better to be prepared. Always wrap it. They're also lubricated. You're welcome."

Unfortunately, the next words out of Nick's mouth were, "But we're both virgins!"

The skin under Dad's left eye twitched. "That doesn't matter. Use condom sense, Nick."

Nick slumped against the door, legs wobbly. "Did you—did you just make a dad joke about condoms?"

"I did. And I regret nothing."

"Dad, *no*."

"Dad, *yes*. Don't be an idiot, kid. It doesn't matter if you're virgins or not. Get used to needing condoms. The sooner you get that through your head, the sooner you can have something in your—"

"Remember the touching moment we had back at home when you cried and then we hugged?"

"You mean twenty minutes ago?"

"I take it *back*," Nick said savagely.

"Oh no," Dad said. "Anything but that."

"Why is no one answering the damn door?" Nick growled, shoving the condoms in his pocket. He banged his hand on the door again, hoping they hadn't been overheard. Nick almost wanted to tell his father that he and Jazz had already gone and bought condoms last weekend just to see the look on his face, but the less said about that adventure, the better. Suffice to say, it'd ended with Nick throwing crumpled money at the startled clerk at CVS before fleeing, box of condoms in hand. Unfortunately, the automatic sliding doors hadn't opened as quickly as Nick had been running, and Jazz said she'd never seen someone bounce off glass so hard before. Not one of his prouder moments.

"Hold your horses," Nick heard Bob call from inside the house. "I can only move so fast, my goodness." The door opened, and Bob grinned out at them. "About time! Everyone else is already here. Come in, come in. Aaron, nice to see you. Nick, you look—" He choked as Nick stalked inside, suit glittering. "Wow. Now *that* is a suit. Good lord. I don't know what statement you're trying to make, but you sure are making it."

"Thank you," Nick said. "That's very nice of you to say. The color of my lapels is called eggplant, according to the clerk at the suit rental place."

Bob recovered as he shut the door behind him. "The girls are getting their pictures taken. Figure when Seth comes down, we can get a few more before we head out."

"'We'?" Nick asked. It was only then that he noticed that Bob was a little more cleaned up than usual. Gone were his overalls. Instead, he wore a pair of khakis and a nice sweater that hugged his shoulders. "What do you mean *we* head out? Dad's dropping us off at the restaurant, and then we're taking a Lyft to prom. Where are you going?"

"You didn't tell him?" Bob asked, glancing at Dad.

Dad shrugged. "Figured it'd be better if I told him here. That way, he wouldn't yell at me because we're at someone else's house."

"Oh boy," Bob said, gazing intently at Nick. "Okay, I want to see the look on his face. Go ahead."

"Dad?" Nick asked. "What's he talking about?"

"Nothing big," Dad said. "You won't even know we're there."

That didn't sound good. "Know you're *where*?"

"Prom," Dad said cheerfully. "Martha and Bob came up with the idea—"

Bob snorted. "Don't you dare try to pin this on us. It was all you. Wouldn't want to deprive you of the credit."

"We're part of the chaperone team," Dad said. "The school put out a call a few weeks back, asking for parents to volunteer." He shrugged. "I signed up. And then Bob and Martha did too." He smiled. "And I couldn't let Gibby's and Jazz's parents feel left out, so they decided to volunteer as well."

Nick said, "What."

"You won't see us," Dad said. He leaned forward, his face inches from Nick's own, his voice a whisper. "But we will be there, watching your every move." He glanced pointedly at Nick's coat pocket, where he'd put the condoms.

Nick shoved Dad away as he burst into laughter. "I can't believe you—this is such a violation of—do you enjoy seeing me suffer? Is that what this is?"

"Yes," Dad said. "That's exactly it." He sobered slightly. "But also, to make sure nothing happens. Not that I think it *will*," he added as Nick started to sputter angrily. "A precaution, and nothing more, especially with this whole bounty business. I promise I won't try to talk to you. No one will even know we're related. Especially with you in that suit."

"Whatever," Nick said. "I'm done with you." He pushed his way past Bob into the living room, where Gibby's and Jazz's parents were standing in front of the girls. He was about to demand that they find something else to do for the night when Trey and Aysha Gibson moved to the left, and Miles and Joanna Kensington moved right.

Nick's lament died a quick death in his throat at the sight of his girls. He'd already seen their fancy outfits at the shop, but somehow, they looked even better now: Jazz, in her lacy, flowing dress, and Gibby in her old-fashioned tuxedo, her bow tie matching the colors Jazz wore. She'd even found a red wallet chain, which dangled on her right hip. Fixed to her chest was a rose boutonniere, held in place by a safety pin. Jazz had a corsage made up of a rose on a bed of baby's breath.

"Holy shit," Nick breathed. "You two look freaking *rad*."

Gibby tipped her top hat at him as Jazz curtsied wonderfully. "Thank you," Jazz said. "You clean up good too, Nicky." She leaned forward, kissing his cheek before wiping away the smudge left from her lipstick.

"Seriously," Nick said. "Everyone is going to be super jealous of us. We're going to be the best-dressed people there. That's a thing that happens at prom, right? Best-dressed group of four award or something? Because we've already locked that shit down."

Gibby reached out and straightened Nick's bow tie. "I'd like to *not* be the center of attention, at least for one night, if that's all right with you."

"Yeah," Nick said, admiring Gibby's tux. "That sounds good to me. What would make it even better is if our *parents weren't going to be there*."

"What," Jazz said.

"What," Gibby said.

"Surprise!" Miles said. "We all get to go to your prom too." He wrapped an arm around his wife's waist. "Chaperones for the win!"

"Daddy," Jazz said with a pout. "You should've told me. What if I want to do something that you don't approve of?"

"Then you probably shouldn't do it," Miles said. "Seems simple enough."

"You probably won't even see us," Aysha said, snapping photo after photo. "We'll skulk in the shadows with all the other chaperones."

"And we're going to dance too," Trey said. "I've been practicing the worm, and I think I've almost got it. Miles and Aaron are probably going to do it with me."

"Dad, *no*," Gibby said.

"Dad, *yes*," Trey and Miles and Dad all said at the same time.

Martha appeared in the entryway to the living room, smiling widely. She looked around the room, gaze settling on Nick. She crooked a finger in his direction, beckoning him toward her. He went, shooting a glare at his father, who ignored him as if he couldn't feel the heat of Nick's eyes.

"Look at you," Martha said when Nick stopped in front of her. "Only you could pull off a suit like that. Quite handsome."

"Thank you. I'm getting that a lot. It's hard being this pretty." He sighed as he looked her up and down. She wore a dress the color of storm clouds. "You look nice, too, but I guess that means that you're doing the whole chaperone thing. Neat."

"I'll ignore that last part and say thank you for the compliment." She steered him toward the stairs. "He's a little nervous."

Nick blinked. "Seth? Why?"

Martha chuckled. "He's got it in his head that tonight has to be perfect to make up for the last few weeks. I told him he shouldn't worry too much, but you know how he is."

Nick did, and while he hadn't exactly been nervous before, he was now. He didn't know why. "As long as we're together, nothing else matters."

Martha watched him for a long moment before sniffling. "Oh, I promised myself I wouldn't cry, but you don't know how much I needed to hear that. Thank you, Nick."

Nick was confused. "For what? I didn't do anything."

She wiped her eyes. "Never you mind. Keep on being you, no matter what. That's all I ask for."

"I don't know how to be anyone else," Nick said honestly. "Warts and all."

"I like what you call your warts. They're part of the boy you are, and I happen to love that boy very much."

"Oh," Nick said, flushing as he shuffled his feet. "I—uh, I love you too?"

Wrong thing to say, seeing as how Martha hugged him tightly, her chest hitching once, twice before she pulled away, shaking her head. "I'm happy he has someone like you. Protect each other. Care for each other, and you'll never be left wanting."

"We always do," Nick said, ready for the explosion of parental emotions to be over. "Is he still upstairs? Do you want me to . . . go . . . get . . . *wow*." The last word came out breathy and soft, a sigh that crawled from Nick's throat.

Seth Gray stood at the top of the stairs, looking down at them, a question on his face as he glanced at his aunt. She waved him off, taking a step back, but she might as well have disappeared for all Nick knew, because everything disappeared—the sound of the people in the living room, the house itself, the city, the world. All that existed was Seth. Heart in his throat, Nick tracked every step Seth took down the stairs.

His slacks pulled tight against the muscles in his thighs, his suit coat buttoned up the front of his broad chest. His purple bow tie (*Eggplant*, Nick thought hysterically, *such a gross food*) matched the pocket square folded into the top pocket of the suit. His shoes were shiny, and Nick couldn't think of a single phrase that didn't involve something the adults in the room wouldn't appreciate, seeing as how much of it was aggressively filthy. He watched as Seth's curls bounced, the ends of which looked wet, as if Seth had just come from the shower.

Nick realized his mouth was hanging open as Seth reached the bottom of the stairs.

"Hi, Nicky," Seth mumbled, looking down at the floor between them.

"Oh my god," Nick breathed. "How dare you look that hot without a damn warning first. What in the actual hell are you doing with *me*?"

Seth chuckled as he glanced up shyly at Nick over the tops of his glasses, something Nick didn't know was a kink of his until right this very moment. Seth seemed pleased, his cheeks reddening as he reached out and tugged on the lapels of Nick's coat. "I'm with you because I want to be. And because you're pretty hot yourself."

"I won't question your tastes then," Nick croaked out. "Because

I'm wearing a dead magician's suit and don't want to make you change your mind."

"I wouldn't," Seth said. "Even though you're wearing a dead magician's suit."

Nick knew it was almost time. Almost time to tell Seth everything he felt, everything that was practically bursting in his head and chest. Not quite yet, but soon. Tonight. When they were slow dancing, perhaps in a corner away from everyone else. He'd say those three little words that scared the hell out of him, but that he knew he felt down to his bones.

"Nick?" Seth asked.

"Sorry," Nick said hastily. "Sorry. Just . . . thank you."

Seth arched an eyebrow. "For what?"

"Existing," Nick said honestly. "For being my best friend. For being my boyfriend. For being you."

Seth laughed bright and loud, and Nick was entranced. He watched Seth lean forward until he was kissing him sweetly. Seth tasted like toothpaste. Nick was going to devour him.

It was only then that Nick saw the clear plastic box in Seth's hand. Inside sat two violets held together by a pin and wrapped in a black band of satin. "Is that for me?"

Seth nodded, fumbling with the box, fingers shaking. "Yeah. Uh, the boutonniere, like we talked about?"

Nick panicked. "Right. Right. The boutonniere. Like we talked about. That one. I'll . . ." Oh crap. Had he forgotten it? It was in the fridge, and he couldn't remember if he'd taken it out. Dammit. Prom was going to be ruined because Nick couldn't keep his head on straight, and Seth was going to be disappointed when—

Something was thrust into Nick's hand, and he looked back and saw his father standing behind him, holding Nick's backpack. Nick looked down, and there, in his hand, was a plastic box like the one Seth held.

"Thanks," Nick said, breathing a sigh of relief. He lifted the box to pull the boutonniere out, but his hands were shaking too hard, and he almost dropped it. Dad and Bob appeared before he could stab Seth in the chest with the pin. Dad took the box from Nick, Bob from Seth. Then they exchanged them, the plastic crackling. They pulled them out at the same time, and Martha stepped forward, taking the empty boxes. Nick heard everyone gathering in the entryway, but he couldn't focus on them because Dad was in front of him, pinning the boutonniere against his chest. Bob did the same to Seth, whispering quietly to him, words just for them as Seth nodded, head jerking up and down.

When they finished, Nick was stunned to see Bob—grizzled, kind Bob—tearing up as he stepped back. "Look at you," Bob said roughly. "You look like your father. I wish they could be here to see all that you've become."

Seth smiled a watery smile. "Me too. But I've got you, so I think I'm doing okay."

More tears fell from most of the adults in the room as they posed for photographs. The only person *not* outwardly teary was Miles, but even he had to blow his nose into a kerchief as Jo took pictures of Gibby standing behind Jazz, hands on her waist.

Finally, Jazz said, "We need to go. Our reservation is at six, and I don't want our war against Ireland to be in vain."

"War?" Bob asked, brow furrowing.

"She's kidding," Miles said. "Sort of. A diplomatic issue, but I've taken care of it. We're all good. Get appetizers. Get all the appetizers you want."

The adults gathered on the porch, calling out to them, waving and saying they'd see them all soon. Jo continued to take photo after photo. Nick made to follow his friends down the stairs but stopped when Aysha grabbed Dad by the arm.

"We're trusting you with our daughter," Aysha said in a low voice, the warning clear. "We care about you, Aaron, but please don't mistake our affection for forgiveness. We're not happy with what you kept from us, or what you represent. It's going to take us time."

Nick bristled, and at one point, he might've come to Dad's defense, but he shoved his irritation away. She and Trey were right to say what they did. Dad had messed up, and not only because of what he'd kept from Jazz's and Gibby's parents. It went much further than that. Nick couldn't defend his father against their words, not when they spoke the truth.

Dad nodded. "I understand, Aysha. I have to work to earn back your trust, if I ever do. I know it may not seem like much, but you have my word that I'll protect them as much as I would Nick."

Aysha paused a beat before nodding and dropping her hand. "All right. We'll hold you to that promise." She sighed when Trey took her hand. "We can worry about the rest later. Get our kids where they need to go. Don't want a war with Ireland. We'd probably lose."

Dad nodded before descending the stairs, nudging Nick along.

"She's right, you know," Nick muttered as they walked toward the SUV where Gibby had opened the door for Jazz, bowing low, much to her delight. "Both of them are."

"I know," Dad said quietly. "They're absolutely allowed to be angry with me, same as you. I messed up. The best thing I can do now is own it and make sure it doesn't happen again."

"Can you do that?"

Dad stopped and glanced at Nick. Nick didn't look away. "I'm gonna tell you the same thing I told them at our meeting."

"Support group meeting," Nick said with disdain.

"Do you want to hear this or not?" He waited a moment as Nick closed his mouth. "I told them that I—okay. Not *understand* where they're coming from, because that isn't fair to them, but that I was listening. It's not up to Aysha and Trey to teach me anything because that takes the weight of it off me and puts it on them, and they don't deserve that. I have to be the one to make things right as best I can."

"What does that mean?" Nick asked.

"I don't know yet," Dad said. "But when I do, I'll let you know. I promise."

"I'll hold you to that," Nick said, nudging his shoe against Dad's.

Dad laid an arm around Nick's shoulders as he chuckled. "I'm counting on it, Nicky. Let's get you where you need to be. And remember what I told you: no one in their right mind pays twenty bucks for a glass of water. But if you really have to, I've put money in your account."

"Thanks, Dad."

Dad pulled him close. "Anytime, kid."

17

They didn't talk about Simon Burke.

That was something Nick would remember, despite all that would happen this night.

They didn't talk about Simon Burke. They didn't talk about Owen Burke. They didn't talk about superpowers or fanfiction. They didn't talk about potential Extraordinary names for Nick. They didn't talk about Miss Conduct or TK or anyone else out in the world who could do things that most only dreamed about. They didn't talk about Lighthouse or Team Pyro Storm or any battles on bridges. No one mentioned Jenny Bell or Guardian or dads who made deals with the devil in order to keep their children safe. There was no discussion about pills that gave people powers or pills that took powers away. No one mentioned ADHD or flying cups or secret lairs hidden behind pocket doors.

For eighty-seven minutes, Nick and Seth and Jazz and Gibby did what most teenagers did on prom night: dressed up in their best and ate at a restaurant whose menu was *not* laminated and instead was the size of a cell phone, with tiny print listing things that no one aside from Jazz could pronounce and didn't have any prices. They made fun of Seth when he decided he was going to order something called Wagyu bolognese that cost eighty bucks and ended up tasting like Hamburger Helper.

They gagged when Jazz ate oysters, the meat sliding from the shell into her mouth, juice dripping down her chin.

They grinned when Nick drank twenty-dollar water only to find out it tasted exactly like water from the tap.

They applauded when Gibby decided that life was too short and ordered calamari, complete with suckers still attached to the fried, rubbery tentacles. She ate them all, and by the end announced that they were her favorite food.

They blushed (at least, Nick and Seth did) when a man with a violin appeared at their table, the music sweet and romantic, Seth reaching under the table and taking Nick's hand in his, squeezing tightly, his eyes glittering in the low light as he looked at Nick.

And dessert! They ordered dessert—chocolate something—that ended up being too rich. They ate all of it anyway, spoons scraping against the plate on the table between them. Jazz fed Gibby, getting chocolate on her nose and cheek. Gibby didn't seem to mind, even if she grumbled about it.

And through it all, they just . . . existed. Seth and Jazz and Nick listened as Gibby plotted out her future, the plans still tenuous but her excitement palpable as she waved her hands. They listened as Jazz gushed about the speech Gibby was writing when she would take the stage as valedictorian, though no manner of begging would make Gibby recite what she'd written so far. Nick watched her roll her eyes at his insistence and laughed until he couldn't breathe.

As the last of the dishes were taken away, Seth raised his glass of sparkling cider and said, "A toast."

The others raised their own glasses, watching, waiting.

He said, "I don't know where I'd be without all of you. For the longest time, I thought I had to do this alone. That it'd be easier. I was wrong. The only reason I've gotten as far as I have is because of you. Thank you for being there for me. For being there for each other. We may not be popular or know what the hell we're doing, but as long as we're together, I know we're gonna be all right."

"Damn right we will," Gibby said. "And even though I'll be at a different school next year, I'm not going to let you idiots get in trouble without me. Yeah, I'll be in college and therefore much more mature, but I promise I'll still make time for my friends."

"Then we'll graduate too," Jazz said. "And we'll follow Gibby and get an apartment in the city where we'll live together and protect people from other people making stupid decisions, like trying to take over Nova City by murdering all of us horribly."

They laughed and then looked to Nick.

Nick, who was so full of love for each and every one of them, so much so that the words were stuck. He swallowed thickly, shaking his head. Clearing his throat, he said, "Paths diverge. People change. There may come a day when we go off in different directions, but today isn't that day. And I don't want to be anywhere else but right here, with you."

They clinked their glasses together, each of them drinking deeply.

Their waiter appeared out of nowhere, eyeing Nick's suit with what could either be disdain or absolute jealousy. Nick preferred to think it was the latter. The waiter smiled at them before setting down a small black folder on the table. "Whenever you're ready," he said, taking away their discarded plates and silverware.

Nick made to grab the folder, only to have it plucked out of his hands by Jazz. "Don't worry about it," she said. "It's on me."

"Oh, thank god," Nick said. "I mean, are you sure?"

Jazz rolled her eyes. "What's the point of having parents who are rich if you don't take advantage of it?" She paused, considering. "Besides, we still have an entire night ahead of us, and I won't have that ruined by you overreacting if you saw how much the bill is."

"It can't be that bad," Gibby said, grabbing the folder and looking down at it as she opened it up. She then snapped it closed immediately and handed it back to Jazz. "Okay, it was that bad. What the f—"

Jazz sniffed daintily. "No need for that kind of language."

"Now I want to see," Seth said. He took the folder from Jazz, and Nick looked over his shoulder. When he found the total at the bottom of the receipt, the blood drained from his face.

Jazz sighed. "See? That's why I said to let me handle it."

"Ireland is going to straight-up murder us," Nick said, getting riled up. "They're going to come here with their storied history and their elegant way of speaking and kill us all until there's nothing left but bone and gristle, and we'll *deserve* it."

He startled when Seth burst out laughing. He looked over to see Seth wrapping his arms around his stomach, tears leaking from his eyes as he laughed. Nick's diatribe melted almost immediately at the sight of Seth Gray laughing, laughing, laughing, as if he didn't have a care in the world. Maybe this was his super-power. Forget the ADHD or the telekinesis, at least for a moment. Maybe Nick's superpower all along had been his ability to make Seth laugh like nothing else mattered. Not a bad power to have, in the long run. And one most people didn't possess.

They stood in front of the restaurant, bundled up against the cold as they waited for the car to arrive. People moved around them, Gibby standing behind Jazz, her chin hooked over Jazz's shoulder. Nick and Seth were side by side, their hands joined between them. They spoke of nothing in particular, Nick closing his eyes and letting the sounds of his friends and the city wash over him.

Something tickled the back of his mind, a light caress from ghostly fingers, familiar and sweet. He opened his eyes, brow furrowed. He looked around. No one was there. He looked up at the buildings that rose above them. Nothing.

"Nick."

He lowered his head. Gibby and Jazz were walking toward a white SUV that had pulled up to the curb. Seth was looking at him, a question on his face. "What's up?"

Nick forced a smile. "Nothing. I thought—" He shook his head. "Doesn't matter. Got lost in my own head."

Seth nodded slowly. "You sure?"

"Yeah. Jazz, Gibby, move your butts over because we're both getting in the back seat with you."

As Seth climbed into the SUV, Nick looked around once more. Nothing.

He followed his friends into the SUV.

Centennial High had been transformed. It was still obviously just the cafeteria where they ate lunch every day, but it looked as if it'd been given a makeover involving an entire cadre of dead magicians.

A banner above the entrance to the cafeteria announced STARRY NIGHTS! WISH UPON THE STARS AND ALL YOUR DREAMS WILL COME TRUE! Nick thought it was a little over the top, but then he'd never been on a prom committee. It absolutely did not help that underneath those words were smaller words that read ALSO FIERY NIGHTS, JUST IN CASE PYRO STORM SHOWS UP!

Nick glared at the banner as they handed their tickets over to a particularly disgruntled woman who looked like teenage happiness was the bane of her existence. "No drinking," she told them. "No drugs. No dirty dancing. No fornicating. Keep it clean, keep it safe."

"Darn," Nick said. "What am I going to do with all these tabs of acid that I'm obviously joking about, so please stop rising from your chair like you're going to kick me out. Oh my god, I was *joking*. I don't even know where to get acid."

The woman sat back down, glaring at Nick. "No drugs!"

"He was kidding," Seth said hastily. "He doesn't do drugs."

"Only the legal kind," Nick promised her. "That were prescribed by a doctor not associated with Burke Pharmaceuticals. I need them because of my brain."

"Stop. *Talking*," Gibby growled. "If you get us kicked out before we even go in, I'm going to let Jazz stab you with one of her heels."

"Go through security," the woman barked, waving them away. "No funny business!"

"Some people can't take a joke," Nick mumbled as they got in the line that led toward the cafeteria. At the front of the line were three teachers going through purses and pockets. "Remember when we could go to school without worrying about people wanting to kill us?"

"No," Jazz said. "Because I can't remember a time when I didn't have to walk through metal detectors in order to get to class."

"Or people not liking the color of my skin," Gibby said.

When it was finally their turn, Nick didn't argue as he was patted down (though he did snap to be careful with his suit), watching as Jazz's purse was riffled through.

The usual lunch tables had been removed, replaced by round tables covered in tablecloths that shimmered under the strings of lights that had been stretched all around the cafeteria. Atop the tables sat bunches of fake white flowers, each of their petals covered in sequins not unlike those on Nick's suit. The tables lined one half of the room, the other half left open as a dance floor, though only a few were dancing so far, the DJ against the wall trying to hype everyone up to no avail. The ceiling had been covered with glow-in-the-dark stars, an entire galaxy complete with a wombat constellation, though it looked diseased and was missing a limb. Someone had apparently thought a fog machine was a good idea and white smoke billowed across the floor, swirling as people moved through it.

Waiters in snappy dress clothes and bow ties moved between the tables, carrying trays of sparkling water and little sandwiches that Nick thought were probably made in the cafeteria.

The heating system was apparently on full blast, and Nick wiped sweat from his brow as Seth led them toward an empty table near the back, pulling a chair out for Jazz and then one for Gibby, who snorted but didn't say anything as she sat down next to Jazz.

Not to be outdone, Nick did the same for Seth, who grinned at him before taking a seat. As Nick sat down, he looked around the cafeteria, trying to see where their parents were so they could actively avoid them at all costs. It was crowded, the sounds of voices and terrible dance music bouncing off the walls around them. Nick thought he saw Bob and Martha against the far wall, but there were too many people to be sure. He was distracted by one of the waiters who moved between the tables, expertly carrying a tray. The man was slim and moved with the grace of a dancer. Nick couldn't quite make out his face in the low light. He didn't know why, but the man seemed familiar somehow.

"What is it?" Seth whispered to him, bringing his attention back to the table.

"Thought I saw someone I knew," Nick said. "One of the waiters."

Seth turned to look out at the crowd. "Who did you think he was?"

Nick shrugged. "Don't know. Probably seeing things. No big deal."

"It better not be," Jazz said, "because I have plans tonight. First, I'm going to dance with Gibby—Seth, you'll be with Nick. Then we're going to switch partners and dance with each other. I want at *least* two dances with the both of you. Gibby, you get more because you're my girlfriend and I want to get freaky."

"Your mom and dad are here," Nick reminded her.

Jazz scoffed. "That's not my problem. If they didn't want to see it, then they shouldn't have come here."

"But"—Nick sputtered—"but—your *virtue*."

"Took care of that a long time ago," Gibby said, leaning back in her chair and grinning smugly. "Broke it into pieces without a twinge of regret."

"Speaking of regret," Nick mumbled. "I'm having a few of those right now for even asking."

"As you should," Jazz said. "Most everyone here is straight. It's our responsibility as the token queer kids to make sure everyone is slightly uncomfortable to the point where they'll need to have an honest conversation with themselves about their biases."

They stared at her.

"What?" she asked. "Do I have something on my face?" She reached into her purse, pulled out a compact, and snapped it open. She pursed her lips at her reflection. "Nope. I look amazing, as expected." She put the compact back in her purse. "What about the two of you?"

"What about us?" Seth asked.

Jazz sighed as if she couldn't deal with the stupidity of boys. "Are you two going to . . . you know." She waggled her eyebrows.

Confused, Nick asked, "Going to what?"

Gibby turned her face toward the ceiling. "It's like we're dealing with puppies. Sweet, dumb little puppies."

"Nick," Jazz said. "We've talked about this. Tonight is a magical night. Perhaps you and Seth will be slow dancing, and then he'll lean closer, and you'll lean closer and whisper—"

"Oh my god," Nick said loudly. "Are you talking about the *sex*?"

The occupants of the tables closest to them turned and looked at them.

Seth waved at them. "Hey. Having a good night? Us too. Obviously."

Panicking, Nick blurted, "My dad made a dad joke when he gave me condoms and I don't know how to feel about that. Like, mad? But also, a little proud? Because it shows the measure of a person to commit to a bit that hard. Also, that was a pun because of *hard* and *sex* and—"

"Your dad gave you condoms?" Seth said, face going pale. "Does he know what they're for?"

"Oof," Gibby said. "I really don't want to be here for this conversation."

"Of course he does," Nick said. "They're for making my life a living hell, just so he can get his kicks. They're in my pocket right now. I'll show you."

Seth grabbed his arm as Nick started to dig through his pocket. "Don't. We believe you. You don't need to show us condoms—and notice I'm not even asking *why* you have them."

"That's what I said. We're both virgins. You're not going to give me HPV, and even if you did, roughly eighty percent of sexually active people have it, and we could seek treatment togeth—"

Seth sighed. "Not what I meant, Nicky."

"Yeah," Gibby said. "I don't want to leave anymore. This is fine." She leaned forward, chin resting on her hands as she stared at Nick. "Keep going, Nicky. Did he give you lube too? Because you're not going to get too far without—"

"Just because you can make your own doesn't mean you need to relish in my discomfort," Nick snapped. Then, "Wow. I wish I hadn't said that."

Gibby squinted at him. "You really don't know anything about female anatomy, do you?"

"Of course not! I'm a gay man! Why the hell would I need to know about how you can—*mmph*!"

"Nope," Seth said, covering Nick's mouth with his hand. "Not today, not ever. Gibby, stop it. You're doing this on purpose."

"Try and prove it, Gray," Gibby said, her smile growing entirely too evil for Nick's liking.

"Dancing!" Jazz said shrilly. "There's going to be dancing, and whatever happens after will be between two consenting people, or it doesn't need to happen at all."

"I don't know about that," Gibby said gleefully. "Nick brought a condom, after all."

"I know how to make dental dams!" Nick announced rather hysterically. "My dad taught me! He—"

"—is coming over here!" Seth hissed, blood draining from his face. "Please stop talking about condoms and dental dams before he hears you!"

Nick whirled around in time to see Dad pushing his way through the crowd. When he saw Nick looking at him, he waved. "Nick! Hey, *Nick*! It's me, your dad! Your father! The man who helped create you!"

"Oh my god," Nick moaned, turning back around and slumping in his chair as if that would help. "My life is over."

"Nah," Gibby said. "It's not like you had much of a life to begin with."

"Just you wait," Nick warned her. "You and Jazz are going to be getting *freaky* and your parents will be right there, watching your lesbian mating dance. They'll probably even be taking pictures."

Gibby made a face. "Not cool, Nicky."

Before Nick could retort, Dad appeared at the table, looking far too pleased with himself. "Hey, didn't you hear me shouting for you? You looked right at me. Wasn't sure if you heard me or not."

"I heard you," Nick muttered. "Everyone heard you."

"Good," Dad said, patting Nick on the shoulder. "Then my job here is done."

"Which means you can probably leave, right?" Nick asked hopefully. "No need to stay any longer. You're old, which means you need sleep. Why don't you head on home and take the rest of the night off."

"Sorry, kid," Dad said. "I take this chaperone thing very seriously. We even got a ten-minute speech about what to watch out for and everything. Can't walk away from that." He plucked a glass from the tray of a passing waiter, raising it to his nose and sniffing. "Good. Hasn't been spiked, as far as I can tell. Don't take a drink and then leave it unattended. That's how they'll get you. Seth, you look like you're about to pass out. You all right?"

"*Dad.*"

"*Nick,*" Dad said in the same tone. "Yeah, yeah. I wanted to say hi. You won't even see me for the rest of the night." He smiled at Seth. "But I'll be seeing you. You can bet on that." He laughed as he ruffled Nick's hair before disappearing back into the crowd.

"He knows," Seth moaned. "He knows about the condoms."

"Well, yeah," Gibby said. "He's the one who gave them to Nick—which, I mean, I get the whole safe sex thing, but that feels like a boundary that shouldn't have been crossed. You guys have a weird relationship. Full offense."

"He's trying," Nick said as he deflated. "Maybe a little too hard. He thinks he needs to make up for all the crap we've been through."

"Is it working?" Jazz asked.

Nick wasn't sure. He hoped so, but he wasn't there yet. "I don't know." He looked at Gibby and Jazz. "How're things going with your parents?"

"Nice deflection, Nicky," Jazz said. She glanced at Gibby. "It's going. My parents are still a little—I don't know—starstruck, I guess, about what Seth can do."

"Mine are still pissed," Gibby admitted. "I think the support group helped a little, though. Dad said that Nick's father seemed to be listening to him and Mom. He's angry, but—"

"Can you blame him?" Nick asked. "Because I can't."

Gibby arched an eyebrow. "You've seemed to have done an about-face with the whole cop thing."

Nick picked at the tablecloth as he muttered, "Better late than never." He sighed. "No, that's not good enough. It shouldn't have taken this long. I have, like, years of hero worship to dismantle and work through that has nothing to do with Extraordinaries. I thought . . . I thought it was black and white, you know? Good guys, bad guys, a divide between them. I'm trying to figure out how to handle what happens when the good guys *are* the bad guys. I'm getting there, but it's harder than I expected it to be." He looked up at Gibby. "He's my dad, you know? It's confusing. I'm angry with him, but I also want to believe that he can still make things right."

"I hope so, Nicky," Gibby said quietly.

"We'll figure it out," Seth told them. "We have to, because it's the only way we'll make it through this."

"And it'll still be waiting for us tomorrow," Jazz said. "Tonight is about us." A new song began to play, some pop mess that grated on Nick's ears. Jazz, however, lit up, grabbing Gibby's hand and rising from her chair. "I love this song! We're going to go dance. Coming?"

Seth said, "We'll be there in a minute. I want to talk to Nick."

Jazz nodded, pulling Gibby toward the dance floor. Nick and Seth watched as Jazz threw her hands around Gibby's neck, pulling her close and rolling her hips expertly. Gibby bent forward, pressing her forehead against Jazz's, moving back and forth with the beat.

"I can't dance like that," Nick told Seth. "I think the bones in my hips are fused together, so—keep that in mind."

"Condoms," Seth blurted.

Nick turned slowly to look at him. "Uh—yes? What about them?"

Seth fidgeted in his chair. "Do . . . do you want to use them?"

Oh. *Oh.* Crap. Not where Nick thought this was going to go. And since Seth looked like he was borderline panicking, it was up to Nick to remain calm and levelheaded. Which is why he said (like a goddamn *boss*), "You want some of the Nick Experience?"

Seth gaped at him.

Nick winced. "That sounded a lot better in my head."

"Did it?" Seth asked. "Did it really?"

Nick took a deep breath, letting it out slow. "We don't have to do anything you don't want to."

That didn't seem to placate Seth in the slightest, especially since he began to pop his knuckles, something he only did when he was nervous. "What do *you* want?"

"I . . . don't know? Which might be an answer in and of itself." Nick stopped Seth from attempting to break his own hands. "Hey. Look at me."

Seth did, eyes wide.

Nick grinned at him. "We don't have to do anything we're not ready for. And even *if* one of us is ready, that doesn't mean the other has to be. This isn't a one-time thing. We've got the rest of our lives to figure it all out, so why worry about it now?"

"The rest of our lives," Seth repeated.

Nick shrugged. "Sure. So long as we don't wait until we're both thirty. I want to do things before then. Like, together."

"No, that's not—you really think we'll be together for the rest of our lives?"

Nick squinted at him. "Yes? Is that—isn't that what you want?" Uh-oh. "Or maybe you *don't* want that, and we're about to break up because you think you need to push me away to keep me safe, and I swear to god, Seth, if *that's* what this is, I'm going to complain so much, you'll regret ever thinking something so dumb. Don't you dare do—"

Seth laughed, a low sound that Nick felt down to his bones. Nick was in awe of him—the way the corners of his eyes crinkled, the way his teeth flashed, smile wide. "You're an idiot. I'm not going to break up with you." His smile faded slightly. "We've never—we've never really talked about what comes next."

Nick frowned. "Yeah, we have. All the time. Remember? We're going to go to school together, and then I'll open up my private investigation agency–slash-bakery, and you'll write true crime books or fiction or be a lawyer who makes sure people listen to voices they've dismissed for so long."

"You remember that," Seth whispered.

"Of course I do," Nick said. "Just because things have changed for the both of us doesn't mean we still can't have that. And honestly, I don't care what we do or where we go, as long as I'm with you."

"You mean it?"

Nick nodded. "We're in this together, Seth. And I'm not talking about the Extraordinaries thing. We're in this *life* together because we choose to be. You and me, we're a team. We have been ever since I found you on the swings. I need you to be by my side to make sure I don't do anything stupid that either gets me arrested or crushed by a Buick flung at me by a stupid villain."

"Those are two very different things."

"Figure I should cover all my bases," Nick said. He squeezed Seth's hand. "What I'm trying to say is that I go where you go. And until you tell me otherwise, that's the way it's gonna be."

"I won't," Seth said, cheeks reddening. "Tell you otherwise, I mean. I like that we're a team. I couldn't imagine it being anyone else."

"Damn right," Nick said. He looked around as the beat to the song slowed dramatically, the people on the dance floor coming together and swaying slowly.

He was about to point out to Seth that Jazz and Gibby were looking like they were about to make out aggressively when Seth stood from his chair, seemingly determined. Seth held out his hand and asked, "May I have this dance?"

Completely and ridiculously charmed, Nick said, "Yeah. Yes. But remember, I learned from Cap, and he wasn't messing around."

Seth pulled him up, walking backward, eyes on Nick as the crowed parted behind him. "Then I guess you'll be giving me a teaser of the Nick Experience."

Mouth dry, Nick could only nod.

Seth led them away from most of the other dancing couples and found an unoccupied corner of the dance floor. Unsure if he was supposed to lead or let Seth have the honor, he stood awkwardly, hoping for some last-second inspiration. The choice was taken from him when Seth positioned Nick's hand on his own waist. Seth then mirrored the position with his own hand on Nick's hip, bringing them close together with only a whisper between them. He clasped Nick's other hand, capturing it between them, his thumb brushing the skin of Nick's palm.

"Show me what you got, Nicky," Seth whispered, and Nick thought the rising temperature had nothing to do with whoever had cranked the heater up to ninety degrees.

They danced. Here, in this little corner of the world, they danced. It wasn't perfect, but then, Nick thought beautiful things didn't always have to be. The truth was in the awkwardness, the imperfection. It was in the way their knees knocked together, in the way Nick stepped on Seth's feet a time or two. About to apologize, Nick stopped when Seth leaned forward. "It's all right," he said, mouth near Nick's ear. "You're doing fine. You got this, Nicky."

He didn't know how much he needed to hear it until this very moment, and even though it was just a dance, it gave Nick courage. It gave Nick hope, something to hold on to, and there, on the tip of his tongue: those three little words like a lighthouse guiding him home.

They danced for what felt like hours, everything else falling away.

Perfect? Never.

Good? Always.

The song ended.

Seth grinned at him as he stepped back. And because he was the best sort of person, he bowed low in front of Nick, one hand behind his back, the other flourishing in front of him. Nick laughed—not at him, never at him. He laughed because he was happy.

A new song started, another infectious pop travesty where the bass rumbled through the floor and walls, crawling along Nick's sweat-slicked skin. Seth was pulled away by Jazz, and she shouted in joy as he spun her out expertly, their arms snapping. Before Nick could react, Gibby stood before him, a devilish smile on her face. "Let's see what you can do, Nicky," she said, taking her hands in his.

It wasn't like it was with Seth. The beat was faster, insistent, and Nick wasn't sure what to do with his arms or legs—especially when Gibby started moving like liquid smoke, something Nick would never be able to emulate, even with years of practice. But instead of worrying about how he looked, he let go. He raised his arms above his head, shimmying his hips, much to Gibby's delight.

Then she was gone, and Jazz was in front of him. She put her hands on his shoulders, and Nick blushed furiously when she slid down his front, dropping low before rising back up slowly. She turned her back to him, her hair in his face as they moved together. Nick placed his hands on her deadly hips, feeling them as they swayed from side to side. There were others around them, the dance floor now crowded, but Nick paid them no mind, his sole focus on the way Jazz felt against him, Gibby and Seth in their periphery, Seth's hands around the back of Gibby's neck, hers on his waist. They all bumped together, moved together, dancing, dancing, and in the back of Nick's mind, a thought like a comet shooting through his head—

We'll always stand together. No matter what. Nothing can stop us. Not now, not ever.

Another slow song. He danced with Gibby, neither of them speaking.

Another fast song. He danced with Jazz, her eyes sparkling.

And then Seth was in front of him again, and Nick knew it was time. It had to be. It was now or never. Seth deserved it. He deserved everything good, and if Nick could add to that, if he could be part of it, then he had to give Seth his all.

He was nervous, yes, but it was a *good* kind of nervous, the kind where the butterflies in his stomach felt like they were on fire. He was burning from the inside out, and it had nothing to do with Extraordinaries or Pyro Storm. It was because of Seth.

Nick took a deep breath, letting it out slow as he and Seth swayed from side to side.

He said, "Seth?"

Seth smiled quietly at him. "Yeah?"

"I need to tell you something. Something big."

"Okay."

"Okay?"

Seth shrugged. "Okay."

Nick nodded. His palms were sweating, and his breath caught in his chest. They stopped moving. He looked at Seth, standing in the middle of the dance floor, his bow tie slightly askew, his glasses fogged up from the heat. Now, now, *now.*

Nick squared his shoulders. He held his head up high. He looked at Seth and said, "I l—where's my dad going?"

Seth blinked. "What?"

Nick frowned as he looked beyond Seth, watching as his father practically ran from the cafeteria, heading for the doors that led further into the school. Dad looked as if he had his phone pressed against his ear, but Nick couldn't be sure. It was probably nothing. Cap, maybe. Or Officer Rookie. It didn't matter. It wasn't supposed to matter. Tonight was about *them*, not anything else.

Still. Something tickled at the back of Nick's mind, a feeling he couldn't quite place. It felt . . . off, somehow. Nick had learned a long time ago to trust his intuition. It might have led him astray a time or two, but often, that flutter in the back of his mind, that slick twist in his stomach, was something he'd learned to pay attention to.

"Stay right here," Nick said. "Don't move; I mean it. I'll be right back. Need to check if my dad is okay."

"You want me to go with?"

Nick shook his head. "Nah, it'll only take a minute. When I get back, I'm going to tell you something you need to hear." And because *Cosmo* taught him to always leave them wanting, he added, "Prepare to be amazed." With that, he pushed by Seth.

He didn't look back as he moved through the crowd, getting bumped and jostled, Seth calling after him, people looking annoyed as he apologized for an errant elbow. The music picked up again, vibrating down to his bones, the beat pulsing. He ground his teeth together as the pressure in his head began to build like he was getting one of his headaches. He hadn't had one of those in a few weeks, not since he'd gotten on the new meds.

He cleared the dance floor and glanced back to see Seth talking to Gibby and Jazz, saying something Nick couldn't hear.

As he was turning back toward the doors Dad had gone through, he crashed into someone. A waiter, his tray tumbling from his hands, glasses shattering on the floor, spraying liquid. The people closest to them turned and stared as Nick stuttered out an apology to the waiter, bending over to help him pick up the broken glass.

"It's all right," the waiter said with a sigh. "Happens to the best of us, honeybunch. Don't worry about it."

Honeybunch.

Nick raised his head slowly.

It was the same waiter he'd seen when they'd first arrived, the waiter who had looked familiar in ways Nick couldn't quite place. Even crouched down, the man was tall, slender, his dark hair falling over his forehead. He picked up the pieces of glass, setting them on the tray on the ground. He must have felt Nick watching him, because he looked up.

And realized exactly what Nick had.

"Oh shit," the man breathed.

"Miss Conduct?" Nick mouthed.

The man's eyes widened. "*Nick?* What the hell are you doing here?"

"This is my school! What are *you* doing here?"

The man—Miss Conduct—said, "Working. This is one of my jobs. I . . . oh my god. Is he here? Is Pyro Storm here too?"

"No," Nick said quickly. Miss Conduct arched an eyebrow. "Wait, yes, but that's not—why didn't you tell us you were going to be working at our prom?"

Miss Conduct rolled his eyes. "Do you know how many high schools there are in the city? How could I have possibly known I'd be working at yours? Besides, it was a last-minute thing. Got a message to pick up some hours. Someone called in sick or their goldfish died in a house fire or something, I don't know." He frowned. "The number wasn't one I recognized, but I don't usually ask questions when it comes to getting paid."

"That's the *perfect* time to ask questions!"

"Riiiight," Miss Conduct said, plucking up the last pieces of glass as he looked Nick up and down. "Killer suit, Nick. I approve."

"Oh, thank you. It belonged to a dead magician."

"That I believe."

"Miss Conduct, I need to—"

"Stop calling me that," he hissed. "Someone might hear you, and I thought we were supposed to be laying low. My name is Mateo."

"Mateo," Nick said, mind racing. "I'm sorry, but I have to go. I have to find my dad. He—"

"Go," Mateo said, lifting the tray from the ground as he stood. "I have work to do. We can talk later." He disappeared into the crowd, never looking back.

Nick stood, too, ignoring the people staring at him, whispering to each other. Something was wrong. He didn't know what, but he was going to find out.

18

The hallways of the school were mostly empty. Nick had never been at school this late before, and the sounds of his footsteps echoed around him, causing him to flinch even as the walls vibrated with the music coming from the cafeteria.

A woman was walking toward him, her head bowed, dark hair hanging around her face, large sunglasses covering her eyes. She wore jeans and a thick coat, a large purse dangling off her shoulders. Who the hell wore sunglasses indoors at night? She must have been one of the chaperones, on her way back from the restroom.

He stopped where one hallway intersected with another, head swiveling. Looking left, he saw a pair of doors that led to the back fields of the school. Two people stood in front of the doors, their backs to Nick. He couldn't see what they were doing, but they weren't Dad, so he looked right.

There, at the other end of the hall, was Dad.

He was pacing back and forth, shoulders stiff, phone still pressed against his ear. Nick hurried toward him, shoes squeaking along the linoleum.

A few other kids were standing near a row of lockers, the girls talking excitedly, the boys pretending to be cool and aloof with their suit coats hanging over one shoulder, chests puffed out like they were preening show dogs. None of them paid Nick any attention as he rushed by.

Dad raised his head at the sound of Nick's approach. The blood drained from his face. He looked as if he were going to say something, but whoever was on the other end of the phone distracted him. "I *get* that, Rook, but we can't be too careful. I need you to call Cap, you hear me? Call Cap and tell him—"

"Dad?" Nick asked, out of breath as he stopped in front of his father.

Dad held up a hand. "I know, Rook. But I don't think there's much we can do about it now. It's out of our jurisdiction. The police upstate will have to handle it until we get some idea of what he's planning. Right. Right. Keep me in the loop. I'm going to stick around here, just to be safe. I don't think he'll show his face, but it's better that we prepare."

Prepare for what? Whatever it was, it didn't sound good.

Dad said, "Right. Talk soon. No, don't worry about it. I'm glad you called. I'll—" The phone beeped against Dad's ear, and he frowned as he looked at the screen. "That's . . . weird. I lost service. What the—" He shoved the phone in his pocket, shaking his head, scowl deepening. "Nick, what are you doing out here? Go back inside with your friends."

"What happened?" Nick asked.

Dad hesitated. Nick could almost see the way his mind worked and the moment he decided to tell Nick some version of the truth. "It's . . . probably nothing, okay? And there's nothing we can do about it tonight, so go back inside."

Nick glared at him. "Would you tell me?"

"Kid, I—"

"We talked about this, remember? No more secrets."

Dad sighed, shaking his head. He looked exhausted, as if he'd aged years in the last ten minutes. "It's Owen. He broke out of the hospital earlier tonight. I don't know specifics because it's still early, but Rook was at the precinct when the call came in. He hurt a few people on his way out. One of the hospital staff, they . . . it doesn't look like they're going to make it."

No, no, no—"Burke," Nick choked out. "It was Simon Burke who—"

Dad shook his head. "That's what I asked, but no one knows anything right now. Maybe he had something to do with it, but do you really think Owen would want anything to do with his father after what he did?"

Nick couldn't breathe. His vision began to narrow as he gagged, bending over and clutching his waist. Bile rose in the back of his throat, acidic and hot. His brain shorted out, a synapse misfiring in an electrical snarl.

A hand on his back, strong and warm, rubbing up and down. "You're okay," he heard a voice say near his ear. "I've got you. Breathe, Nicky. Just breathe. In. *In*, kid. There you go—and— hold. One, two, three. Out. One, two, three. Again. Yeah, good. In—hold it—and out. Breathe with me. Big breaths. You got this."

Nick gasped, sucking in air. His lungs expanded painfully, but his head started to clear, the fog dissipating slightly. "H-how did this happen?"

"I don't know," Dad said again. "He was supposed to be under constant watch. All those lights." He paused. "Did Owen ever use his powers without the benefit of the pills?"

Nick shook his head, sweat trickling down his cheek. "He couldn't. It was only because of the pills that he could do what he did. Why?"

"Because of the shadows," Dad said quietly, still rubbing Nick's back. "Rook said he was told that Owen used shadows to—it doesn't matter. We'll figure it out. Regardless, there's no way Owen could get back here tonight."

"Bullshit," Nick spat. "If he has his powers again, that means he can fly. For all we know, he's on his way here right now. We have to tell the others."

"Sure, Nicky. Yeah, we'll do that, okay? Let's take a moment to—"

"Hello, Nick!"

Nick and his father spun around, looking down the hall from where the greeting had come.

The group of kids still stood against the lockers, but they hadn't been the ones to call out. They were looking further down the hall, toward the doors. The doors where two people stood, the same two people Nick had noticed when he'd come from the cafeteria.

A woman faced them, familiar even at a distance, hand raised in greeting as if she were the one who'd called out Nick's name. Crouched next to her, facing the doors, was a man, hand running along the seams between the two doors, leaving a thick coat of ice, freezing the doors together.

"Oh no," Nick whispered.

The twins. Christian and Christina.

Smoke and Ice.

Mr. Burke sends his regards.

Dad took a step toward them. "You there! Are you students here? What are you doing to the doors?"

Ice rose to his feet, joining Smoke. They wore matching suits, black with white dress shirts. Smoke's tie was a dark gray, and Ice's was blue. Smoke smiled wickedly as she cocked her head. "It's nice to see you again, Nick."

"Yes," Ice said. "So very nice."

Dad took another step toward them. "I don't know how you think you know my son, but I—I won't—" He stopped. "Where have I seen you before?"

Ice and Smoke exchanged a look before they both laughed, a flat, dull sound that echoed along the hallway. "Familiar?" Smoke asked.

"Yes," Ice said. "We are familiar, Aaron Bell. Very familiar."

"What's going on?" one of the boys at the lockers asked. "Is this part of the dance? I didn't know there was going to be a show too." He elbowed his friend. "Look at them."

His friend—a douchebro if there ever was one—laughed. "Weird, right?" He pushed himself off the locker, puffing out his chest. "Hey, freaks! What's wrong with you? Why are you talking like that?"

"Stop it, Micah," one of the girls said, sounding annoyed. "Don't be a dick. Nick's dad is right there."

"And?" Douchebro said. "What's he gonna do?"

"He's a cop."

Douchebro turned around, eyes wide. "Oh shit. The weed isn't mine! Please don't call my parents. Cornell will rescind my acceptance!"

"Get out of here," Nick snarled at them. "Tell everyone they have to get out of the school while they can!"

They went, the boys running as quick as they could, leaving their dates behind. One of the girls sighed irritably before motioning her friend to follow. She glanced at Ice and Smoke before looking at Nick and his dad. Nick thought she was going to say something else, but her friend pulled her along, back toward the cafeteria.

Ice and Smoke followed their exit, barely blinking. "Children," Ice said. "I like the children."

"No," Smoke said sharply. "Focus. We are here for the boy."

"What boy?" Dad asked.

Ice and Smoke snapped their heads toward Nick and his father. Without thinking, Nick took a step back. "Dad?"

"You shouldn't be here," Dad barked. "This is school grounds. You aren't welcome . . . here . . . what did you do to the door? Is that *ice*?"

"It is," Ice said. "Door's frozen. Like all the other doors. There is no escape. For you. For the boy."

"Dad!"

Dad looked back at Nick, frowning. *"What*, Nick? I'm trying to—"

"That's them!" Nick cried. "That's Smoke and Ice! They're working with Burke!"

Dad didn't hesitate. He went for his sidearm, cursing when he realized he didn't have it. He'd left it at home. It wasn't allowed in school, especially since he was off duty. Nick had watched as he'd stored it in the gun safe earlier that afternoon before they'd left the house. Instead, he moved in front of Nick, shielding him. Nick gripped his father's coat, hanging on for dear life, breath rattling in his chest.

"You can't have him," Dad snapped. "This is *my* kid. You want him, you'll have to go through me. And I promise you it'll be the last thing you do."

"Challenge," Smoke said, a small smile forming on her face. "We have been offered a challenge."

"We accept," Ice said. "We will go through you, Aaron Bell. You are expendable. And then we will have the boy. Pyro Storm will have no choice but to reveal himself. He will come, and we will be waiting."

They raised their hands in unison, palms facing Nick and Dad. Their fingers twitched. Behind them, Nick thought he saw someone peer around the corner. He only saw her for a moment. The woman he'd passed in the hallway. Dark hair. Sunglasses. The sunglasses were now sitting on top of her head, and in her hands, she held what looked like a small camera, pointed in their direction.

Rage like he'd never experienced before flooded his entire body, and he snarled, "Holy shit, you are the goddamn *worst*, Rebecca Fire—"

"Run!" Dad shouted as he spun on his heels. He grabbed Nick by the wrist, jerking him off his feet as he took off, running away from Smoke and Ice. Nick stumbled, looking back over his shoulder to see black clouds beginning to billow around Smoke's hands, ice crystalizing out of the air and floating in sharp spikes above Ice's head. Dad pulled Nick around the corner just as the spikes were hurtled toward them. One hit a row of lockers, denting the metal as the spike shattered. Another embedded itself into the wall, the plaster cracking.

Dad's grip tightened on Nick's arm to the point where Nick thought he'd be bruised if they survived this. "We have to lead them out of the school!" Nick cried. "Away from everyone else!"

Dad whipped his head back. "Where?"

Nick took the lead, Dad still holding onto him. The music still thumped through the walls, the bass heavy. Nick tore through the school, Dad close on his heels. They ran past darkened classrooms, past stairs that led to the second floor. Nick gave brief thought to getting the higher ground but dismissed it. He couldn't take the chance of getting trapped. He led Dad toward a side entrance the teachers used to access the parking lot.

"Work," he muttered to himself. "Goddammit, why don't you work?" He shook his free hand, trying to get his powers to do *something*. He squawked when Dad shoved his head down, another ice spike flying over his head and colliding with the wall in front of them. Particles of ice hit Nick's face as they rounded the corner. His teeth chattered at the sudden cold.

Ahead, the pair of double doors. The windows showed the parking lot outside, bathed in an angry shade of yellow-orange from the sodium arc lights that lined the lot.

"Yes!" Nick cried, running full tilt toward the doors. "Yes! Screw you, assholes! You can't—*dammit!*"

The doors were frozen shut, the ice thick over the handles and locks. Nick slammed into them, hoping the ice would shatter. The doors barely budged.

Trapped. They were trapped.

Dad let Nick go, hurrying toward the nearest interior door, but it was locked. He took two steps back before lifting his leg and slamming the bottom of his foot against the door. It rattled in its frame but didn't open.

A cloud of black smoke billowed around the corner before re-forming into Smoke. Ice appeared at her side, eyes glittering darkly. "Run, run, run," he said. "I do like it when they run." His smile stretched so wide Nick thought his face would tear in half.

"There," Smoke said. "Nowhere else to go. You tried, Aaron Bell. But we will have the boy. Pyro Storm will reveal himself. And then everyone will see who they both truly are."

Dad stepped in front of Nick once more. "I told you, you aren't going to touch him. I don't need powers to kick your asses."

"No?" Ice said. "Let us show you otherwise."

The air above Ice's head began to shift, hazy and snapping. Ice crystals appeared, gathering together, the temperature dropping around them. The particles swirled, forming the biggest spike of ice Nick had ever seen. It was at least four feet long, the end needle-sharp and aimed directly at them.

Rebecca Firestone skidded to a halt behind them, camera still pointed in their direction. Her cheeks were flushed, her wig sitting lopsided on her head.

"Help us!" Nick shouted at her.

"I can't!" she called back. "I'm a reporter, I can't get involved."

"Oh my god," Nick muttered. "I hate her so much."

"Bigger things to worry about, kid," Dad growled, never looking away from Smoke and Ice.

"Mr. Burke regrets that it has come to this," Ice said as his eyes slid unfocused, the spike hovering above his head as it grew even larger. "But you took from him, Nicholas. And now he will take from you. Say goodbye to your father."

Ice jerked his head, the spike quivering before hurtling toward them. Time slowed down around Nick, each second five beats of his heart. He watched as the spike grew bigger and bigger the closer it got, the sharp point glistening. Dad turned, but not away. Never away. He wrapped his entire body around Nick, clutching him tightly, Nick's face against his shoulder, eyes burning.

Shielding him. His father was shielding him. "I love you," Dad whispered in his ear. "Yesterday. Today. Tomorrow. I'll love you forever."

Mom laughing as the wind blew through her hair, the salt from the ocean thick on their tongues.

Nick between them, little Nick learning to walk, little Nick holding onto both their hands, demanding that they swing him up. They did.

The phone ringing, Dad on the other end saying *Nick, oh my god, she's gone, she's* gone.

Dad coming into his room late at night, Nick screaming in his sleep, a nightmare where she reached for him and he couldn't get to her. "You're all right," Dad whispered as his son sobbed against his chest. "I've got you."

Mom, dancing in the kitchen, an old song playing on the radio. "Nicky!" she cried happily when she saw him watching her. "Come sing with me." He went, of course.

The three of them walking through the city, Nick telling them a story that went on and on and on, but no one was telling him to shut up, no one was telling him to stop talking. *More, kid, tell us everything.*

Dad standing next to him, the lighthouse in the distance, an urn clutched between them.

All I ever wanted was to keep you safe.

"*No.*"

Nick lifted his head as he spoke, looking over Dad's shoulder, the knot in his head and chest untangling with ease, the strands sliding loose as he pulled and pulled and pulled. And there, in his chaos, a spark, burning brightly.

The ice spike stopped. Less than a foot away from Dad's back, the sharp point glistened. A drop of water fell from the tip, landing with a splash on the floor. Nick breathed in and Nick breathed out, and there, in his head, a tremendous pressure, deliciously painful. He grasped onto it, gritting his teeth against the heavy wave of hurt that flooded his head. But he was bigger than it was, stronger. He hadn't always been, but he was now. The pressure increased, and he pushed against it. It rippled like the surface of a lake. Resistant, but not so much that he couldn't force his way into it, to sink beneath the surface and submerge himself in all of it.

So that's what he did.

It closed up and over his head.

He should've drowned.

He didn't.

He was alive, *alive*, the spark in his head the beginning of a great fire. He didn't know how he hadn't seen it before. He was—

"In control," he whispered, and with all his might, he *pushed*.

The ice spike exploded with a fierce crack, the shards hitting the floor and bouncing away. Nick gently pushed his father to the side, Dad uncurling himself, the lines on his face smoothing out when he realized he hadn't been run through by the spike. He turned slowly as Nick moved around him.

Smoke and Ice watched Nick, and for the first time, they looked . . . unsure. No fear—not yet—but they hadn't expected Nick to be able to do what he'd done.

Good. They'd underestimated him. It would be their undoing.

"I knew it," Rebecca Firestone breathed. "I goddamn *knew* it! You're an Extraordinary too. You're—"

"You shouldn't have tried to hurt my dad," Nick said in a low voice. He glanced at the rows of lockers lining the hallway and *pushed* against the spark. The doors began to rattle, the metal clanging loudly. The rattling moved swiftly down the hallway until all the locker doors were bouncing, bouncing, and *there* was the fear. It started with Smoke, her eyes widening as she took a step back. Ice was frowning; he didn't yet understand what was happening. He raised his hands again, as if to send another spike their way.

"Don't," Nick warned.

But Ice didn't listen. His fingers twitched, ice forming in the air above him once again.

Nick pushed again.

The locker doors squealed as they tore from their hinges, metal creaking and groaning. Ice cried out when one of the doors slammed into his hip, almost knocking him off his feet. The lights in the hallway began to flicker as Ice was struck by another door, and then another, this last one drawing blood from the back of his hand, a cut that sprayed droplets against the wall.

Smoke dissipated, turning into a voluminous black cloud as the locker doors flew through her, hitting Ice again and again. Except now, the doors didn't bounce off Ice. No, they began to wrap *around* him, molding against his body. Two hit his legs, the metal shrieking as the doors folded around his feet and ankles, holding him in place. More doors crashed into his legs, then his waist, arms, pinning them to his sides. Ice cried out as the metal dug in, but Nick didn't stop. He couldn't stop. He didn't *want* to stop. One night. They couldn't even have *one night* where they weren't running or screaming or fighting for their lives.

It would be easy, Nick knew. So easy. All he had to do was wrap one of the locker doors around Ice's face and cut off his air. The metal would squeeze around Ice's head, and he'd be *terrified*, begging Nick to *stop, please, stop, please, I don't want to die.* Nick wouldn't listen. He wouldn't listen because this man, these people, had tried to hurt Seth. They had tried to hurt Miss Conduct and TK. They'd tried to kill his father.

And there, standing behind them, looking as scared as he'd ever seen her, was Rebecca Firestone, somehow still recording. He could finish her too. She'd made Seth's life miserable. She'd spread lies about the both of them. She was here, which meant she knew something. Maybe she was working with Burke. Maybe she was just stalking Nick. It didn't matter. If he took care of Smoke and Ice, he could handle Rebecca Firestone.

The lights flickered violently, the entire hallway rumbling, the floor cracking as Smoke's arms re-formed, pulling against the metal wrapping around Ice. Another door slammed against Ice's chest, crumpling and molding until it looked like he was wearing a metal straitjacket. Only his head was left. One more door. One more door and it would all be over for him. Then Nick would move on to Smoke, and he would be a hero. Rebecca Firestone had the footage, and though she looked like she was about to run, Nick could catch her. Stop her. Make her feel every ounce of suffering she'd brought down on his family, and then, oh, and *then,* he'd find Simon Burke. He would find him and make him pay for everything he'd done. For all his lies, for saying the name of Nick's mother like he had any right to, and when he begged for Nick to spare him, Nick would laugh in his goddamn *face,* and—

"Look at me," a voice said through the storm, through the sounds of the hallway breaking apart around them. "Look at me, kid. *Nick.*"

Familiar hands on his face, rough and warm and kind, thumbs rubbing against his cheeks. Nick blinked slowly as he broke through the surface, as the spark in his hands burned and burned and burned.

Dad said, "No, Nicky. No, no. That's enough. No more. Look at me. *Look at me, Nick.* I'm here. I'm here with you. We're okay, I promise."

"Dad?" Nick whispered as his father came into focus, brow furrowed, the worry lines deep. He looked *scared,* but Nick couldn't tell of what. Smoke? Ice? Nick himself? He didn't know, but it was enough to startle him, as if waking from a vivid dream.

Dad nodded. "There you go. It's all right."

Nick breathed in and out, the pressure in his head lessening slightly, enough so that he could think. It'd been close. So close.

"Listen to me," Dad said. "The ice broke on the doors. Go.

Don't call 911. I don't know who'll answer, and we can't take that chance. Call Cap directly. But *run*, you hear me?"

Nick was already shaking his head, even before Dad finished. "No. I can't leave my friends here. I can't leave *you* here——"

Dad jostled him. "They're coming for *you*, Nick. They want you and Pyro Storm, and I won't——"

For years after, Nick would remember the exact look on his father's face the moment a band of black smoke wrapped around Dad's chest. Shock and disbelief and anger. The nightmares Nick would have—brutal. His father was ripped away from him, flying backward as he reached forward for Nick. It happened so quickly. One moment, Dad was inches away from Nick, and then he was gone, hurtling through the air toward Smoke, her arms extended like smoky tentacles. Ice fell to the floor at her side with a metallic *thunk*.

"*DAD!*" Nick screamed.

Black smoke wrapped around Dad's mouth, cutting him off. He struggled—oh, how he struggled—but it was no use. The smoke that held him was too strong. For a moment, Nick flashed back to a bridge, to shadows rising around him, but it was lost in the storm in his head.

"No," Smoke said, and she sounded *furious*. "Not another step. You move, and I will crush him. Do you want to see what your father's insides look like?"

"Let him *go*," Nick snarled, the lights flickering again, the hallway rumbling.

"Strong," Smoke said, looking up at the lights. "He knew you'd be strong. But this is more. Mr. Burke will help you. Come—come with us. Let him show you the way. If you do, your father will be safe. If you do not, he will die. Your friends will die. Everyone at this school will die. It will be your fault."

"Kiss my damn ass," Nick growled, and reached for a small, red-and-white box embedded in the wall. He grabbed the handle, pulling it as hard as he could. It slid down with an audible snap. The second before the alarm blared, Nick, ever the badass, said the greatest mic drop in superhero history, in his most humble of opinions. "Where there's smoke, there's *fire*."

The alarm shrieked. The sound caught Smoke off guard. The column holding Dad loosened and he slipped toward the ground, the tips of his shoes scraping the floor. "Nick, goddammit, *run*!" Dad cried. Before he could say more, the band tightened around him again, covering him almost completely. Smoke pointed her other hand toward Ice, black clouds falling from her palm, landing on top of Ice and lifting him up off the floor, still surrounded by metal. Ice glared at Nick as he rose, floating next to Smoke.

Screams from the cafeteria as the dance music cut off. Startled, Nick jerked his head toward the sound.

Smoke used the distraction to turn and run back down the hall, Ice and Dad floating after her, the black clouds around them shifting angrily. Rebecca Firestone pressed her body flat against the wall, face screwed up in fear. They ignored her. Nick screamed for his father, but they had already rounded the corner, out of sight, leaving Nick standing alone in the ruined hallway, alarm blaring, lights flashing, rows of lockers bent and hanging at odd angles off the walls.

He glanced back over his shoulder. The ice covering the door had shattered. He could go. Do what Dad said. Call Cap. Call for help. It would be safer. It would be smarter.

Except this was Dad.

And Seth.

Gibby.

Jazz.

Their parents.

Mateo too.

Heroes didn't run away. They didn't leave their people behind. He was terrified, but it didn't feel important.

What was important was the way they took care of each other, had each other's backs no matter what. They were a team. They were a lighthouse, a beacon in the dark.

He turned away from the doors and took off down the hall where Smoke had disappeared with Dad and Ice, toward the sound of screams. As he ran, he found the name on his phone he was looking for and hit the call button, ready to bring in the cavalry.

The phone beeped in his ear. He pulled it away, looking at it in horror as he skidded to a stop. He had no service. He'd always had service in school, but now? No bars. It was useless.

He took off again, about to put his phone back in his pocket when it was knocked from his hands as he collided with a group of people running in the opposite direction.

Boys and girls, all dressed to the nines, their faces bloodless and panicked. Nick was shoved against the wall as his phone fell to the ground. It landed a few feet away, but before Nick could grab it, a tall boy stepped on it as he fled. The screen went black as it broke, pieces chipping off as it was kicked away.

Nick groaned. He'd just gotten that damn phone.

He tried to push himself up but was knocked back by the rushing crowd. He pressed his hands flat against the wall, ready to do what he had to in order to get to his father, when a hand wrapped around his wrist, pulling him up. He was about to thank the person when he saw who it was, and the words turned to dust and blew away.

Rebecca Firestone grinned at him, chest heaving. Her cheeks were flushed, her eyes sparkling. She must have chased after him down the hall. "I guess that makes us even."

Nick glared at her. "Are you out of your damn mind? Get the hell out of here with that nonsense, you hack. I saved you from falling off a bridge. We're not *close* to even. What are you doing here?"

"Following a story," she said, pushing a button on her camera before pointing it in Nick's face. "Care to explain what happened in the hallway? Quite a display of powers. When did they manifest? Is it telekinesis?"

"If you don't get that camera out of my face, I'm going to shove it up your—"

More screams from the cafeteria. Nick pushed by Rebecca Firestone, wishing that she'd be forced out with the crowd of people trying to flee. Whatever was happening, he hoped the fire alarm had given people some warning. As he pushed his way through the tide rushing against him, he looked for his team. No sign of any of them.

He winced as people crashed into him, elbowing him, hitting him in the chest, face, and stomach. He kept his head down as he continued, trying to yell above the noise for everyone to get out of his way.

Eventually, he made it to the doors that led to the cafeteria. They hung on their hinges. People stampeded through the doorway, practically climbing on top of each other. A girl fell to her knees, her dress tearing. Her cheek had a smear of blood on it, and Nick bent low, grabbing her by the arm and pulling her up. She gasped as he brought her to her feet. "Go!" Nick shouted at her. "Get out of here!"

She nodded and ran, never looking back.

Nick rushed into the cafeteria and stopped dead in his tracks. Rebecca Firestone crashed into his back, cursing.

Groups of students were huddled together against the walls, high schoolers clinging to each other as they looked on in horror.

Teachers and other chaperones stood in front of them, shielding them as best they could. The ones closest to the doors were shepherding people through, but most were cut off, trapped. The adults gathered the students close, holding them together.

And there, standing in the middle of the cafeteria, eyes blazing, was Pyro Storm.

He wore a costume Nick had never seen before: sleeker, tighter. It was black with red piping that ran up the sides of his legs and chest. He didn't have a cape, but a familiar flame symbol sat in the middle of his chest. His helmet was smoother, the lenses glowing a fierce shade of red that looked like fire. He bared his teeth, and he glanced at Nick rushing toward him, expression softening briefly.

"Where the hell did you get that?" Nick demanded breathlessly as he came to a stop in front of Pyro Storm, briefly ignoring the thundering chaos happening around them. "And when did you have time to *change*?"

"Kept it hidden from you at school," Pyro Storm growled, gaze still fixed upward. "Someone told me that sequels needed new costumes, so I've been waiting for the right moment to debut it."

"Where's—"

"Look *out*!" Pyro Storm shouted, shoving Nick. It felt like Nick had been hit by a truck as he flew back and hit the floor. Right where he'd been standing, a spike hit the ground, embedding itself into the floor, the ice glistening as water dripped from it.

Nick looked up.

Smoke and Ice floated near the ceiling. The metal that had covered Ice had fallen away, and he wasn't smiling. His face twisted in anger as he formed more spikes around his head. And there was Dad, pinned to the wall near the ceiling, dozens of feet above the floor, covered in a roiling black cloud. He struggled to no avail.

Hands gripped Nick's arms, pulling him up. Nick panicked and tried to pull away until he heard Gibby say, "Nick, *stop*, it's us!"

He looked around to see that Jazz and Gibby were supporting him. Gibby's suit coat was gone and her bow tie hung in tatters, the outer layer of lace on Jazz's dress had been torn away, but otherwise, they appeared unharmed. Furious, but unharmed.

"What the hell is going on?" Gibby demanded.

"Assholes," Nick snapped. "They're trying to unmask Seth."

People screamed when a heavy block of ice smashed into the ground, causing Pyro Storm to vault away before getting flattened. "Is that Rebecca *Firestone*?" Jazz demanded. "What is she doing here?"

"Forget her," Nick said. "My powers are on. I have to help—"

"Go," Gibby said. "If they're after you, we'll get everyone out and come back and help. Distract them."

Nick nodded. "Get everyone through the doors to the teacher parking lot. They should still be open. Don't do anything stupid. Stay low, stay hidden. Help is on the way."

"On it," Jazz said. "We'll—"

"*Jasmine!*" Miles roared.

Nick lifted his head in time to see a column of black smoke hurtling toward them. He didn't have time to react when Jazz shoved them both with surprising strength, causing him and Gibby to stumble back, Gibby grunting as the smoke sliced through the air where they'd just stood, Jazz on the other side, a ferocious snarl on her lips. Before Nick could recover, the smoke snapped back and swung against his chest, knocking him off his feet. He slammed into a wall, the back of his head causing the plaster to crack. He gasped, dazed, lights flashing before his eyes. The smoke spread to his arms and legs, lifting him up off the floor, holding him in place. He tried to push against it, but it was too heavy.

Smoke appeared in front of him, a thin smile on her face. She wasn't corporeal, more smoke than human, and she collapsed and re-formed in front of him until her face was inches from Nick's own.

"Hello," she whispered. "You're so much stronger than he expects. Good. He will need you. And you will let him have you. But first—you hurt my brother. And now I will hurt you."

Nick tensed as he waited for the smoke to tighten around him, to crush his bones, but the moment never came.

Smoke laughed at the expression on his face. "Not you." She spun slowly, raising her head upward. "Him."

Dad cried out as the smoke constricted around him. His head rocked back, the cords in his neck sticking out. His eyes were bulging, and Nick screamed.

Then a voice rang out, fierce and strong. "Bitch, I'm trying to *work* here, and you think you can come in and stop me from getting paid? You're in for the shock of your whole damn *life*. And yes, that's a catchphrase, so kiss my fantastic ass."

Smoke's entire body began to seize as bright blue electricity slammed into her, arcing over her arms and legs and chest. The smoke holding Nick collapsed, causing him to slide to the floor. He landed on his feet, looking up to see the smoke holding Dad beginning to dissipate. Nick took off at a run, tearing toward his father, passing by Mateo, the only thing hiding his identity being the mask around his eyes. He snarled as electricity snapped around Smoke, her limbs extended, fingers flexed and trembling.

The smoke holding Dad lessened even more, and he fell a few feet before stopping, still far above the ground. If he fell all the way down, at the very least he'd be seriously hurt, but if he landed wrong, he could die.

He passed Pyro Storm, the heat from his fire blowing over Nick's skin. Pyro Storm was locked in battle with Ice, the villain moving quickly, blocking the fireballs with walls of white. Nick heard Pyro Storm shout his name, but he ignored it, lost in a wave of panic bowling over him as more of the smoke holding Dad disappeared, causing him to plummet toward the ground.

"*No!*" Nick shouted, and the pressure in his head increased to the point where he thought it was about to explode. He *pushed* and felt the spark grow as bright as the sun. He raised his hands, hoping against hope that his powers wouldn't fail him, that he'd be the hero his father needed.

Except he never made it.

A column of ice exploded from the ground. He couldn't stop in time and skidded into it, the impact jarring, pain igniting in his shoulder. The spark dimmed, and he cried out in horror as the last of the smoke disappeared.

Dad fell. He didn't make a sound.

But Trey and Miles and Bob did, with Trey shouting, "I've got him!"; Miles bellowing, "You better not be as heavy as you look!"; and Bob muttering, "I'm too old for this shit." They appeared underneath Dad and he landed on top of them, causing them all to hit the floor. Bob pushed himself onto his hands and knees as Ice sent a wave of hundreds of tiny spikes toward Pyro Storm, causing him to flip away to avoid being impaled. Ice turned toward the fallen men, hovering above them. Rebecca Firestone stood in a corner, hunched low over her camera, pointing it toward the dazed men.

"Foolish," Ice said mildly. "And now you will suffer because of it."

He raised his hands.

His fingers trembled.

"You'll have to go through us first," a voice said, and then Martha appeared, hands on her hips. Next to her stood Aysha and Joanna, both holding what looked like butter knives from the tables. In front of them were Gibby and Jazz, Gibby's hands curled into fists, Jazz barefoot, her high heels in her hands, wielding them like weapons. All in all, not the best-outfitted group, but if Nick was facing them, he'd be terrified. If looks could kill, Ice would already be straight-up murdered.

But since he apparently didn't know who he was dealing with, he said, "You are nothing. I will go through you. Right through *all* of—"

A high heel bounced off his forehead with an audible *thunk*, the skin splitting, blood dribbling down to the bridge of his nose. He reached up and touched his face, his hand coming away wet with a red smear.

Jazz squinted up at him. "Are you serious? No wonder the patriarchy failed. You always underestimate what women are capable of. Sucks to be you." She raised her arm, the other shoe gripped tight in her hand. Ice reared back. Nick didn't blame him; he'd never seen Jazz look so hardcore before.

But it was all an act, the distraction they needed. Ice, his attention so focused on the group of women and the men they shielded, didn't see Pyro Storm rising behind him. Fire bloomed around Pyro Storm, the air crackling. Raising his hands, Pyro Storm gathered the fire in a swirling ball before he hurled it at Ice. At the last second, Ice turned his head, eyes widening.

Nick was about to throw his hands up in victory when Ice *caught* the fireball. The flames froze in a blue sheen of frozen particles between his hands.

"Oh shit," Pyro Storm breathed, and then Ice hurled the ball *back* at him. Pyro Storm managed to dodge just in time, the ball exploding on the ground, ice sliding along the floor. A piece bounced against Nick's shoe, and he looked down at it as the other people still trapped in the cafeteria screamed. He glanced toward the closest group, stunned to see Rebecca Firestone standing in front of them. For a moment, he thought he'd gotten her all wrong and that she was protecting them. But then he saw her pointing the camera in their faces, going for extreme close-ups of their fear, and Nick knew—even now, as he was fighting literal villains—she was the most terrible human being in existence.

A cry came from behind him. He whirled around to see a column of smoke slamming into Mateo, an arc of electricity shooting up toward the ceiling, striking the lights. The bulbs shattered, glass and sparks raining down everywhere. A section of the ceiling holding up prom banners—thin metal struts that crisscrossed—broke off. Nick covered his head with his hands and bent over, trying to make himself as small as possible. He closed his eyes, sure he was about to be crushed, and he felt his mind *twist*, the sensation filled with a mix of pain and pleasure at the same time, and he loved it, he loved the way it made him feel, the way it warmed him from the inside out, the way it—

He opened one eye.

He wasn't dead.

He opened the other and looked up.

Glass and metal and dozens of sparks swirled above his head like a field of stars. He reached up and touched one of the sparks. He hissed when it singed his finger. He pulled his hand away, shaking it out. He swayed his head from side to side, choking on a laugh when the glass and metal and sparks swayed with him.

He turned slowly toward Smoke. He grinned at her. He puffed out his chest, put his fists on his hips, and said (in a ridiculously deep voice), "It's time to take out the trash." Rebecca Firestone better have gotten that on film because he was going to rewatch the *shit* out of it.

"Nicky, *no*," Gibby shouted.

"Nicky, *yes*," he growled, like a badass.

And then he moved.

He ran for Smoke, now solid. The sparks and glass swirled furiously, attaching to the metal struts, causing them to glow and glitter. Mateo's eyes widened as he saw Nick coming and raised his own hands, electricity snarling across his fingers. Nick jerked his head, sending the ember-hot struts flying toward Smoke. As they hurtled toward her, electricity flew from Mateo's fingertips, the snap and snarl of blue light racing next to the struts. If their aim was true, they'd clip her, not kill her, which would hopefully be enough to give them the upper hand.

But her body turned to smoke, and the struts and arcing electricity flew right through her, metal quivering as they hit the wall in a shower of sparks, the electricity snapping into nothing.

Nick tried to stop, but the floor was wet with melting ice. He slid into Smoke right as she became corporeal. He bounced off her, but before he could fall to the ground, she wrapped a hand around his throat, lifting him up, his feet kicking into empty air. She raised him above her as he choked, her fingers digging in as he slapped at her arm, trying to get her to let him go. No use.

"You," she said, mouth twisted in a sneer. "I have had enough of *you*."

"Feeling is mutual," Nick managed to say. Her grip tightened, cutting off his air. Inky-black splotches began to filter into Nick's vision, and he couldn't breathe, he couldn't *breathe*—

With a yell, Gibby appeared behind Smoke, running toward them. When she was still six feet away, she leapt, hands clasped above her head in one fist, bringing them down to smash Smoke's head. Which would have been *epic* as all hell, except before the impact hit, Smoke vanished in a black cloud, causing Gibby's hands to smash into Nick's shoulder as she collided with his chest, knocking them both to the ground. Gibby landed partially on Nick, who blinked slowly up at the ceiling.

Smoke re-formed above them. Her expression was pinched as she said, "I hate children."

And then she screamed, whirling around, slapping at her back. Behind her, Jazz stood, lowering her hand, hair fluttering around her face. Sticking out of the middle of Smoke's back was one of Jazz's heels, the tip embedded in her skin.

"It's about time I got to stab something," Jazz snapped, helping Gibby up as Smoke fell to her knees. "Try that again, and the next shoe goes in your damn *eye*."

Nick gasped when Pyro Storm crashed down next to him, rolling violently, costume torn on his shoulders and chest, drops of blood leaving a red smear on the ground. He landed on his stomach, grunting as he pressed his hands and feet flat against the ground before pushing *up*, legs kicking out as he flipped back onto his feet. He swung his arm out in a flat arc, fire shooting from him, melting a block of ice hurling in their direction.

"Get up," Pyro Storm spat, grabbing Nick by the arm. Dizzy, Nick clung to Pyro Storm, their faces inches apart. They breathed the same air, in and out, in and out, and if they were going to die, if these were going to be their last moments on earth, Nick wasn't going to waste them.

He said, "Dude, I lo— *Look out!*"

Nick shoved Pyro Storm as hard as he could. The Extraordinary fell back, a sheet of ice flying between them, missing both of them by inches. Nick was about to rush back toward Pyro Storm when hands grabbed his shoulders, turning him around.

Smoke grinned at him. "Hello." And then she punched him in the face.

Nick fell back, lip split, blood arcing as he collapsed backward to the floor, bright lights flashing before his eyes. He heard someone shout his name, but it was faint, negligible. He felt like he was underwater, moving slowly. His limbs were heavy. He wanted to close his eyes. Sleep, maybe. Forget about all of this. Everything hurt, but it was fading, fading. He closed his eyes.

And then a hand gripped his throat, jerking him up. He was spun around, his eyes unfocused. He coughed, blood dribbling down his chin.

"Oh," Smoke whispered in his ear. "*This* is familiar, isn't it? Yes. We've been here before."

Nick's vision began to clear. And when he saw what lay before him, his heart sank to his feet.

Pyro Storm, standing in the middle of the cafeteria, fire moving around him in hot waves.

Ice, on the other side of the cafeteria, in a similar position. Only instead of a stranger on the street, he held a girl, a kid from their school. She was crying, her makeup streaking. It took Nick a moment to place her. Megan. Megan Ross, the one in charge of the prom committee who had tried to get Nick to bring Pyro Storm.

"Let them go," Pyro Storm commanded, though the implied threat was undermined when his voice broke. "Don't hurt them."

"We can," Smoke said. Then, raising her voice, "Don't move. You stop *right there*."

Nick turned his head to see Trey and Miles holding Dad back, his face stricken as he demanded they let him go, let him go *right* now. Mateo stood in front of the largest group of kids, trying to herd them toward the exits. Jazz and Gibby were next to their parents. Martha was holding Bob up, wiping a trickle of blood off his forehead. Rebecca Firestone was still there, still recording, standing near the back of a smaller group of students.

His team.

They did good.

Whatever happened next, they did good.

(Except for Rebecca Firestone. She could suck it.)

"Who will you save?" Ice taunted him, shaking Megan, her head snapping back and forth.

"Oh, *come on*," Nick snarled as he struggled against Smoke's hold on him. "Are you freaking kidding me? You know what? Screw all of you. Hey, Pyro Storm!"

Seth turned toward him, tense and afraid. Nick didn't need to see all of his face to know that. There was only one way to make this better.

Nick bared his teeth in a ferocious grin and said, "I love you."

And *oh*, how Seth smiled. Not Pyro Storm. Not the Extraordinary. *Seth*. The boy from the swings. The boy who wore chinos and sweaters and bow ties. The boy who Nick thought hung the moon and the stars. The boy whose glasses got fogged up when it was too cold outside. The boy who Nick thought the world of, the boy who Nick would do anything for.

He said, "I love you too. Always."

"Hell yeah, you do," Nick said. He turned his gaze to Ice, glaring at him. "Let her go, you dumbass. She's innocent!"

And then Megan stopped crying, as if a switch had flipped inside her. Something crossed her face, something that sent a chill down Nick's spine. "Bullshit," she spat. "I'm not *that* innocent."

"Holy shit," Nick breathed. "That was a *catchph*—"

Megan brought her leg up, her sparkly high heel catching the light. She brought it back against Ice's shin. The Extraordinary bellowed in pain, letting Megan go. She stumbled forward as Pyro Storm shouted, "Nick! Backflip of Chaos!" He hurtled toward Ice as Megan fled.

You want to learn to fight, you've got to prepare for anything. Help won't always come. How do you get free?

I don't know.

Here, a weak point. Use enough force, and you might be able to get them to loosen their grip on you.

With a strength he didn't know he was capable of, Nick brought his arm up and shoved it back as hard as he could, elbow smashing into Smoke's side. Smoke exhaled explosively in his ear. Without giving her the chance to recover, Nick jerked his body forward as hard as he could, the muscles in his back protesting angrily. As he bent over, he grabbed the hand around his throat and yanked, lifting Smoke up and over Nick. It happened so quickly, she didn't have time to react. She hit the ground hard, grunting as her breath was knocked from her chest. Nick cocked his fist back, ready to let it fly right in her stupid face. Never, ever hit a woman, unless she's a villain controlling smoke, crashing a prom, and ruining what should have been a perfect night.

She vanished, and Nick punched the floor. He howled and jumped back, shaking his hand. "Son of a *bitch*. What the *frick*. Ow, ow, *ow*. Oh my god, I hate you so, so much. Why won't you freaking *die* already?"

She re-formed in front of him and backhanded him across the face. Nick was thrown backwards, skidding through water until he stopped at the feet of Jazz and Gibby. They helped him up just in time for him to see Pyro Storm locked in battle with Ice, steam hissing.

And then they began to lose.

Ice grabbed Pyro Storm by the arms, spinning on his heels, flinging him away. Before Pyro Storm could course correct, Smoke was there, jumping up and bringing her elbow down on Pyro Storm's chest, smashing him to the floor, which cracked upon impact. Nick screamed for him, struggling against the hands holding him back. Pyro Storm lifted his head, mouth bloodied, but then Smoke kicked him in the stomach. Pyro Storm curled in on himself, trying to make himself smaller, but Smoke continued to kick him over and over, Pyro Storm's mouth leaking blood.

Nick pulled free as Ice put his hands back on Pyro Storm, one on his right thigh, the other on his left ankle. The scream Pyro Storm let out knocked Nick's breath from his chest as ice spread along Pyro Storm's front, freezing his body.

Nick charged, the only thought in his head was to kill, kill, kill before they killed Seth.

Someone ran next to him. He looked over.

Mateo, a furious sneer on his face, electricity crackling.

Except Ice lifted his head. He stood slowly. He smiled.

And then, almost quicker than Nick could follow, he punched the floor. The tile split apart as thick walls of ice burst up around them. The last Nick saw of Pyro Storm—Seth—was Smoke kicking him viciously. And then they were lost behind the ice.

"No!" Nick cried, smashing his hands against the ice. "No! Let him *go*!"

No use. The ice was too thick.

Ignoring everyone shouting around him, Nick pressed his hands flat against the ice, gritting his teeth, trying to find the spark, the pressure, the pain, *something* to call upon his powers. But his mind was a storm. He couldn't think. He couldn't focus. He had failed, and Seth was suffering because of it. Seth, who only wanted to keep people safe. Seth, who never hurt anyone.

Seth, Seth, SethSeth*SethSeth*—

A loud crash from above.

Nick raised his head, as if in a dream.

The ceiling of the cafeteria cracked, then broke apart, the pieces floating in air as the night sky appeared above them, the stars blinking coldly. Then the stars were blotted out by a figure appearing through the hole in the ceiling.

His costume was the same as it'd been before, black and bulky, the front of his helmet opaque. The large sections of broken ceiling swirled around him as he lowered to the ground. Once his feet hit the floor, he turned his head slowly toward Nick. And though he couldn't see his face or eyes, Nick knew he was looking right at him.

"How did you know?" Nick whispered, a tear trickling down his cheek.

TK said, "I've been watching. You wanted a lesson? You've got one." He held out his hand toward Nick.

Without hesitating, Nick took what was offered. TK pressed Nick's hand against the ice.

"Nicky!" he heard his father cry, but it was so far away.

"Focus," TK whispered, hand on top of Nick's. "Feel it. It's there; I know it is. You know it is. Hold tight. It'll try and break free, overtake you, but it's part of you and you can control it. It's yours. And remember: it's easier to stand together than it is to struggle apart. Now *push*."

He did. It was easier than he expected it to be. The pressure built, but there was an ebb and flow to it, like waves on a beach. Nick closed his eyes, and there, in the remains of the tangled knot: the spark, burning like the sun. He closed his hand around it gently. It struggled against him, trying to break free, but he held it close, whispering to it that it was safe, that *they* were safe, that it was okay, everything would be all right.

The spark pulsed once. Twice.

In his mind, Nick opened his eyes, and then his hand.

The spark floated above his palm. It rose a few inches above his hand, near his face. It moved forward, brushing against the tip of his nose before it began to vibrate. It shook and trembled, and then it sank down to his hand.

Into his hand.

Warmth like Nick had never experienced barreled through him, covering every inch of him with a prickly heat. It wasn't comfortable, but the further it spread, the more it merged with him, the easier it became. His. It was all his. He didn't need it to be extraordinary, but there it was, all the same.

In the ruins of the cafeteria, he opened his eyes, looking at TK's gloved hand pressed against his. The ice was cold, water sluicing against his palm.

And then he pushed. He felt when TK did the same, and it felt like music, harmonious and strong. A wave of energy rose through Nick, meeting one that came from TK. It was familiar, synchronous, and for a moment, Nick thought of a lighthouse, the cold, salty air.

The ice shattered. All of it shattered with a mighty crack, the ice wall turning into powder, falling like heavy snow.

And through the remains, Ice and Smoke, standing above Pyro Storm, battered and bloodied.

Still holding TK's hand, Nick moved forward, ice particles trailing against his face. Smoke's eyes widened as Nick pushed again. The air around them stuttered before Smoke was knocked off her feet, sliding along the ground. Ice shouted for her but was cut off when Nick stared at him. He jerked his head to the right, and Ice crashed into the ground next to his twin.

Letting go of TK, Nick rushed toward Seth, who was pushing himself up off the ground as he spat out a thick wad of blood.

"Nick," Seth muttered as Nick helped him up. "You . . . thank you."

"We're getting out of here," Nick told him, putting an arm around Seth's waist. "We need to—"

"Look *out*!" TK shouted.

A column of smoke burst between them, knocking them away from each other. Seth crumpled to the ground, head bouncing off the floor. Nick landed on his back, blinking up at the hole in the ceiling. The stars looked brighter than he could remember. The metal struts in the ceiling hung uselessly, and as he pushed himself up, his hands slipped in the water on the floor.

Water.

Smoke.

Ice.

Metal.

Fire.

His eyes widened. "Oh my god," he whispered. "I just had a terrible idea."

He jumped up, rushing toward TK, who stood his ground

against an onslaught of ice being flung toward him. Nick almost slid into him but managed to stop before he crashed. "I need you to trust me," he hissed as TK broke another wave of ice.

TK didn't hesitate. "Whatever you're thinking, do it and do it *now*."

Nick lifted his head, taking a deep breath. He turned, pressing his back against TK's, letting the Extraordinary handle the attack so he could focus. He let his breath out slow and raised his hands toward the ceiling.

He pushed.

Nothing happened.

Again.

Nothing.

"Come on," he muttered. "Come *on*."

Nothing. It didn't work. He couldn't do this. He couldn't—

"Nick!"

He looked toward the sound of his name.

Dad, near a pair of doors, pushing kids out and into safety. Dad took a step toward him, chest heaving. "You've got this!" Dad shouted at him. "You can *do it*."

Nick grinned. "Damn right I can."

He stretched his hands higher and pushed again. This time, the metal struts above him began to move from side to side, creaking and groaning. He ground his teeth together as the pressure built in his head, but it wasn't as big as it used to be. It didn't hurt. It felt *good*, and at least a dozen struts of varying lengths broke off in a metallic shriek. They hovered near the ceiling, wobbling until they smoothed out.

Nick stepped out from behind TK, hands still raised in the air.

Smoke and Ice stood side by side.

Nick said, "I'm about to show you why you *never* fuck with queer people." He dropped his hands quickly, slapping them against his legs.

The struts hurtled toward the ground, the air whistling around them. The first struck the floor in front of Smoke, breaking through the tile, standing upright and quivering. Then another.

Then another. Then another, slamming into the ground again and again, surrounding Smoke and Ice, who snarled angrily. The last strut hit the floor. Smoke and Ice were surrounded by metal bars, most of which still shook from the impact.

"This will not hold us," Smoke said.

"You have lost," Ice said, taking a step toward them, feet sliding through the water on the floor.

Nick rolled his eyes. "Oh my god, do you ever shut up?"

Smoke began to dissipate, moving to pass through the bars.

Ice gathered the air around him, another spike forming above his head.

Nick startled when Jazz and Gibby appeared on either side of him. "Pyro Storm!" Gibby shouted. "Miss Conduct! Hit them with all you've got!"

"TK," Jazz said. "Nick. Hold those struts in place. Don't let them move."

Without hesitation, Nick and TK raised their hands toward the struts. The symphony rose between them again, and the struts quivered before sinking further into the floor with a loud *crack*.

Ice and Smoke screamed as a tornado of fire rose around them in a roar, the heat immense, causing the metal struts to flash molten hot, the spike of ice shattering and hissing as the water splashed to the floor. Lightning arced down the metal bars, striking the water. Ice began to seize as electricity coursed through him, limbs stiff, head rocked back.

The column of smoke was halfway through the metal bars when they were struck by the combined powers of Nick and TK, Pyro Storm and Miss Conduct. The smoke began to shudder as it morphed into a roiling ball of black. It tried to force itself through the struts, but Nick ground his teeth together as he forced the struts closer together. The ball of smoke pulled back abruptly before it battered against the struts, causing them to creak and groan, but it was already too late. The moment it touched the metal, the ball re-formed into a woman, and she screamed as she was electrocuted. Nick wanted to push harder, make them regret hurting his friends, his family, his people. Kill them both for—

"No," Gibby whispered near his ear. "Let it go, Nicky. Just let it go."

And so he did.

The fire and electricity snapped and snarled before it flickered out, leaving only dark wisps and the smell of burnt air. Smoke and Ice stood for a moment longer before they both collapsed inside the metal prison. For a moment, Nick thought he'd gone too far, that they'd killed them both, but then Ice groaned, eyes fluttering, and Smoke's chest rose up and down, up and down.

Nick collapsed to his knees, strength draining from him as Jazz and Gibby hugged him tightly. His body hurt and his head felt like it was splitting in half. Panic was there, along the edges, reaching for him, ready to pull him under. But Jazz and Gibby were there, telling him to breathe in, breathe out. Again, Nicky. In. Out. In and out. He took their strength and held it close, the vise grip on his lungs eventually loosening as his vision cleared.

"You did good, kid," a voice said, and Nick and Jazz and Gibby looked up.

TK stood above them, his helmet reflecting Nick's tired face back at him. TK looked like he was going to reach for Nick but took a step back instead, hand curling into a fist. His chest heaved.

"Yeah," Nick said tiredly. "Thank you. For coming. For being here. For trusting me."

TK nodded but didn't speak.

A memory, flitting about Nick's head like a little bird. He blinked slowly. "You said—you said that it's easier to stand together than it is to struggle apart. Where did you hear that?"

But TK didn't answer. Someone called Nick's name, and he turned his head to see Dad running toward them, a terrified expression on his face. Gibby's and Jazz's parents were doing the same, their daughters rising to their feet and going to meet them halfway. Nick looked back to TK only to see the Extraordinary rising above him, arms spread like wings. Just as he disappeared through the hole in the ceiling, Dad lifted Nick up, holding him close, his face buried in Nick's neck. Nick's feet barely touched the floor, and he said, "Dad, I'm okay. I swear."

If anything, Dad squeezed him tighter. "Let me have this."

Beneath the tough exterior, Dad was nothing but a marshmallow, so Nick allowed it. And if he shed a tear or two of relief, well, that was just between them. Close. It'd been so close again.

But that was the life of a hero, Nick knew. Danger was always going to be part of being an Extraordinary.

Dad finally set Nick down, cupping his face, searching for what, Nick didn't know. "Who was that?" Dad asked in a hushed voice.

"TK," Nick said, turning his face in his father's hands. "He's . . . like me."

Something crossed Dad's face, something that looked like hope mixed with grief. Nick didn't understand. "He? Who is he?"

"Don't know. Never seen him outside of his costume. He's—"

"*Nick!*"

He pulled out of his dad's arms and turned toward his friends. They rushed toward him, Seth and Jazz and Gibby all shouting incoherently. Then Seth was in his arms, kissing his mouth and cheeks and chin and forehead. Gibby jumped on Seth's back, legs wrapped around his waist, fists pumping in the air, Seth taking a hard step back to keep from falling. Knees weak, Nick slumped to the floor again in front of them, Jazz's hand tugging on his hair as she smiled down at him. "You did it."

"No," Nick said quietly, suddenly exhausted. "*We* did it. All of us."

"Team Pyro Storm," Jazz agreed.

"Goddamn Lighthouse," Gibby said.

"The best superhero team that has ever existed," Seth said. He was still in costume, though it was torn in places, one of the lenses in his helmet cracked and dim. Nick reached up and brushed a thumb against Seth's bloodied lips.

Then, his eyes widened and he tried to sit up. "Mateo. Holy shit, we need to—"

"Gone," Seth said, pushing himself up off Nick with a groan. "Said he'd meet up with us later. Wanted to get out of here before anyone asked questions." He sat down on his butt, pulling his knees to his chest. "What are the chances that he'd be here?"

Nick said, "I don't know. It was weird, right? It's like—like—"

Do you know how many high schools are in the city? How could I have possibly known I'd be working at yours? Besides, it was a last-minute thing. Got a message to pick up some hours. Someone called in sick or their cat died in a house fire or something, I don't know. The number wasn't one I recognized, but I don't usually ask questions when it comes to getting paid.

"It's like it was planned," Nick whispered. What if . . . no. That couldn't be. He wouldn't . . .

"Nicky?" Gibby asked, sounding concerned.

"Burke," Nick said, stomach twisting slickly. "Simon Burke. That's what Smoke and Ice said. They were trying to draw us out. Draw *Pyro Storm* out. Something Mateo said—he wasn't supposed to be here tonight. Got a message from a number he didn't recognize. What if that was part of Burke's plan? To get us all here to . . ." He scowled as he looked around wildly. "Where is she?"

"Who?" Jazz asked.

He stood quickly. Dad was standing in the middle of the cafeteria, looking up toward the hole in the ceiling, face pale. Smoke and Ice lay unconscious in their metal prison. Trey, Aysha, Jo, and Miles were helping stragglers who hadn't been able to escape, kids who looked scared as they stared at Nick and his friends, including Megan, who looked shaky but able to stand on her own. Bob was sitting in a chair, Martha above him, fussing over a cut on his forehead.

Gone. She was gone. She was—

Trying to mix in with the kids leaving with Jo and Miles.

"Stop!" Nick shouted and took off running. He heard the others call after him, but he ignored them. He jumped over broken chairs and tables, his muscles protesting. Right before she walked through the doors and out into the hall, he reached her, grabbing her by the arm and spinning her around.

"Let me *go*," Rebecca Firestone snarled, her sunglasses missing a lens, a bright eye glaring murderously at Nick.

"You knew," Nicks spat. "You *knew* what was going to happen, and you did nothing to stop it."

"Nick?" Miles asked. "What's going on?"

"Rebecca Firestone," Nick snapped. "She was here before the attack. She was filming everything. She knew this was going to happen. How? Burke? Are you working with Simon Burke? Holy shit, you are the *worst*."

She smiled. "I have no idea what you're talking about. And even if I did, you have no proof." Her eyes narrowed as she leaned forward. "I knew it. About you. I *knew* you were like them. Like Pyro Storm. Like Owen. You may have everyone else fooled, but once they see the footage I took, you won't be able to escape. The life you had is *over*. Unless—"

"Unless?"

She stood upright. "Interview. Exclusive. You, me. All on the table. Any questions I want to ask."

"And if I refuse?" Nick asked.

Her smile widened, flashing teeth. A shark's grin. "Then it'll be my word against yours. Who do you think people will believe? You'll never know peace again. Do you really want to do that to your father? It's over, Nick. Everything you've kept secret will be dragged into the light. I can help you. I can make it better. Why would you— Get your hands *off* me!"

"Huh," Jo said, tearing Rebecca Firestone's purse from her shoulder. She overturned it, spilling the contents on the ground as the reporter struggled against Nick's hold. A wallet, eight lip balms, makeup, a package of tissue, a tin of mints, Tylenol, and a camera. The same camera she'd used to record everything.

Nick let Rebecca Firestone go and picked up the camera, testing its weight in his hands. Such a little thing. "What's the school's Wi-Fi password?"

Rebecca Firestone snarled, "How should I know? I don't go to this stupid school."

Nick grinned at her. "So you weren't able to upload the footage to a cloud. Which means this is all the leverage you have."

Her face twisted. "I will end you if you—" She screamed as Nick pivoted on his heels, cocking his arm back and letting the camera fly. It smashed against the wall, shattering into pieces.

"I'll kill you!" Rebecca Firestone cried, her sunglasses falling to the floor, eyes narrowed into slits. "You hear me? You're *dead*. You're—"

"Are you threatening a minor?" Trey asked, taking a step forward.

She laughed, a choked sound that grated against Nick's nerves. "You're damn right I am. This little shit broke my camera!"

"I don't think that's what happened," Aysha said with a frown. "In fact, all I saw was Nick picking it up for you after Jo accidentally dropped it."

"I'm so clumsy," Jo said airily. "Always have been."

"It's one of the things I love most about her," Miles said, winking at his wife. "And Nick here has the same tendencies. It slipped, isn't that right, Nicky?"

"Yep," Nick said, grateful for these people in his life. "Slipped right against the wall."

"So you see," Trey said, "Nick has witnesses. You don't. Maybe you'll try to spin this some way, but trust me when I say hell hath no fury like a pissed-off parent. You come for Nick—you come for *any* of our kids—and I'll make sure everyone knows the part you played here. I'm sure your viewers would love to hear how you didn't lift a finger to help any of the kids at this school while they were being attacked."

"You won't get away with this," she snarled. She turned her fiery gaze to Nick. "I've seen it for myself. Everyone will know; I'll make sure of it. You hear me? *Everyone will know.*" And with that, she shoved her way through them, heading for the exit.

Strangely, Nick almost felt sorry for her. He didn't know why; she didn't deserve his sympathy. Everything she'd done had put the people he loved in danger. Which was why he was surprised when he called after her. "Hey, Firestone!"

She stopped but didn't turn around.

Nick took a step toward her as the parents stood at his back. "I don't know what he promised you," Nick said, and she stiffened. "But I do know that while I despise everything you are, you're not stupid, at least not completely. Burke is only in this for himself.

Once you've served your purpose, he'll toss you aside because you mean *nothing* to him. And I think some part of you knows that."

Rebecca Firestone walked out the door, Nick staring after her.

They left together: Nick and Seth, Jazz and Gibby, Martha and Bob, Jo and Miles, Ayesha and Trey. Dad, crowding against Nick as if he thought Nick would get attacked again. They were all dirty and battle-weary, but not broken. They held their heads high.

"Ready?" Seth asked as they reached the doors that led to the parking lot.

No. No, he wasn't. He was more scared than he'd been in the cafeteria. But he couldn't back down now. He lifted his head and nodded. "Ready."

They stepped out of the school and into chaos.

The parking lot was filled with people: students, faculty, parents, guardians, police and EMTs and firefighters. Lights spun atop emergency vehicles as reporters shouted from behind sawhorses set up near the edge of the parking lot. Cameras flashed, and one of the photos—the one showing Nick and his people as they walked down the stairs together—would be on the front page of the *Nova City Gazette* the next morning under a single word: SURVIVORS. But that would be on the bottom half of the front page.

The top half would be something else entirely.

Nick flinched when people began to whisper, students and teachers all staring at him, eyes wide as Pyro Storm gripped his hand, holding it tight. The whispers grew louder, saying, *That's him* and *It's Pyro Storm* and *Did you see what they did?* and *Is Nick Bell an Extraordinary?* and *No, it wasn't him, it was the other one, the one in black, the one who could fly.*

Once upon a time, Nick would have given almost anything to have this. To have people think he could do something extraordinary. And he had; they all had. His friends. Their parents, Martha and Bob. TK and Mateo. And maybe he did feel strong for a moment, powerful. But this was tempered by the fact that Ice and

Smoke had been sent for them. If it wasn't for Nick, if it wasn't for Seth, none of this would've happened. Sure, the blame rested solely on Simon Burke and his lackeys, but all that had happened had been *because* of Nick and Seth. If they hadn't been here, the dance would've gone on, the night filled with music, dancing, laughter, and happiness, without a care in the world. Any sense of victory he might've felt was quashed under how close it'd been, how many more people could've gotten hurt. Or worse. And for what? To let Nick and his friends have a moment where they could be like everyone else?

They weren't. They hadn't been for a long time.

Being a hero was vastly more complicated than he'd expected, and he didn't know how to reconcile it with all he'd thought it'd be. It didn't help that everyone was staring at them with a look of fear tinged with wonder. A part of him wanted to bask at the attention, to allow himself to fill with joy at what he was capable of, what they could do when they worked together.

But a bigger part of him was strangely realistic, knowing how much everything would change from this point on. He'd dreamed of this moment for so long, and now that it was here, he realized that some dreams were infinitely more complex, even when they came true.

He cringed as the voices rose around him, as the cameras shuttered and clicked, as everyone tried to look at him, standing on their tiptoes, craning their necks to catch a glimpse of him. He tried to curl in on himself, but it was no use. He was here, exposed. In front of everyone.

"It's all right," Dad whispered in his ear. "We'll deal with it. Let's get you out of here, okay?"

Nick nodded blindly, squeezing Seth's hand like a lifeline. He stepped forward again, only to stop when Seth did. He looked back as people began to crowd around them, cops appearing and pushing them back as everyone screamed for them, saying *Nick, Pyro Storm, what happened? What did you do? What are you?*

"What is it?" Nick asked, voice trembling.

Seth smiled. "You told me you loved me."

Nick gave a watery smile. "Yeah. I guess I did."

"And you meant it too."

"Every word."

Seth nodded, taking in a deep breath and letting it out slow. "You and me." He leaned forward, pressing his forehead against Nick's.

"You and me," Nick whispered to him. "Always."

Seth pulled back, but not before he kissed Nick's forehead. He turned toward his aunt and uncle and said, "It's time."

Martha covered her mouth with her hand, eyes shining.

Bob put his hand on Seth's shoulder. "Are you sure? You won't ever be able to take it back."

Nick had no idea what they were talking about. He was about to ask when Seth said, "I know. But remember when Gibby's and Jazz's parents came over to the house? Nick told them he was Pyro Storm because he wanted to protect me. He did it without thinking. He only cared that I was safe. That's the kind of person he is. I have to do the same for him." His voice broke when he said, "Are you going to be mad at me?"

"Never in your life," Martha said, dropping her hand and pulling Seth into a hug. "We're so, so proud of you. My brave, wonderful boy."

"We're with you, no matter what," Bob said roughly. He sniffled and wiped his eyes. "Knew this day would come. We're ready if you are."

"Detective Bell, you need to *move*," one of the cops called, trying to hold the crowd back.

"We gotta go," Dad said, trying to lead Nick away.

"Wait," Seth said, and when he turned back around, he held his head high, his shoulders squared. People gasped around them when fire began to leak from his hands, cascading down to the ground. The crowd took a step back as he rose in the air, hovering above them. Nick stared up at him in wonder, heart so full he thought it'd burst. His throat constricted when Seth looked down at him, smiling that one smile only meant for Nick. "I love you. And I've got your back."

Nick's eyes widened. "No, no, you don't have to—"

Seth raised his voice, causing everyone else to fall silent as they looked up at him. He said, "I don't want to hide anymore. I don't know how I can do what I can do, but this—this thing in me is powerful, and you deserve to know who it is that can do the things I can. I'm done hiding behind a mask. I'm done staying in the shadows because I have fire and it can help chase the darkness away. You know me as Pyro Storm, but it's just a name, and not even my real one." He raised his hands to either side of his helmet. He didn't hesitate as he pulled it off, his curls springing free. He let the helmet drop to the ground as cameras flashed and people gasped, the sound rolling over them like the wind. This was the picture that would be on the top of the front page and would spread across the world: Seth floating above the crowd, fire burning around him, faces turned up toward him in wonder. It would successfully divert the attention from Nick, though for how long was anyone's guess. The headline read what was said next, and nothing would ever be the same. "My name is Seth Gray. I'm a student at Centennial High. And I'm the Extraordinary called Pyro Storm."

BREAKING NEWS

Transcript from interview between Rebecca Firestone and Simon Burke

Rebecca Firestone

It's been two weeks since the attack on Centennial High School. While the investigation is still ongoing, many questions remain. Why was the school attacked? Who was the intended target? What did Seth Gray, the Extraordinary known as Pyro Storm, have to do with what happened?

And what of Simon Burke? Simon Burke—whose son, Owen Burke, was revealed late last year to be Shadow Star and has since escaped from custody—remains a central figure in this mystery. Rumors of underground labs and pills that could turn anyone into an Extraordinary ran rampant after anonymous allegations spread following the Battle at McManus Bridge. Burke denied these allegations, and investigators found nothing of consequence when they searched Burke Tower. However, it must be noted the Extraordinaries now known as Smoke and Ice stood with Burke when he launched the Save Our Children initiative. Smoke and Ice, twins, who worked for Simon Burke. Why then, did they attack the school?

I sat down with Simon Burke for a wide-ranging interview in his office at Burke Tower. No topic was off-limits. From the whereabouts of his son to the revelation that a student at Centennial High is the Extraordinary known as Pyro Storm, Burke was gracious and informative.

Rebecca Firestone

Thank you for agreeing to the interview.

Simon Burke

Of course, Rebecca. I'm happy to speak to you. In my line of work, transparency is paramount.

RF

I appreciate that. Let's start with a big one. Where is Owen? Your son escaped from custody, killing one and injuring six.

SB

First, let me say that my wife and I send our sincerest condolences to the family of Jacob Lee. It is a tragedy, what has occurred, and the guilt Patricia and I feel over this is overwhelming. We are working with authorities to assist as best we can, but unfortunately, I have no idea where my son is. He has not attempted to contact me, nor have there been any sightings of him.

RF

Mr. Lee is the third person Owen allegedly killed. As a reminder to our viewers, last fall, *Action News* lost two of its members in a helicopter crash caused by Shadow Star, the name Owen adopted when he became an Extraordinary.

SB

Yes, and it's terrible. As we did with your fallen colleagues, Burke Pharmaceuticals will be taking care of the families of the victims. Anything they need, all they must do is ask. We have already set up scholarship funds for Mr. Lee's children.

RF

That's kind of you.

SB

I don't see it that way. It's not a kindness. It's a necessity. Owen is my son and therefore my responsibility. He is also a murderer—a dangerous one at that. I only hope that no one else will suffer because of his actions.

RF

You don't know where he is?

SB

No.

RF

If he watches this interview, is there anything you'd like to say to him?

SB

Yes. Owen, if you're watching, turn yourself in. Enough of this. Let us help you. Your mother and I love you very much, but the only way we can set things right is by dealing with the consequences together as a family. You've hurt people. But you're still my son, and I will do whatever I can to help you. Excuse me. I didn't think it would get to me as much as it has. I—ah, there's the tissue. I—

RF

It's all right. I can only imagine what you and Mrs. Burke are going through.

SB

I'm sure anyone who is a parent has the same fears. You do what you can for your children, try to raise them right, give them a future that most can only dream about, but then something happens, and . . . I don't know. I'm scared for him.

RF

For him? Or of him?

SB

For him. I'm not scared of my son. And he should know he has nothing to fear from me.

RF

You'd turn him in if he came to you?

SB

Without hesitation.

RF

Two months ago, you stood with the Extraordinaries known as Smoke and Ice as you announced a bounty on Pyro Storm. They—

SB

Christian and Christina Lewis.

RF

Yes, them. Both are currently in custody, awaiting trial. It's expected you'll be called as a witness in the case against them.

SB

Terrible business, that. I thought they were people I could trust. We vetted them. Extremely intelligent, the pair of them. They worked for Burke Pharmaceuticals, but it wasn't until they'd been employed with us for close to a year that they came to me, revealing their abilities.

RF

Why did you allow them to join you onstage?

SB

Because I thought they were good people, people who wanted the same things I did. I thought they could put a face to the word *Extraordinary*. I was wrong. Unbeknownst to me, they had an agenda of their own, though I'm unclear as to what that agenda was, specifically.

RF

Sources have told me that they haven't said a word since they've been in custody.

SB

Yes, I've heard the same. I don't know if we'll ever know what their purpose was, what they hoped to achieve by attacking Centennial High. I'm grateful there was no loss of life. And that's apparently thanks to Pyro Storm.

RF

Seth Gray.

SB

Yes, Mr. Gray.

RF

Who was friends with your son.

SB

Curious, isn't it? It makes you wonder if there is anyone else hiding something in that school.

RF

I'm sure we'll find out sooner rather than later.

SB

You were there, weren't you?

RF

Yes. Unfortunately, I'm under a gag order, as I might be called as a witness. What do you make of Seth Gray revealing his identity? Especially knowing that he fought against Owen numerous times.

SB

I'm sure Mr. Gray had his reasons—I won't say a calculated move, per se. He's a child, after all. I wouldn't ascribe him any sort of dark machinations. But I do wonder about the timing of it. He could have just as easily fled, keeping his identity a secret, the same as his counterparts—the Extraordinary who could conduct electricity and the other one, the one with telekinesis.

RF

Speaking of that night, there have been allegations levied at the NCPD for their late response to the attack on the school. Some are suggesting that cellular service was cut to disallow anyone to call for help, that the attack was planned using police resources. And further, Rodney Caplan, the former chief of Nova City Police, claimed during the press conference announcing his resignation that he believed officers conspired to prevent an emergency response. He said, and I quote, "Something is rotten in the state of Denmark," while also making not-so subtle allusions that you were somehow involved in what transpired at Centennial High. Would you like to respond to this?

SB

I thank Rodney Caplan for his service with the NCPD. His is a storied career, the first Black chief of police Nova City had, and while we've disagreed on many issues, I know his heart has always been in the right place. To be honest, I'm a little flattered he thinks I have any level of control over the NCPD. That being said, his unfounded accusations cast a pall over his legacy and the NCPD as a whole. These are hardworking men and women, and to have their former boss fling such aspersions on their characters is at best unfortunate, and at worst dangerous. I have met with many of the officers who protect this city, and I can assure you that none of them would ignore a call to help the people who need them most. They are all just as devastated by what transpired, and I know any investigation will prove that. They cannot and should not be blamed for their response, given how fluid the situation was, and how chaotic. I told them the same thing I'll tell you: I trust them and will do everything I can to help them. And not only them. I want to help everyone, Extraordinaries included.

RF

With what? What would you do for them?

SB

I—I hadn't expected to say this, but I suppose the time is right. As I said previously, transparency is important. And as a parent of an Extraordinary, I know what it's like to be scared for your child. With this attack of a high school prom, it's becoming evident that Extraordinaries are among us and that they're capable of doing tremendous harm, especially if they're unable to control their powers. What if a child could control the weather, and they became angry? Or what if a child could move things with their mind and were neurodiverse, say, for example, having attention deficit hyperactive disorder? That could lead to chaos and destruction—people getting hurt or worse. Pure speculation, of course, but the things we've witnessed suggest that it's within the realm of possibility. After the events of McManus Bridge, I instructed my scientists to work around the clock in order to understand our Extraordinary brethren. I followed this with the Save Our Children initiative, hoping that different types of Extraordinaries would come into the light. The more we know, the better off we'll be. I'm pleased to announce that as of last week, we have successfully cured our first Extraordinary.

RF

Wait, what? What do you mean, "cured"?

SB

A child was brought to us by their parents. This child, who we call Eve to protect their anonymity, exhibited signs of telekinesis. From a young age, Eve could move things around their house. The parents were frightened. At first, they thought their home was haunted. It wasn't until the child grew older that they realized Eve was the cause. Rightfully concerned, they came to me after we announced the Save Our Children initiative. Following weeks of testing, we all agreed to proceed, especially seeing how Extraordinary powers aren't considered medical and therefore do not need to be overseen by organizations like the FDA. There was no risk to the child. The treatment is non-invasive, and Eve is doing fine. I spoke with their mother this morning. There have been no signs of telekinesis since they completed treatment.

RF

That's incredible. How on earth did you achieve that?

SB

Ah, trade secrets. We're not quite ready to disclose the type of treatment Eve underwent, though we hope to soon. But the bigger thing to focus on is that we could potentially heal anyone with powers. Eve was just the first. We're in the process of attempting to replicate the results with a different test subject, a man in his late fifties who came to us after years of hiding what he was capable of. He was in tears when he told us his story. All he wants is to be normal. And if we can help him achieve that dream, then who am I to say no?

RF

What would you say to people who will accuse you of playing God?

SB

I would listen to them, of course, and understand where they're coming from. However, my rebuttal would be that this is a voluntary treatment. We aren't holding people against their will. Anyone who participates in these early trials knows there's no guarantee, and that they can stop at any time. We aren't trying to play God. We're trying to keep people safe. We want to help those who cannot help themselves.

RF

I'm sure it doesn't hurt that after the attack on Centennial High, public polling is showing a shift against Extraordinaries. *CNN* released a national poll that showed fifty-two percent of people were against Extraordinaries. That's up ten points since the Battle at McManus Bridge.

SB

Yes, I saw that. People are scared, as they should be. We don't know what these people with powers will do or what they're capable of. You have Extraordinaries like Seth Gray, who can create fire out of nothing. What if there's an Extraordinary out there who has the capability to split atoms? To raise the levels of the oceans? I choose to believe in the good in people, but is that naïve? I thought my son was good until I saw evidence to the contrary. What'll we do if there's an Extraordinary who can cause nuclear explosions and will do so if we don't bend to their demands?

RF

And so you want to try to develop a way to stop them.

SB

No. Not stop. Help. I only want to help. I want to make sure that no one suffers like my family has. I . . . years ago, a dear, dear friend of mine revealed herself to be an Extraordinary, and I was so consumed by what she could do, I never stopped to think of the ramifications for the rest of us. She was kind and just and good, but what if she hadn't been? What if she'd been evil? I should've helped her. I wish I had. She's gone now, but there isn't a day that goes by that I don't think of her, which is why, because of her and all those like her, I want to help.

RF

And for those who don't want your help? Seth Gray, for example. Do you really think he'll meet with you after you put a bounty on his head?

SB

The bounty was a regrettable mistake. I apologize for that. I should have known better. Some problems cannot be solved by throwing money at them. I won't force him into anything. He knows where I am. All he needs to do is reach out, and I'll gladly listen to whatever he wants to say. That goes for anyone around him too. Anyone at all.

RF

Say, perhaps, another teenager capable of moving things with his mind?

SB

Exactly. And I would urge them to heed my words. The tide is changing. People will not stand idly by while their lives are disrupted by Extraordinaries. Soon, it may become a requirement for Extraordinaries to register. I know legislation has failed in the past, but the more we know, the safer we'll be. See something, say something. And that will be the forefront issue in my campaign.

RF

Because you have another announcement, don't you?

SB

That I do, Rebecca. I'm formally announcing my intention to run for mayor of Nova City. For too long, our leadership has failed us. It is time for fresh blood and new insight to bring our glorious city into the future we all deserve, one where we can live in harmony without fear of fire raining down from the sky or buildings falling on top of us. The current mayor has done nothing to stop the repeated attacks against Nova City. If elected, I promise that I'll do everything in my power to keep citizens safe from harm.

RF

And you've already received a powerful endorsement from the Fraternal Order of Police. Not only are they endorsing you, they released an internal poll showing that eighty-one percent of the NCPD support your candidacy.

SB

Yes, and I'm grateful to our men and women in blue, and not only for their support. They understand that while people like

Pyro Storm may seem like they want to help, they cause more harm than good. People have died because of their actions. Who knows? If Pyro Storm hadn't done what he did, perhaps my son wouldn't have felt the need to become Shadow Star.

RF

It sounds like you blame Seth Gray.

SB

No, not entirely. I'm merely speaking in hypotheticals. Mr. Gray is a seventeen-year-old boy with abilities that defy imagination. But there's a reason he hasn't been allowed to return to school. Parents are scared for their children. It's no longer just about gun violence. It's about people manifesting powers that could mean the end of life as we know it. Seth Gray is only one piece of the puzzle. But the picture is becoming clearer.

RF

Thank you, Mr. Burke. This has been most illuminating.

SB

Of course. Thank you for giving me an opportunity to speak. And I hear you have an announcement of your own?

RF

I do. This will be my last interview with *Action News*. For the past ten years, I have reported from the streets of Nova City. I love my job and I love my coworkers, but it's time for me to move on, to do something new. I'm excited about the future.

SB

Congratulations. I can't wait to see where you end up.

Two weeks later:

PRESS RELEASE
FROM THE SIMON BURKE MAYORAL CAMPAIGN
IN BURKE WE TRUST!

We are pleased to announce that Rebecca Firestone has joined the Simon Burke for Nova City Mayoral Campaign as press secretary. Ms. Firestone, a Nova City native, brings years of experience from her work as a journalist with *Action News*. Recognizable, trusted, and hardworking, Ms. Firestone has a level of expertise few have achieved.

"I look forward to working with Rebecca," Mr. Burke said in a statement. "She will only add to the growing movement of our campaign. She, like my wife and I, believes it's time to take our city back. We're better off because she has joined us. I'm delighted to have her."

"I'm honored," Ms. Firestone said. "While I'll miss holding a microphone and reporting from the streets, this new endeavor will allow me to use my knowledge of Nova City to ensure that Mr. Burke will be our next mayor. In Burke we trust!"

EPILOGUE

The valedictorian said, "And when we look back on our time spent here, I hope it's with joy and light, and that we never forget the lessons we learned. Thank you." He left the stage as the audience cheered.

"It should have been Gibby," Nick muttered as he clapped.

Seth and Jazz could only nod.

Megan Gardner . . . Justin Garrett . . . Lola Gibson—"

Nick flew to his feet, screaming at the top of his lungs. The people around him did the same: Seth and Dad, Jazz and her parents, Bob and Martha. But it was Trey and Aysha who were the loudest of all as their daughter walked across the stage, her graduation gown flowing around her. She rolled her eyes at the ruckus they were making but grinned when her diploma was given to her as she shook the principal's hand. When she reached the other side of the stage, she flipped her tassel from one side to the other. Before she descended the stairs, she raised her arms above her head, pumping her fists.

Nick and Seth stayed back, while Gibby's parents and Jazz clung to her with no small amount of tears. Nick sniffled, wiping his eyes with the back of his hand. Seth laughed quietly, reaching over and wrapping an arm around Nick's shoulders. They both ignored those staring at them, whispering behind their hands. They were getting used to it by now.

"Soft," Seth said. "So soft."

"I'm just proud of her," Nick grumbled. "Shut up."

"I think it's cute."

"I should hope so. I'm the cutest."

"No question." He looked around. "It's weird."

Nick glanced at him. "What is?"

"Being back here. I can't believe it's already been two months."

Nick scowled. This topic wasn't his favorite. After the attack on the school and Seth's reveal to the world that he was Pyro Storm, things had changed. The NCPD—in conjunction with the Nova City Department of Education—launched an investigation into what exactly had happened to allow two superpowered villains to enter the school and cause chaos. Seth was at the center of the investigation, and though there were dozens of witnesses (mostly students) who came forward and said Seth—Pyro Storm—was only trying to protect everyone, the school board had decided Seth couldn't return to Centennial High for the rest of the year. The board said it was not only for the safety of their students, but so they could have time to understand what precautions needed to be taken with an Extraordinary walking the halls.

Nick, Jazz, and Gibby had been outraged. Seth? Not so much. He took it in stride as he always did and told them it would be okay. Nick felt enormously guilty, and there were days he came close to blurting out that he was like Seth, that he, too, was an Extraordinary, just to fling it in their faces rather than have them continue to believe that everything he'd done had been because of TK. The reasons he didn't were twofold: first, Seth asked him not to, telling Nick that while he appreciated the solidarity, he didn't want Nick to reveal himself for Seth but rather on Nick's own terms when he was ready to do so. Nick's rebuttals were weak and half-hearted. He knew Seth was right.

The second reason? Nick was a coward.

Dad told him he wasn't; Seth, Jazz, and Gibby too. And while Nick appreciated them saying so, he really was one. He'd seen what had happened to Seth after he'd revealed himself. Martha and Bob had to have their house phone number changed after they got repeated death threats telling them that Seth was a freak and deserved to die. It didn't help that for weeks following the attack on prom, reporters had camped out in front of the Gray brownstone, trying to catch a glimpse of Seth and his aunt and uncle. There were long stretches of days when Seth never left the house, tutors coming to him to help him finish out the school year at home, since he wasn't allowed back in the school.

And it *really* didn't help that there was a rising wave of anger against Extraordinaries in Nova City and across the country. People had watched from all over the world in horror at the footage of the aftermath of the Attack at Centennial High (capitalized by the media, just like the Battle at McManus Bridge) and the moment Pyro Storm removed his helmet, revealing himself to be a seventeen-year-old high school student. At a special meeting with the school board, angry parents said that if the board didn't remove Seth Gray from the school, they would pull their own kids.

Seth went without so much as a fight, much to Nick's dismay.

There was talk that he'd be allowed to return for his senior year, but Bob and Martha were looking into homeschooling Seth in case that didn't go through. The upside would be that he could potentially graduate early if they went that direction.

The downside?

He wouldn't get to spend his senior year with Nick and Jazz. Nick knew it bothered Seth, though he put on a brave face. He'd had to get permission to be allowed to come to Gibby's graduation.

There had been protests on his behalf, and then counterprotesters against *those* protesters, all of them holding signs that said things like LET THE KID LIVE, DAMN! (Nick agreed wholeheartedly) and GOD CREATED ADAM AND EVE, NOT ADAM AND PYRO STORM (what did that even *mean*?) and PYRO STORM IS AMAZING (damn right!).

And then Burke had given his interview with Rebecca Firestone, which made Nick feel even worse. Burke appeared untouchable. They all knew he'd been controlling Smoke and Ice, but they had no proof. Cap and Dad had decided to go after Burke hard, but they'd been shut down by the mayor, who was concerned with public perception and how it would look against her own campaign for reelection. What would people think if it seemed as if the mayor had weaponized the police force to investigate a political opponent? Dad had been furious, especially when he was removed from the Extraordinaries Division by the acting chief of police after being accused of covering for Pyro Storm, now revealed to be Seth Gray, the boyfriend of his son.

What Aaron Bell had done next had made Nick prouder of his father than he'd ever been before. They had been sitting in their kitchen, dinner half-eaten between them, talking about nothing and everything. Nick had thought Dad was working up to something, but he didn't know what.

He'd been proven correct when Dad cleared his throat and said, "Nicky? I need to talk to you about something. It's important. It affects the both of us, and I want to run it by you before I do anything."

Nick had set down his fork and looked at his father expectantly. "Yeah, okay. Go for it. I'm listening."

Dad had looked down at his hands, the circles under his eyes like bruises. Nick hated to see him so beaten down, which was why he was surprised that when Dad lifted his head, all he'd seen was firm resolve. "I want to follow Cap's lead."

Nick had nodded slowly. He'd had an inkling this was coming, especially after what Cap had done. It still scared the shit out of him. "You're resigning."

"I am," Dad had said. He'd reached across the table, his palm up, fingers curling in invitation. Nick had laid his own hand on top of his father's. Both gripped each other's wrist. "I—I can't be part of this anymore. I don't . . ." He'd huffed out a breath. "I don't recognize the people I work with anymore. And no matter what happens, I'll always be associated with Seth. My superiors will never see beyond that again."

Nick had bristled. "Oh no. You don't get to put that on—"

Dad had squeezed his wrist. "I'm not. I promise. It's a good thing, Nicky. Because I would rather stand with him—with *you*—than anything else. But it's not only about that. It's about me too.

The things I've done. The harm I've caused." He'd blinked rapidly as his chest hitched, his pulse stuttering under Nick's fingers. "I should've quit a long time ago. I had no business having a badge when I . . . hurt someone like I did. I lost sight of what being an officer is supposed to mean. I don't want to be that person anymore. I need to figure out a different way to create change for the better, and I don't think I can do that staying with the NCPD."

"Are you scared?" Nick had asked quietly.

Dad had laughed as he wiped his eyes. "Hell yes, I'm scared, but it's the right thing to do. And I don't want you to worry about money or anything like that. Your college fund is going to stay untouched. I've . . . " He'd sighed. "I think I've been planning this for longer than even I knew. I've squirreled away enough for us to get by until I figure things out. And we still have money from—from your mom's life insurance." He'd chuckled. "Still watching over us, even now."

"I can get a job," Nick had said, heart in his throat. "Help out."

Dad had shaken his head. "Nah. Well, maybe for the summer, but when school starts up again, I want you to focus on graduating and nothing else. We'll be all right, I promise."

"This feels like giving up," Nick had admitted. "You and Cap. I know it's not, but—"

"It's not," Dad had said firmly. "I won't speak for Cap, but for me, it's about accountability. How can I help fight to change things when I can't even hold myself responsible? And I can't have that for myself or for you, because I'm your dad, Nicky. I need to lead by example, so you become the man I know you'll be."

Nick had sniffled. "You're doing all right so far. What are you gonna do next?"

Dad had smiled at him. "Cap and I have some ideas. Nothing we're ready to talk about yet, but once we know the direction we want to go, you'll be the first we tell. You and Seth. Gibby and Jazz. Their parents and Bob and Martha. All of us to—"

"—stand together so we don't have to struggle apart," Nick had whispered.

Dad had nodded, pleased. "Exactly, kid. We'll be okay. I promise."

Nick had believed him. And it had gotten him thinking about who he was supposed to be, the man he'd become.

Which was why when he'd found himself at the Caplan house the next week—Dad and Cap locked away in Cap's office, making plans, he came to a decision. Not for Dad. Not for Seth. Not for his friends, but for himself.

"They'll keep going all night if we let them," Mary Caplan had said with a laugh. Nick and Dad had come over for dinner at Mary's invitation. Gluttons for punishment, even until the end, seeing as how Mary had delightedly told them she'd found a new recipe for pot roast. It'd tasted like sawdust mixed with tears. Nick had choked it down.

"It's never going to get easier, is it?" Nick had muttered as he helped Mary clear the table.

She'd paused, rubbing her hands with a dish towel. "Remember what I told you when your dad was in the hospital?"

He did and didn't. Those were hazy days when all he'd known was panic and fear, worried that his father would never wake up.

"The price," Mary had said, "for loving a hero is a steep one. But we're a lighthouse. A beacon to help them find their way home. What Cap and your father did was brave, Nicky. Don't let anyone tell you otherwise. They're going to need us now more than ever, but I know we'll rise to the challenge."

Nick had said, "Can I tell you something?"

"Of course, Nick. You can tell me anything."

"Well, I guess showing you is probably easier."

She'd leaned against the counter, arching an eyebrow. "Show me what?"

He'd taken a deep breath and let it out slow. He'd raised his hand, brow furrowing as he searched for the spark within. It was coming easier now. The pressure built in his head, but it didn't hurt as it once had. He barely had to push anymore.

All the dishes that remained on the table had floated upward, spinning slowly as he moved them toward the sink. Mary gasped, hand at her throat, watching her plates and bowls and silverware float by her face and stack neatly in the sink. Once the last plate settled, Nick had lowered his hand.

"Cap knows," Nick had said quietly, nervous but trying not to show it. "Dad too. Gibby. Jazz. Seth, of course. Their parents and Bob and Martha. But you're the first I've told since—since prom. I'm an Extraordinary."

Mary had stared at the dishes in her sink for a long moment. Then she'd shaken her head, a determined look upon her face. She'd marched right up to Nick and pulled him into a fierce hug. "Thank you for telling me," she'd whispered. "I'm honored. But you should know I already thought you extraordinary."

Nick had sniffled. He heard movement near the entryway and saw Dad and Cap standing there, watching them both. Cap had grinned at him, mustache twitching. Dad had nodded slowly.

Now, as people moved around them on the football field, looking for their loved ones in a sea of graduation caps, Nick lay his head on Seth's shoulder. He didn't know how many of his peers actually believed that he'd had nothing to do with what they'd seen at prom, but no one had pushed him.

And now the school year was over, and they had a long, glorious summer stretching before them. Nick was going to use the time to listen to Seth, to let him talk about what *he* wanted. He hadn't suited up as Pyro Storm since prom night, fearing retaliation, and Nick hadn't pushed. He wouldn't, not with the weight of his own powers resting firmly on his shoulders. It sucked that it had taken Nick coming into his own for him to realize how heavy the weight could be, and he promised himself that he'd never again try to push Seth into something he wasn't ready for.

And Simon Burke.

The chill Nick had felt when he watched that interview felt like Ice had come back and frozen him solid. A cure. Burke said he had a cure. And he already seemed to have the police in his pocket, even though he hadn't been elected yet. Add to it the fact that

Owen Burke was out there, somewhere, and the future was a scary thing.

They watched Gibby and Jazz standing in the middle of the milling crowd, their foreheads pressed together.

Let them come, Nick thought as Seth kissed the top of his head.

Later, the four of them sat on the bleachers, watching the cleanup crew stack chairs and pick up discarded mortarboards, the tassels tangled and knotted. They were going to meet up with everyone later for Gibby's celebration dinner at her house. Miles and Jo were hosting a barbecue with just those in the know so they could speak freely. Nick needed to go home and change first, but he had time. There was nowhere else he wanted to be.

"It should have been you," he said, and they looked at him. He shook his head. "It should have been you up on that stage, Gibby. You earned it."

She shrugged. "Yeah, I guess, but I'm over it already. In six months, no one is going to remember who gave what speech. Who cares?"

Nick did. He cared very much. His fury at the school's decision to disqualify Gibby from being valedictorian, given her participation in protecting the school, was only rivaled by his rage at the decision to kick Seth out for the rest of the year. Gibby's parents had raised holy hell, but the school board wouldn't budge, even under the threat of legal action. They were still investigating, they said. Gibby was part of that investigation. And until the investigation was complete, she couldn't represent her class as valedictorian. Nick thought that was bullshit and hated Ice and Smoke and Burke even more. It was only later that Jazz had confided in him that Gibby had cried that night, angry tears at the unfairness of it all. Jazz had also told him that Gibby said she would do it all over again if she had to. Keeping people safe was all that mattered. Once a member of Team Pyro Storm, always a member of Team Pyro Storm.

"I care," Nick said. "And I know Seth and Jazz do too."

"We do," Seth said. He brightened. "Wait. Hold on. You could do it now."

She blinked. "What?"

Seth grinned at her. "Come on. I know you worked on a speech. Jazz said you practiced with her." He pushed his glasses back up his nose, a curl of his hair hanging on his forehead. "And I bet it's as amazing as you are."

"Hell *yes*," Nick crowed. "Seth, you have the best ideas. Gibby, you earned this. I want to hear what you have to say."

Gibby shook her head. "I'm not going to—"

"You don't have to do the whole thing," Jazz said, kissing Gibby's cheek. "Just do the last part. It's my favorite."

"Pleeeeease," Nick whined. "Gibby, Gibby, GibbyGibby*Gibby-Gibby*—"

"Oh my god, *fine*," she said with a scowl. "I'll do it if you shut up. You're so annoying."

"It's his superpower," Seth said. He paused, considering. "One of his superpowers."

"Hey!"

Gibby snorted as she stood, smoothing her graduation gown. The metal bleacher creaked under her boots. "I didn't finish it," she warned them. "And no matter what Jazz says, it's not very good."

"She's so modest," Jazz said. "It's perfect. Start with the part about living life to—"

"Yeah, yeah," Gibby muttered. "I know." The sun beat down on her head as she pulled herself to her full height. For a moment, Nick could almost see the adult she was becoming: lovely and formidable, capable of anything she put her extraordinary mind to. The world wasn't ready for Lola Gibson. She was going to change everything for the better.

And then she began, her voice growing stronger as she went on.

"This life isn't one I expected. I never expected to be the strong, queer Black woman you see standing before you all. I never expected to have the friends I do, people I would do anything for because I know they would do anything for me. It's scary, thinking about where we go from here, leaving this behind. And it doesn't help that the world is scary, too, filled with people who would do anything to make sure we don't succeed. But I'm here to tell you that no matter how loud those detractors get—no matter how angry they are, how spiteful—our voices are louder. Our voices are stronger. And there is nothing we can't do if we raise our voices together, if we lift each other up. The fight for change is never easy, but in the end it's worth it, especially if those who come after us are able to live in a world that accepts them for who they are, no matter what that may be.

"So, when we leave here, I ask that you remember something: a world without hope isn't a world at all. Hope is a boon. Hope is a necessity. Hope, when need be, is a weapon, one to be wielded with a firm but just hand. These are my hopes for you, for me, for all of us.

"I hope when you look back on the life you lived and the memories you built, you're happy with the person you've become. I hope you're floored by the simple things in life—a pretty girl smiling at you and only you, the sounds of your friends' laughter, the way your parents hug you and push you to become a better person. Acing a test you thought you'd bomb. Believing in a person because he wants to be extraordinary, even if he goes about it by putting a cricket into a microwave. Watching a friend bring the fire to chase away the shadows. Fighting to protect others, not because you want to be a hero, but because it's the right thing to do.

"I hope you're brought to your knees by love—love for your family, love for your best friends, love for a girl who believes in you more than anyone else. We're here, we're queer, and you better get used to it."

They laughed, even while tears streamed down their faces.

And then Gibby said, "And I hope you remember this time we had together. Maybe it wasn't the best time for you. Maybe you were ostracized because you were a person of color, or because you were queer, or because you had ADHD. Maybe you kept secrets because you wanted to keep those you loved safe. Maybe you wished high school was over a long time ago. And it is. It's over. This is an end, but it's not *the* end. When you leave here today, look back but remember to look ahead. The future is waiting for all of us, to make of it what we will." She grinned. "Screw anyone who doesn't think we're capable, because we're gonna make this world a better place, with or without their help. And to those who will try and silence us, a message: you will fail, and fail hard. There is nothing we can't do. There is nothing *I* can't do. And I plan on showing you just that." She sighed, scrubbing a hand over her face. "Uh, that's it. That's the end."

She squawked in outrage when they all tackled her and landed in a pile on the bleachers. They stayed there in the warm spring sun, holding onto each other.

Eventually, Nick looked at his friends and said, "We're alone in this."

Gibby glanced over at him, her head in Seth's lap, her feet on Jazz's legs, the toe of one of her boots pressed against Nick's thigh. "What do you mean?"

Nick shrugged. "Everything that's coming—we can only trust in ourselves and each other. We don't have the cops. We don't have a lot of the people. It feels like everyone is against us."

Gibby sat up, leaning against Seth, who wrapped an arm around her shoulders as she drew her knees to her chest. "Bullshit."

Nick blinked. "What?"

"That's bullshit," she repeated. "It was never going to be easy. But I promise you there are so many more of us than there are of them. Screw those people. Screw the cops. *We* know what we are, and what we're capable of."

"She's right," Jazz said as she patted Gibby's arm. "It may feel like we're alone right now, but it won't always be that way, so long as we remember what we're fighting for. And maybe that puts a weight on us that we didn't ask for, but I know us." She looked at each of them in turn. "I know we can build the world we want to live in. It's up to us to see that through."

"We can," Seth agreed, "and we will." He smiled at Nick. "We owe it to each other and to ourselves."

Paths diverged, Nick knew. What was true one day might not be true the next. And yet, when he looked at his friends, he thought they had a point. While he didn't want to think about the possibility of one day not having these wonderful people in his life, he would never forget what they'd taught him. Maybe that was the point of all of this—to make the most of everything with the time they had. And if there was one thing he'd learned in his short, dramatic life, it was to never let things go unsaid. You never knew when it might be the last time.

"I love you guys," he said quietly. "More than you know."

"Ditto," Seth said.

"Ditto twice," Gibby said.

"Ditto three times," Jazz said, and Nick laughed until he could barely breathe.

D ad!" Nick called when he walked into the house. "You home?"

"Upstairs!" Dad said from somewhere above him. "All right?"

"Yeah! Gonna get changed so we can go. Gibby said to remind you that I'm not allowed near the grill because she likes my eyebrows as they are."

Dad appeared at the top of the stairs. "Noted. But if Seth hasn't already burned them off when you two were grinding on each other, I think you'll be all right."

"*Dad!*"

Dad rolled his eyes. "What? It's not my fault you two were on the couch like that when I got home."

Nick scowled at him. "You didn't have to put plastic on the couch. That was overkill."

"Boy stains," Dad reminded him.

Nick threw up his hands. "Whatever. Keep on making my life miserable, why don't you."

"I'm funny," Dad said.

"That is a flat-out *lie*. There's nothing funny about you!"

Dad crossed his arms. "I made you, didn't I?"

Nick was startled into laughter, though he tried to cover it up. It didn't go well. It sounded like he was trying to hack up a lung. Dad looked too smug for his own good.

"Mail for you," he said, turning back around, heading toward his room. "Left it on the kitchen table. Package was delivered earlier. I swear to god, if it's a sex toy, you better not have used my credit card. I'm all for expressing yourself, but I don't need to know if you bought something to be inserted into someone else."

Nick screeched in outrage. How *dare* his father suggest something so . . . so . . . huh. Sex toys. Nick had never thought of that before. Did Seth want a sex toy? Maybe they could—

He blushed furiously. One thing at a time. They needed to have *sex* first before considering silicone assistance.

And mail? Who was sending him mail? Curious, he set his backpack on the bottom stair and headed toward the kitchen. He paused at the entryway. Sitting on the table was a white rectangular box with a blue ribbon wrapped around it. It was heavier than he expected it to be when he lifted it to shake it. He set it back on the table, untying the ribbon and lifting the lid.

Inside was tissue paper. On top was an envelope with his name written on the front in a stylish flourish. He lifted the envelope, opened it, and pulled out the paper. He unfolded it and glanced down at the signature at the bottom.

Miss Conduct

He paused. He hadn't seen the Extraordinary since the attack at prom. Seth had a couple of times and they'd all exchanged messages through the app, but Mateo was lying low, worried about the same things the rest of them were. No one had seen or heard from TK, however. Dad had seemed weirdly frustrated when he'd grilled them about the other telekinetic hero, especially when they hadn't been able to give him much information.

Nick went back to the top of the page and read:

Nicholas—

I've thought about this for a long time—whether giving something like this to you was the right thing to do. In the end, I figured it's better for you to have it, just in case. Before you decide, please read this note in its entirety.

A hero is called upon when they're needed most, not

when they're most prepared. I know it may not seem like it, but I learned a lot from you and our fiery friend, and not only from the disaster that was your prom night.

If you're anything like me, you're worried about the future. Everything we're hearing about Extraordinaries is scary. People are angry with us. Those in power are trying to track us. That asshole Burke thinks we need to be cured. We don't. There is nothing wrong with us. We are as we're supposed to be. I'll always believe that. Giving ourselves permission to be human is hard, but that's what we are. We just have something a little . . . extra.

It's not about the costume, but the person who wears it. I know about your mother. I know she was once the hero the city needed. A guardian. The Guardian. I hope you don't mind, but I put together a little something for you, with help from Seth and Gibby and Jazz. I tried to find as many pictures of Guardian as possible so I could honor her memory. Girl was elusive; mad props to her. I know she'd be proud of you.

If you decide to become the hero this city needs, I hope you'll wear this with pride. I hope you'll live with pride, because pride is a riot. We fight because we can. We love because we can. We become a lighthouse to guide others home. We become guardians to stop evil in its tracks.

Guardian, Nick.

A perfect name for a new hero, don't you think?

Love,
Miss Conduct

The letter fluttered to the table. Hands trembling, Nick reached for the box and pulled out the tissue paper.

And there, sitting inside, was a cerulean-blue costume.

It was like the one his mother had worn, though with noticeable differences. The material was stronger, lined with white stripes that crisscrossed along the chest and legs. The boots were stiff and shiny.

And the helmet.

Nick lifted the blue helmet from the box. It was heavier than he expected it to be. The lenses were white and appeared to be made of some sort of thick plastic. He turned it over in his hands and thought he saw something blinking inside. He frowned, squinting at the tiny light. It called to him like a lighthouse in the distance, leading him home.

Without a second thought, he slid the helmet over his head.

He breathed and breathed and *breathed*—

White light exploded. He stumbled and bumped against a chair, whirling around as numbers, shapes, and words flitted in front of his eyes, running faster and faster. Lines of code flew as a deep chime sounded around him. Then it was gone, Nick's vision clearing—except everything was sharper, more in focus. He could see the grain in the table and chairs, the chips in the cabinets, the crack in the wood of the windowsill. Before he could react, a voice spoke in his ear.

"Guardian," it said. "This is Lighthouse. Do you copy?"

Nick gasped, dumbfounded "*Seth?*"

"Gibby here!"

"And Jazz!"

Seth's voice was warm when he said, "Guardian, you're coming through loud and clear."

"What is this?" Nick whispered, a tear trickling down his cheek.

"The future," Seth said. "For you. For me. For all of us. You're a hero, Nicky. An Extraordinary. It's about time you had a costume to show that."

"Oh my god," Nick breathed. "Do you realize what this means?"

"What?" Gibby asked, her voice crystal clear.

"We have a ship name!" Nick cried. "Holy shit, we're PyroGuard! Wait, no. That sounds like medicine for a foot rash. GuardStorm! StormGuard? GuardPyro!"

"Nicky, *no*," they all groaned.

"Nicky, *yes!*"

"Nicky, yes," another voice said, and Nick startled. He removed the helmet and smiled at Dad, who was standing in the entryway to the kitchen. His eyes were wet, but he was smiling. Nick set the helmet on the table before flinging himself at his father. Dad caught him. He always did.

"Guardian," Dad whispered into his hair. "My guardian."

CREDITS

When I released *The House in the Cerulean Sea* and *The Extraordinaries* in 2020, they were my first books with my new publishers, Tor and Tor Teen. Acknowledgments are written well in advance of publication, so while an author knows who the people working on their books are, when it comes to the first book(s), you don't quite know just how hard people work on your behalf until the books come out.

This is just a long-winded way of saying that without the following people working their butts off on my behalf, my stories wouldn't have reached even a fraction of the audience they have. I am the writer, yes; but these lovely people are the ones working behind the scenes to *get* my books to you. They deserve all the praise.

First is Deidre Knight, my agent, without whom none of this would be possible. She worked tirelessly to find my books the best possible home, and I have never felt as lucky with a publisher as I do with Tor and Tor Teen. Thanks to Deidre and the team at the Knight Agency, including Elaine Spencer, who handles all the foreign rights to my books. If one of my titles is getting translated into a different language, you can bet that's because Elaine is working behind the scenes to make that happen.

Next, Ali Fisher, who is—without question—the best editor I've had the pleasure of working with. Not only does she get me (my sense of humor can be a little . . . out there, as you probably know if you've made it this far), but she also believes in the stories I want to tell. Without her guidance, I'd be a floundering mess and using, commas, after, every, word. Also, OxfordComma4Life.

Also on the editing side is assistant editor Kristin Temple. Kristin keeps me sane, which isn't an easy task. Any time I get an email from her, I know I'm going to get to see something ridiculously awesome, and she is a true cheerleader for my books. Thanks, Kristin.

To the sensitivity readers, Margeaux and Jon Reyes—who read the book and provided wonderful feedback—thank you. Your insights were not only welcome but necessary and invaluable. You both made this story better, and I am profoundly grateful for it.

Saraciea Fennell and Anneliese Merz are the best publicists, full stop. I am responsible for at least sixteen thousand emails in their in-boxes on a monthly basis, and they never reply with *TJ, KNOCK IT OFF, YOU DON'T HAVE TO EMAIL US TO ASK IF IT'S OKAY TO TWEET WHAT YOU HAD FOR DINNER.* Instead, they hold my hand and tell me everything will be all right. Also, every public appearance I make—every panel I participate in or book tour stop I make—is because of their planning. I don't know how they do it. They're the real Extraordinaries.

The higher-ups—though the exact opposite of Extremely Upper Management—are Tor Teen Publisher Devi Pillai; President of Tom Doherty Associates Fritz Foy; Vice President, Director of Marketing Eileen Lawrence; Executive Director of Publicity Sarah Reidy; Vice President of Marketing and Publicity Lucille Rettino; and Chairman/Founder of TDA Tom Doherty. My books exist with Tor and Tor Teen because *they* exist. Thank you for letting me tell queer stories the way I want to. These people are some of my biggest cheerleaders, and I adore them.

Anthony Parisi is the marketing lead, and it's because of him that you see my face and book covers a lot (perhaps more than you'd like to, but that's okay; my covers are great, and I do like my face). Anthony is a delight, and he comes up with the best ideas. Thank you, Anthony.

Isa Caban works with Anthony as the marketing manager, and she is a rad person doing rad things. I wish I could be as rad as her.

An additional marketing lead is Becky Yeager. Though she

mostly works on my adult books, I want to thank her here too because she rocks and deserves to be mentioned. Hi, Becky!

Sarah Pannenberg—the digital marketing coordinator—runs Tor Teen's social media accounts, so if you ever see me snarking at them, you know Sarah is on the other side, rolling their eyes as they play along with me. Thank you, Sarah!

On the production side of things, you have production editor Melanie Sanders, production manager Steven Bucsok, interior designer Heather Saunders, and jacket designer Lesley Worrell. See how pretty this book looks? That's because of them. Thank you.

Also, thank you to Lynn Schmidt and Mia Gardiner for beta reading. They're the first to read my books, and they are excellent at what they do while also telling me I might be pretty good at this whole writing thing. Thanks, ladies.

I would also like to thank Shawn O'Neal and Jennifer Ho, professors at the University of Colorado Boulder. Though we've never met, I am in their debt. They taught the online course I took called Anti-Racism—it was humbling and illuminating, and it should be a requirement for all white people.

And to you, dear reader. Thank you for coming along on this journey with me, Nick, Seth, Jazz, and Gibby. They'll be back for one last ride before you know it, and I can't wait for you to see how it all ends.

TJ Klune
March 25, 2021

(Oh, and one more thing: turn the page, won't you? Because *Flash Fire* isn't *quite* over yet. Someone's been keeping secrets . . .)

STUNG

Aaron Bell stood on a windswept roof, the collar of his coat up around his neck to keep the rain away. The moon was hidden behind storm clouds, the lights of the city stretching out below him. He'd come here night after night since the attack on the prom, hoping against hope.

Foolish, he knew. He was chasing a ghost.

He sighed, hands brushing against a piece of paper in his pocket. He pulled it out and looked down, anger flooding through him. It'd come the day after Nick had received his costume. Remembering all the hate mail the Grays had received, he'd decided to open it himself, just to be sure. If it was nothing, he'd hand it over to Nick. Better to be safe than sorry.

He was glad he did.

He'd waited until Nick was out with his friends before tearing the envelope open. There was only one piece of paper inside, and on it were three words above a black scribble that had been scratched into the paper. At first, Aaron thought it was smoke—perhaps a threat from someone associated with Christina and Christian Lewis. But then he looked closer at the black scribble and saw that underneath, someone had drawn a familiar sigil.

A star symbol. But why had they covered it in—

No. Not smoke.

Shadow. The star was covered in shadow.

The three words?

SEE YOU SOON!

He crumpled the paper and shoved it back in his pocket. He'd had Officer Rookie test it, his man on the inside. Chris had been nervous but determined. It'd taken longer than Aaron had hoped, but Chris had put himself at great risk, pushing this through. If anyone knew he was loyal to Cap and Aaron, he'd be canned quicker than he could blink, so Aaron took what he could get. Especially since the Rook continued to feed them information about what was happening with the NCPD.

The results, while disappointing, hadn't surprised Aaron. No trace evidence. No fingerprints. No DNA. Nothing.

But he knew who it was from: Owen Burke.

He looked out at the city once more, chiding himself for keeping this from his kid. They'd promised each other no more secrets, but what Nick didn't know was that being a parent meant doing *anything* to keep their kid safe, no matter what. If he could find Owen before he tried something, they'd all be better off for it. Simon Burke claimed to not know the whereabouts of his son, but Aaron didn't believe a damn word that came from his mouth. He didn't talk to Burke. Not anymore. Not after all he'd done.

Officer Rookie was the only other person who knew about the letter. He'd promised to keep it to himself with the caveat that Aaron would eventually need to tell Nick and his friends. "We can't keep this from him," Rook said. "Owen is planning something."

Good kid, Officer Rookie. Aaron didn't know where he'd be without him. He hoped Chris would never get a reason to regret helping them.

He glanced down at his watch. Half past eight. He'd texted Nick a little while ago, letting him know he'd be home soon. Nick—always and forever Nick—had responded in all caps and exclamation points. He was halfway convinced Aaron had been seeing someone, going out on dates, especially since he was coming home late a couple of nights a week. Aaron had been stunned when Nick told him this. It had never even crossed his mind.

"It's okay if you are," Nick said. "I—I know that you have to move on sometime. I hope whoever it is, they make you happy."

He'd assured Nick that wasn't the case at all. He wasn't seeing anyone. He'd managed to hold it together until Nick went upstairs before he broke, face in his hands as he rocked back and forth. Grief was never far away, even three years later.

Which was why he was here.

They were in the After. But they'd once been in the Before, and not the Before Nick knew. Before even him.

This was where he'd come, waiting for Jenny to finish her rounds at night, moving through the city, watching over it, doing what she could to help people. This was where she'd find him, laughing as she landed on the roof, always managing to startle him. She'd tear off her helmet and kiss him deeply, smelling of clean sweat, her face flushed, her hair billowing. Oh, how alive she was, how beautiful. She'd scared him. She'd scared him so much, but he'd never loved a woman like he'd loved her. Like he still loved her.

Which was why he was here.

He'd seen the Extraordinary known as TK standing with his son against Smoke and Ice. He'd seen the way TK had moved with Nick, like they were two sides of the same coin. They moved together like they'd done it for years. And when Nick told him that he didn't know who TK was, only that he was a man, Aaron had believed him. Jenny was gone.

She'd died instantly in the bank, a gunshot to the face. Cap hadn't let him see her after. She'd been identified by her fingerprints. Her body was cremated. They'd spread her ashes at the lighthouse.

So why was he here?

"Stupid," he muttered to himself. "So stupid." He turned to head home. Nick was waiting for him. Nick was still here, still alive. He needed his father at home, not standing on a roof chasing ghosts.

He stopped. A figure stood between him and the roof access door.

Dressed in all black, helmet on his head, opaque as ever. TK.

Aaron took a step back as TK cocked his head. Even though he couldn't see TK's eyes, he knew he was being watched. Studied.

"Who are you?" Aaron demanded roughly.

TK didn't speak.

"Why did you help my son?"

Nothing.

"Where did you come from? Did you know my wife? I—" His chest hitched as his voice broke. "You helped Nicky. I saw it. You're telekinetic. Like him. Like she was. How did you—"

"Aaron," TK said, voice heavily modulated.

And just like that, Aaron knew.

He *knew*.

He sank to his knees there on the roof as TK bowed his head. TK's hands went to his helmet, and he lifted it off slowly.

Not he.

She.

Oh my god, a voice whispered in his head, a meteoric rise of memory. *I'm so sorry! I was trying to reach a book on the top shelf, and I slipped off the ladder. Are you hurt?*

No. I'm . . . okay. Hi, I'm Aaron.

Aaron, huh? Hello, Aaron. I'm Jenny. And apparently still lying on top of you.

I don't mind. Take your time.

Wow. Did you expect that line to work?

I don't know. You'll have to tell me thirty years from now when we're celebrating our anniversary.

And she'd *laughed*.

As an air of unreality washed over him, Aaron gasped when she lifted her head, helmet clutched in her hands, eyes wide as she looked at him, a lock of her short blond hair falling over her forehead. "Hi, honey," Jennifer Bell said quietly. "I'm home."